A5+

P9-BZY-409

THE BESTSELLING NOVELS OF
Tom Clancy

RED RABBIT

Tom Clancy returns to Jack Ryan's early days—in an extraordinary novel of global political drama . . .

"AN OLD-FASHIONED COLD WAR THRILLER."

—*Chicago Sun-Times*

THE BEAR AND THE DRAGON

President Jack Ryan faces a world crisis unlike any he has ever known . . .

"INTOXICATING . . . A JUGGERNAUT."

—*Publishers Weekly* (starred review)

RAINBOW SIX

Clancy's shocking story of international terrorism—closer to reality than any government would care to admit . . .

"GRIPPING . . . BOLT-ACTION MAYHEM."

—*People*

EXECUTIVE ORDERS

Jack Ryan has always been a soldier. Now he's giving the orders . . .

"AN ENORMOUS, ACTION-PACKED, HEAT-SEEKING MISSILE OF A TOM CLANCY NOVEL."

—*The Seattle Times*

continued . . .

DEBT OF HONOR

It begins with the murder of an American woman in the back streets of Tokyo. It ends in war . . .

"A SHOCKER!"
—*Entertainment Weekly*

THE HUNT FOR RED OCTOBER

The smash bestseller that launched Clancy's career—the incredible search for a Soviet defector and the nuclear submarine he commands . . .

"BREATHLESSLY EXCITING!"   —*The Washington Post*

RED STORM RISING

The ultimate scenario for World War III—the final battle for global control . . .

"THE ULTIMATE WAR GAME . . . BRILLIANT!"
—*Newsweek*

PATRIOT GAMES

CIA analyst Jack Ryan stops an assassination—and incurs the wrath of Irish terrorists . . .

"A HIGH PITCH OF EXCITEMENT!"
—*The Wall Street Journal*

THE CARDINAL OF THE KREMLIN

The superpowers race for the ultimate Star Wars missile defense system . . .

"*CARDINAL* EXCITES, ILLUMINATES . . . A REAL PAGE-TURNER!"
                                    —*Los Angeles Daily News*

CLEAR AND PRESENT DANGER

The killing of three U.S. officials in Colombia ignites the American government's explosive, and top secret, response . . .

"A CRACKLING GOOD YARN!" —*The Washington Post*

THE SUM OF ALL FEARS

The disappearance of an Israeli nuclear weapon threatens the balance of power in the Middle East—and around the world . . .

"CLANCY AT HIS BEST . . . NOT TO BE MISSED!"
                                    —*The Dallas Morning News*

WITHOUT REMORSE

The Clancy epic fans have been waiting for. His code name is Mr. Clark. And his work for the CIA is brilliant, cold-blooded, and efficient . . . but who is he really?

"HIGHLY ENTERTAINING!"   —*The Wall Street Journal*

Novels by Tom Clancy
THE HUNT FOR RED OCTOBER
RED STORM RISING
PATRIOT GAMES
THE CARDINAL OF THE KREMLIN
CLEAR AND PRESENT DANGER
THE SUM OF ALL FEARS
WITHOUT REMORSE
DEBT OF HONOR
EXECUTIVE ORDERS
RAINBOW SIX
THE BEAR AND THE DRAGON
RED RABBIT

SSN: STRATEGIES OF SUBMARINE WARFARE

Nonfiction
SUBMARINE: A GUIDED TOUR INSIDE A NUCLEAR WARSHIP
ARMORED CAV: A GUIDED TOUR OF AN ARMORED CAVALRY REGIMENT
FIGHTER WING: A GUIDED TOUR OF AN AIR FORCE COMBAT WING
MARINE: A GUIDED TOUR OF A MARINE EXPEDITIONARY UNIT
AIRBORNE: A GUIDED TOUR OF AN AIRBORNE TASK FORCE
CARRIER: A GUIDED TOUR OF AN AIRCRAFT CARRIER
SPECIAL FORCES: A GUIDED TOUR OF U.S. ARMY SPECIAL FORCES

INTO THE STORM: A STUDY IN COMMAND
(written with General Fred Franks)
EVERY MAN A TIGER
(written with General Charles Horner)
SHADOW WARRIORS: INSIDE THE SPECIAL FORCES
(written with General Carl Stiner, Ret., and Tony Koltz)

Tom Clancy's
Op-Center™

SEA
OF
FIRE

Created by

Tom Clancy and Steve Pieczenik

written by

Jeff Rovin

BERKLEY BOOKS, NEW YORK

This is a work of fiction. Names, characters, places, and incidents either are the product of the author's imagination or are used fictitiously, and any resemblance to actual persons, living or dead, business establishments, events, or locales is entirely coincidental.

TOM CLANCY'S OP-CENTER: SEA OF FIRE

A Berkley Book / published by arrangement with
Jack Ryan Limited Partnership and S & R Literary, Inc.

PRINTING HISTORY
Berkley edition / July 2003

For information address: The Berkley Publishing Group,
a division of Penguin (Group) USA Inc.,
375 Hudson Street, New York, New York 10014.

ISBN: 0-425-19091-9

BERKLEY®
Berkley Books are published by The Berkley Publishing Group,
a division of Penguin (Group) USA Inc.,
375 Hudson Street, New York, New York 10014.
BERKLEY and the "B" design
are trademarks belonging to Penguin (Group) USA Inc.

PRINTED IN THE UNITED STATES OF AMERICA

10 9 8 7 6 5 4 3 2 1

Acknowledgments

We would like to acknowledge the valuable assistance of Martin H. Greenberg; Larry Segriff; Denise Little; John Helfers; Brittiany Koren; Lowell Bowen, Esq.; Robert Youdelman, Esq.; Danielle Forte, Esq.; Dianne Jude; and Tom Colgan, our editor. But most important, it is for you, our readers, to determine how successful our collective endeavor has been.

—Tom Clancy and Steve Pieczenik

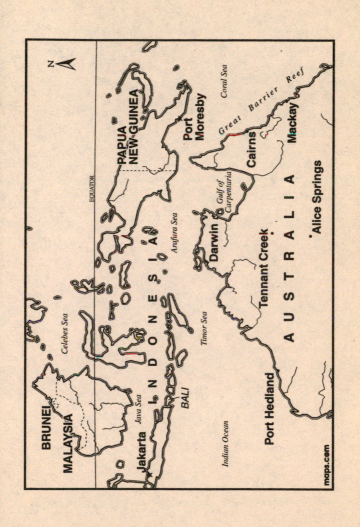

ONE

The Celebes Sea
Tuesday, 4:19 A.M.

There were three things that swarthy, dark-eyed Singaporean Lee Tong knew very well.

One of those was the sea. The lanky but muscular Lee was the son of the late Henry Tong, a hardworking mate on a timber carrier. The elder Tong's vessel, the 100-ton capacity *Lord of the Ocean*, was a container ship. It took regular runs of hardwood cargo from their home port in Singapore to India. On the return trip it would carry teak logs that had been shipped from the Ivory Coast to Bombay. These were bound for Hong Kong and Tokyo. Lee's mother had died of food poisoning when the boy was five. Rather than live with his grandparents in Keluang, on their inland farm, Lee often traveled with his father. By the time Lee was thirteen, he was working full time as a cabin boy for the first mate.

Traveling the timber route, Lee learned the different moods of the waters. The clean smell of the Andaman Sea was different than the tart, oily smell along the coast of the South China Sea. The currents of the East China Sea caused a sharper rocking than the heavier, lofting swells in the Pacific Ocean. The storms were different, too. Some were sudden and ferocious. Others came from afar with enough warning that the pilot could steer around them. Lee also learned about men on these odysseys. What pleased them, what bothered them, what bothered them enough to kill. He learned that money, undemanding women, cigarettes, drink and the camaraderie of drink, and the loyalty of friends were the only things that really mattered to him. By the time the elder Tong died of liver failure, Lee had only managed to get a lot of smoking and drinking done. He would never get much more as long as he worked on the *Lord of the Ocean* or a vessel like her, which was why Lee Tong took up the next profession he did.

When Lee was sixteen, several years into his own career on the timber ship, he met two other young sailors who did not want to end up like their own fathers. Who were unhappy working for three dollars a day, seven days a week. Eventually, in port, they sat down with other dissatisfied young men from other professions. That led Lee to the second thing he knew very well.

Piracy.

Lee was standing in the steep raised prow of the sampan. The vessel was not of Singaporean design. It was a squat Shanghai Harbor model, also known as a *mu-chi* or hen boat. The name was a result of the sampan's resemblance to the bird. Built mostly of softwood, which aged well and was extremely light, the *mu-chi* was eighteen feet long with four compartments, including a galley. There was an engine for rapid travel and four *yulohs*—thirteen-foot-long oars—for silent travel. That was how the five sampan pirates were traveling now, with Lee's crewmates rowing two men to a side. They had bought the sampan in China, legally, just over two years before. They had paid for it with cash, most of it borrowed from Lee's grandparents. The loan was repaid within a year. Buying the sampan was the last lawful act the men had done.

Early in their career the men learned how to mingle with harbor traffic to select their prey, how to track them until dark, and how to come alongside swiftly and quietly. They learned how to prowl the shipping lanes with their backs to the setting sun so that they would not be seen. Former police sergeant Koh Yu kept both a 500-channel scanner and a world band receiver on board to monitor restricted police and military communications. He had stolen them before resigning from the Special Operations Command of the Singapore Police Force. After sampling all kinds of ships, they focused on yachts and fishing charters. The take was usually good, and resistance was limited to indignant words. Since most of those words were English, Lee didn't understand what was being said. Among them, only the unflappable Koh spoke English. And Koh did not care what was being said. None of the men felt remorse about the work they did. On land, the large took advantage of the small. The fat had their way with the lean. At sea, the sharks ate the tuna. Lee Tong had tried both lives.

He preferred being a shark.

They began by waylaying small pleasure boats, tour ships, and party vessels out of Hong Kong and Taipei. The men didn't even have to board the ships to rob them. They came alongside and pressed plastic explosives low on the hull. The soft, explosive patties were homemade from concussion-ignited mercuric fulminate—a mixture of mercury, alcohol, and nitric acid—paraffin, and linseed oil to keep the wax pliant. That was a contribution of eight-fingered Clark Shunga, a former demolitions man for the lumber industry. Trees that were too difficult to cut down were blasted down. When he lost two fingers to a faulty detonator cap, he was fired with meager compensation. The Woo See Lumber Company was afraid that he would kill someone by mishandling explosives. He showed them that he could still play the guitar, but they were unimpressed. Clark put all of his severance pay— fifty dollars—toward the sampan.

The pirates would carefully place the plastic explosives fore and aft, a few feet above the waterline. That would keep them dry. It would also make it difficult for anyone to try to dislodge them with a pole or net. They would have to stand there, on the rocking deck, while the pirates shot at them. After the explosives were placed, the sampan would withdraw to a safe distance of between fifteen and twenty feet. Using a megaphone, they would order that valuables, jewels, and occasionally a female hostage be sent over the side in a rowboat or dinghy. They would enjoy the woman's company for a short while and then set her adrift. If the orders were not followed, they would turn on the laser sight and fire a bullet from one of the M8 pistols that each man carried. The shot would ignite the explosive. To date, the pirates had never found it necessary to destroy a ship.

The Celebes Sea was still relatively new territory to Lee and the others. They had been sailing this region of the Western Pacific for just two months, since the Singapore navy increased its patrols in the South China Sea. The shipping lanes were different, and the sea itself was different. The waters did not heave up and down or from side to side like other bodies of water. They pitched you back and then drew you forward, thanks to a very strong and constant undertow. It reminded Lee of something his father once said about life: that it lets you move one step ahead and then knocks you back two.

The sampan was traveling dark. The cabin lights were off, and even the phosphorescent compass was covered with a canvas cloth, so that it would not be seen when they came alongside. They were headed toward two beacons roughly a quarter mile away, the fore and aft running lights of a yacht. It was an eighty-foot two-masted sailing yacht they had spotted while heading to port the previous day. The men had tracked the low, sleek vessel as it headed southeast. It was on an easy course with just a few people on board. It was probably a weeklong charter that cost some fat Aussie or Malaysian about fifteen or twenty thousand dollars, American. It was the perfect prey. This was the third thing Lee Tong knew well: spotting perfect targets. Since organizing the others on that hot, humid, hard-drinking night in Hong Kong, Lee had never picked a loser.

Until tonight.

TWO

Washington, D.C.
Monday, 7:45 P.M.

The Inn Cognito was located at 7101 Democracy Boulevard in Bethesda. Paul Hood had never been to the new hot spot, but Op-Center's attorney, Lowell Coffey III, had given it an enthusiastic recommendation. Hood and his undemanding palate were happy with something less chichi. He could do without TV monitors showing tape of blinking eyeballs and snapping fingers. But he was not here alone. He was with Daphne Connors, founder of the cutting-edge Daph-Con advertising agency. The forty-one year-old divorcée had also gotten a thumbs-up from Coffey, who knew the family of her former husband, attorney Gregory Packing, Jr.

The name of Daphne's firm appealed to Washingtonians. Especially to the military. The blond-haired Daphne also appealed to Beltway insiders. She had the stylish poise and intensity of a CNN anchorwoman. In addition to handling various Army accounts, she represented hotels and restaurants, including this one. That was how they managed to get a reservation.

Daphne was quite a contrast to Hood, whose job as the director of Op-Center demanded quiet, steady leadership. The husky-voiced woman was extremely high-energy. She reminded Hood of the late Martha Mackall, Op-Center's go-get-'em political liaison. Martha had been confident, poised, and always stalking. He didn't know what she was hunting or why. He was not sure she did, either. But she never stopped.

Maybe that's what Martha was really searching for, Hood thought. *Understanding.*

Tragically, terrorist bullets ended the life of the forty-nine-year-old African-American woman. Hood was sorry he had not gotten to know her better. From a strictly managerial point of view, he also wished he could have learned how to harness her intensity.

Hood tried to keep up with the hard-driving Daphne as she described how she established her agency in college with commissions she earned from selling ad space in university newspapers. She told him how it had grown to a global organization that employed over 340 people in the United States alone. In ten minutes she must have used the words *push* and *drive* a dozen times each. Hood found himself wondering how their respective organizations would fare if they switched jobs. His guess was that Daph-Con would end up being sold to some insipid conglomerate and homogenized. Op-Center would probably swallow the NSA, the CIA, and possibly Interpol.

Well, it might not be that extreme, Hood thought. But he had served as mayor of Los Angeles. He had worked on Wall Street. And eight years ago he had returned to government. Hood was fascinated by the different management styles in the public and private sector. He enjoyed the give-and-take of a team, the challenge of reaching a consensus. The need for self-expression that drove someone like Daphne was foreign to him. It was also a little off-putting—not because he disapproved but because he felt intimidated. His former wife, Sharon, had been introspective and very satisfied to go with the family flow. Even the presidents and world leaders Hood had known found it necessary to be team players.

"Paul?" Daphne said over her ducksalad appetizer.

"Yes?"

"I've been to enough pitch meetings to know when someone's brain is wandering," she said.

"No, I'm here," Hood replied with a smile.

She gave him a dubious look. It had playful corners around the eyes and mouth, but just barely.

"You were telling me about the pro bono work you do for the Native American Chumash in California, so that their sacred caves in the Santa Ynez range are protected."

The woman relaxed slightly. "All right, you heard me. But that still doesn't mean you were listening."

"I assure you, I was," he said. "That glazed, unfocused look you saw was the glazed, unfocused eyes of Paul Hood at the end of a long day of bureaucratic conflicts."

"I see," Daphne said. She smiled now. "I understand. Totally."

Still, Hood knew that she was right. Years ago, an actor friend in Los Angeles had taught him a trick of the trade. It was called "floating" lines. It was done when performers did not have adequate rehearsal time. You let words into your short-term memory, where they could be accessed. That left the rest of the brain free to observe, muse, and—yes—wander. Hood used the technique to memorize speeches when he was mayor. Since coming to Washington, he had developed floating to an art by attending endless policy briefings that were anything but brief. He could listen, even take notes, while thinking about what he needed to do when he got back to Op-Center.

Daphne pushed her plate aside and leaned forward. "Paul, I have to confess something."

"Why?"

She laughed. "Funny. Most people would have asked, 'What?' "

He thought about that. She was right. He did not know why he said that.

"I haven't been on a date in seven years," Daphne said, "and I'm afraid I've turned this into something of a dog and pony show."

"If it helps, I'm enjoying what you have to say."

"You're sweet, but *I* don't like it," Daphne said. "I'm acting like I'm at a client pitch. I'm trying too hard to sell myself."

"No—"

"Yes," she insisted. "You've been very patient for the last half hour."

"I told you, I'm interested," he answered truthfully. "I

don't meet many people who run businesses."

"No, you meet people who run countries," Daphne said.

"Most of whom are not as interesting as you are," Hood replied. "And that wasn't a line," he added.

That caught her with her guard down. "Talk to me about that."

"Most of them had to sandblast their most distinguishing features, make everything smooth to get where they are," Hood told her. "What's left is guided by constitutions or surrounded by domestic and international watchdogs, constituents, and special interests."

"Is that a bad thing?" she asked.

"Not necessarily," Hood replied. "It prevents dictatorships. But it also slows progress to a glacial pace. The individual leader can't move without the entire system moving with him or her."

"Still, what they do affects more than the bottom line of a very minor privately held company." She sat back. "What about you?"

"What do you want to know?" he asked.

"How you do it," she replied. "You don't seem to be one of those bureaucrats who's always on the make, looking for access."

Hood selected a bread stick from the basket. He dabbed it in a dish of olive oil and took a bite. He was not good at this either. When Sharon used to ask him how his day went, he never said much. There was no point starting a lengthy conversation because there were always interruptions. The phone, the kids, something on the stove or in the oven.

"I'm interested in having the access it takes to do my job, not in collecting it," Hood replied.

"An idealist."

Hood shrugged a shoulder.

"Is that a yes?" Daphne pressed.

Hood looked at her. Daphne had a nice smile. It started at the eyes and made its way down. "Let's say I try to do what's right," he replied. "When I screw up, it's not out of malice."

"So you don't possess the revenge gene that most people in big government have," she said.

"No," he said. "Bastards invariably cause their own downfall."

"And that really works for you?" she asked.

"It leaves me free to do more constructive things," Hood said.

Daphne laughed. "Lord, we are very different people. I hate SOBs or discourtesy or people who beat me at anything." She regarded him. "I still don't believe you have absolutely no bloodlust. Tell me if I'm overstepping some kind of first-date rule with this, but I read about those men who took the children hostage in New York. The ones you and your team killed. Didn't you hate them?"

"That's a good question," Hood replied.

Daphne was referring to the renegade United Nations peacekeepers who had seized the Security Council during a party. Several children, including Hood's daughter Harleigh, were among the young musicians providing entertainment. Hood and his number-two man, General Mike Rodgers, entered the chamber and, in a bloody gun battle, freed the captives.

Daphne was regarding Hood intently.

"I certainly hated what they did," he told her.

"But not them?" she asked.

"No," he answered truthfully. "They lost. Victory cost us something. Life always does. But it cost them everything."

"So you see it as a net gain for our side," Daphne said.

"I'm not quite that dispassionate about it, but yes. More or less," Hood told her.

"You're more philosophical about confrontations than I am," Daphne told him. The woman leaned forward again. "I hate my enemies, Paul. I despise them from my nose to my toes. And I track them. I follow their activities in the trade magazines and through the cocktail-party circuit. If they are executives in a public company, I check the stock several times a day. Each time it goes down,

I'm a happy woman. I don't miss an opportunity to cut their hamstrings. In fact, I go out of my way to get them."

"Well, that's business," he said.

"No, Paul. It's personal. I personalize it. I personalize everything. You don't understand that, do you?"

"It seems a little obsessive to me," he admitted. "Or maybe that should be *for* me."

"It is obsessive!" Daphne agreed. "Who says that's a bad thing?"

"Well, there will always be more enemies," Hood replied. "You can't vanquish all of them."

"Probably not," she said.

"So I don't see what the benefit is to an ongoing high-intensity conflict," Hood said.

"Living," she said. "You feel passionate about something every second of every day."

"The hate doesn't eat you up?" Hood asked.

"That's the point!" she said. "It only eats you up if it stays inside. I channel it, use it as fuel for other things."

"I see," Hood said.

Not only did Daphne remind Hood of Martha Mackall, but she would get along terrifically with Op-Center's intelligence chief Bob Herbert. Herbert hated fast and deep and enthusiastically. Hood admired, respected, and trusted him. But if Herbert didn't have someone to keep him in check, he would constantly struggle between what was right and what was satisfying.

Daphne sat back again. "So. Now that I've turned you off completely, talk to me about whatever you do that isn't classified."

"You didn't turn me off," Hood insisted.

"No?"

Hood shook his head as he took another bite of breadstick. "Some of my best friends are sociopaths."

The woman gave Hood a twisted little smile.

That's promising, Hood thought. *She can laugh at herself.*

Hood answered Daphne's question as she finished her appetizer. He explained that Op-Center was the epithet for the National Crisis Management Center. It was housed in a two-story building at Andrews Air Force Base. During the Cold War, the nondescript, ivory-colored structure was one of two staging areas for flight crews known as NuRRDs—nuclear rapid-response divisions. In the event of a nuclear attack on the nation's capital, their job would have been to evacuate key officials to safe command centers outside of Washington, D.C. With the fall of the Soviet Union and the downsizing of the NuRRDs, emergency air operations were consolidated elsewhere. The newly evacuated building at Andrews was given over to the newly chartered NCMC.

Hood told Daphne no more or less than was described in Op-Center's public charter.

"The NCMC has two primary functions," Hood said quietly. Speaking in a loud whisper was a habit he had developed whenever he discussed even declassified Op-Center business in public. "One is preventative. We monitor intelligence reports as well as the mainstream press for possible 'hot button' incidents. These are seemingly isolated events that can trigger potential crises or terrorist activities at home and abroad."

"Such as?" she asked.

"The failure of Third World governments to pay their troops, which can lead to revolution and attacks on American interests," Hood said. "The seizure of a large cache of drugs, which can spur retaliation against law enforcement officers. We make sure local personnel are aware of potential dangers."

"So there's a lot of profiling, intelligent guesswork, that sort of thing," Daphne said.

"Exactly," Hood said. "The other function of Op-Center is to deal with situations that have already started to burn. I can't go into details, but it's along the lines of what we did at the United Nations."

"Killing bad guys," Daphne said.

"Only when necessary," Hood replied. He said no more.

Until eight months ago, the crisis-management process

relied heavily on the rapid-response military squad known as Striker. After Striker was decimated in Kashmir, Hood decided to rely instead on the surgical insertion of deterrent personnel. This allowed Op-Center to undermine enemies from the inside. It might take more time, but it risked fewer lives. If a military presence were required, Rodgers would call in an outside special ops unit.

The conversation turned to their private lives. Daphne told Hood about her ex-husband and how he was not ambitious enough to satisfy her.

"He was a partner in his father's law firm, a very powerful and high-profile firm," she said. "But he preferred riding horses to working with cases. I tried to get interested in that, but the smell and the empty shmoozing just drove me crazy. Especially since that was as high as he ever aimed."

"Didn't you know what kind of man he was when you married him?" Hood asked.

"I was twenty-two," she said. "I didn't know anything. I had spent my teenage years building my little advertising business. I thought it would be fun to hook up with a man who knew how to relax and had the means to do so. I didn't count on losing respect for him."

Hood laughed. "I had just the opposite problem," he said. "My wife wasn't happy with the way Op-Center monopolized my time. I actually quit for a few days, but I couldn't stay away."

"Did you know it was costing you your marriage?" Daphne asked.

"Not until the account was overdue," Hood said. "I knew Sharon was unhappy, but I didn't think she was *that* unhappy."

"So she initiated it?"

Hood nodded.

"How do you get along now?" Daphne asked.

"Okay," Hood said. "She's flexible with visitation and all that. But we were never really best friends. I suppose that was a problem all along."

"I agree," Daphne said. "You have to like someone to

be their friend. You don't have to like them to be married to them. Actually, I've developed a simple test for that."

"Have you?"

"Yes," she said. "I call it the sandbox test. If you and your potential mate were dropped in a sandbox, could you have fun there for twenty-four hours? Could you build castles or have a little Zen garden or pretend you were on a beach? Could you improvise a game of Battleship or draw pictures? Could you do something other than have sex or wish you were somewhere else? If the answer is yes, then that's a person you should consider being with."

"Does it have to be a sandbox?" Hood asked. "Why not just a hotel room or some form of transportation?"

"You would have TV in a hotel room," Daphne said. "Or magazines and food in an airplane or train. A sandbox demands imagination. You have to look at a mound of sand and see a dune or a mountain or a castle. It requires the ability to play well with others and to be a little silly. It requires the capacity to access the child inside you. Otherwise you can't be in a sandbox at all. Or a fun relationship. You also need to be able to communicate. If you don't have all of that, you'll be incredibly bored. Or else you'll end up bickering. Those same qualities are necessary for a successful relationship."

"And how did you arrive at this concept?" Hood asked.

"When I was doing a national campaign for an insurance company," the woman said. "It was set in a sandbox, with two people growing old together. It started me thinking."

Now Hood thought, too. He could never have spent a day in a sandbox with Sharon. He could not imagine himself playing in a sandbox with former Op-Center press liaison Ann Farris. After his separation, he had a fling with her. But Hood could have spent a day in a sandbox with the woman he was dating before, Nancy Jo Bosworth. The love of his life. A woman who walked out on him and shattered his heart. Hood thought about the way Bob Herbert talked about his wife, a fellow CIA operative who was killed in the Beirut embassy blast in 1983. He could imagine them playing together in a sandbox. Hell, that was essentially what they were doing together in Lebanon when she died and Herbert lost the use of his legs.

"It works with most of the ladies I've known," Hood told the woman. "But it sounds as if your former husband would have been a great one for playing in the sandbox."

"He would have been," Daphne agreed. "If it were a really big sandbox and he was with a Thoroughbred. Gregory would have felt self-conscious, uptight, and bored with just me. Like Lawrence of Arabia without a camel. That's the key, Paul. Would you enjoy a silly experience like that together? Is the idea of being together more important than where you are?"

"I get it," Hood said.

The sandbox test was an absolute. Daphne was obviously a woman of extremes, and life demanded more compromise than she seemed willing to allow. Yet it was sad to think that very few people Paul Hood knew could pass the test. Especially himself and Sharon.

Hood did not know whether he and Daphne Connors would enjoy a day in a sandbox. And it was much too early to worry about that. Still, they had spent an agreeable time having dinner and discussing very different philosophies of life.

They had not come to blows.

That was a good start.

THREE

The Celebes Sea
Tuesday, 4:34 A.M.

The sampan rocked vigorously from side to side as it neared the yacht from the stern. Lee Tong had moved aft. Clark Shunga had passed out plastique to Lee and one of the other men. Koh Yu continued to monitor the radio while the men silently oared the sampan closer.

Lee was poised on the horseshoe-shaped aft section of the boat. His feet were bare, and his legs were spread wide to help him keep his balance. Two curved wooden arms rose three feet above a seat to which the keel was attached. Lee worked the long *yuloh*-shaped keel with his left hand. The water whispered across the paddle of the keel. The sound always calmed him, especially before an assault. In his right hand he held a fist-sized chunk of plastique. The explosive was sealed in a sheet of plastic food wrap. The covering prevented the sea spray and Lee's perspiration from coating the plastique. The dampness would make it difficult for the waxy substance to adhere to the hull. The pirates had slung six large canvas sacks filled with sand over the port side of the sampan. This quieted the impact in case the vessels happened to bump one another.

Lee's pistol was tucked in a worn leather holster attached to his belt. He wore the gun low on his right hip. Once the explosives had been placed and the sampan pulled away, Koh would come from below with a megaphone. He would call out to the passengers on the yacht. If necessary, Lee and Clark were the ones who would fire at the plastique.

The sampan was just a few meters from the yacht. The

ship was not at anchor, and the sampan was rocking slightly in its wake. Lee skillfully maneuvered the keel while the other men oared forward. At the bow, Clark watched the yacht with night-vision glasses. Virtually every pleasure ship that sailed these waters had a deadman's watch from dusk until dawn. Even so, a ship traveling dark and silent was virtually impossible to see or hear. Especially if it came from the bow or stern. Most sentries tended to stay in the midsection of the vessel and watch the horizon. That was especially true in this region. Most sailors did not yet consider the Celebes Sea to be dangerous.

The sampan eased ahead. The yacht was more than four times the length of the pirate vessel. They would sail alongside, close to the hull, and place the explosives in reverse order. Clark would attach his explosive to the rear of the vessel as they passed. Then the sampan would continue forward. If the pirates were spotted, Lee would be able to aim his weapon at the plastique Clark had placed. When they reached the bow, Lee would use a rag to wipe sea spray from the vessel. Then he would place his charge against the hull. Then the sampan would move off to the side.

Clark continued to scan the ship slowly from bow to stern. As far as Lee could tell, there was no one on deck. Suddenly, Clark stopped. He was looking at a spot low on the forward mast.

"Retreat!" Clark said in a strong whisper.

Lee turned the keel to the port side. The *yuloh* men immediately switched to backwater strokes. Lee bent at the knees to brace himself for the lurch he knew would follow. The sampan shook as it braked. The streamlined boat steadied quickly as the men began to row in reverse.

Lee opened his eyes very wide. He tried to see into the darkness. He searched the spot where Clark was still looking. He could not see anything.

"It's tracking us," Clark said. His voice was louder now.

"What is?" Lee asked.

"A security camera with a night-vision lens," Clark said. "It's three meters up on the mast."

Lee looked up. He still did not see the surveillance camera. But there was no time to worry about it. Just as the sloping prow of the sampan cleared the stern of the yacht, several figures came on deck. They were about four meters up. Lee could not see them, but he could hear them. He could also hear the distinctive slap of clips being loaded into automatic weapons. An instant later, the soft, black night was pocked with yellow flashes, deadly stars on the deck of the ship. A sound like balloons popping rolled from the deck. And then there were screams. The screams of the men on the sampan.

Lee felt the backward movement slow. The *yuloh* men must have been hit. He did not dwell on that. He released the tiller and ran forward. Realizing that he was still holding the plastique, Lee tossed it overboard. He did not want to risk having a bullet strike the explosives by chance. His chances of surviving the attack were remote enough without the added risk.

As the wooden deck spat splinters of wood at him, Lee scurried on hands and knees to the middle of the vessel. The belowdecks compartments were covered by a long, inverted U-shaped shelter. This was made of Foochow pine covered with bamboo matting. The roofing would provide some protection as Lee made his way below-decks. The pirate's intention was to hide there and hope that the yachtsmen did not board the sampan. If they did, he still had his pistol. He would use it against them if he could. If not, he would turn it on himself. He did not intend to spend any time in a Singapore prison.

Lee screamed as a bullet hit his right ankle. The shot cut his Achilles tendon and caused his leg to straighten. He flopped flat on his belly as a hot, cramplike pain raced up his right side all the way to his neck. As he fell, a second bullet drilled into his left calf. That sent a wave of fire up the other side. Lee bit down hard to keep from screaming and giving his location away. Desperately, he tried to pull himself forward on his flat hands. Perspiration stung his eyes. He felt as though his body weight had tripled as he dragged himself ahead. He sucked air through his teeth and fought to keep his eyes open.

Suddenly, that effort was no longer necessary.

There was a sound from the bow like a rock going through glass. He knew that sound. It was plastique. Lee felt himself rising. The sound was followed by intense heat and white light, both of which hit Lee like a fist. He couldn't hear, see, or feel anything but that for an endless moment.

And then he heard, saw, and felt nothing.

FOUR

Sydney, Australia
Thursday, 8:30 A.M.

Lowell Coffey liked a good intellectual fight. He loved joining them. He loved causing them. Typically, there were two ways they came about.

One way was by giving speeches. Communicating his strongly held ideas as concisely and effectively as possible. Being the attorney for Op-Center allowed him to do that from time to time. He spoke on issues of international rights and national security, of civil liberties and the loss of privacy. If the thirty-nine-year-old attorney had the thick skin required for politics, he would have run for office. But he had a stubborn, confrontational nature when anyone criticized his views. In politics, Coffey knew he would get it from both sides. The Southern California native believed in a very strong and aggressive military. That was his conservative side. He believed very deeply in human rights in all their forms and variations. That was his liberal side. He would never form any kind of coalition to get himself elected, which was unfortunate. Unlike many politicians, Lowell Coffey III had what he jokingly referred to as a "substance abuse" problem. He was addicted to issues that had meat on strong bones. His interest in substance was what drove him to international law. His father would have preferred that he join the successful entertainment law firm of Coffey and O'Hare, based in Beverly Hills. But while Coffey liked his Armani suits, Rolex watch, and Jaguar—which was in the shop more than it was out—he had needed substance as well. He found it first as an assistant to the California state attorney general, then as deputy assistant to the United States solicitor general. Since joining Op-Center six years ago, he was up to his cleft chin in substance. There was hardly a nation on earth or a division of the federal government Coffey had not dealt with since joining the National Crisis Management Center. Sometimes those dealings were adversarial, as when Striker was caught in the struggle between India and Pakistan, or when Paul Hood and Mike Rodgers shot up the United Nations to end the hostage standoff. Often he ended up learning on the job. But even international confrontations gave him satisfaction he would not have gotten from negotiating product placement in movies for deodorant or beverage brands. Coffey's personal and professional integrity did not prevent his coworkers from referring to the sandy-haired Californian as Percy Richkid. It was a tease, and he rolled with it. Besides, Coffey could not help the financial stratum in which he was born. He took pride in the fact that he had never used family connections to get anything. Coffey had worked hard at every school he attended, and he had earned every position he held.

The second thing the tall, blue-eyed attorney enjoyed was travel. Unlike most travelers, however, seeing new sights was not what appealed most to Coffey. Back in the early 1980s, the attorney had attended Oxford for postgraduate studies in international law. Being on campus had exposed him to ideas that were not only contrary to his own but often anti-American. Coffey knew things to be true viscerally. He enjoyed having the opportunity to defend them intellectually. He discovered that classrooms, coffeehouses, even train stations and airport lounges gave him an opportunity to jump into conversations and state his views. After graduation, traveling around the world for the state of California and the federal government gave Coffey the chance to exercise his skills. Happily, every region was different. Coffey encountered debates in London that were unlike those he found in Montreal, Moscow, Tokyo, or Damascus.

And now, Sydney.

Coffey was standing outside the front door of the Park

Hyatt Sydney on Hickson Road. He had arrived the night before and gone directly to bed. From his room at the rear of the hotel he could see across Sydney Cove to the spectacular Sydney Opera House. Standing here, along the broad avenue, he was able to look out at the wharves on Walsh Bay. Sydney was a clean, vibrant, spectacular city. Coffey was only scheduled to be here for three days. Most of that time would be taken up by the Conference on International Oceanic Sovereignty. Coffey hoped he would have time to see some of the city.

Even though Coffey had his sunglasses on, it was still a blindingly bright morning. The sun bounced off the water and the clouds. It was reflected from every silver tower and white structure in a city full of them. The sun and air felt different here than they did in the United States or Europe. Maybe the heat was softened by the constant sea breeze. Maybe the ocean kept the air clean as well. Whatever it was, Coffey found it invigorating.

Tourists came and went from the hotel as Coffey waited for his ride. Penny Masterson was chairperson of the Asian Rim Relocation Organization. Coffey had met the woman in Washington several years earlier at a seminar hosted by Amnesty International. ARRO was a not-for-profit group dedicated to assisting refugees from Indonesia, Malaysia, and other nations close to Australia. Many of those refugees ended up in Australia, most of them illegally. Those who were caught or subsequently identified were returned to their homelands. If there was anything worse than being an illegal immigrant deported from a nation, it was being an illegal emigré returned to one of those countries. Charges of treason, followed by lengthy prison sentences including hard labor were not uncommon.

The petite, strawberry-blond Penny was the perfect person for the job. The twenty-nine-year-old was sweet, she was bright, she was compassionate. She had grown up being teased about her maiden name, which was Penny Date. Boys would ask if that was how much she charged. As a result, Penny had the thickest skin of anyone Coffey had ever met. She could run for public office and win. But she wanted to help people and not, as she put it, "run a football team whose primary adversary is itself."

Penny pulled up in her old red pickup. The doorman opened the battered door. It groaned.

"Sorry, Lowell," Penny said as he climbed in. "It isn't exactly the red-carpet treatment."

"It's charming," Coffey replied diplomatically. The truth was, the truck smelled of fertilizer, and there were what Bob Herbert called HVICs on the windshield—high velocity insect casualties. The only thing charming about the vehicle was the driver. Penny's accent had little silver bells in it. Her smile gleamed like those little silver bells. And her eyes were as brilliant as the sunshine. If she were not married, he would be engaged in a very serious long-distance courtship.

"The truck is functional," Penny said. "Unfortunately, I hadn't quite mastered some of the narrow turns when that happened," she added, nodding to the dented door.

"But you have now?" Coffey asked anxiously as he buckled himself in.

Penny laughed. That was music, too. "I wouldn't put Gaby in here if I hadn't," she replied as she pulled away from the hotel.

"Gabrielle must be what, now—a year old?" Coffey asked.

"Thirteen and a half months," Penny said. "And she's a peach."

"I have no doubt," Coffey replied. "What about your husband? How is he doing?"

"Charlie is doing great," Penny said. "He quit the parks service seven months ago and became a self-employed gardener."

"Which explains the truck instead of a minivan," Coffey said.

"We've got a fleet of three!" Penny laughed. "Charlie just couldn't take it anymore. He spent more time figuring out how to implement budget cuts in his field crew than he did actually landscaping. As he put it, 'I was tired of trying to move heaven. I'd rather move earth.' "

"We've got that same problem at Op-Center," Coffey said. "Do you work with him at all?"

"On weekends I use this truck to help him transport trees, shrubs, and soil around the city and suburbs," Penny said. "I have to say, I enjoy getting my hands dirty in a wholesome way."

"It probably takes your mind off the more unpleasant things in life," Coffey said.

"It does," Penny agreed. "But I found that it also serves a purpose in my own work. When I drive up to meetings or detainment centers, people don't automatically assume I'm a homemaker who is using ARRO as something to fill the daytime hours."

Penny turned off Hickson Road. Tools rattled in the open back of the truck. Penny did not even seem to be aware of the sounds. *There was something sweet about that,* Coffey thought.

"How is the conference shaping up?" Coffey asked.

"It's going to be the largest of the four we've held here," Penny said. "Thirty-two nations, one hundred and eleven representatives. And the breakfast reception at the State Parliament House is going to be a first. They're finally acknowledging that we're a force to be counted. When that's done, we'll go over to the Sydney Convention Center. You'll be speaking after dinner, which means that everyone will be well-fed and ready to sit back and listen."

It also meant that Coffey would have time to mingle, eavesdrop, and find out what other people were thinking. He would have time to address up-to-the-moment issues in his speech.

"Will our nemesis Brian Ellsworth be there?" Coffey asked.

"He was invited, of course," Penny said. "But he declined as usual."

"I'd be honored to take it personally," Coffey said.

"Your keynote speech in Brisbane last year was not in his nightstand reading stack, I'm sure," Penny said. "But

I do believe his disinterest is spread across the entire organization."

Ellsworth was chief solicitor for the Australian Maritime Intelligence Centre. Based in Darwin, Northern Territory, the MIC was the first line of defense against illegal aliens trying to make their way into Australia. They maintained that nationals who desired amnesty typically defected to foreign embassies in their own countries. As far as Ellsworth was concerned, every boat, plane, or raft that came through the back door carried drugs, smugglers, or terrorists. According to ARRO's research, just over 65 percent of those craft did. The other 35 percent transported people who were poor, terrified, and searching for a less oppressed life. The "Australia first" MIC had a great deal of influence in parliament. By law, illegal immigrants were typically returned to their point of origin within twenty-four hours. ARRO and the MIC were constantly fighting one another for a way to make the process more equitable.

As Penny spoke, her cell phone beeped. The young woman excused herself and answered it.

"It could be the baby-sitter," she said apologetically. She punched the hands-free phone that was bracketed to the dashboard. "Hello?"

"Mrs. Masterson?" asked a man's voice.

"This is she."

"Mrs. Masterson, is Mr. Lowell Coffey with you?"

"I'm Lowell Coffey," the attorney said. "Who is this?"

"Sir, this is Junior Seaman Brendan Murphy in the command of Warrant Officer George Jelbart, MIC," the young man replied. "I have your name from Mr. Brian Ellsworth. Sir, Warrant Officer Jelbart was wondering if you might have some free time today."

"I'm here for a conference," Coffey replied.

"Yes, sir, we know."

"What did Mr. Jelbart have in mind?" Coffey asked.

"A flight to Darwin," Murphy replied.

"That's clear across the continent!" Coffey declared. "Why does he need to see me?"

"We have a situation, sir," the officer replied. "One that he needs to discuss with you face-to-face."

"What kind of situation?" Coffey asked.

"A *hot* one, sir," the caller replied gravely.

The way the MIC officer emphasized *hot* led Coffey to believe that he was not referring to the temperature or an imminent event. That left just one interpretation.

"There are some people I should talk to before I agree to anything," Coffey said, glancing at Penny.

"We are a little squeezed for time," Murphy said. "You are the first and hopefully only call I'm making about this."

"If I decide to come, when can you arrange for transportation?"

"A P-3C patrol craft has been dispatched to Sydney Airport, Mr. Coffey," the caller replied. "It will arrive within the hour. As I said, sir, the warrant officer would like to talk to you in person."

Penny and Coffey exchanged looks. She tapped the Mute button.

"That doesn't sound like an invitation," she said.

"No," Coffey agreed. It sounded like an order.

"What do you want to do?" she asked.

"That doesn't seem to matter, does it?" he asked.

"Why not?" she asked. "You're a civilian and an American. You can tell the junior seaman, 'No thanks,' and hang up."

"Then I wouldn't find out why Ellsworth recommended they call," Coffey said. "I have a feeling the MIC is interested in talking to Op-Center, not just to Lowell Coffey."

"What makes you say that?" Penny asked.

"I'd rather not say until I'm sure," Coffey replied. It was not that he did not trust Penny. But he was an attorney. A cautious one. He did not like to say anything he did not believe or know to be true.

Coffey disengaged the Mute button.

"Where will the plane be waiting?" Coffey asked.

"If you go to the domestic cargo terminal, someone will meet you," the caller said.

"All right," Coffey said. "I'll be there."

"Thank you, sir," the junior seaman said. "I'll inform the warrant officer."

And Coffey would inform Hood.

He apologized to Penny. She said that she understood completely. He said that he hoped he would be back soon.

In his heart, though, he sensed that would not be the case. Especially if "hot" meant what he thought it did.

FIVE

Darwin, Australia
Thursday, 8:42 A.M.

Fifty-two-year-old Warrant Officer George Wellington Jelbart had seen and experienced many extraordinary things in his thirty-two years of service in the Royal Australian Navy.

Jelbart spent his first twelve years of military service with the Hydrographic Force. Based in Wollongong, just south of Sydney, he and his team constantly updated charts of the 30,000 kilometers of Australia's coastline as well as adjoining waters. He loved being out in ships and planes, producing maps that covered nearly one sixth of the world's surface. Even when his team was caught in a tropical cyclone, a category five hurricane, or a tsunami, he relished the work he was doing. As his naval officer father once described it, "The Navy puts muscle in your back. Danger keeps it strong."

The next nine years were radically different and much less muscular. Because Jelbart was so familiar with the geography surrounding Australia, Deputy Chief of Navy Jonathan Smith moved him to the Directorate of Naval Intelligence. That was during the 1980s, when the influx of Japanese businessmen and investors brought an influx of Japanese criminals. There, in a windowless office, Jelbart helped signal personnel pinpoint the direction and location of broadcasts coming from local waters and surrounding nations. He did that out of duty, not love. Finally, on his fortieth birthday, Jelbart requested a transfer. He needed to be back on the sea or at least in the sunlight. Smith agreed to a compromise. He gave Jelbart a promotion and shifted him to the Maritime Intelligence Centre. There, the newly minted warrant officer would be out-of-doors and dealing with a wider range of illegal activities than he had in his previous posts.

That was where Jelbart encountered the unexpected on a weekly basis. Some of it was heartbreaking. There were the Malaysian slavers who abducted Aborigine children via cargo plane. There were refugees from war-ravaged East Timor who were dropped offshore using World War II–surplus parachutes. Most of them were young. All of them were inexperienced jumpers. Fifty of the sixty-seven of them drowned. There were the Australian drug traffickers who used surfboards with high-tech listening devices to spy on MIC aircraft. Jelbart had even investigated sea-monster sightings in the Gulf of Carpentaria. Those turned out to be Chinese submarines conducting maneuvers.

But in all his years in the Royal Australian Navy, the sandy-haired, six-foot-four-inch Brisbane native had never heard anything like this. The implications were chilling.

Jelbart had arrived at his office in the Australian Central Credit Union Building, 36 Mitchell Street, at seven A.M. Throughout the early 1990s he had arrived early to hear phone messages and go through the mail. Since the late 1990s he had to come to the office early to slog through E-mails. If he could eliminate the E-mails from fellow officers who were compelled to forward bad jokes, he could do the job in an hour. Unfortunately, he had to open every correspondence on the off chance it had something to do with naval matters.

Shortly after Jelbart arrived, the phone beeped. His aide, Junior Seaman Brendan Murphy, answered. Murphy forwarded the call. It was from Captain Ronald Trainor of the Freemantle-class patrol boat *Suffolk*. They had found a man floating in the Banda Sea twelve miles east of Celebes.

"The fellow was barely conscious and clinging to a section of waterlogged pine," Trainor reported. "He's dehydrated and lost a lot of blood. He had been shot twice in the lower legs and managed to rig some crude bandages from his shirt. We assume he's a pirate whose mission ended badly."

"That's a possibility," Jelbart said.

Jelbart was confused. This was a routine rescue on international waters. It did not require the ship's captain to report to him personally.

"But what drew us to him was extremely unusual," the captain went on.

Jelbart grew concerned as Trainor explained. What they found was not only unusual, it was inexplicable. The warrant officer wanted a complete investigation. Trainor told him that they would search for the rest of the vessel and crew, as well as whoever attacked them. In the meantime, the injured man was going to be airlifted to the Royal Darwin Hospital along with the remnants of his vessel. Jelbart said that he would meet the helicopter there to take charge of the evidence and arrange for security. When he hung up, Jelbart realized that he would also have to notify Chief Solicitor Brian Ellsworth. Ostensibly, the Banda Sea castaway was being brought to Darwin for medical care. But Captain Trainor's other discovery made that a secondary issue from the MIC's point of view. The man had to be questioned. There were complex legal issues surrounding the interrogation of a foreign national recovered in international waters.

Ellsworth was in the shower when Jelbart called. The civilian official lived with his newscaster wife in the exclusive La Grande Residence on Knuckey Street.

At the warrant officer's insistence, Mrs. Ellsworth summoned him to the phone. Jelbart explained the situation as it had been explained to him. The forty-three-year-old solicitor thought for a minute before replying.

"I will meet you at the hospital," Ellsworth replied. "But there is someone else I would like you to call."

"Who?"

"A gentleman named Lowell Coffey," Ellsworth said. "He is in Sydney for a conference on international civil rights."

"That's the ARRO symposium?"

"Yes," Ellsworth said. "Mr. Coffey works for the National Crisis Management Center in Washington."

"Op-Center? Do we really want a foreign intelligence service involved in this?" Jelbart asked.

"We want the NCMC for three reasons," Ellsworth told him. "First, we'll want to get a very quick read on this situation. The NCMC can help us. Second, one of their best people is already in Australia. I don't agree with his politics, but he is smart and well-informed. Finally, holding this shipwrecked alien could backfire. Especially if the explanation turns out to be something very innocent. If that happens, we have someone to share the blame."

That last was not entirely honorable, Jelbart thought, but the solicitor did have a point.

Ellsworth had told Jelbart how to get in touch with Lowell Coffey. He was to call Penny Masterson, who was Mr. Coffey's host for the ARRO conference. The warrant officer passed the information to Brendan Murphy. Jelbart also told Murphy to dispatch a plane to Sydney. If the American agreed to come, Jelbart did not want to waste any time.

While the junior seaman made the calls, Jelbart composed an E-mail explaining the situation. He sent the message coded Level Alpha to Rear Admiral Ian Carrick at Royal Australian Navy headquarters in Canberra. The Level Alpha clearance guaranteed that only the rear admiral would see it. When that was finished, Jelbart checked his computer to see what appointments he would have to cancel today. And possibly tomorrow. He hoped this took no longer.

If it did, what Jelbart hoped was just an incident could turn out to be a crisis.

SIX

"What do we know about the hair up Shigeo Fujima's nose?" Paul Hood asked.

Hood, Bob Herbert, and Mike Rodgers were sitting in Hood's office. It was the end of an uneventful day in the middle of an uneventful week. As much as Hood had often wished his plate were not so full, he felt restless when it was empty. Especially since he did not have a family to go home to. Ironically, it was his overpacked schedule that had cost him his family.

Paul Hood's question hung in the air like a high, arching fly ball. Shigeo Fujima was the head of the Japanese Intelligence and Analysis Bureau at the Ministry of Foreign Affairs. Fujima had helped Op-Center resolve a recent crisis in Botswana without explaining why he knew what he knew. Or why he was interested. That did not sit well with Hood. Especially since the young officer was not returning Hood's calls.

"We know nothing," Herbert replied, finally calling the catch.

"What have we done to find out?" Hood asked.

"Last time I checked, which was about two hours ago, everyone in the tech lab, including Matt Stoll, had been unable to get into the IAB computers," Herbert went on. "Stoll says that all the files we want to look at are apparently in dedicated systems."

"I'm not surprised," Hood said. "The IAB does not play well with others." Daphne Connors's sandbox reference popped into his head. Maybe the woman had something there after all.

"Do we want to send someone to Tokyo?" Rodgers asked. "Check the files after hours?"

General Rodgers had recently established a human intelligence team at Op-Center. It consisted of international operatives who had worked with Op-Center in the past. Three of the members had distinguished themselves on the inaugural mission to Botswana.

"Who would you assign?" Hood asked.

"I've been talking to the guys we worked with during the Korean missile crisis," Rodgers said. "They gave me the names of people they have used. I talked to several of them. One in particular seems a good candidate. Bibari Hirato. She's based in Tokyo."

"This makes me nervous. What's she got against her own country?" Herbert asked.

"Japan isn't her country," Rodgers said.

"I see," Herbert said.

"Bibari is the daughter of a Korean comfort woman. Her father is one of three or four hundred Japanese sol.diers who used her early in the war. Bibari's mother gave her a Japanese name so she could go over if she chose to."

"And mess with them," Herbert said.

"In a word, yeah," Rodgers said.

"Objection withdrawn," Herbert said.

"Mike, why don't we have Bob run a check on her?" Hood said. "If she's clean from our point of view, let's do it."

"It was on the to-do list for tomorrow," Rodgers said.

As the men were chatting, Hood's phone beeped. Hood's assistant, Bugs Benet, said Lowell Coffey was calling from Australia.

"Thanks," Hood said.

"What time is it there?" Herbert asked.

"Late tomorrow morning," Rodgers said.

"Too early for Lowell to have pissed off anyone at a breakfast meeting," Herbert said.

Herbert fell silent as Hood took the call.

"Morning, Lowell," Hood said. "How are things Down Under?"

"Surprising," Lowell replied. "I'm on my way to the airport."

"Why? What's up?" Hood asked.

"I'm not entirely sure," Coffey said.

"Lowell, Bob and Mike are here," Hood said. "I'm putting you on speakerphone."

"Good," Coffey said. "I may need their help."

Hood punched the button and sat back. "Go ahead, Lowell."

"A few minutes ago, I got a call from an aide to a Warrant Officer George Jelbart of the Maritime Intelligence Centre," Coffey said. "He told me they have a hot situation up in Darwin. From what I was able to get over an unsecure line, 'hot' probably means one thing."

"Radioactive," Hood said.

"Right," Coffey replied.

Hood felt a chill in the small of his back. "Did he give you any context, a scenario of some kind?" Hood asked.

"Zero," Coffey said. "But I was on a cell phone, and he obviously didn't want to say very much. All I was told is that there's an airplane waiting to take me to Darwin."

Herbert had already swung up the laptop computer attached to his wheelchair. The intelligence chief had lost the use of his legs in the Beirut embassy blast that had killed his wife. He had wireless Internet on the laptop, as well as the ability to tap any of Op-Center's computers using LEASH—Local Executive Access Secure Hookup. The technology only worked within a radius of 500 feet from the personal computer in his office. While Coffey was speaking, Herbert had gone to the Australian Department of Defence file. He found the dossier on Warrant Officer Jelbart and read it.

"What do you know about Jelbart?" Rodgers asked.

"He's a heavyweight," Herbert said. He spoke loud enough for Coffey to hear. "He's fifty-two, a career officer, divorced twice, no kids. He runs the coastal intelligence network and has a background in mapping and signal recon. Commendations up to his eyeballs."

"Bob, are there any nuclear submarines in the Darwin area?" Rodgers asked. "I'm wondering if there could be a leak."

"I was not given that information."

"It could also be a plutonium-powered satellite that fell to earth," Hood suggested.

"I suppose," Coffey agreed. "But why would Jelbart call me for either of those? My first thought was that there might be civilian casualties resulting from an accident of some kind—"

"Possibly American civilian casualties," Rodgers pointed out.

"Right. But wouldn't they go to an embassy first?" Coffey asked.

"Not necessarily," Hood said. "If they were negligent in some way and wanted to cover their asses, having an internationally known human-rights attorney on site would be a nice cosmetic touch."

"Gentlemen, before we go to war with Australia over this, I'd like to check both possibilities," Herbert said.

The intelligence chief went to the United States Department of Defense secure file and accessed the naval intelligence Red List—an up-to-the-minute listing on the whereabouts and status of nuclear-capable craft. It was the list that gave the Pentagon the first warning that the Russian submarine *Kursk* had gone down in August 2000. The list also showed the status of the nine cruise missiles that had been removed from the submarine and taken to the top secret Nerpa shipyard located at the mouth of Olenya Guba Bay in Murmansk. The list included vessels with nuclear-powered engines and nuclear missiles. Herbert told the others that only the Chinese People's Liberation Navy had a vessel operating in the region, a Xia-class ballistic missile submarine. There was no suggestion of any problems on board. Then he went to the National Reconnaissance Office site to check on nuclear-powered satellites and exploration craft. Herbert reported that the list of deorbiting hardware was free of alerts.

"I sure was hoping it was one of them," Herbert said.

Hood did not have to ask why. Absent an accident, that left the probability of illegal nuclear activity, possibly the transportation of weapons or raw nuclear material.

"Lowell, are there any nuclear power plants in the Darwin region?" Rodgers asked.

"I already asked my host," Coffey told him. "She said she does not believe there are."

"I'm with you, Lowell," Herbert said. "Nothing personal, but I'm bothered by the fact that they asked for you instead of an official representative of the federal government."

"I am, too," Coffey said.

"Do we know that they didn't do that as well?" Hood asked.

"I was told that I was their one-and-only," Coffey said.

"Jelbert's aide may not have been in possession of that information," Hood pointed out. "For all we know, the American embassy has been notified. We're going to have to let this play out until we know more."

"There obviously has to be a legal issue involved," Herbert said. "Something that requires Lowell's expertise in international affairs."

"That does seem to make sense," Hood said. "Lowell, how long until you reach the airport?"

"About fifteen minutes," Coffey replied.

"Maybe we'll know more by then," Hood said. "Lowell, let us know what you find out as soon as you can."

"Of course," he said.

Hood wished him well and hung up. He looked at the others. "Bob, is there any history of nuclear trafficking in that region?"

"The answer is, 'possibly,'" Herbert said.

"Jeez, I remember when intelligence agencies used to deal in probablies," Rodgers said.

"When you were a greenhorn in 'Nam, they did," Herbert said. "We still had human intelligence resources in every backwater den you could imagine. Then the electronic intelligence guys came in and said there was no reason to risk lives anymore. They were wrong. Satellites can't do belowdecks imaging in a freighter or oil tanker."

"What about those possibilities, Bob?" Hood asked, getting them back on subject.

"We suspect that terrorists and rogue states in the Pacific Rim have used commercial ships and private vessels to transport nuclear weapons or components," Herbert told him. "But we have no evidence of that. For the last few years a bunch of navies and air defense forces around the world, including Australia, have been placing radiation-detection equipment on their vessels. These gizmos measure gamma radiation or neutron fields, depending on whether they're looking for raw radioactive material or weapons, respectively. But they haven't found anything."

"Which doesn't mean much," Rodgers said. "Adequate lead shielding will hide that."

Herbert nodded. "That's why we need more people watching potential traffickers on the shipping and receiving ends. The CIA and the FBI are working on that, but we're nowhere near up to speed yet."

"All right," Hood said. "The system has a lot of holes. But you're saying the Aussies have the capacity to pick up hot cargo?"

"That's right," Herbert said. "And if that's what happened, there are a lot of reasons they might want someone like Lowell to have a look."

Hood suggested that Herbert and Rodgers return to their offices to see if there was any other intelligence they could dig up. He would notify them as soon as Coffey called.

As they left, Hood looked at the photo of Harleigh and Alexander on his desk. He wished he could roll back the clock ten minutes. The responsibility of fighting nuclear terrorism was an unimaginable burden. The price of failure would be appalling.

Still, whether Hood wanted it or not, that responsibility might be his. Hopefully, this would prove to be something far less dire than he could imagine.

SEVEN

Sydney, Australia
Thursday, 10:01 A.M.

It was like talking to stone.

When Lowell Coffey did not get the service, respect, or answers he was looking for, his inclination was to stand and fight. Quietly, but with unshakable determination. Jaguar dealers or presidents, it did not matter.

This was a rare exception.

Coffey and Penny arrived at the domestic cargo terminal. It was a vast, low-lying building that looked as if it had been built in the 1960s. It was situated away from the main terminal area. Penny parked the pickup among rows of semis with container rigs. They walked to the front office, which sat just inside the main hangar. There they were met by a petty officer from the MIC. He was a fresh-faced kid whose name tag said Lady. That name must have got him teased a lot more than Date. Coffey judged him to be about twenty-five. The petty officer checked Coffey's passport, thanked him for coming, and said he would show the attorney to the aircraft. He removed a small point-to-point radio from his belt. Lady was pleasant, efficient, and uninformative. Unacceptably so. Coffey refused to follow the young man into the hangar.

"Petty Officer Lady, before I board the aircraft, I would appreciate some information," Coffey said. "Specifically, I'd like to know why I'm going with you." He had to speak loudly to be heard over the forklifts that were moving barrels and containers.

"I'm sorry, sir," the young man replied. "I can't tell you that."

"Then I can't go with you," Coffey insisted.

"No, sir. I mean I can't tell you because I don't know," Lady said. "What I can do, sir, is put you in touch with my CO if you'd like. But I can assure you that he doesn't know anything more than I do. This is a Level Alpha operation. Information is on a need-to-know basis."

"Well, I need to know, and so do my superiors," Coffey said. He held up his cell phone and wiggled it back and forth. "What do I tell them?"

"Sir, I wish I could help you. But that information is at the other end of a two-hour flight," Lady said. He held up his own radio. "What shall I tell the pilot, sir? He is waiting to take off."

If the kid had wiggled the radio, the attorney would have turned around and left. But he did not. He was respectful. And he had effectively called Coffey's bluff.

The American turned to Penny.

"It looks like I'll be taking a two-hour flight," he said. "I'll let you know as soon as I have some idea what's going on."

"Don't worry about it," Penny said.

"I do," Coffey said. "I just hope this isn't an elaborate Ellsworth plot to keep me from giving a speech."

"He's a duck-shover," she said, "but if that turns out to be the case, just E-mail me the speech. I'll read it for you."

Coffey thanked her and indicated for Petty Officer Lady to lead him to the plane.

"Duck-shover?" he said, turning back to Penny.

"My dad drove a taxi," the woman shouted ahead. "That's what they used to call drivers who cut other taxis off or muscled them out of the way."

"I love it!" Coffey called back, waving as he headed toward the back of the hangar and the door that led to the field.

The Lockheed P-3C was a big, gray, cigar-shaped four-engine prop plane. It was 116 feet in length with a wingspan of nearly 100 feet. Coffey had only been in a prop plane once before, when he traveled with the regional Op-

Center mobile office to the Middle East. He had not liked the noise and vibration then. He did not think he would like it now.

Because this was a transport mission, not travel to a combat zone, the P-3C had gone out without a tactical coordinator. The TACCO's station was located in the rear of the aircraft. After Petty Officer Lady turned Coffey over to the crew, the captain gave him the coordinator's seat. According to the pilot, it was the warmest, most comfortable place in the plane. The plane was taxiing before Coffey had even buckled himself in to the threadbare red seat.

The attorney faced the port side as the aircraft rumbled its way into the air. He was sitting in a cubicle shaped like half a pentagon. The sun-faded blue metal walls were covered with displays, buttons, and old-fashioned switches and dials. Coffey sat with his back to the open window as the sun burned across his neck and the equipment. An hour ago, if Coffey had to guess all the places he could conceivably have found himself this morning, the rear end of a Royal Australian Navy patrol craft would have been nowhere on the list.

The strangeness of it all was outweighed by Coffey's curiosity as to what he would find on the other end. The attorney was thrilled by the fact that he was in the right place to do something about whatever this was. He relished the opportunity and the challenge. It reinforced one of his strongest convictions: that an individual did not have to be in the big, bulging belly of politics to have a positive impact on society.

For the duration of the 116-minute flight, no one came back to check on the attorney or offer him coffee. Or a pillow. Nor was the flight all that comfortable. Coffey wondered if they had stuck him back there just so he would not bug anyone for answers. Sitting there, he found himself thinking about Paul Hood's managerial style.

Hood did not always have information that people wanted to hear. But he never kept them out of the loop. Sometimes he was not at liberty to say what he did know.

But he always told people that. Stonewalling was dehumanizing. Hood had his flaws, but he always treated people like people.

The plane landed at Darwin International Airport. The airport consisted of one large central structure that looked like a shopping mall in Anytown, U.S.A. The building was all white. Coffey wondered if everything in Australia was white. Located less than four miles outside the city, DIA was both a commercial airport and a Department of Defence airfield. It was used primarily by the Royal Australian Air Force. However, the MIC also flew reconnaissance missions from here.

Coffey was not taken to the terminal. The plane pulled off onto an apron where several F-18s were parked. The pilot walked him down the aft staircase to a waiting black sedan.

"Tell me, Captain," Coffey said as they crossed the short, windy stretch of tarmac. "Did you folks strand me back there on purpose? An unadorned yes or no will suffice."

"Yes, sir, we did," the captain replied.

"Follow-up question," Coffey said. "Why did you leave me alone?"

"Because we were told to, sir," the pilot said.

Okay, Coffey thought. *At least that was honest.*

The pilot turned him over to the petty officer who stood beside the car. The men exchanged salutes, and then the pilot left. The petty officer opened the door, and Coffey got in. There was a glass partition between the front and back of the car. Obviously, they did not want him talking to the driver, either.

The car sped off, carrying Coffey past a forest of tall, colorful stone poles that stood in a small, green plot beside the building. Coffey recognized these from the tour book he had read during the flight to Australia. They were Tiwi Pukumani burial poles—a tribute to the Aboriginal peoples who dwelt in the Northern Territory. They were used as mourning totems during funeral ceremonies. Afterward, they remained standing above the grave as a memorial to the dead. These particular poles were carved to honor all native dead. Coffey thought about how moving it must be for a sculptor to work on interpretive likenesses of deceased individuals from his tribe or village. The process made more sense to Coffey than a marble worker impersonally hacking names into stone.

Also, the burial poles were not white. They were brightly painted, a celebration of life.

As the sedan headed toward downtown Darwin, Coffey looked out at the gleaming waters of the Timor Sea. He found it ironic that since leaving Sydney he had encountered a pilot, a driver, and a series of totems. All of them were mute, but only one of them had any eloquence.

The one that was made of stone.

EIGHT

The Celebes Sea
Thursday, 12:12 P.M.

If anyone had been watching the two vessels, it would have seemed like a chance encounter. A passing ship or plane, even a spy satellite, would see it as an offer by a decommissioned cutter to lend assistance to a yacht. The two ships stayed together briefly, less than fifteen minutes. Then the cutter pulled away, its captain waving grandly to a fellow seafarer.

In fact, the encounter was anything but innocent. Or accidental.

Forty-seven-year-old Peter Kannaday, owner and skipper of the *Hosannah*, was supposed to have made the rendezvous with the privately owned cutter when night was upon the sea, and no one could have seen them together. But the explosion on the sampan had opened a crack in his hull. Actually, it had blown an oar, pieces of hull, and the body of a pirate against the bulkhead of the yacht. They were what had caused the breach. The crack was less than a meter long and was well above the waterline. But where it had hit was very inconvenient for the captain. Inconvenient and extremely dangerous. They had to stop and repair it. Fortunately, there had been no other ships in the area. That was one of the reasons Kannaday had selected this route in the first place.

The Australian sea captain watched as the red-hulled cutter moved away slowly. The diesel-electric motors growled loudly as the 200-foot-long ship crawled forward under a perfect blue sky. The cutter was formerly owned by the Republic of Korea Navy, bought from the United

States in 1950. Now it was the property of Mahathir bin Dahman of Malaysia, who used it as part of his global waste-disposal operation. The ship's captain, Jaafar, had said that Dahman had been very concerned about the risks of a daylight pickup. Jaafar had assured him that it would be all right. Dahman decided to trust his man on the scene. Jaafar was right. Everything went well.

Kannaday did not think that his own boss would be as understanding. It bothered Kannaday that he had to worry about that. The ship had a security officer for this. One who had been appointed by the boss himself.

Kannaday turned from the deck and went below. He pulled a hand-rolled cigarette from his shirt pocket. He lit it and took a few quick drags. The five security officers had gone down ahead of him. They were in the process of returning their automatic weapons to the gun racks. They were always on high alert during a transfer.

The rest of the crew was going about their business of sailing the yacht back to Australia.

The yacht belonged to Kannaday, and some members of the crew had been with him for nearly seven years. They were loyal, though not necessarily to him. They liked the untaxed money they made and the job was easy. Most of the time the *Hosannah* pretended to be conducting coastline tours or fishing runs. They wanted to be seen in as many places as possible. Crew members posed as paying customers. Between those essentially idle cruises, the crew were veterans of countless independent smuggling operations. They had transported people and goods all across the southern hemisphere, from Australia to South America.

The security people did not work for him. They worked for John Hawke, who worked for Jervis Darling. A thick mist of distrust circulated between them and Kannaday's veteran crew. Kannaday's men had never had to defend their vessel and their cargo. But they could and would, if necessary. Hawke's team had never sailed a yacht. Yet each team believed they could do the other's job better. Seamen always felt that way. Unfortunately, what had happened the night before stoked the frustration in both camps. The seamen felt the security team should have seen the sampan coming before dark. They had radar and sonar, installed in the radio room by Darling's technicians. Unfortunately, the sampan was so small it literally slipped under the radar. Kannaday's crew felt that once the threat was identified, the security people should have anticipated that there might be explosives on board. They could have changed course to avoid the threat, as they always did before going to work exclusively for Darling. Unfortunately, the schedules of Darling and his partners did not allow time for flight. They were to load and off-load the materials as soon as possible.

The miserable irony was that except for the explosion, everything had gone perfectly. The security system and defensive response had worked. An hour before they were supposed to meet Jaafar, the sophisticated marine radar had picked up a blip. Darling's nephew Marcus had reported it to Kannaday, who had watched the seven-inch color monitor in the communications room. They had observed the sampan's approach on the night-vision security camera attached to the mainmast. They decided that the crew were pirates preparing to board. A security team went on deck and took them out. So as not to hit fuel supplies or stockpiled ammunition, they aimed at the men, not at the sampan. Though they took precautions, a replay of the security video showed what had happened. Bullets struck explosives one of the pirates had been carrying. Perhaps the pirates had intended to try to cripple the yacht and forestall pursuit. In any case, the handheld explosive had blown up and damaged the yacht. There was no way to have seen that. No way to have anticipated it. And, unfortunately, no way to protect against it.

The yacht was divided into ten rooms. Six of those were for the crew, one was for munitions, one was for Kannaday, and one was for communications. The tenth room, the room that was damaged, was for their cargo. Kannaday walked down the carpeted central corridor to the room where repairs were still ongoing. Fortunately, all of the internal walls had held secure. Kannaday stopped beside thirty-one-year-old John Hawke, his security officer.

Hawke was a contrast to the tall, prematurely silver-haired Kannaday. The sinewy, five-foot-nine-inch Hawke was what the people of his native Cootamundra, South Australia, used to call a Mong—a mongrel, the son of a Canadian father and an Aborigine mother. However, no one who knew Hawke used the disparaging term. The taciturn sailor wore a wommera tucked in his sash belt. The traditional Dharuk weapon was a hooked wooden stick used for hurling darts with force and accuracy. The dart was placed in a hollowed end and then flung, like a jai alai ball. Kannaday had seen Hawke use the weapon on sea birds for practice. Their eyes were his favorite target. Their squawks were like sylvan music to him, producing the only smile Kannaday ever saw.

Hawke's own eyes were pale gray set in a face of dark rust. His hair was black and curly and worn in a shoulder-length ponytail. He moved with the steady, fluid grace of a man who had spent most of his life on a ship's deck. The oddest thing about him was that he was almost always whistling. Except for when he was on deck at night, he would whistle native melodies. No one ever asked him why, and no one asked him to stop. Not only was he a formidable presence, but he had been handpicked by Darling.

Right now Hawke was standing outside the cargo door. He was wearing a radio headset. He was speaking with the three crew members who were inside the room. Kannaday offered Hawke a drag from his cigarette. Hawke declined with a single shake of his head.

"How is it going?" Kannaday asked.

"Mr. Gibbons says they'll have the outer hull sufficiently repaired to get us safely to the cove," Hawke told him.

"Good," Kannaday replied. "Thank the lads for me. I'm going to report to the chief."

Hawke did not respond. Kannaday had not expected

him to. If something did not need to be said or indicated, Hawke did nothing.

Kannaday moved past him down the corridor. He shouldered by the security personnel who were returning from the munitions room to their cabin. The lab had been made from the forward port-side guest cabin. The radio room was assembled in the rear starboard guest cabin. In the center of the yacht was the saloon. Walls had been erected in the center of the dining area. The security team slept in hammocks slung in the port-side section. Kannaday's crew slept in the starboard section. Kannaday's own cabin was astern. Except for transfer times or emergencies, the security team remained below. To all outward appearances, the *Hosannah* was simply a pleasure yacht on charter.

Kannaday knocked on the door of the communications shack. Without waiting for a reply, he slipped his large frame through the small doorway of the windowless cabin. The rush of air from the belowdecks ventilation duct filled the room. The vent was located port side of a crawl space that ran the length of the yacht. That was where emergency supplies were kept. It was also where nonlethal contraband such as drugs or political refugees were kept.

The green-haired communications officer looked up from his cot. Marcus Darling was the chief's twenty-five-year-old nephew. The heavyset young man had an advanced degree in electronics and the arrogance that comes from nepotism. Most of the time he lay here or on deck reading science fiction and fantasy novels or watching DVDs on his laptop. Occasionally, he took the flare guns from the compartment above his station and checked them. In case of an accident, he was in charge of all forms of rescue signaling. But what the kid really wanted to do was run one of the boss's movie-special-effects facilities in Europe or the United States. Uncle Jervis told him that after he put in a year on the yacht, he would send Marcus wherever he wanted to go.

Marcus was the one who had built the *Hosannah*'s secure radio system three years before. At the time, the young man was still in college, and Jervis Darling was just beginning to plan this operation. Marcus had hacked a classified NATO web site to get a list of components the organization used in their field-communications setup. The heart of the system was a digital encryption module that could be interfaced with analog radios. Run through a personal computer, the DM continually modulated the frequencies while communicating the changes to a computer on the receiving end. It was virtually impossible to decrypt the communication without the computer software.

Marcus set aside the science fiction novel he was reading. He rose from the cot as Kannaday shut the door. The radio operator was on call all day, every day, and this was where he slept. The room was a tight squeeze with the radar equipment where the porthole used to be and the radio gear on the wall across from the cot. Kannaday backed against the door while Marcus moved toward the desk. It was actually a wide shelf built directly into the wall. The desk ran the length of the cabin. The young man eased into the canvas director's chair in front of the radio.

"I didn't hear any shooting this time, Peter," Marcus said.

"We get things right on occasion," Kannaday replied. He had long ago given up explaining himself or trying to get the kid to refer to him as Captain Kannaday. Fortunately, Marcus did not do it when other crew members were around. This was just the young man's private dig.

"Don't be modest," Marcus said. "You and your crew get things right most of the time."

"There's a 'but' in your voice," Kannaday said.

"You've good ears," Marcus said. "The 'but' you hear is that Uncle Salty likes things to be right all of the time. He doesn't like movies that flop, magazines that don't make a profit, and real estate that loses value."

Salty was the Australian media's nickname for Jervis Darling. It was inspired by the big, stealthy saltwater croc-

odile of the Northern Territory. Kannaday had no idea
whether Darling liked the epithet or not.

"This is a different kind of business," Kannaday said.
"There has to be leeway for the unexpected."

"I suppose that's true," Marcus said as he activated the
system. He picked up the headset and hung the earpiece
around his left ear. "Unfortunately, we can't really afford
that leeway, can we?"

"What do you mean?"

"Failure can result in more than a financial loss for
everyone concerned," Marcus said.

As much as Kannaday disliked giving Marcus his due,
the kid was right. Failure in this enterprise could result in
death or the kind of jail term that would make death the
preferred option. On the other hand, like all the men on
board, Kannaday obviously felt that the risk was worth it.
Kannaday was earning 75,000 dollars a week. His men
were taking in 6,000 each. Darling put the money in an
escrow account in the Cayman Islands. At the end of each
two-year stint, the money would be theirs. They had six
months to go on this leg. And they did not have to do
any other kind of smuggling for this employer. No drugs,
no guns, no terrorists. They already knew the handful of
players in this game, so there were rarely personnel
changes and very few surprises. The only thing that made
no sense to Kannaday was what was in this for Jervis
Darling. The captain did not understand why a multibil-
lionaire would be interested in taking a risk of this magnitude.

Marcus contacted Jervis's personal secretary, Andrew
Graham. Andrew was at the Darling compound in Cairns.
The secretary said he would transfer the call to Jervis
Darling's private line. Marcus handed Kannaday the headset. Kannaday placed the entire unit over his head. Marcus
did not get up, so Kannaday leaned on the metal desk. He
looked at the thermometer-like spectrometer on the wall
in front of him. One cable ran from the base of the unit
to Marcus's computer. Another ran to a battery pack on
the desk. The device ate up a lot of electricity, but they

could not afford to be without it. This room adjoined the laboratory. If there were a leak, software in Marcus's computer would notice a photopeak on its internal graph. That would cause an alarm to sound.

The connection would take about five seconds. They were five very long seconds. Kannaday drew hard on the cigarette. Most of the time, the sixty-two-year-old Darling was a soft-spoken man. But that was misleading. The Australian native could communicate more with a delay or with silence than most people could with speech. Darling had been very quiet when he was told about the explosion. He had told Kannaday simply to "take care of it." The captain had been chilled by Darling's monotone, by the way he pronounced "take" and "care" as distinct words instead of running them together. Hopefully, word of a successful transfer from Dahman's ship would mollify him.

"Go ahead," Andrew said.

"Sir, the transfer has been completed," Kannaday said. They never used Darling's name over the air. Unlikely though it was, there was always a chance that the signal could be intercepted and interpreted.

"All right," Darling replied. "We will talk about this when you arrive . . . Captain."

There was a click. Kannaday felt as though he had been punched hard in the gut. Darling had hung up. Kannaday had not expected absolution, but he had been hoping for neutrality. He did not get that. There had been a pause between "arrive" and "Captain." Kannaday did not know whether that meant *It was your responsibility to protect the ship,* or *Enjoy the title while it's still yours.* Kannaday removed the headset.

"Did Uncle Salty take a bite?" Marcus asked.

"Without even opening his bloody mouth," Kannaday replied. He opened the door.

"Don't worry," Marcus said. "Maybe my uncle will let it go at that. If you don't catch the first wave, often you won't catch it at all. When I was a kid, I saw him do that on one of his movies. His star was scratching away at a part like she was chipping for gold. Three days into the shoot, the director was already six days behind schedule. Uncle Salty couldn't yell at his big-name star, so he went after one of her wardrobe mistresses. He showed up on the set one morning and chewed her out for being slow. Chucked a micky, big time. Uncle Salty's star worked a lot faster after that."

"I'll make sure to warn my dresser," Kannaday said. "This is not a motion picture. Your uncle cannot afford to let things slide. He cannot write off a failure on his taxes."

"That's true," Marcus said as he returned to his cot. He shrugged. "I was just trying to give you some hope. Forget I said anything." Marcus picked up his novel and resumed reading.

Kannaday left the communications room. He should have known better than to engage in any kind of dialogue with Marcus. Not only did the kid like to tweak him, but Kannaday believed that Marcus and Hawke had something going. It was nothing he could pin down. It might not be anything more than simpatico. But every time Kannaday came upon them together, it looked as though the two men had just finished setting a bear trap. Hawke was typically implacable, but Marcus was always watchful, cautious, guarded.

Kannaday went to his small cabin in the aftermost section of the yacht. The hardwood floorboard creaked slightly. He shut the door and stared out the tiny rear porthole. He did not see the sea or the sky or the glare of the sun on the bulletproof glass. He was only aware of one thing: *How would Darling react when they were face-to-face?*

Kannaday knew too much about this operation for the magnate simply to dismiss him without the rest of his pay. Besides, Darling would have to get himself another boat. If he tried to take this one, the new captain of the *Hosannah* would have to explain what happened to the old captain. There would be an inquiry. Anyway, Kannaday did not believe that Darling would kill him. There were rumors about past activities of that sort, but Kannaday's crew was not stupid. If something happened to Kannaday, they would not wait around. They would take the yacht to sea and lose themselves at the first crowded port. Kannaday also did not think Darling would risk the setup he had.

Of course, there might be larger issues for Darling to consider. Issues that might override these other concerns. Darling might feel as if he needed to teach an object lesson to the men on this or other operations. That accidents could not be tolerated.

That possibility worried Kannaday. There was only one way he could be sure it did not happen.

That was to strike first.

And Kannaday had an idea just how to do it.

NINE

The Celebes Sea
Thursday, 12:33 P.M.

The cutter had proceeded northwest at seventeen knots. It reached the designated area quickly. Fortunately, the delay had not impacted Jaafar's scheduled drop-off. International Spent Fuel Transport, a division of Dahman Waste Management, had clearance at the site for noon until three-thirty every two weeks. There were 112 visits to this site each year. The next ship would not visit here until the following morning. The International Nuclear Regulatory Commission assigned the slots so that each ship would have a comfortable window for getting in and out of the area. The time slots were created to minimize the chance of collisions. And if an accident occurred on one ship, it would not threaten the crew of another.

Jaafar watched from the bridge as his crew worked the winch on the forward section of the cutter. The eight crewmen all wore radiation suits. They worked slowly and carefully as the fifty-foot crane removed a concrete block from the forward hold.

The block weighed three tons and was roughly the size of a compact automobile. It was designed to contain just three ten-gallon drums of waste. Each radioactive rod was sealed inside a mixture of absorbent lithium chloride, potassium chloride, and alkali metal chloride salts. These were packaged inside cesium metal containers within reinforced ceramic and steel drums. Once the concrete block was in the water, it would be lowered slowly to a ledge feet below. A fiber-optic camera on the line would guide the winch operator. He would take care not to nick or damage any other block while placing his. Each week, the

INRC sailed through this region to make certain none of the blocks were leaking.

This area of the Celebes Sea was one of twelve oceanic regions where the INRC permitted radioactive waste to be deposited. The seabed here was geologically stable, and fishermen did not regularly sail these waters. Any leaks would not have a high impact on any peoples or economy. Of course, security was a relative state of mind. The waste would be highly radioactive for ten thousand years. But it had to be disposed of and, for now, this was one of the best places for that. Especially since scientists were discovering that even the strongest containers buried on land were subject to erosion from microbacteria. Many of these organisms had been buried in volcanic flows millions of years ago and remained dormant inside the rocks. Just a whisper of radiation from materials such as cobalt 60 caused them to be revived and eat through rock and metal.

The olive-skinned, black-bearded Jaafar watched with pride as his men went about their task. The thirty-seven-year-old had worked closely with the physicists hired by Mahathir bin Dahman. They had designed a safe and efficient process for off-loading waste. The walls of the bridge were decorated with documents from the INRC commending the Dahman operation.

Jaafar remained at his post until the operation was completed. He radioed the home office in Kuala Lumpur to tell them that everything had been successful. Then he went below to thank the crew and have lunch.

And to enjoy, as always, one delicious snack.

The irony of those INRC citations.

TEN

Darwin, Australia
Thursday, 12:05 P.M.

Royal Darwin Hospital is one of the finest, most modern facilities in Australia. A ten-story white structure, it has a unique mission. Because the population it serves lives across a vast region, with varied racial backgrounds and difficult climatic conditions, the hospital must be ready to deal with almost any kind of illness or injury.

Medically, they were ready for Lee Tong. Psychologically, no one was ready for him. Or what he brought to Australia.

The staff car rolled up to the front entrance of the hospital. As it did, an officer stepped from the lobby. He was a big man with hair the color of straw. Coffey was not up on his Royal Australian Navy chevrons, but this man had the carriage of a high-ranking officer. The driver ran around and opened Coffey's door. The petty officer saluted as the other man approached the car.

"Mr. Coffey, I'm George Jelbart," the man said in a very thick Australian accent.

"Good afternoon, sir," Coffey said.

"Thank you for coming," Jelbart went on. "I hope the ride was not too uncomfortable."

"It was fine, except for the curiosity burning a hole in my head," Coffey replied.

"Please forgive the secrecy," Jelbart said. "You'll understand why that was necessary."

"I'm sure," Coffey said. "Thing is, I hate calling my boss and telling him that I don't know why I'm going someplace. It looks bad, us being an intelligence agency and all."

"I understand. Again, you'll see why it was necessary."

The men entered the hospital lobby. They walked past the casualty area toward the elevators, and went up to the fifth floor. There, toward the end of an L-shaped corridor, two leading seamen stood at ease on either side of a door. They each wore a sextant patch on their sleeve. When Coffey asked, Jelbart told him that the badge was from the navy's hydrographic survey branch. Both men wore handguns and no-nonsense expressions.

Hydrographic survey and maritime intelligence, Coffey thought. Science and counterespionage were working together on this. That reinforced what he had been thinking all along. He only hoped that the situation was not as bad as he imagined.

The men saluted as Warrant Officer Jelbart arrived. He returned the salute as he opened the door. Directly inside was a lead screen made up of three vertical panels. It was similar to the ones Coffey had seen in X-ray laboratories. The screen did not surprise him, but it did sadden him. A human being was lying on the other side of the screen.

There was a small window in the center. Jelbart gestured for Coffey to look through. The attorney stepped up and studied the patient in the bed. He was a dark-skinned, muscular-looking man with an intravenous needle in his arm and an oxygen mask on the lower half of his face. There were bandages over his bare chest, shoulders, arms, and portions of his face and scalp. Several monitors were hooked to his arms and temples.

"We think he's from Singapore," Jelbart said.

"Why?" Coffey asked.

"It's his general physiognomy," Jelbart told him. "Also, he's wearing clothes usually worn by dockworkers at Keppel Harbor. His shark and anchor tattoos look like the designs they do there as well. At least, the portions that weren't burned away."

"I see," Coffey said. "How did he get here?"

"He was picked up by an RAN patrol boat," Jelbart said. "They found him clinging to a few planks from what may have been a sampan. That's what the wood and curve of the wood suggested. He had third-degree burns over twenty percent of his body and a bullet hole in each leg. Ironically, the burns cauterized the wounds. Otherwise, he would probably have bled to death. He was out there for eight or nine hours before they found him."

"He's lucky they found him at all," Coffey said.

"Lucky is a relative term," Jelbart said.

"How so?"

"Our patrol boats are equipped with radiation detectors," Jelbart went on. "They watch for anyone who might be trying to smuggle nuclear weapons through the region. They got a reading from our friend."

"From him or from the wreckage?" Coffey asked.

"Both," Jelbart replied. "The doctors don't think he received a lethal dosage. There are tests, of course, though I understand the best sign will be if he actually wakes up. I'm told you know Brian Ellsworth."

"Yes."

"He is downstairs in the morgue with some local security officials and the wreckage," Jelbart told him. "We bathed the victim, but we don't want to clean up the planks until they've been analyzed."

"So you're keeping it isolated," Coffey said.

Jelbart nodded.

"Has anyone contacted the authorities in Singapore?" Coffey asked.

"Yes," Jelbart replied. "We're hoping they can help to identify this individual."

"But he will be too sick to transport back to Singapore," Coffey said knowingly.

"That happens to be true," Jelbart told him. He faced Coffey. His voice was barely above a whisper now. "But you're right, Mr. Coffey. We don't want him leaving here just yet. If this man was involved in the transport of nuclear materials, we don't know who else in Singapore might be involved. It could be members of the government, the military, or private industry. We don't want anything to happen to him until we can question him."

"You know that you can't hold this man if he asks to be released," Coffey said. "He was found in international waters and committed no crimes that you're aware of. For all you know, he was a victim."

"I understand that," Jelbart said. "Now let's talk about reality. This region is the world's best-traveled route for nuclear traffic. Your government has been at war with potential nuclear terrorists here and in Africa and the Middle East. But it's been on our shoulders to try to stop the goods in transit. That's not easy. Without trace radiation or known perpetrators, we have no right to board ships in the open sea. The coastline is another problem. Watching that eats up a lot of time and resources. I don't know what we're going to find out about this man. Air and sea patrols are searching the region where he was found. They're looking for more of the wreckage. So far, nothing has turned up. A few extra hours in the water may have diluted the radiation and the wreckage sufficiently to make detection difficult."

"What about other vessels that may have been in the region?" Coffey asked.

"We're checking charters, radio transmissions, even cellular phone calls that were made before dawn," Jelbart said. "According to the doctor, the victim was injured about four or five A.M. Perhaps another vessel saw or heard something. But then, we assume they would have reported it."

Coffey nodded. "Of course, if there was something illegal going on, this man's shipmates would have steered away from other vessels," he said.

"Most likely," Jelbart agreed. "There's one other scenario we have to consider. The accident occurred near the Ryder Ridge, a region for nuclear waste disposal. It's remotely possible this man and his shipmates were trying to salvage some of that material."

"In a sampan?" Coffey asked.

"I said 'remotely possible,' not 'likely,' " Jelbart pointed out. "Which brings me back to what I believe is the case. That they were transporting nuclear material in some form and were attacked. Maybe it was a deal gone wrong. Maybe they pushed their engine and it overheated. But we need to find out more, which means holding this man until such time as he can speak to us."

Coffey looked at the unconscious victim. "What are you asking me to do? Ignore his rights?"

"Involving you was Mr. Ellsworth's idea," Jelbart said. "I don't know what he wants you to do. But I'm telling you, Mr. Coffey, this has me scared. We have in the past intercepted troublesome cargo. Components for nuclear weapons. Fake passports for the transit of rogue nuclear scientists. Plans of nuclear power plants here and abroad, including the routes they use for the transportation of spent fuel. But this is the first time we have encountered clear evidence of radioactive materials close to our shores."

"The point is, you *did* find it," Coffey said.

"By luck."

"Nonetheless, you know where to look now," Coffey said. "By examining the wreckage, you may even know what to look for. What kind of ship, where it came from. This man may not know anything. You can't treat him as if he's a terror mastermind."

"Sir, we can't afford to treat him as if he isn't," Jelbart replied. "Do you want to know what I'm asking you to do, Mr. Coffey? I am asking you to consider the rights of the twenty million people living in Australia and the countless millions living around the globe. I'm asking you to consider their right to live lives free of nuclear terrorism."

"People should live free from any form of terrorism," Coffey said. He nodded toward the man in the bed. "That includes state-sanctioned terrorism, physical or psychological."

"No one is going to hurt him," Jelbart said. "Which is something else you should consider. Whatever treatment this man receives while he is our guest will be preferable to what they would do to him in Singapore. If the government wants information, they will beat or drug him to get it. If someone wants to silence him, they will do that, too." Jelbart looked at his watch. "I told Mr. Ellsworth I would bring you to him. I suggest we go downstairs now. The representative from Singapore is also due any moment."

The men returned to the elevator.

Coffey was torn. In theory, he could disagree with nothing the warrant officer had said. In practice, he could not shake a quote by Calvin Coolidge that he had memorized. It was commemorated in a plaque in one of the lecture halls at the UCLA School of Law where Coffey had been a student. It said, "Men speak of natural rights, but I challenge anyone to show where in nature any rights existed or were recognized until there was established for their declaration and protection a duly promulgated body of corresponding laws."

Jelbart was wrong. Bend the law, and the rights of all people suffered.

But then, Coffey was a good lawyer. As such, he could not help but wonder if there was a loophole in this instance. Nuclear terrorism, even the threat of it, removed part of what made him want to protect this man.

It took the word *human* from *human rights*.

ELEVEN

Darwin, Australia
Thursday, 12:17 P.M.

The RAN Iroquois helicopter carrying Female Naval Defence Technical Officer Monica Loh of COSCOM, the Coastal Command of the Republic of Singapore Navy, landed on the helipad at the Royal Darwin Hospital. The pad was typically used by the Rescue Birds—helicopters that brought patients from the regions surrounding Darwin. Formerly an officer with the Explosive Ordnance Disposal Group, the five-foot-seven-inch Loh walked several paces ahead of the two shorter male Naval Defence technicians who had accompanied her. The vessel to which Loh was attached, a 360-ton mine countermeasure vessel, was still at sea. Warrant Officer George Jelbart had dispatched the helicopter to get Major Loh to the Darwin hospital as quickly as possible.

Brian Ellsworth had sent a scanned photograph and fingerprints of an injured seaman to the Police Coast Guard at the Tanjong Pagar Complex in Singapore. Ellsworth had wanted any information the PCG might have on this individual. He was Lee Tong, a registered former seaman on the *Lord of the Ocean* container ship. The PCG wanted to know why Ellsworth needed this information. He told them, at the same time inviting someone from COSCOM to join the investigation. Since FNO Loh had experience in that area of the sea, as well as with explosive devices, she was sent to Darwin. The last time she had been involved with Australian officials was three years before. That was when the two nations had joined with Malaysian authorities to raid a warehouse on the Malaysian coast. They broke up a DVD pirating ring that the Australian

Film and Video Security Office said was costing Hollywood producers over twenty-five million dollars a year in lost revenue.

Everyone wants to be in show business, she thought bitterly at the time. To carry out the raid, Loh's superiors had pulled her off a coinvestigation with the Home Affairs Ministry involving Lebanon's Hezbollah guerrilla group recruiting Singaporean Muslims. These individuals were being used to spy on the American and Israeli embassies in Singapore. Fortunately, the Singaporean Muslims decided the risk was not worth the rewards. They quit the Lebanese terror unit before carrying out their mission.

Loh and her two aides were met by a pair of RAN leading seamen and escorted to the back of the hospital. They were informed that a service elevator would take them to where the "items" were being stored.

It felt strange to be on land. Loh was used to the rocking of the MCMV, where she spent much of her time. Even the helicopter had felt more comfortable than solid, unmoving asphalt. It was also unusual for Loh to be in the sunshine. While the bulk of the twenty-eight-person crew searched for mines, she conducted signal intelligence operations in a segregated area of the ship. She listened for communiqués that might suggest smuggling operations. If she detected anything unusual, the appropriate police or military unit was sent to investigate.

The fact that just the opposite was happening here did not surprise her. The thirty-four-year-old Loh did not share the viewpoint of many of her fellow female naval officers. They regarded the RSN nomenclature as dismissive, since male naval officers were simply referred to as *naval officers.* Loh did not agree. She sincerely believed that men had created the distinction for a reason. So that they would have somewhere to turn when things got difficult. Like now. Loh's father, Vendesan, was an officer with Singapore's Criminal Investigation Department. His specialty was gathering intelligence on the powerful secret societies that ran the nation's gambling, prostitution, and drug rings. Her father was very smart. But whenever Ven-

desan was baffled, he discussed the situation with his
wife. Monica would often lie in bed, listening to their
conversations. Her mother, Nurdiyana, was a school-
teacher. More often than not, the woman would have sen-
sible solutions to her husband's problems. It was the same
with the FNOs. When roaring and mane shaking failed,
the RSN lions sent in the smarter, cagier lionesses.

Not that Loh's father was like that. He respected
women. And he respected intellect. Chinese, Malay,
Tamil, and English were all official languages in Singapore. He spoke them all. At his insistence, Loh had
learned them in school. He himself had taught her Japanese.

"Arms can subdue, but often at great cost," her father
had once told her. "But languages can infiltrate and control. If used correctly, they give you power over groups
and individuals."

Her father had been proof of that. He had survived
forty-five years with the CID before retiring.

The Singaporeans and their escorts entered the spacious
elevator and rode down three floors. The doors opened on
a metal desk with a security guard seated behind it. A
senior member of the Darwin Police Force was standing
beside him. The officer tipped his hat to Loh as she
walked past. If she were out of uniform, she would have
found that sweet. In uniform, it made her uncomfortable.
She would have preferred a salute. They walked a few
steps to the morgue. The hospital guard buzzed them in.
The two leading seamen did not enter.

The morgue was about twenty by twenty feet. There
were refrigerated cabinets with stainless steel doors on the
left-hand side. On the right side were shelves with chem-
icals, tools, and electronic equipment. There were two
doors in the rear. In the center of the room was a row of
gurneys. Dark aprons covered several of them. Loh assumed that these were lead-lined and that the remains of
the boat were beneath them.

There were four other people in the brightly lit room.
One of them walked over briskly and introduced himself.

He was Brian Ellsworth, a short, rotund, balding man. Dressed in a black three-piece suit, the pale official looked as though he were dressed for his own funeral. Ellsworth introduced Warrant Officer George Jelbart, attorney Lowell Coffey III of the National Crisis Management Center in Washington, D.C., and Dr. Maud Forvey, a physicist at the Northern Territory University.

Loh introduced herself and her two aides.

"I want to thank you all for coming," Ellsworth said. "Frankly, we aren't sure precisely what we've stumbled upon. We hope you can help."

"You received the data from the Police Coast Guard," Loh said.

"Yes. We did, just now, thank you," Ellsworth said. "We have people checking to see if there is additional information about Mr. Tong."

"I would like to visit him," Loh said.

"We'll take you to his room in a minute," Ellsworth said. "First, if you don't mind, we'd like to know if there is anything you can tell us about the wreckage. We understand you've been at sea for ten years."

"That's right," she said.

"Mr. Jelbart believes it's from a sampan, but we aren't certain," Ellsworth said. "By the way, Dr. Forvey has checked the flotsam for radioactivity. It is extremely low level, perfectly safe for a brief exposure. Just don't handle any of the pieces without the proper attire."

Loh walked over to the gurneys. Dr. Forvey put on thick yellow gloves. She raised the end of one of the lead covers. The Singaporean officer looked at the charred pieces of planking.

"That's Foochow pine," she said.

"Are you certain?" Ellsworth asked.

"Absolutely. The Chinese use it to make *mu-chi* sampans."

"Do you ever see these in Singapore?" Warrant Officer Jelbart asked.

"Occasionally," Loh said. "They're mostly used for river travel."

"Why is that?" Ellsworth asked.

"The *mu-chi* sampans have a very low profile and can pass easily under most bridges," Loh informed him.

"Are they motorized?" Jelbart asked.

"They can be," she replied.

"Obviously this one was," Ellsworth said. "The question is, why take one of them to the middle of the Celebes Sea at night?"

"Piracy," Loh replied. "That's what sampans are used for in the South China Sea."

"That would make sense," Jelbart said. "The low profile would make it extremely difficult to spot on the horizon and difficult to pick up on radar. If they waited for nightfall, they could quietly oar their way to a ship."

"That's exactly what they do," Loh told him.

"What about using the sampans for smuggling?" Ellsworth asked.

"That is uncommon," Loh said. "There is not a lot of storage capability. They would not be very efficient when weighted down. Doctor, could you raise the apron a little higher?"

Dr. Forvey did so. Loh examined the wreckage for a long moment.

"There is something else," Loh said. "I don't believe that the explosion of a diesel engine caused this wreckage."

"How can you tell?" Ellsworth asked.

"The engine would have been located in the rear," she said. "The curve of these planks suggests they came from the front section. Something would have had to explode close to the planks to do this kind of damage. Also, the foxing along the sides of the wood is unusual. Petrol explosions produce sharp, splintering cracks. This wood was pulverized."

"Suggesting what?" Jelbart asked.

"That a powerful explosive device was on board," Loh said. "There have been reports over the last few years about a band of pirates who place explosives on the hulls of ships. The pirates threaten to destroy the vessels unless they turn over their cargo."

"Do we know anything about these pirates?" Jelbart asked.

"No," Loh replied. "They always attacked in the dark and stayed out of range when making their demands. Any hostages they took were hooded or killed. It is conceivable they could have used a sampan for these attacks."

"How did they collect their plunder?" Jelbart asked.

"The cash and jewelry were put in a dinghy or sometimes a bag, which one of the pirates would swim over to collect," Loh replied.

"That would not have been a convenient way to move nuclear materials around," Dr. Forvey noted. Carefully, she lay the heavy apron back across the battered pieces of wood.

"That assumes this was the same group of pirates," Coffey said.

"The only way we're going to find that out is by talking to the survivor," Loh said. "I would like to do that as soon as possible."

"He's unconscious," Ellsworth told her.

"Then we'll have to wake him," Loh replied.

"Officer Loh, that's something we will have to discuss with his doctors," Ellsworth said.

Loh glared at him. "*You* can discuss it with his doctors," she suggested firmly. "I am here to find out why a sampan and one of its operators were exposed to radiation."

"We can try to do both," Coffey suggested diplomatically.

Loh turned and walked toward the door. There was nothing to hunt down here.

The lioness was moving on.

TWELVE

The Celebes Sea
Thursday, 1:08 P.M.

The yacht was about to cross south into the Molucca Sea when Captain Kannaday summoned John Hawke to his cabin. Fifteen minutes later, the security chief knocked and entered.

Kannaday was seated at a small rolltop desk against the port-side wall. It was an eighteenth-century piece. There were laminated charts marked with grease pencil and a laptop with nautical data. When Kannaday sat here, it made him feel like the captain of an old-time frigate or whaling ship. How many of those men also dealt in contraband? he often wondered. Back then it would have been slaves and arms and opium.

Hawke shut the narrow door behind him. The bright light from the porthole moved with the slow sway of the he pryacht. One moment the sun shone brightly on the officer's long face. The next moment he was in sharp-edged darkness. Hawke did not blink in the direct light of the sun. He removed his headset and hung it over his shoulder.

There was a deck chair beside the bed. Kannaday did not invite him to sit. The captain swiveled his own chair toward the newcomer.

"You took your time getting here," Kannaday said.

"I was busy with the repairs," Hawke replied.

The man had a voice like sea spray. It was soft and feathery, a combination of his mother's drawling Aborigine accent and his father's lyrical Canadian inflection. Considering the setback they had suffered, it was also disturbingly confident and untroubled.

"What is the status of the lab?" Kannaday asked.

"The hole has been welded shut," Hawke replied. "The area is free of leakage."

"Leakage of seawater or radiation?" Kannaday asked.

"Both," Hawke replied. "However, damage to the processing equipment has been extensive."

"Are you saying the materials cannot be processed by the time we reach Cairns?" Kannaday said.

"That is correct," Hawke informed him. He waited a moment, then asked, "Is there anything else?"

"Yes. You don't seem very upset," Kannaday said.

"I cannot change what is," Hawke said.

"The chief did not want us ever coming into port with the cargo," Kannaday reminded him.

"The only other option is to dump the drums," Hawke said. "We have already radioed ahead for new equipment. It will be waiting at the compound when we arrive. We will sail in, collect the gear, then sail out."

"Are you certain there are no other options?" Kannaday demanded. "Nothing we can jury-rig?"

"The destruction was extensive. You can get a radiation suit and go to the laboratory and look for yourself." Hawke removed the headset from his shoulder. He held it forward. "Or you can ring Dr. Mett and ask him."

"I'm asking you," Kannaday said.

"Asking? It sounds as if you are accusing me," Hawke said.

"Perhaps you're feeling guilty," Captain Kannaday said. "What is the problem, exactly?

Hawke's unhappy gray eyes were fixed on the captain. He replaced the headset. "Even crude reprocessing requires nitric acid to dissolve the spent elements," Hawke replied. "All of our containers were shattered in the explosion. We also need a functioning centrifuge to separate the remaining materials into daughter products. The blast dented the swing arms. They will not turn correctly. Our partner is expecting three pounds of enriched uranium in pellet form. Three hundred and fifty pellets, roughly. If we cannot distill the material, we cannot turn it over to our partner, nor he to his clients." Hawke paused. He was beginning to seem restless, annoyed. "I feel obligated to add, Captain, that the crew feels we are lucky to still be afloat."

"I agree, Mr. Hawke. And I don't much care for luck," Kannaday said.

"We took every reasonable precaution," Hawke pointed out.

"Apparently not," Kannaday said. "Our hull was breached."

"Once again, did you order me here to take some of my skin off?" Hawke asked.

"No, Mr. Hawke," Kannaday replied. "The truth is, I asked you here for something else. I'd like your resignation as head of security."

The shifting light fell full upon Hawke's face. After a few moments, his expression changed. He no longer appeared to be impatient. He seemed almost amused by Kannaday's pronouncement.

"You expect me to fall on my sword for what happened?" Hawke asked.

"Those are your words, not mine," Kannaday said.

"But that's what you're asking."

"We were unprepared. The men who attacked us were not novices," Kannaday said. "There must have been reports of previous raids."

"Quite possibly," Hawke agreed. The amusement vanished as swiftly as it had come. He was growing angry now. "But whenever our computer boys hack about for classified information, they risk leaving a trail. Every time we pay someone to look up police records on a particular sea lane or harbor, we bring someone else into our circle. It is more efficient and ultimately more secure to deal with a rogue or two if and when they show up."

"That's an excuse, not an answer," Kannaday replied. "I want your resignation."

"And if I choose not to give it?"

"Then you will be dismissed," Kannaday said.

"With or without the chief's approval?" Hawke asked.

"When we sail into the cove with those drums of raw nuclear waste on board, the chief will not dispute what I have done."

"Are you so sure, Captain?" Hawke walked forward. "I work for him, not for you."

"The chief dislikes failure," Kannaday said. "He'll back me."

"Because you're the captain?" Hawke pressed.

"Because I'm looking out for his interests," Kannaday replied.

"I see. This decision has nothing to do with your being a full-blood?" Hawke demanded.

"That's irrelevant," Kannaday said.

"Because you say so?" Hawke asked.

"Because it's true!" Kannaday replied. "I have never judged you by your background."

"But when you have your audience with the chief, you will tell him that I was inattentive and uncooperative," Hawke said. "White shorthand. Those are the usual charges against native Australians. You might even get him to believe you. He has never been a friend to Aboriginals or their issue."

"Your background has nothing to do with my decision," Kannaday insisted. "You failed in your responsibility. That is not something we can afford. You will be paid for the work you have done thus far. That's a considerable sum, I should add. With a resignation, you can run security for another operation. This won't affect your career."

Hawke drew the wommera from his sash. The four-inch-long darts were in a closed canvas sack that hung beside it. Kannaday was not concerned. There was not enough room to use them in here. And the stick was neither solid nor thick enough to use as a club.

"I refuse to resign," Hawke said. There was steel in his jawline, in his voice. "Now. How will you enforce your decision?"

"I have weapons, too," Kannaday said. "And I have the men to use them. More men than you have."

"You have sailors," Hawke said. "I have killers."

"Half of them are Aboriginal and half of them are white," Kannaday said. "How do you know they won't turn against each other in a showdown?"

"My people are loyal to me," Hawke said.

"Your people? Your killers still work for the chief, and they will want to get paid," Kannaday assured him. "Now get out. I have to inform the Indonesians that we will not be making the rendezvous in the morning. Then I'm going to turn over security operations to one of my people, Mr. Henrickson. You may have free run of the ship as long as you agree not to work any mischief."

"I will not resign," Hawke said.

"Then you are dismissed," Kannaday said. He glanced at the wommera as he rose. "And if you're thinking of taking me on personally, I've tangled with monkeys like you my whole life. Up and down the islands, in bars and down alleys, on and off board ship."

"Monkeys," Hawke said contemptuously.

"Yes," Kannaday said. "Annoying little creatures. Now leave before I throw you out."

"Like trash," Hawke said.

Kannaday had had enough of this. Everyone felt oppressed these days. He reached for the security chief's shoulders. As he did, Hawke jerked the wommera as though he were cocking a shotgun. The top quarter of the stick flew off. Beneath it was a scalpel-sharp five-inch steel blade. Hawke thrust the slender knife forward. He pressed it into the soft flesh just below Kannaday's larynx. The blade was pointed up. Hawke forced Kannaday to the balls of his feet. Kannaday had not known the wommera had a concealed blade. He felt stupid. That was worse than feeling helpless.

"Don't *ever* assault me," Hawke said. "I'm not your dog . . . or monkey."

Kannaday said nothing. At moments like these it was best to listen. That provided information as well as time.

"Maybe you're telling the truth," Hawke went on. "Maybe you hate me for myself, not for my background.

Or maybe you were just protecting your ass like you've done before. For your information, I did conduct research before signing on. I looked up your personal history. I know about the lawsuit your former partner Mr. March filed when you stole this ship by changing national registries. He could not get you into court because he could not find you. I know about the counterfeiters you betrayed in Auckland to save yourself from a smuggling charge, and I know about the wife you abandoned in Sydney. The chief needed someone to run this route, and you were the perfect bastard. But I knew it would be wrong to trust you too far."

Hawke leaned into the wommera. The captain felt a pinch at his throat. He backed against the rolltop desk. Hawke followed him. Thick drops of blood fell slowly onto Kannaday's trousers. The captain had anticipated that Hawke might attack him. He kept a .45 in his desk drawer for protection. But he was up against the drawer and could not reach it.

"You asked why I was late just now," Hawke said. "I was speaking with my men. They may be mixed, Mr. Kannaday, but they understand loyalty. They also understand necessity. If they cannot trust their fellows under fire, they will not survive. So here is my proposal. I will allow you to keep your ship and your command. If the chief dismisses you, we will refuse to sail with anyone else. He will not want to lose us both." Hawke moved in closer. He did not press the blade further. "We can all ride out this unfortunate incident. The key to your personal survival, Captain, is not to find a goat. It is to be allied with a hawk. Someone who can watch over you."

"You have a sword at my throat," Kannaday rasped. "You haven't left me any options."

"Did you leave me any?" Hawke demanded. "How does it feel?"

The blood was running thicker now. Kannaday thought about trying to grab the shaft.

Hawke seemed to read the captain's mind.

"Think this through," Hawke warned. "No one needs

to know about our exchange," Hawke told the captain.
"When you see the chief, you can tell him you were injured in battle. He may even respect you more for it. I
will tell my men that you never threatened me. I will say
that we simply agreed on what you would tell the chief.
You can wear a turtleneck to conceal the wound."

"I see. And we just go on as we were," Kannaday said.

"We do," Hawke replied. "You don't have to like me
or our arrangement. But this is what necessity demands.
You will live with it."

Hawke backed away. He relaxed the blade slightly. A
moment later he removed it entirely. That was intended,
no doubt, to be a show of trust. Or perhaps of confidence.
The two were often related.

Kannaday removed a handkerchief from his pocket. He
dabbed it against the shallow wound. He stepped away
from the rolltop desk. The captain could reach the .45
now. Hawke had attacked him. Kannaday had the wound
to prove it. And the weapon.

The sheath of the wommera was attached by a slender
leather thong. Hawke replaced the cap and returned the
weapon to his belt. Then he turned away and walked
slowly toward the door.

Kannaday could easily reach the gun. Hawke obviously
knew that, too. He had to suspect that the captain kept a
weapon in his quarters. But to stop Hawke now would
mean shooting him from behind. To kill him that way
would probably cause even his own sailors to turn on him.
They would understand discipline and self-defense but not
cowardice.

Hawke paused by the door. He turned back and faced
the captain full. "Is there anything further you wanted?"

"No," Kannaday replied.

Hawke lingered a moment longer. Then he reached behind him, twisted the knob, and left the room.

Kannaday's shoulders dropped. He had not realized
how tense he was until they did. He checked the handkerchief and saw that it was thickly stained with blood.
He pressed it back in place and went to get a first-aid kit.

He kept one in the locker at the foot of his bed, along with his private store of scotch. As soon as he patched the cut, he would open the bottle.

Kannaday was shaken. The captain was also angry at himself for underestimating Hawke. The man had poise. And courage. And a purpose: To end this encounter leaving Kannaday feeling something less than a captain. And a man.

Kannaday sat on the bed to clean and bandage the wound. He gazed into the mirror on the inside of the lid. The gash was a quarter inch long and bleeding slower now. But it went deep. Right down to his dignity.

As Kannaday uncapped the antiseptic cream, he reasoned that he had not come from this empty-handed. If he had not confronted Hawke, there was no guarantee the man would have stood by him. Still, Kannaday promised himself this much. If John Hawke failed to back him up with Jervis Darling, honor and pride would not save him. Kannaday would take him down anywhere and any way he could.

Even if that meant shooting him in the back.

THIRTEEN

Washington, D.C.
Thursday, 11:09 P.M.

"I feel like I'm in Oz," Coffey said into his cell phone.

"You are," Hood reminded him.

"I mean the other one, the Emerald City one," Coffey replied. "The one where an out-of-towner walks around with a strange collection of personalities, looking for something that's really tough to find."

Hood was alone in his office. Bob Herbert and Mike Rodgers had just gone home, but their teams were still looking for intelligence. They were seeking any leads about radioactive materials missing or currently being trafficked through the region. They had not yet turned up anything new or relevant. As Herbert had reported before leaving, governments or components thereof were often involved in this trade. Unlike individuals, nations like China and the Ukraine were very good at covering their activities.

"I'm standing down the hall from the pirate's hospital room," Coffey went on. "Three people just went inside. One was Brian Ellsworth. You can read about him in my files. The other two are Warrant Officer George Jelbart of the MIC and Female Naval Defence Technical Officer Monica Loh of the Singaporean Coastal Command."

Hood entered the names on his computer as Coffey spelled them. He forwarded the information to Bob Herbert. Hood knew that the designation *female* had been part of the title in Singapore for decades. The military services were fully integrated, and discrimination was not permitted. Nonetheless, high command liked to keep their combat unit leaders weighted toward men. This was an easy way to keep track of the balance.

"Is the patient conscious?" Hood asked.

"No, which is why I didn't go in with them," Coffey said. "Ellsworth said they'd notify me if he came around. Meanwhile, I'm using the secure phone I borrowed from Jelbart. Switch to code DPR1P."

"Hold on," Hood said.

He entered the code for AMIC into his desk unit. Op-Center telephones were preprogrammed to decrypt calls from over two hundred allied intelligence services around the world. The Australian Maritime Intelligence Centre was one of these. The only thing required to secure the line was an access code for the individual AMIC phone.

"Done," Hood said. "So what do you make of all this?"

"I honestly don't know yet," Coffey admitted. "The wreckage is definitely that of a sampan, and it is definitely radioactive. It was probably destroyed by explosions that occurred on the sampan itself. Apparently, pirates have been working the Celebes Sea sporadically for years. They use explosives to hold crews hostage while the vessels are robbed."

"So this could have been a premature detonation," Hood said.

"It's possible," Coffey agreed.

"But that doesn't explain the radioactivity," Hood added.

"Exactly. As far as anyone knows, these pirates have never dealt in nuclear material. That's making everyone around here pretty jumpy."

"Why?" Hood asked. "Nuclear trafficking has been going on for years in the region. The MIC knows that."

"They also know that there isn't much they can do about it," Coffey said quietly. "If word gets out about this, there will be pressure to do something. Only no one knows what, exactly. It's the same problem the United States has faced for years. How do you monitor every point of access? It's tough enough catching drug shipments. Radioactive materials are even more difficult."

Coffey was right. There was not much that anyone could do about it. A terrorist could use a lead-lined fountain pen or pocket watch or even a rabbit's foot on a key chain to slip plutonium into a country. Just a few grams of weapons-grade material would be enough to kill thousands of people or contaminate tens of thousands of gallons of water.

"Has the press been all over this?" Hood asked.

"Not yet. The government is trying to keep this as quiet as possible," Coffey said. "Patients and visitors are being kept away from the man's room, but this is a big hospital. Someone is certain to hear that something unusual happened. The game plan is to deny that anything hot was involved."

"Is there anything else we can do?" Hood asked.

"I'll let you know," Coffey replied. "Right now it looks as though someone's motioning for me. I think they want me in the room. Paul, I'll call you back when I can."

"I'll be here another hour or so," Hood said. "Then you can get me on the cell or at the apartment."

"Very good," Coffey said and hung up.

Hood placed the phone in the cradle. He sat back and thought about what was happening on the other side of the world. It was strange how events like this caused the globe to shrink. Conceivably, what Coffey and the others were dealing with could impact the United States within hours. Nuclear material could be transported clandestinely by sea and then loaded onto an aircraft anywhere in the region. The plane could be flown to a small airfield in Washington or New York or Los Angeles. A small amount of nuclear material could be walked into the terminal and left in a waste can. Or dropped on the floor under a bench. The human toll would be extraordinary. A larger amount of nuclear matter could be attached to a makeshift explosive. Perhaps homemade plastique or cans of spray paint triggered by a car flare. The human toll of the dirty bomb would be unthinkable.

All of that could be in progress right now, Hood

thought. The realization came with a keen sense of helplessness.

There were always crises. That was why Op-Center had been chartered. They were the National Crisis Management Center. But the personality of these disasters had changed over the years. The speed, the scope, and the frequency of them were terrifying. And though more resources were being applied to combat them, those resources targeted existing patterns and likely perpetrators. A methodology had not yet been created to anticipate what Bob Herbert called "kamikaze genocide"—the piecemeal extermination of Westerners by suicide attacks.

Several years ago, when Op-Center was combating neo-Nazis, Herbert said something that had stayed with Hood.

"When the brain doesn't have enough information, only your gut can tell you what to do," the intelligence chief said. "Fortunately, since some depraved sons of bitches blew up my wife and my legs, my gut has been able to digest some pretty sick thoughts."

Hood suddenly felt energized. He and his team would figure this out. They would figure out everything that came along. Every deviant variation, every monster. They had to. It was necessity but also something more.

It was stubborn, blessed American pride.

FOURTEEN

Darwin, Australia
Friday, 12:47 P.M.

"Madam, we are not going to inject the patient with anything!"

The speaker was a man in a white tunic. Probably the attending physician. He was standing in a tight circle with Ellsworth, Loh, and Jelbart. Ellsworth was the one who had motioned Coffey over. The man's strident voice was the first thing Lowell Coffey heard as he approached the closed door.

"Doctor," said Loh, "we have a situation that needs to be resolved as swiftly as possible—"

"And I have a patient who needs rest," he interrupted.

"You have one patient now," she said. "How will you feel when this ward, including the hallways, is lined with beds?"

The doctor looked at Ellsworth. "Is she right about that? Is it possible?"

"Such a scenario does not appear imminent," Ellsworth replied crossly. He was looking at Loh.

"There is radioactive material abroad," Loh persisted. "We have to know whether this man was transporting it, receiving it, or merely stumbled upon it. We have to find out if there is radioactive material still at sea, poisoning the fish that may feed some of your patients. Or poisoning some of your future patients. Doctor, we need to know what happened."

"If I do as you ask, you may kill him," the doctor said, shaking his head. "Then you will never get your answer. And there is no guarantee that he will say much, or even anything, if we wake him."

"That is a risk worth taking," she replied.

"Easy for you to say," the doctor said.

"Before we even consider whether to take this rather extreme step, let's find out if we're free to do so," Ellsworth said. He turned to Coffey. Ellsworth was visibly upset. Coffey could not decide which was worse for the Australian official: the responsibility of having to make a controversial decision, or the fear of what they might discover. "Lowell, this is your bailiwick. What do you say, keeping in mind that we are not entirely certain of our guest's nationality? Have we the right to do anything to him?"

"Apart from administering medical care," the doctor added.

Coffey glanced at the physician's name tag. "Dr. Lansing, if this man is a Christian Scientist or a Buddhist, even that could be considered a violation of his rights."

"You've got bronze for brains!" the doctor exclaimed. "The patient was shot twice and had third-degree burns! He would have bled to death if we didn't patch him up!"

"That may be," Coffey said. "However, the International Resolution on Oceans and the Law of the Sea says that absent a victim's ability to choose, the dispensation of care is a decision to be made by his family or by the ranking representative of his nation, in that order."

"And if we don't have those?" Jelbart asked.

"In that case, the host nation calls the shots, isn't that true?" Ellsworth said.

Coffey nodded.

"That would be us," Ellsworth said.

"Correct," Coffey said. "But the host nation is also liable for citation in any civil-rights violations that may arise from the execution of that decision. And the host nation is required to exercise what is called 'humanitarian caution' in administering curative drugs or techniques."

"Which means we don't give him norepinephrine cocktails to try to wake him," Dr. Lansing said with finality.

"Not necessarily," Coffey said. "If this man is suspected of what is classified as a 'high crime' involving the international transport of drugs or other contraband, the questioning of him by responsible authorities is permitted."

"Go question him!" Dr. Lansing said. "It appears I can't stop that. Just don't ask me to wake him!"

"I cannot believe you are debating this when there may be radioactive waste spilling into the sea," Officer Loh said.

"And I can't believe your nation canes people nearly to death for spray-painting graffiti, but there we have it," Dr. Lansing charged.

"Doctor, the IROLS is rather specific on the question of interrogation," Coffey said. "It doesn't say 'ask,' it says 'question.' The regulations presume that the individual is awake."

"If he is not?" Dr. Lansing asked.

"Then frankly, the peremptory issue is one of summum bonum, the supreme good," Coffey said. "Will the public welfare benefit from taking reasonable security measures? The only guidelines that apply are whether there is just cause for the pursuit of the information and, if so, that the questioning be done in a humane manner, without coercion or threats."

"I'd say a radioactive man is reason enough to infer the presence of dangerous nuclear material," Jelbart said.

"And you do have the weight of at least one other nation behind your decision," Coffey said, nodding toward Loh.

"Whoa. Just one?" Ellsworth asked him.

"Officially, yes," Coffey said.

"Will the United States back whatever decision we make, emphasis on the *we?*" Ellsworth pressed.

"You've got sound legal grounds, and my office agrees that there are real security concerns," Coffey said. "That's as close to a yes as this attorney can give you right now."

Dr. Lansing looked from Coffey to the others. He shook his head unhappily. "Attempting to wake this man may kill him. You understand that?"

"We do," Loh said.

"I'm absolutely opposed to it," Lansing said. "I want that known."

"Noted," Ellsworth said.

"I also want to tell you, not as a doctor but as an interested observer, that the one man to whom this matters most can't say a bloody word! I don't think that's right."

"Why do you assume he would be opposed?" Coffey asked.

"Good point!" Jelbart said. "Maybe he would want us to snatch whoever did this."

Lansing looked from Ellsworth to Jelbart. "I have other patients. Which of you two is going to sign the consent form?"

There was a long moment of silence. Jelbart turned to Ellsworth. "Is this going to be a military or government matter?" the warrant officer asked.

That is a good question, Coffey thought. If this were classified as a military issue, the armed forces would have a legal leg up to launch a military response. The transport of nuclear material would automatically be classified as a security threat and not simply illegal traffic. If Ellsworth signed, Canberra would be obligated though not bound to pursue a diplomatic resolution.

Coffey was not surprised when Jelbart answered his own question a moment later.

"I'll sign the form," the warrant officer said. "Let's see what our guest can tell us."

Dr. Lansing summoned a nurse. He turned Jelbart over to her while he went to the medical supply closet on the opposite side of the corridor. Officer Loh went silently into the hospital room.

"Thank you, Lowell," Ellsworth said.

"You're welcome, Brian," Coffey replied.

The government official looked pale. He went to the water cooler on the opposite wall.

"Would you like some?" Ellsworth asked as he filled a cup.

"No, thanks," Coffey said.

Ellsworth drained the cup and refilled it. He drained

that, too, then crumpled the paper cone and tossed it in the trash.

"Is there anything you haven't told me?" Coffey pressed.

Ellsworth shook his head.

"Is there anything else I can do?" Coffey asked.

"Yes. Would you mind sticking around?" Ellsworth asked. "I know you have that convention in Sydney. But we really could use a third-party voice."

"What would you have done if I had gone against you?" Coffey asked.

"I didn't think you would have," Ellsworth replied, sounding somewhat defensive. "I feel that we have the jurisdiction to do this."

"You didn't answer me. What would you have done?" Coffey asked.

"We would have done exactly what we are doing," Ellsworth admitted. "We don't have a choice. This is a scary business, Lowell. It has to be dealt with aggressively." He looked at Coffey and smiled slightly. "But it's good to have you on our side."

Coffey smiled. It was strange to hear Ellsworth talk about dealing with things aggressively. Just a minute ago he had frozen when it came to taking responsibility for drugging their guest. What the chief solicitor meant, of course, was that he must aggressively authorize others to take action and responsibility. It was a strange new world for people like Brian Ellsworth. Men who enjoyed the perks of power without the shoulder-bending weight of liability.

In the meantime, though, Lowell Coffey found himself in agreement with Ellsworth on one point, at least.

This was a scary business. And he had a feeling it would get a lot more terrifying before it was through.

FIFTEEN

Darwin, Australia
Friday, 12:59 P.M.

FNO Loh stood between Warrant Officer Jelbart and
Dr. Lansing. The three wore rubber gloves and surgical
masks. The Singaporean naval officer watched dispas-
sionately as the physician injected a clear solution into the
patient's intravenous needle. He had already turned off a
valve to the drip in the patient's thin but sinewy left arm.
Brian Ellsworth and Lowell Coffey stood behind the lead-
lined screen near the doorway.

The balding physician shook his head. "This poor chap
is going to get a double dose of wake up," Lansing said.

"How so?" Jelbart asked.

"I've had to shut off the flow of painkillers. Morphine
inhibits the uptake of norepinephrine," the doctor informed him. "In a perverse way, though, that may help to
save him. I'm giving him a moderate dosage of levarter-
enol. I'm hoping that the combination of pain and stim-
ulant will be enough to wake him without damaging him."

"Why would he be damaged? What does this norepinephrine do?" Jelbart asked.

"It is an energizer," Lansing told him. "This patient is
suffering from hypotension."

"Shock," Jelbart said.

"That's right," Lansing replied. "The sudden jump from
systemic underactivity to overactivity could easily drive
him to cardiac arrest."

"I see," Jelbart said. "What about the radioactivity?
How has that affected him?"

"It's too early to say," the doctor replied. "There would

not be many symptoms this early, and we still don't know what the original exposure levels were."

"Then how can you treat him?" Jelbart asked.

"He's still alive," the doctor said dryly. "So we can infer that the dose was not lethal."

"True," Jelbart said.

"There are standard responses, regardless of the exposure," Lansing went on. "I've given him Melbrosin pollen, a natural radiation-sickness therapy. We can treat the results, the nausea and weakness. But this boosts the capability of the bone marrow to produce red and white blood cells. It won't affect the pharmacological treatments he's receiving for his wounds. If there is good news in any of this, it is that the burns appear to have been caused in the explosion, not as a result of the radiation."

"How can you tell?" Jelbart asked.

"The body responds differently," the doctor replied. "You see a more extensive form of blistering with radioactive burns."

"What about the levels of radiation the patient himself is generating?" Jelbart asked.

"They are extremely low," Lansing assured him. "We won't be contaminated in any way if we stay for less than a half hour or so. And we will be here for far less than that, I assure you. That lead screen is primarily for the nurses who walk by all day."

The man in the bed began to moan as the drugs entered his system. FNO Loh leaned toward him.

"Don't bother talking to him yet," Lansing cautioned. "He won't hear you. This is only the pain talking. You'll know he's conscious when you see his eyes begin to move under the lids."

Loh stood up again. She tugged on the hem of her jacket and absently ran a hand down the front.

The room was warm, and there was the faint odor of antiseptic. It smelled sanitary rather than fresh. To FNO Loh, dirty mop water on the deck of a patrol ship smelled fresh. Salty sea air, rich with fuel from the engine room, smelled fresh. This smell was void of life, of character.

The young woman looked at the patient. He was starting to breathe more rapidly. She felt a pinch of sadness. It took suffering and horror to put him in what was probably the cleanest bed he had ever been in. Whatever his nationality, there were thousands of other young Asian men and women just like him. Maybe he was running from something. Maybe he did not want to be like his father. Perhaps he was running to something. Perhaps he had seen European or American movies or television shows and wanted to live like that.

The officer felt compassion for him, but she also felt contempt. It was not a crime to want to escape from terrible oppression and poverty. To desire money and freedom. Yet there were other ways to earn money. Legal, honorable ways. Service in the military was one. Working on a farm was another. Apprenticeship in a trade was yet another. People like him were devious rather than smart, indignant rather than industrious, violent rather than strong. They deserved the disaster they ultimately brought on themselves.

The patient's eyes opened slightly. They crinkled with discomfort. His dry lips parted and moved wordlessly. He began to shift about, then started thrashing weakly as he moaned. Loh leaned close to his ear. She lightly touched his unbandaged cheek and forehead.

"Don't move," Loh said softly in Malay. She repeated it in Chinese and then in English.

"Who—?" he said in Malay.

"You are safe," she said. "I am Monica. You are in a medical facility. Where are you from?"

The patient writhed and opened his mouth in silent pain.

"Where are you from?" Loh repeated.

"Singapore," he said.

"What is your name?" she asked.

"Name," he said drowsily. "Lee."

"Lee what?" she pressed.

"Tong," he replied.

"Lee Tong, what were you doing at sea?" she asked.

"It hurts," the patient said. He closed his eyes. Tears fell from the sides. "My skin, my feet . . . on fire."

"We will make the pain stop when you answer my questions," Loh said. She was glad the doctor could not understand her. He would only waste time with misguided pity. "What were you doing at sea?"

"They fired at us," he said.

"Who did?" Loh asked.

"They saw in the dark," he went on.

"The boat you were attacking?" she asked.

"Yes," he replied. "They hit . . . plastique."

"Your plastique?" she asked. "You had plastic explosives on board?"

He nodded.

"Lee Tong, were you trying to take something from the other vessel?" Loh asked.

He began to pant.

"Did you attack another vessel?" Loh demanded.

"It hurts . . . help me!"

"Did you attack another vessel?" she shouted.

"Yes—"

Dr. Lansing was checking the heart monitor to the right of the bed. "Ms. Loh, his blood pressure is rising, two ten over sixty. His heart rate is two twenty."

"Meaning what?" Jelbart asked.

"He's approaching ventricular tachycardia," the doctor said. "That can cause hemodynamic compromise—clots, air bubbles, death."

"You're saying you haven't got much time," Jelbart said.

"I'm saying *he* hasn't got much time," the doctor replied. "It's time to stop this, Ms. Loh."

Loh refused to move. "Lee Tong, what did you want from the vessel?" she demanded.

He did not answer. He simply moaned.

"Did you want to hijack it? Did you want to steal something?" the naval officer asked.

"Money," he replied.

"You just wanted money?" she asked.

"Jewelry," he said. "Goods."

"What kind of goods?" she pressed.

"Electronic," he replied.

"Nothing dangerous?" she asked. "No nuclear waste?"

He shook his head weakly.

They were just pirates, then, she told herself. Pirates who picked the wrong vessel to try to board.

Lee Tong began to cry. He struggled against the straps that held him to the bed. A nurse came over to help restrain him.

"Officer Loh, this has got to stop," Dr. Lansing said. "Nurse, he needs a beta-blocker to stabilize. Push more propranolol IV. The rest of you—out."

Loh ignored the physician. "Lee Tong, were you in the Celebes Sea when this happened?"

"Yes," he replied.

"Can you describe the vessel you attacked?" she asked.

"Too dark," he said. He began to shiver and become more active. His eyes opened suddenly. He forced out a raw, hoarse, inarticulate scream.

"That's enough!" the physician said.

Dr. Lansing moved in front of the woman. He turned the morphine drip on again. Almost at once the patient began to calm.

Loh maneuvered around the doctor. "Can you describe the boat?" she asked. "Did it sink?"

"Did not sink," the man said as he drifted off. "Explosion . . . kept going . . ."

Lee Tong relaxed and sank back into the bed.

"Why did you do that?" Loh asked the doctor.

"Because his heart rate was approaching two hundred and thirty-five beats a minute," the doctor said. "In his weakened condition, we could lose him. Now step aside, Ms. Loh. Let me do my job."

The naval officer moved back. As the physician moved in with his nurse, Jelbart took FNO Loh by the arm. He walked her around the lead screen and into the corridor. The other men gathered around her.

"What did he tell you?" Ellsworth asked.

Loh looked at the others. She took a short breath. "His name is Lee Tong, and he is Singaporean. He was at sea with other pirates, and they attempted to rob a vessel at night. They only wanted those goods they could spend or fence. That is typical of the breed. Judging from the radioactivity, it appears they happened upon a vessel that was carrying nuclear waste."

"What kind of ship?" Jelbart asked.

"I don't know," she said. "But these people do not routinely attack the kind of vessels that would transport nuclear materials."

"Legal nuclear materials," Coffey pointed out.

"That is correct," she said. "The pirates obviously tried to stop the ship and were repulsed by weapons fire, probably by a team with night-vision capability. Lee Tong said they were cut down in the dark."

"By professionals," Jelbart said.

"It appears so," Loh agreed. "In the course of that exchange, the pirates' own plastique was detonated. It must have punched a hole in the target vessel and sprayed the sampan with radiation. He said that the ship is still afloat. Perhaps it was crippled in the explosion and is at anchor not far from where it was attacked. I'm going to search for it."

"Before you leave," Coffey said to Loh, "I am obligated to point something out."

"Yes?" she said.

"Whatever the patient told you cannot be used in fashioning a legal case against him," Coffey told her. "Mr. Tong did not have an attorney present, and he was under the influence of medication."

"He is also guilty of piracy," Loh replied flatly.

"Perhaps," Coffey admitted. "And if you are inclined to prove that, you will have to do it some other way."

The woman's aides were standing at the far end of the corridor. Unschooled and very young, they both knew virtue from criminal behavior better than these older, highly educated men beside her. Knowledge and liberality had crowded common sense from their brains.

"Gentlemen, I am returning to my patrol ship," she said. "It is probably not a coincidence that this event occurred where it did."

"What do you mean?" Ellsworth asked.

"You're thinking about the 130-5 site, aren't you Officer Loh?" Jelbart asked.

"I am," Loh replied. "I would like to go there and look for evidence of a conflict or perhaps the target vessel itself."

"Excuse me, but what's the 130-5 site?" Coffey asked.

"It's the point of intersection at one hundred and thirty degrees longitude, five degrees latitude," Jelbart replied. "That's where Japan and China are permitted to dump their nuclear waste."

"But Officer Loh just said these pirates wouldn't have attacked a vessel of that sort," Ellsworth said.

"They would not have," the Singaporean agreed. "What I'm afraid of is something else."

"What?" Ellsworth asked.

"That they attacked a vessel that may have just done business with one of those vessels," Loh replied.

SIXTEEN

Washington, D.C.
Thursday, 11:55 P.M.

Paul Hood was about to leave when the phone beeped. It had been nearly five hours since he turned over the running of Op-Center to the evening shift. That was the only time he got to catch up on E-mails, intelligence briefings, and personal matters.

He snatched it up and sat on the edge of the desk.

"Evening, Paul," Coffey said.

"Good afternoon," Hood replied. "So? Did your patient wake up?"

Coffey told him he had. Before the attorney briefed him, Hood conferenced in Mike Rodgers and Bob Herbert. Both men were at home. Rodgers was up watching old action movies, as usual. Usually John Wayne or Charlton Heston. Herbert was getting ready to turn in.

Nothing Coffey said surprised Hood.

"Do you have any information about the bullets they pulled from the pirate or the wreckage?" Rodgers asked.

"Yes, I wrote that down," Coffey said. "Jelbart had one of his men come over and take a look at them. He just received word that they were from a .380 double-action semiautomatic. The initial forensics tests said that the bullets were remanufactured with a tungsten-polymer coating—"

"Which means that they're doubly difficult to trace," Rodgers said.

"How so?" Hood asked.

"Remanufactured, meaning that the shell and casing came from different places," Rodgers said, "and designed so as not to retain evidence of the rifling from the barrel that shot them."

"Bullets without fingerprints," Herbert said.

"More or less," Rodgers replied.

"Would it take considerable financial resources or a special laboratory to create ammunition like that?" Hood asked.

"Not necessarily," Rodgers replied. "Depends on what scale they're making these things. A few dozen, even a few hundred could be done in a shack with easily obtainable gear."

"So that's pretty much a dead end," Hood said.

"There is one thing that we need to talk about," Coffey said. "Brian Ellsworth, the chief solicitor for the Australian Maritime Intelligence Centre. He is very keen to have the United States as a part of this investigation."

"Officially, you mean," Rodgers said.

"That's what I mean," Coffey said. "I'm here as an independent adviser, not as a representative of Op-Center or the United States."

"What is Mr. Ellsworth looking for?" Hood asked.

"A formal commitment that we are a part of this investigation," Coffey told the others.

"Why should that matter?" Herbert asked. "There isn't a convenience the Australians need or a challenge that scares them."

"They could certainly do this by themselves," Coffey agreed. "At the same time—"

"They would prefer not to go it alone," Hood interrupted. "Especially if they need to put pressure on Singapore for access to intelligence or background information on this pirate."

"On Singapore, Malaysia, China, anyone who could be involved in this," Coffey replied.

"Frankly, I don't think the pirate is going to matter much anymore," Herbert said. "He and his guys were just unlucky."

"Possibly," Hood agreed. "I'm curious what they'll do if they discover that any Australians are involved in this."

"I'm sure that's another reason Ellsworth wants us involved," Coffey said. "If there is an Australian component to this, we can help pressure anyone in Canberra who might be in denial. That's one thing they don't do very well, Bob. Self-examination. There's a very strong blue-wall component in their thinking. It's them against the Rim, fighting for European values in an Asian world. They don't like attacking their own."

"Is anyone going out to the site of the attack?" Rodgers asked.

"Loh and Jelbart are both going on separate vessels," Coffey said. "I'll be joining the Australians."

"Lowell, if these pirates had attacked a vessel involved in the legitimate transport of nuclear material, there would be a record of the transit. Isn't that correct?" Hood asked.

"Yes," Coffey said. "Also a report would have to have been filed about the attack. The International Nuclear Regulatory Commission demands that an accident or attack involving any nuclear vessel, military or civilian, must be reported to both the home and destination port. That hasn't happened."

"How do you know?" Rodgers asked.

"Because the INRC must put out a bulletin immediately, warning of potential dangers to shipping or possible radioactive contamination," Herbert said. "The Australian Department of Defence, the Department of National Emergency Services, and the Communicable Disease and Public Health Center are among those institutions that would be notified."

"And have not been," Hood said.

"Right," Coffey said.

"Are the public health people down there taking any special precautions?" Hood asked.

"They're going to increase coastline patrols off the major cities," Herbert said. "They'll be looking for radioactivity, of course, as well as any ships that look as though they've been damaged."

"Bob, is there anything the National Reconnaissance

Office can do to help look for the mystery ship?" Hood asked.

The National Reconnaissance Office was the highly secretive government agency that controlled and processed satellite imagery as well as other electronic surveillance capabilities.

"We're talking about a very large area with a great deal of shipping," Herbert said. "We don't know which way the other ship may have gone or exactly where the sampan was. I'd like to try to narrow the search area before we ask the NRO to tie up resources."

"Isn't this what those resources are for?" Coffey asked.

"Actually, no," Herbert replied. "Those satellites are for watching Chinese naval maneuvers, missile tests, and picking out terrorist activity in the hills and jungles of Indonesia. All of that affects American military and foreign policy on a daily basis."

"I see," Coffey said.

"You don't sound happy, Lowell," Hood suggested.

"Well, I was hoping to give the Australians something," Coffey said.

"Does it have to be practical or can it be political?" Herbert asked.

"I suppose both is out of the question?" Coffey said.

"Only since the days of Julius Caesar," Herbert said. "Will Mr. Ellsworth accept a gesture of solidarity?"

"Most likely," Coffey said. "What did you have in mind?"

"Going over there myself," Herbert said. "It would be awkward sending Mike into a situation that is already bristling with soldiers."

"And I'm not sure the Pentagon would approve," Rodgers added.

Hood had to agree with that. Though Rodgers was second-in-command at Op-Center, he was still a soldier. The Australian press might assume that the unscheduled arrival of a military adviser was a prelude to a regional military buildup. Extreme ideas tended to grow in the fertile ground of unprecedented situations. They could not afford that kind of attention, not just from foreign governments but from the White House. Op-Center's needs might conflict with the administrations short- and long-term plans in the region.

"Mike, what about some of your special ops people?" Hood asked.

"If I sent Maria off on another mission now, Darrell would start a war of his own," Rodgers said.

Darrell McCaskey was Op-Center's liaison with the FBI and various international law enforcement groups. He had recently married former Spanish Interpol agent Maria Corneja. Shortly thereafter, Rodgers offered her a spot on his new intelligence-gathering unit named Op-Center Reconnaissance, Intelligence On-Site. ORION had been assembled to put spies on the ground, where the crises were happening, instead of relying on electronic surveillance. Maria accepted the assignment and was immediately sent to Africa along with her new teammates David Battat and Aideen Marley. McCaskey had not been happy about that.

"The other operatives are out of town, tying up personal and professional matters before moving down here," Rodgers said, "and I haven't had any face time with my Asian intelligence man, Yuen Chow."

"Where is he now?" Hood asked.

"At home in Hong Kong," Rodgers said. "He'll be here next week. We're still running security on him. He spent seven years working in the movie business in Shanghai. It's tough finding out which of these boys may have had ties with the Guoanbu in Beijing or the Triads in Hong Kong."

"Or both," Herbert said. "Frankly, I'd want some of that take-no-prisoners muscle in my corner."

"So would I," Rodgers said. "But I would hate having to hire a shadow to make sure my spies weren't double-dealing."

The Guoanbu was short for the Guojia Anquan Bu, the Chinese Ministry of State Security. They were a ruthless intelligence service with irrevocable ties to Chinese nationals around the world. The Guoanbu thought nothing about imprisoning people at home to gain the cooperation of family members abroad. The Triads were the equally amoral gangsters who had organized in Hong Kong over a century before. They took their name from a three-sided good luck symbol that stood for heaven, earth, and man.

"So that leaves us with me," Herbert said. "I can go to Darwin and lend a hand collecting and crunching intel."

"Lowell?" Hood asked.

"It sounds like a good idea to me," Coffey said.

"Run it past Ellsworth," Hood suggested. "In the meantime, Bob, why don't you get ready—"

"I've been making the reservations on-line as we speak," Herbert told him. "Air New Zealand to Darwin. I'll be there Saturday morning."

"By way of how many cities?" Rodgers asked.

"Five," Herbert replied. "D.C. to New York to Los Angeles to Sydney to Darwin."

"Screw that. I'll call over to the travel office at the Pentagon," Rodgers told him. "I'm sure we can hitch you a ride and get you there with less hassle."

"What, on one of those butt-cold, avalanche-loud, flying metal rib cages that you guys call airplanes?" Herbert asked.

"Actually, I was going to requisition Air Force One," Rodgers said. "But I don't want you going soft."

"Gentlemen, I'm going home," Hood told them.

"And I've got to go hitch a ride with Jelbart as soon as he's finished with Ellsworth and Officer Loh," Coffey said.

"What are they talking about?" Hood asked.

"Whether we're going to have two investigations or a coordinated operation when we get out to sea," Coffey replied.

"Jeez," Herbert sighed. "This is how the world will be lost. There will be a skirmish that bloodies someone's nose followed by a world war that has nothing to do with that. We'll kill each other debating how to find some son of a bitch instead of just laying waste to him and his kind."

"You said it before," Hood reminded him. "It's either practical or political."

"Well, let's see if we can make it both," Herbert said.

"How?" Hood asked.

"By understanding," Herbert replied.

"That's it?" Hood asked, amused.

"Yes," Herbert said. "Understanding that the only way to get rid of me is by doing this thing right."

SEVENTEEN

Cairns, Australia
Friday, 7:00 P.M.

The tranquillity of the cove was just what Peter Kannaday needed. Like any long-time sailor, his emotional state was strongly affected by the sea.

The sun was going down as the *Hosannah* entered the mouth of the cove. The effect was like a candle on the sea. There was a long, rippling, waxy-yellow streak on the water. It ended in a burning yellow wick on the horizon. Kannaday watched it from the stern as they entered the cove. Directly above him the blue-green skies were already spotted with early stars.

To all other sides of him was Darling Cove. The inlet was located in the northern reaches of the Great Barrier Reef. Over 2,000 kilometers in length and up to 125 meters thick, the reef is separated from the mainland by a shallow lagoon. The massive structure was born at the end of the Ice Age when oceanic polyps began to thrive in the region. The polyps created protective multicolored shells that survived when the animals themselves perished. Coral built upon coral for over 10,000 years, providing a home for each new generation of tentacled creature. It also became a haven for countless species of fish, giant turtles, humpback whales, manta rays, dolphins, and dugongs—marine cousins to the elephant.

The helmsman steered the yacht into the calm, wide-mouthed inlet. Kannaday looked down at the stained-glass blue water. Then he walked forward as sweet, warm air washed over the deck. It carried the hint of grapes from the Darling vineyard located to the southwest. Immediately to the northwest was a limestone formation scooped from a hundred-meter-high cliff by ancient storms. The rock glowed rust orange in the twilight.

The high reef concealed the cove from the open sea. To access the inlet a sailor had to know to come around the reef well to the north. The mouth itself was less than a half kilometer across. It was just about 200 meters to the far shore. There was a long stone wharf ahead and deep stretches of tawny white sand on all sides. Two motorboats, a motor yacht, and a pair of sailboats were at anchor. Security cameras were concealed in the 200-foot-tall karri trees that ringed the cove. Kannaday knew that microphones were hidden in the trees as well. They rarely heard more than the wind, the soft breakers, or the cry of a lost dolphin. For boaters who happened by, there were signs at the entrance to the cove. The oak boards, floating on moored buoys and mounted to posts, announced that this was the private property of Darling Enterprises. There were no posted warnings, no threats. Anyone who knew of Mr. Darling knew to keep out. Those who did not were arrested within two minutes of entering the cove. Guards lived in a small cabin just beyond the beach. Most of the time they surfed the Internet or played tiddledywinks. Darling held twice-yearly competitions among the staff with a sizable purse.

It did not escape Kannaday that the object of that game was to gather all the different chips in one cup. A cup that was controlled by Jervis Darling.

Kannaday took another moment to watch the sun set. This was the ninth or tenth time he had sailed into this cove. The quiet, majestic beauty of this place thrilled Kannaday for a moment. It always did. But this time it also made him angry. He felt as though he should own the seas he had just traveled. Kannaday had a yacht, and he was on the way to having enough wealth to keep him comfortable for the rest of his life. Instead, all he could think about was the displeasure of Jervis Darling. A man whose name alone on a placard was enough to frighten would-be trespassers. Kannaday resented the man's power and feared his disapproval. The captain also hated his own resentment and fear.

The yacht would be anchoring in a few moments. Kannaday would take a motorized dinghy. He would be met there by a Humvee. There was no need to radio ahead. The guards would have seen him. As the yacht slowed, Kannaday wondered if Jervis Darling feared anything. The billionaire probably feared failure. Also death, most likely. And almost certainly in that order. A man like Darling would only accept defeat at the hands of God himself.

If only I could have God as an ally, Kannaday thought bitterly. Instead, he had John Hawke.

The security officer was belowdecks with his men. They were probably watching action movies on DVD. That was all they ever did. There was no curiosity about the world, no desire for self-improvement. Perhaps that was why Kannaday had assumed Hawke would take his offer and go. It was easy.

Men like Hawke liked things easy.

Kannaday walked to the port-side winch that held the dinghy. He waited as one of the crewmen lowered it to clear water. The hum of the motor echoed through the cove. Kannaday's stomach began to burn.

Even though John Hawke had physically threatened the captain, Kannaday did not fear him. Fear did not come from known threats. It did not come from fear for one's physical well-being. For a man of the sea, the adrenaline kick that came with danger carried the captain through moments like those. Even when he had the knife at his throat he was not fearful. He had been focused on surviving, which was not the same thing.

Fear came from one thing above all. It came from the unknown. It grew from the anticipation of something debilitating. A loss of freedom. The inability to realize one's vision.

Darling represented that kind of power. Kannaday was not looking forward to this meeting. He considered calling Hawke's bluff. Would that little man have the courage to seize the yacht? And would Darling accept Hawke as commander if he did?

Sun-bronzed first mate Craig McEldowney ambled over. The big, thirty-nine-year-old New Zealander stopped beside Kannaday. The two had been together for two years. They had met in a bar in Surabaya, Java, where McEldowney was washing glasses. The former dock-worker had just served five years' hard labor for stealing shipments of tobacco and selling it at a discount to the locals.

"It's going to be all right," McEldowney said. "The chief isn't going to blame you for what happened."

"Who will he blame?" Kannaday asked.

"Nobody," McEldowney replied. "Captain, these things happen. Just like they did to me."

Kannaday grinned. McEldowney was a decent but dull-witted man. That was why he had been caught.

Kannaday left his first mate in charge and swung down the aluminum ladder into the blue-gray dinghy. The rungs were damp with sea spray. He had to hold on tight to keep from slipping. He reached the sturdy little boat and sat on the aft bench. He released the winch cable, switched the engine on, and sped toward the wharf. The guards were already driving down the sloping, wooded path. The crunch of wood chips and the growl of the Humvee engine added to the noise.

This is how chaos is built, Kannaday thought. *One noise at a time.*

The question before Kannaday was simple. What was the best way to prevent his own situation from becoming more chaotic? Unfortunately, only one man had the answer.

And that answer was unknown.

EIGHTEEN

The Celebes Sea
Friday, 7:33 P.M.

When Lowell Coffey was eight years old, something wonderful happened. His father took him to see the circus in Sherman Oaks. What was most memorable, however, was not the show itself. What Coffey remembered best was sticking around to see the circus being broken down. The deconstruction had been a mesmerizing sight, awesome in its scope and complexity.

The departure of the Singaporean and Australian ships from Darwin reminded Coffey of that. Banners flying and large vessels setting out. Instead of roustabouts, sailors were putting the big machine in motion. Instead of elephants, there were helicopters and motorboats being moved into position. Instead of the smell of horses and sawdust, there were diesel fuel and ocean air. The scope and logistics of both were memorable. There were, however, two major differences. After the circus was packed and moving, the young Lowell Coffey had gone home with his father. The boy had felt sad and disconnected. This morning, the adult Lowell Coffey had gone with the seagoing convoy. He felt plugged into a great and powerful enterprise. It was invigorating.

For about three minutes.

Unfortunately, the adult Lowell Coffey was also desperately nauseated. He was sick from his high, hammering forehead down through his vacant gaze to his sloshing stomach. Even the joints of his knees felt as if they were rolling in their sockets. And the attorney was sitting down.

Coffey was on the small, claustrophobic bridge of the MIC corvette. George Jelbart was in command and seated in a swivel chair to his right. The medic had given Coffey two dimenhydrinate tablets, a generic form of Dramamine. It did not make Coffey feel better, but at least he got no worse. There was only one exception. Whenever Warrant Officer Jelbart swiveled in his seat, Coffey tasted his own breakfast for a moment. There was something very disorienting about the officer's side-to-side movement.

The swift, modern warship had departed Darwin minutes after Loh's patrol boat had set out. Ellsworth did not join them. He had gone back to his office after intensive dockside discussions about how to manage this joint investigation. Since this was Loh's plan, it was agreed that she and her crew would conduct the initial phase. Jelbart would lend whatever support was necessary in terms of equipment, manpower, or technical capabilities. Coffey had told them that Op-Center's intelligence chief, Bob Herbert, was coming to Darwin. Herbert would be prepared to assist with analysis of whatever they did or did not find at sea. Ellsworth had been happy to hear about the NCMC's involvement. He was grateful for the intelligence resources, of course. But Ellsworth was more interested in America's support. This could turn out to be an isolated incident, in which case everyone would be relieved. If it were something else, though, the more weight Ellsworth had behind him, the happier he would be.

Jelbart removed the small, compact headset he was wearing. He hung it around his neck. "How are you doing there, Mr. Coffey?" he asked.

"The situation has stabilized somewhat," he said with a weak smile. He looked down. Unlike the horizon, the floor of the bridge was not moving. Attorneys were meant to be in quiet wood-paneled offices where the only movement was the pendulum of a grandfather clock.

"You'll get used to it," Jelbart promised. "By the time we get back to Darwin, it will feel unnatural to be on ground that doesn't move."

Coffey had to take that on faith. Right now it did not seem plausible.

The radio operator leaned in. He was located in a cubicle just off the main control center.

"Sir?" he said. "Incoming from FNO Loh."

Jelbart slipped the headset back on. He adjusted the mouthpiece. "Jelbart here," he said.

"We have reached the target area," she said.

Jelbart glanced at the control panel. There was a small black monitor to his right. It had an electronic grid overlay in light blue. Ships were red dots. Jelbart had previously explained to Coffey that this was an adjustable global positioning display. They could pull back as far as five hundred square kilometers or move in as tight as ten square kilometers. The area currently being displayed was twenty square kilometers.

Jelbart turned to his right. "Helm?"

"Yes, sir," said one of the two men seated there.

"Coordinates ten-five-nine west, three-four-two north," Jelbart said, reading from the grid. "Backwater standby, on command."

The helmsman repeated the coordinates, acknowledged the command, and set the course accordingly.

Coffey looked up. He was confused. "I can see them out the window," he said. "Why don't you just follow them?"

"We have been," Jelbart told him. "But if something happens to officer Loh's vessel and we lose visual contact, we want our computer to know exactly where they are."

"I see," Coffey replied. It was an unpleasant thought but a practical one.

The Singaporean patrol boat came to a complete stop. Jelbart ordered the corvette to half speed. He came alongside the other vessel, keeping 300 meters to port. After a moment, the corvette stopped. With one axis of motion removed, Coffey immediately felt a little better. Able to look out now without feeling sick, the attorney watched the prow of the Singaporean vessel. Using fishing nets, sailors had lowered several black boxes into the water. They looked like laptop computers.

"What are those?" Coffey asked.

"They're grannies," Jelbart replied. "Gamma ray and neutron irradiation saturation detectors. I learned about them in the physics course MIC gave its personnel. Impressive little units."

"What do they tell us?" Coffey asked.

"The kinds of materials we are searching for give off three kinds of radiation," Jelbart said. "Alpha particles, beta particles, and gamma rays. Gamma rays are the most powerful. Even mild doses can cook your insides. That's the first thing you want to detect."

"If the sampan encountered gamma radiation, the sailor would not be alive," Coffey suggested.

"Possibly. He may not have been exposed to the mother lode. It's good to keep a watch out for it. That's also the reason I gave the backwater standby command. In case we have to get out of here in a hurry."

"I like that option," Coffey said.

"Neutron irradiation tells you something about the elements involved and the size of the nuclear sample," Jelbart went on. "Officer Loh checked with the INRC to determine the size of the drums deposited out here. There is always trace radiation, however tightly these things are secured."

"That's reassuring," Coffey said.

"The levels are not dangerous unless exposure is cumulative," Jelbart added. "That's one reason to put it out to sea or deep in caves."

"What about the ecological impact?" Coffey asked.

"The fish are tested regularly. As long as they aren't affected, I don't think anyone in the area cares very much," Jelbart said. "The point is, given the time the last vessels were here and the amount they off-loaded, Officer Loh knows exactly what the readings should be."

"What was the last ship to come out here?" Coffey asked.

The computer monitor was located in front of Coffey.

Jelbart swung toward it. His swivel was quick and unsettling. The attorney looked down and took a slow, deep breath to try to get his balance back.

"The last vessel to visit here was a Chinese freighter with four twelve-gallon drums of material from a nuclear power plant outside of Shanghai," Jelbart said. "Before that it was a cutter owned by International Spent Fuel Transport out of Malaysia. They deposited three ten-gallon drums of material from a Japanese nuclear power plant. No one was out here for ten days prior to that."

"How will we be able to tell them apart?" Coffey asked.

"They each have a specific drop point," Jelbart replied. "The coordinates Loh sent us represent the Chinese site."

"I see," Coffey said. "I'm still unclear about one thing, though. What does she hope to find? If one of these ships were damaged, wouldn't someone have been notified?"

"Possibly," Jelbart said. "What concerns us is that one of the vessels may have transferred their cargo to another ship. That other ship may have been the one the pirates attacked."

"What do you do if that scenario pans out? Go after the vessel?"

"I don't know," Jelbart replied.

"You don't know? Wouldn't that be a logical step?" Coffey asked.

"Perhaps," Jelbart told him. "It could also tip off whoever has the nuclear material. It might be more prudent to try to find that material, then go back and clean up the relay team itself."

"Doesn't the MIC have simulations and playbooks for this sort of thing?" Coffey asked.

"We have search patterns and seizure protocols, yes," Jelbart replied. "When it comes to tracking radioactive cargo, we're in unfamiliar territory. Just as America has been. The only nuclear materials we've actually hunted were two warheads missing from the Soviet Union's Strategic Rocket Forces. One was from a facility in Kazakhstan, the other from Belarus."

"Did you find them?" Coffey asked.

"The Russians eventually did," Jelbart replied. "There were indications that the warheads had been purchased by Indonesian rebels. Perhaps they were, but delivery was never made. The weapons had actually been moved to a cave in the Ukraine. Russian engineers and physicists hired by a retired general were in the process of dismantling them."

"Lovely," Coffey said.

"We try to rebuild Eden, but the snakes are always there, more persistent than ever," Jelbart said.

"They've had a lot of time to study us from the underbrush," Coffey observed.

"Too true," Jelbart said. "The other thing about this mission, Mr. Coffey, is that we have a partner." He nodded toward the Singaporean vessel. "We don't know how porous their command center might be. We don't know how many secrets we'll be comfortable sharing."

"I wonder if she feels the same," Coffey said.

"Almost certainly," Jelbart said. "Though with her it's as much a cultural issue as a political one. The Singaporeans are aggressively private."

"That's an oxymoron. I'll have to think about it," Coffey remarked.

"You'll see what I mean when you spend more time with FNO Loh," Jelbart promised.

It also sounded racist. Coffey hated even benign generalizations like that. He would try not to hold that against Jelbart.

Ten minutes after the search had begun, Loh radioed that the Chinese site was registering the anticipated levels of ambient radiation. She provided the coordinates for the next site. The patrol boat moved on.

So did the corvette.

And so, once again, did Coffey's stomach.

NINETEEN

Over the Pacific Ocean
Friday, 2:57 A.M.

Once in a very rare while life surprised Bob Herbert.

Mike Rodgers was able to get the intelligence chief on a TR-1 long-range strategic reconnaissance aircraft. The plane was headed from Langley Air Force Base in Virginia to Taiwan with a stopover at the Australian Defence Force Basic Flying Training School in Tamworth, New South Wales. There, the USAF was going to pick up three officers for hands-on experience in surveillance upgrades. The RAAF would give Herbert a lift to Darwin. The TR-1 was leaving at one-thirty A.M., which meant the intelligence chief had to hustle. Herbert drove himself from his waterside home in Quantico, Virginia. There was literally no traffic at that time of the morning. He made the eighty-mile trip in one hour.

There was a small officers' station on board the sixty-two-foot-long aircraft. It was located near the cockpit. The crew removed the seat, and Herbert was able to tuck his wheelchair into the area. There was a power source for the chair batteries and a wireless Internet jack for his computer. Herbert felt oddly like a cyborg, a part of the big, sleek spy ship. Happily, the aircraft was not as noisy as transports he had been on. In fact, it was as quiet as a commercial jetliner.

Life was good, at least for the moment. And since a moment was all anyone could count on, Herbert tried to enjoy it. He did, for a while.

Herbert submerged himself in research and coffee. The coffee was provided by a very considerate navigator. The black coffee did more good than the research. The moment of contentment passed.

Using the plane's secure communications link, Herbert donned his WASTEM screen name. The profile he had created was for a thirty-year-old white female, one who advocated militia uprisings and a suspension of rights for everyone who was not a "pure-blooded American." Herbert had made her a female to attract male sociopaths, men who were looking for someone to share their mental illness with. Through WASTEM, the intelligence officer had been able to break up a supremacist group that arranged tours to Libya. There, for 50,000 dollars, group members could watch prisoners being tortured. For 75,000 dollars they could participate in the torture using whatever means they wished. For 150,000 dollars they could carry out an execution.

Herbert had his wife's picture attached to the profile. Not only was Yvonne a fox, but she would have appreciated having a posthumous hand in destroying cults of hate. A cult like the one that had claimed her life.

As usual, WASTEM had dozens of E-mail messages. Most were from men and women who wanted to go shooting with her or sponsor her at their training camp in this wilderness or that mountain range. Though WASTEM's interests included the acquisition of "red rain," a euphemism for radioactive materials, none of the E-mails offered to sell her any. He spent some time in the Anarkiss chat room, where sickos went for romance. As one of the few "women" in the room, WASTEM was always extremely popular. If anyone seemed to have information he might want, he offered to go private with them. People with something to hide spoke more freely in a chat room for two.

Unfortunately, no one had any leads on nuclear material being trafficked through the Far East or the South Pacific.

Herbert's next stop were charts of the shipping lanes in that region. He got a list of tankers, fishing vessels, ocean liners, and pleasure boats that had been through the area in the past seventy-two hours. When he got the names, he switched to his generic BOB4HIRE screen name. Claiming to be an insurance investigator, he E-mailed the various shipping companies and charterhouses. He asked if any of them had received a report of an explosion in the Celebes Sea. While he waited for the answers, he contacted the National Reconnaissance Office. He asked for an ID listing of all the ships that had accessed global positioning data around the time of the explosion. That information was supposed to be confidential, stored in coded files known only to the vessels and the satellites. However, the NRO had access to the satellite databases, thanks to the Confidential Reconnaissance and Code Satellite. CRACS was one of a new generation of satellites that spied on other satellites. Using sophisticated background radiation detectors, it read incoming and outgoing satellite pulses that momentarily blotted out the cosmic radiation. CRACS ended up with a silhouette of the communication from earth. The satellite was able to translate the pulses into numbers. That, in turn, gave the NRO the code words used by the earth-based planes or ships to contact the satellite.

What Herbert was looking for was an inconsistency. He was hoping to find a vessel that might have been close enough to hear the sampan explosion but did not report it. If he found that, chances were good it was the ship the pirates had tried to waylay.

The data came in slowly over the next several hours. During that time Herbert reveled in the relative comfort and privacy of his little section of the airplane. He was facing the starboard side of the aircraft, and there was a small window to his right. He leaned forward and looked down. The view inspired him. Not because it was a big, beautiful ocean but because it reminded him how people had fought and suffered and perished to explore it. Nothing came without hard work and sacrifice. That fact kept Bob Herbert from slipping into bitterness for what his own public service had cost him.

He received replies from twelve of the twenty-two E-mails he had sent out. No one had reported any explosions in the region. He also learned that there had been at least one vessel in the region at the time of the explosion. It was named the *Hosannah* and was apparently owned by a gentleman named Arvids March. There was a reference to a court case that Herbert could not access. The vessel sailed under a Tasmanian flag and listed six ports of registry. Herbert searched the Tasmanian phone directory online. He could not find an entry for Arvids March. That did not surprise him. Ships from one country were often registered in another for tax reasons. Mr. March could be from anywhere. Or it could be a fake name for a fake enterprise. Herbert did a full Internet search for him and came up empty. He searched under A. March and found over ten thousand references, from "I love a March" to a hip-hop group Ides a March. He sent an E-mail to Op-Center asking them to see what they could find out about the man. A quick check turned up nothing. Obviously not a publicity-seeker or public figure.

Then Herbert took a break. A think break. He had spent hours on this search and had very little to show for it. That was frustrating. Worse, it was dangerous. Herbert knew too well what could happen when people went into a situation with zero intelligence. That was how the embassy in Beirut was hit.

Herbert went back to his computer. The rogue boat was out there.

He wanted to find it.

TWENTY

It was the largest privately owned collection of prehistoric fossils in the world.

Jervis Darling had developed a love and deep appreciation for prehistoric animals forty years before. When in his early twenties he read an article on the Australian Museum in one of his first magazines, *Australian Insider*, he had not realized what a successful reign the dinosaurs had on earth. Each new generation evolved into a more refined version of the last. The carnivores became perfect pack hunters as well as individual predators. The herbivores bonded in family units with complex forms of child care. They had survived over 100 million years. That was 100 times longer than humankind and its ancestors had walked the earth. It was probably 100 times longer than humans would continue to walk the earth.

Unless he had his way.

Darling began buying fossils, from the smallest, oldest marine trilobites to a complete land-ranging allosaurus to a soaring pteranodon. He did not settle for plaster casts, as so many museums did. Only the real thing. He had them displayed in two large rooms on his estate, along with murals showing the animals and their world. It was ironic, he thought. The Australian media had nicknamed him Salty after the northwest crocodile. That was an insult, though not for the reasons they thought. Darling did not mind being compared to a carnivore. But he aspired to be one of the all-time great ones, like tyrannosaurus or gorgosaurus. Not a relatively small contemporary off-shoot.

The moon shone through the large, arching skylight. Small lights illuminated the mounted skeletons, murals, and exhibit cases. Dressed in jeans and a flannel shirt, the six-foot-four-inch Darling stood in the middle of the cathedral-like structure. The bald-headed media titan did not end each day with a stroll through his collection. He did so today, however. He reminded himself that sometimes creatures perished due to things outside their control. The dinosaurs were a perfect example. Apparently they all died out slowly after an asteroid struck the earth. The collision threw incalculable tons of dust into the atmosphere, blotted out the sunlight for years, and created a worldwide ecological disaster. The equivalent of a prehistoric nuclear winter. According to the geological record, these impacts and global extinctions occurred with some regularity.

Portions of the earth were overdue for a similar cleansing, he reflected. It was a concept Darwin would never have imagined. A mixture of natural selection and mass extinction.

Footsteps echoed along an adjoining corridor. A few seconds later, Andrew stepped through the door connecting the mansion with the wing that housed Darling's collection of Ice Age fossils.

"Mr. Darling, Captain Kannaday is coming up the walk," the executive secretary informed him.

"Bring him to the kitchen," Darling said.

"Yes, sir," Andrew replied.

There was no hesitation in Andrew's voice. If Darling had instructed his aide to escort Kannaday to his private observatory, to the garage, or to a guest-room closet, Andrew would have done so without question. Descended from people who lived here during the Ice Age, Andrew Juta Graham was one of the few people whom Darling trusted absolutely.

Darling followed his secretary into the hallway of the 30,000-square-foot estate. This was the east wing, which held the public area of Darling's home. The museum, the dining hall, the ballroom, the screening room, the gym, the indoor and outdoor swimming pools. He made his way through the dining area to the kitchen. He asked the cook and her assistant if they would mind waiting in their quarters for a few minutes. They left at once. Darling went to one of the three refrigerators and removed a large bottle of sparkling water. He leaned against a butcher-block counter and faced the picture window. He opened the water and took a swallow as he stared off at rolling grounds. He wondered suddenly if the dinosaurs ever drank from sparkling springs. They probably did. And did they notice a difference?

Of course, he decided. But it would not have meant anything to them. They did not have the brainpower to look past the initial stimulation. In that respect the dinosaurs were like the terrorists Darling was dealing with now. Locked into narrow patterns of information processing. Impulsive instead of reflective. What made them dangerous also made them easy to manipulate.

A door opened behind him. It was the door that led from the rear of the estate through the servants' quarters. Darling set the water on the countertop and turned. His back was to the window as Andrew left and Kannaday made his way through the appliances. Spotlights from an outdoor patio shone outside the window. Crisp white light washed over the skipper. He was dressed in a black pullover and khakis. Even though Kannaday walked briskly, with his shoulders pulled back, he looked tired. He extended his big right hand. Darling shook the hand and held it.

"Your palm feels warm," Darling said.

"I was on deck, in the sun, Mr. Darling," Kannaday said.

"Palms up?"

"I'm like a solar battery, sir," Kannaday said. "Sunlight hits a spot and shuttles all around me."

"Ah. Would you like a cold beverage?" Darling asked.

"Thank you, no," Kannaday replied.

Darling released Kannaday's hand slowly. "Wine," he said.

"No, thank you."

"I wasn't offering," Darling said, laughing. "I was just wondering if grapes ever fermented in prehistory."

"I would imagine they did," Kannaday said. He seemed stung by having rejected an offer that had not been made.

"Quite right," Darling said. "The liquid may have collected in a pool. A dinosaur might have lapped at it. Perhaps he even became a little inebriated. Quite a thought, wouldn't you say?"

"It is," Kannaday replied.

"I wonder what a prehistoric vintage would demand in the Mahogany Auction Room," Darling said. "An unthinkable sum, I would imagine. Can't you just picture it? Scientists bidding against connoisseurs to buy a mud-crusted and fossilized puddle."

Darling chuckled at the thought. Kannaday smiled uncomfortably. *The man has no imagination,* Darling thought. Then again, he was at something of a disadvantage here. Because Darling was silhouetted by the patio lights, Kannaday could not see him clearly. He could not tell from Darling's expression whether he was joking or being serious. That was how Darling wanted it. He wanted his guest off balance and open. Vulnerable.

Darling crossed his arms and regarded the captain. "I understand that replacement gear is being sent over to the yacht."

"Yes, sir."

"I want you back at sea as soon as possible."

"Of course," Kannaday said.

"Before you go, though, I'd like an explanation," Darling said.

"First, I promise that nothing like this will happen again," Kannaday said. "We should have foreseen it. Your security chief agrees."

"Hawke agrees?"

"Absolutely," Kannaday said.

"And how will you guard against future attacks?" Darling demanded. His mood soured quickly. "A sampan full of sea rats drew close enough to put a hole in the side of your vessel! How did that happen?"

"Sir, the men in the sampan did not cause the explosion," Kannaday said. "We did."

"How?"

"By accident. We hit the pirates hard, fast, and decisively," Kannaday told him. "The attack triggered explosives that were on board the other vessel."

"Why did you let them get so close?" Darling asked. "You have a good radar system on board."

"The sampan did not create a blip that was distinguishable from porpoises or flotsam," Kannaday said. "We failed to identify it until the security camera picked it up. By then it was nearly upon us. At that point we decided not to strike until we were certain that we were facing an enemy," Kannaday replied.

"Why?" Darling asked.

The question seemed to surprise Captain Kannaday. "Sir, are you suggesting we should have attacked what may have been an innocent vessel?"

"Preemptive strikes reduce risk," Darling told him.

"I would have thought that a stealthy passage was more important," Kannaday replied.

"The best way to assure a low profile is to eliminate potential witnesses," Darling pointed out. "Now, you say Mr. Hawke agrees that adequate security precautions were in place?"

"He does," Kannaday said.

"Or am I hearing a case of 'You watch my back, I'll watch yours'?" Darling said.

"Excuse me?" Kannaday asked.

"I don't know Mr. Hawke very well," Darling said. "I doubt anyone does. A good security chief does not share his thoughts. But I cannot believe Hawke would agree that a disastrous operation was, in fact, a competent one. It is an indefensible position."

"Sir, forgive me for repeating myself, but what happened was unforeseeable," Kannaday insisted.

"And *I* say that what happened was preventable!" Darling yelled.

Kannaday said nothing.

"As for Mr. Hawke, you would not misrepresent what he said. That would be easy to check. So we have a contradiction."

"Mr. Darling, you've lost me," the captain said helplessly.

"Hawke has apparently agreed to back your explanation, that this was a freak occurrence," Darling said. "Why?"

"Because it was."

"Do you like Mr. Hawke?" Darling asked.

"No, sir. I don't."

"You do not like him, you did not hire him," Darling said. "This was your chance to blame him and get rid of him. Why hasn't that happened?"

Darling watched Kannaday's face. The blanket glow of the spotlight left nothing in shadow. The captain did not break eye contact or move his mouth. It was unnatural.

Kannaday was concealing something.

It took a long moment for the captain to speak. It must have felt far longer than that.

"You're right," Kannaday said at last. "I called him out for this. I demanded that he surrender his post."

"And what was his response?"

Carefully, the captain rolled down the neck of his sweater. There was a white surgical bandage taped to his throat. In the center of the bandage was an ugly red spot. Jervis Darling was not surprised to see it. Kannaday had to have been wearing the high collar for some reason. Had he been injured in battle, he would not have sought to hide the wound.

"Hawke put a blade to my throat."

Darling snickered. "You let him surprise you just as the pirates did."

Kannaday did not reply.

"Hawke let you survive so you could absolve his team of blame," Darling went on. "On the one hand, I should not care about that. I am only concerned about results. The problem, Captain, is that I like people to meet or surpass my expectations. You have failed in that regard."

"Once!" Kannaday said. There was frustration, not anger, in the captain's gravelly voice. "We've had a single slip in more than a dozen very difficult, perfectly executed missions."

"You had two slips, Captain Kannaday," Darling pointed out. "First the pirates, then Hawke."

"All right," Kannaday agreed. *"I* made two mistakes. I accept that responsibility."

"Wherein lies the problem," Darling said. "Errors can be repaired. Restoring trust is another issue."

"Mr. Darling, I feel like a catboat in a bloody hurricane," Kannaday said. "I need to finish this job. Then I have to look ahead to the other jobs. I can live with the way things are between me and John Hawke. My ego can handle that. But how do I fix it with you?"

"You are the captain," Darling said. "Figure it out."

"Sir, I'm trying very hard to do that," Kannaday said. "In the future we will attack or avoid any ship that comes close. We'll push the *Hosannah* to make up as much lost time as possible. I will work out my problems with John Hawke if you like."

"Captain Kannaday, I don't 'like'!" Darling sneered. "You suffered a mutiny on board your vessel!"

"It was a disagreement, Mr. Darling."

"It ended when Mr. Hawke dictated shipboard terms from the hilt of a blade," Darling pointed out. "That, sir, is a mutiny."

Kannaday was about to respond. Instead, his mouth clapped shut and he looked away.

"And you did nothing about it," Darling went on. "Was his knife at your throat all day?"

"No, sir."

"How did he pay for his crime?" Darling demanded. "What did he say when the wind changed and you put a knife at *his* throat? You did want to do that, didn't you?"

"I did, sir."

"I wish you had," Darling said. "You cannot work for me *and* for Mr. Hawke. The way back, Captain, is to fix that."

The silence in the kitchen was such that Darling could hear the water fizzing in the bottle.

Kannaday held Darling's gaze a moment longer. "I understand, sir. Was there anything else?"

"No," Darling said.

Kannaday nodded. Then he turned to leave. As the captain made his way around the counter, Andrew appeared to escort him from the estate. Andrew had been just out of earshot the entire time. Kannaday respected the secretary's devotion, his discretion, and above all his loyalty. If only everyone in Darling's service were like that.

Darling walked to the counter. He picked up his water and took a quick swig. He did not really care whether Kannaday won back his respect or not. All that mattered was having someone take charge of this mission. To see the rest of it through without event. To make sure he was not bothered on any future aspects of the operation.

Darling finished the water and wondered who that lieutenant would be. John Hawke was a confident man, and strength was a great motivator. Peter Kannaday was a frightened man. Fear could move a man as well, often in strange and unexpected ways.

Which is the greater asset? Darling asked himself.

The big, successful prehistoric predators had enormous power and guile. Sometimes, though, a startled vegetarian like a stegosaurus would swing its spiked tail and fell a mighty tyrannosaur. There were countless cracked skulls in the fossil record.

The tactics never changed. Only the combatants and their weapons.

Darling put the empty water bottle on the counter. He left the kitchen to briefly attend to his other businesses. The safe ones. The ones that had long ago lost their ability to challenge and gratify him. The ones that covered the world and reported on it.

A world that he would have a hand in reshaping.

TWENTY-ONE

The Celebes Sea
Friday, 9:44 P.M.

Monica Loh's patrol boat hovered about the second nuclear waste site. This was where the Japanese government was allowed to deposit material. Tokyo was also free to assign space to other nations, provided they adhered to the International Nuclear Regulatory Commission codes.

The officer did not like coming to the Japanese site. She did not like going to any place controlled by the Japanese. It was a purely psychological reaction but a strong one. People of smaller nations in this region were inevitably caught in the backwash of history created by China and Japan. The Chinese were ambitious, organized, and insensitive. With over a billion people to feed and manage, Loh did not blame them for their totalitarian efficiency. She did not have the same sympathy for the Japanese. They were greedy rather than ambitious. They were domineering, not just organized. And they were cruel rather than insensitive. When the Chinese turned outward it was for land and resources to control. The Japanese looked for people to subjugate.

Singapore had its own forms of overkill. Laws were strict and punishment stricter. Dissent was permitted as long as sedition and abusive language were avoided. Work was hard, wages were low, and the government did not do enough to ease the burden of laborers. The shipbuilders and oil refiners were the backbone of the economy. The government could not afford to alienate them. Since the bulk of the population was of Chinese heritage, they understood the rules. But Singaporeans had, at heart, a gentle nature. Their discomfort about the Japanese came partly from history lessons and partly from a clash of natures. They experienced it on the seas, in the harbors, in the banks, and on the stock exchanges. Whenever FNO Loh was around Japanese sailors, military or otherwise, she felt as though she was on high alert. Even tourists made her uneasy. They seemed to be collecting memories instead of enjoying them.

Loh watched from the deck as the sailors lowered their gear into the water. They were just a few meters ahead of her, port side. They worked in silence as they had been trained to do. Talk was a distraction in military operations. Still, every one of the officer's senses was stimulated. She smelled the oil and salt of the sea. She heard the slapping of the waves against the hull of the patrol ship. Spotlights fastened to the rail played across the water. The net containing the equipment seemed to lose pieces as it descended into the darkness between the bright, patchy crests of sea. A strong, temperate wind pushed at her from the northwest. Though the woman's world was the sea, she had always felt a kinship with the wind. It moved across the ocean, just like she did. It was silent. And it had changing moods that were only noticed by those who got in the way. The stars were partly hidden by high, wispy clouds. They reminded Loh of a waitress she had once seen in Bangkok. The woman had worn a white gown with sequins that sparkled in the light. Now that Loh thought of it, she knew as little about that waitress as she did about the heavens. The world was full of mysteries.

Loh was relaxed as the men and women worked. She did not care whether they found the site to be corrupted or intact. Even no information was information. She would deal with whatever they discovered. Though not a practicing Buddhist, Loh believed in the four noble truths it taught: that existence is suffering; that the cause of suffering is desire; that suffering eventually ends in a state of peace known as nirvana; and that the road to nirvana, the so-called eightfold noble path, consists of the qualities of right resolve, right speech, right action, right livelihood, right effort, right mindfulness, and right concentration. All of those skills did not come easily. And they required one thing above all.

Patience.

Loh had learned that quality by watching her father work on his cases. In the end, the perpetrator would be caught. It only remained to be seen how, when, and where.

After a few minutes, the young male specialist in charge of naval underwater systems jogged over to FNO Loh. He saluted.

"Ambient radiation levels are below normal at the site of the last deposit," he said. "Unless the coordinates are incorrect."

"There is no reason to believe they are," she said. "Go down and see what you can find."

"Ma'am," he said, saluting and turning.

It took just five minutes for the underwater unit to get into the sea. They carried a fluoroscopic scanner. If there were anything hot inside the stencil-dated concrete block, it would show up as a red pattern on the viewfinder.

Ten minutes later the three-person team reached the site. The block that had been deposited registered as cold. It contained no radioactive materials. FNO Loh unhooked the point-to-point radio from her belt. She contacted Warrant Officer Jelbart on the other vessel.

"Then the materials were off-loaded somewhere between the source and the drop-off point," Jelbart said.

"That is apparently the case," Loh agreed.

"And it's possible they were given to the vessel that was attacked by the sampan," Jelbart said.

"That is also likely," she said.

"We'll get the name and registry of the ship that made this drop," Jelbart told her. "Then we'll have a talk with the captain."

"That is worth doing," Loh said. "But I am betting you will not find the ship or the crew."

"What do you mean?" Jelbart asked. "The ship has to be registered."

"That is true," she said. "But that vessel probably has multiple registries. I am guessing they were notified when the sampan attacked their fellow ship. While they were still at sea, the vessel would have been rechristened and the hull repainted. I doubt very much that we will find it."

"Then we've learned nothing," Jelbart said. "Except for the fact that there is a great deal of nuclear waste somewhere in our corner of the world."

"That is not nothing," Loh said. "We will find it."

"I like your attitude. Any suggestions?" Jelbart asked.

"Just one," she said. "Have patience."

TWENTY-TWO

Cairns, Australia
Friday, 9:45 P.M.

Peter Kannaday returned to the yacht a shaken man.

During the meeting with Jervis Darling, the captain had experienced something extremely disturbing. For the first time in his forty-seven years, Kannaday's natural, healthy suspicion had blossomed like a nightshade into poisonous paranoia. And it had happened for a shockingly simple reason. Being buffeted by two forces, Jervis Darling and John Hawke, was troublesome enough. What bothered Kannaday more was the thought that those forces might not be working independently. Hawke had been hired by Darling. They could be working together through Marcus Darling. Perhaps the elder Darling wanted Kannaday to turn on Hawke so that Hawke could eliminate him. Then he could seize the yacht. Kannaday's crew would not turn against a security chief who had defended himself. From Jervis Darling's point of view, this was easier and more secure than purchasing a yacht and leaving a paper trail. Or there could be other reasons. Perhaps Darling was doing this out of nothing more than utter contempt for an easygoing man. Or maybe breaking people was how Darling got his jollies.

These suspicions turned the captain's natural force, his momentum, inside out. It had turned healthy caution into deadly fear. Kannaday had to find a way to get rid of that.

Kannaday also had to get rid of John Hawke. Even if Hawke and Darling were not working together, the captain had not been given any wiggle room on that account.

Kannaday hoped that getting the mission back under way would help restore some of his balance.

The *Hosannah* left Darling Cove at 9:05 P.M. Repairs to the laboratory had been completed by 10 o'clock. The new equipment had been secured and tested. The yacht was ready to make their delayed rendezvous with a fishing vessel from Malaysia. But no sooner had they set out than Kannaday's radio beeped. It was Marcus Darling reporting some very odd radio traffic in the Celebes Sea. Captain Kannaday went below to see him.

John Hawke was already in the radio shack. It was the first time Kannaday had seen him since returning from the Darling estate. The security chief had been working in his cabin when Kannaday returned.

Their eyes barely met. Hawke said nothing to Kannaday, and the captain did not acknowledge the security chief. Kannaday stood behind the radio operator. Hawke was to the left, where the porthole used to be. Marcus had an AltaVista translation file open on his laptop. The program automatically translated incoming messages into English typescript.

"I picked up a communication from a Japanese trawler," Marcus said. "He was asking if it was safe to pass."

"Asking who?" Kannaday asked.

"A Singaporean patrol vessel, judging by the names and ranks," Marcus replied.

"Why would he ask that?" Kannaday asked.

"The trawler is at one hundred and thirty degrees longitude, five degrees latitude," the younger Darling told him. "Obviously, the patrol ship is there as well. And the worst news is, it may not be alone."

Kannaday felt a chill. "Go on."

"The ship from Singapore is apparently talking to another ship," Marcus continued. "I can't hear what the other ship is saying because the message is blacked out."

"Then how do you know the Singaporeans are talking to another ship?" Kannaday asked.

"Because there are short blackouts after every conversation with the trawler," Marcus told him. "They are of roughly the same duration as the initial conversation. It's as if the boat receiving the message is translating and relaying the conversation word for word."

"Why wouldn't another ship just listen in?" Hawke asked.

"Because as soon as the other ship turned on their radio, someone like me would know they were there. And, more importantly, I'd know exactly who they were," Marcus said.

"I see," Kannaday said. "Is that a military tactic?"

"Military or police, yes," Marcus replied.

Military and police vessels did not go to that site on routine visits. The area was monitored by civilian vessels of the International Nuclear Regulatory Commission.

"We need to find out who is there," Hawke said.

"Why?" Kannaday asked. "The dumping grounds are not on any of our routes."

"They are on Jaafar's route," Hawke pointed out.

"Why should that worry us?" Kannaday asked.

"He is an ally."

"By now Jaafar has got the name of his ship repainted and is flying a different flag," Kannaday said. "Those changes would have been made at night or under a tarpaulin. It is very unlikely that anyone would have seen him."

"Then what are one and possibly two military vessels doing at the waste site?" Hawke asked.

"I have no idea, and I'm not sure it concerns us," Kannaday said.

"If they discover that Jaafar deposited empty drums of nuclear waste, it could come back to us," Hawke said.

"They would have to find him first, which is unlikely," Kannaday said. "If Jaafar thinks someone is on to him, he will go into hiding. We can warn him on our secure channel."

"I want to know who's out there," Hawke repeated.

"And do what, exactly?" Kannaday asked.

"Go after those vessels, if necessary," Hawke said. "Do to them what the pirates wanted to do to us."

A preemptive strike, Kannaday thought. Just what Darling might have suggested. Maybe Hawke was sincerely concerned about the patrol ship. Or maybe he was simply trying to provoke a confrontation with Kannaday. In either case, the captain decided to let him have his head on this one.

"How do you recommend we conduct reconnaissance?" Kannaday asked.

"We need a satellite overview," Hawke replied. "We need to see who is there and what they're doing."

"Marcus, can you do that?" Kannaday asked.

"We can do that through Colonel Hwan," Marcus said.

"Who is that?" Kannaday asked.

"Colonel Kim Hwan is my uncle's man at the North Korean Reconnaissance Bureau," Marcus replied. "The NKRB collects strategic and tactical intelligence for the Ministry of the People's Armed Forces. They also eavesdrop on business rivals when my uncle needs them to."

"How long will it take to get information from Colonel Hwan?" Kannaday asked.

"We won't know until we contact him," Marcus said. "He may be able to get the information through normal channels. If not, he might have to go to the Chinese for access to one of their satellites."

"Do it," Hawke said.

Hawke did not bother to ask Kannaday. The captain let that go, too. Kannaday wondered if he was afraid to stop him or letting him run until he hit a reef. He realized now how complacent he had grown as a commander. Maybe he should question this more. Just to flex his muscles.

"You're certain there's no way anyone can eavesdrop on our message or trace the signal?" Kannaday asked.

"It's extremely unlikely," Marcus replied. "My uncle has a direct line to Colonel Hwan's cell comm. We'll patch into that and send E-mails directly to him. Hwan can respond to them immediately. No one would have any reason to monitor those communications."

"And if someone does?" Kannaday asked stubbornly.

"Every message we send is coded and untraceable," Marcus told him. "We'll be safe."

"All right," Kannaday said. "Go ahead."

Marcus accessed the main transmitter in Darwin. He turned to his laptop and accessed the codebook on the hard drive. He looked up Hwan's code name. Once he had that, he took the appropriate diskette from a small safe under the radio stand. He plugged that into the drive.

"Ready," Marcus said.

Hawke dictated as Marcus typed. The security director had not reacted to Kannaday giving the final okay to contact Hwan. Hawke asked the North Korean colonel to find out who was at the waste site and, if possible, why. While they waited for an acknowledgment, Kannaday watched for any sign of bonding between the two men. A glance. Hawke moving closer to Marcus. Something that might indicate collusion. Both men would benefit by Kannaday making a misstep. Hawke could seize the *Hosannah*. Marcus could run certain aspects of the mission, show his uncle leadership chops. They did not seem to be connecting in any meaningful way. The captain felt some wind in his sails.

Many paranoids do have enemies, Kannaday reflected. But he wondered whether, more often than not, it was themselves.

"What do we do in the meantime?" Marcus asked.

"We continue to the rendezvous point," Kannaday said. "Is everything set with the Malaysian crew?"

"I received a radio message while you were with the boss," Marcus said. He accessed the notes on his computer. "They've been crisscrossing the area since we missed our appointment. I told them we had an equipment problem. They are awaiting a new ETA."

"Tell Captain bin Omar we'll be there at one A.M.," Kannaday said. "And thanks for being vague about what happened."

"I didn't have much choice," Marcus said. "It would not have instilled confidence to tell them the truth."

That was true.

Kannaday asked Marcus to let him know when he had any information. Then he went to the deck to chat with the crewmen who were posing as passengers. There was a great deal of sea traffic offshore. Kannaday knew many of the local skippers who ran pleasure boats. Ironically, if they saw Kannaday, if they waved to him, it helped him stay anonymous. No one thought, *Where is Captain Kannaday and what is he up to?*

Kannaday walked the deck. The sea air was unusually misty. The droplets felt good on the captain's face. He felt slightly better than he did before. Hawke had a different project to focus on. That kept the pressure off Kannaday. It also did something else.

It gave him time to figure out what to do about the security chief.

TWENTY-THREE

Washington, D.C.
Friday, 7:17 A.M.

As mayor of Los Angeles and as head of Op-Center, Paul Hood had taken calls from heads of state. During times of crisis he had spoken calmly over the phone with his counterparts in other nations. Even when lives were at risk or lost, Hood had been able to speak without agitation to operatives in the field. He had talked with the wives and mothers of police officers and firefighters who had lost husbands and sons. He had called and visited the families of the Strikers who had perished in the Kashmir conflict.

But Hood was somewhat unnerved when he got around to accessing his personal cell phone messages. Daphne Connors had called at six-fifteen that morning. From the sound of her voice she had just woken up. Or perhaps she was just going to sleep. She often went to client parties that continued late into the night. She reported in a low, smoky voice that she had a dream about him. It had something to do with a stagecoach driver and a tavern owner in the old West. Only Hood was running the saloon and Daphne was running the stage.

Maybe that was true. Or maybe it was a pretext to phone. In either case, the call troubled him. Or rather, it was the tone of Daphne's voice. He had not heard a bedroom voice in years. His former wife, Sharon, had never had one, really. And the one night he spent with Op-Center's former press liaison, Ann Farris, was followed by awkward silence and forced felicity.

Daphne's voice was very feminine, very seductive. It got into Hood's ear, into his mind, into all his nerve endings in a way that made him very uncomfortable. It also made him wonder with dismay whether his discomfort was actually with Daphne. It might be with the idea of anyone getting close. Maybe his marriage had gone just the way he wanted it to. Built around a core of emotional and physical detachment for the sake of stability. It was as if he were running a city government or federal agency.

Hood did not like that thought at all. He chose not to think about it. He had arrived at the office a half hour before, and he was still going through the report from the evening unit. It appeared to have been an uneventful night everywhere except in the Celebes Sea. Hood listened to a call from Lowell Coffey to Hood's evening counterpart, Curt Hardaway. The call had been recorded digitally on Hood's computer.

Coffey reported that the Singaporean patrol ship had discovered an empty concrete block at a nuclear disposal site. The block should have contained radioactive waste. Radiation detectors on board Coffey's ship, an Australian MIC corvette, supported the findings.

"The Singaporeans are not trying to put anything over on us," Coffey assured Hardaway. "We are going to try to locate the vessel that made this drop. The ship that was scheduled to have been at the 130-5 site is owned by Mahathir bin Dahman of Malaysia. Warrant Officer Jelbart has heard of Dahman. He is involved with waste disposal on a global scale."

Hood made a note of the name.

"Jelbart is not hopeful of tracking the missing material from here," Coffey continued. "If the ship sold the nuclear material, the vessel will already have gotten a face-lift. If they were just pawns, it will be difficult to get timely interviews with anyone who may have been involved. The Malaysian government is not known for opening its books, so to speak. Especially when it comes to the country's leading citizens."

Coffey then asked Hardaway if the NRO would have a look at the region. Perhaps they saw something. Hardaway had left Hood a note saying that he had checked with the NRO. They did not routinely watch the Celebes Sea. The only time they would turn a satellite to the region was if they learned the Chinese or Russians were also doing so. Like the United States, those nations often tested their satellite systems using targets in out-of-the-way sectors. New space cameras were often calibrated and focused using targets on ships or submarines.

Hood archived the messages, then put in a call to Bob Herbert. The intelligence officer would have been airborne for a little under six hours. That was just enough time to make him cranky. Herbert enjoyed being in the field. But once Herbert started downloading mission data into his brain, he was anxious to act on it. Waiting killed him.

The pilot of the TR-1 said that Herbert was sleeping. He asked if Hood wanted to talk to him anyway. Hood said he did not. He was sure Herbert would check in when he woke.

As Hood hung up, he got a call from Stephen Viens. For several years Viens had been the Satellite Imaging supervisor at the National Reconnaissance Office.

Viens had been a college chum of Matt Stoll, Op-Center's chief technical officer. Because of their close relationship, Viens had always given Op-Center's needs top priority. Viens was now Op-Center's internal security chief. He still had friends at the NRO, however. Whenever they came across something that might be of interest to Op-Center, they let him know.

"Paul, I just got a call from Noah Moore-Mooney at the NRO," Viens said. "Bob Herbert had put out an APB on activity in the Celebes Sea."

"Curt Hardaway said there's nothing going on there," Hood said.

"There wasn't," Viens said. "Until a few minutes ago."

"What have you got?" Hood asked.

"Our *Shado-3* satellite watches Chinese satellites," Viens said. "When they move, it tracks them. They just saw one shift from Taiwanese shipping lanes in the South China Sea to an area of the Celebes."

"What area?" Hood asked.

"The coordinates are one-hundred and thirty degrees

longitude, five degrees latitude," Viens told him.

"That's where Lowell Coffey is," Hood said, "along with Australian and Singaporean naval vessels. Why the hell would China be watching two small naval ships?"

"How would they even know the ships were out there?" Viens asked. "Flyover?"

"Maybe," Hood said.

It was unlikely that the Chinese would be dealing in third-party nuclear material. They had enough of their own to sell, much of it to Pakistan.

"Stephen, when you were at the NRO, did you come across any cooperative satellite use?" Hood asked.

"You mean would another nation have access to the Chinese satellite?" Viens asked.

"Right."·

"Allies like the Vietnamese or North Koreans asked Beijing for intelligence," Viens said. "But China controlled the hardware."

"All right, Stephen, thanks," Hood said. "Let me know if you get any other information about this."

"Will do," Viens said.

Hood hung up. He looked at his computer clock. He needed to call someone. Someone who had not been returning his calls. But right now it was the only person who might be able to get him the information he needed.

Hood picked up the phone and placed one of those calls he was comfortable making. One he was good at. One where the fate of nations, and not the fate of Paul Hood, was at risk.

TWENTY-FOUR

The Celebes Sea
Friday, 10:33 P.M.

Raja Adnan bin Omar and his radio operator stood in the small dark cabin of the fishing boat. The radio operator was standing beside a shortwave set on a shelf.

The radio operator's legs were bent slightly to help him stand on the rocking deck. Bin Omar was at the wheel. Both men were dressed in heavy black pullovers. Their heads were uncovered, their hair and beards well groomed. A wet wind hissed against the windows. It punched through the old wood of the cabin walls. The two men were accustomed to it. So were the two other fishermen aboard the thirty-footer. One of them was bin Omar's twenty-seven-year-old son. They were below, putting fish in large ice lockers and repairing the nets. They had caught more fish during their zigzagging delay. When they were finished, they ripped the nylon strands on purpose so they would have something to do. In case they were ever boarded, bin Omar wanted them to be busy. Idle men looked guilty, even if they were not. The lockers were stored in a closet at the stern of the vessel. Two of them were made of lead. They were not designed to hold fish.

Automatic weapons were also stored below in case they were needed.

The radio operator removed his headset. "They are just over two hours from us. They apologized again for the delay."

"Did they give you a reason?" bin Omar asked.

"Mr. M said only that the problem was mechanical in nature," the operator replied.

"Ah," said bin Omar. "The excuse that cannot be disproved."

"Perhaps they will tell us more when we are together," the radio operator suggested.

"They will have to," bin Omar said. "Our employers will certainly wish to know more. But it is not our problem. We are merely messengers."

For the first time in more than a year of dealings, Captain Kannaday had failed to make a rendezvous. The sixty-two-year-old fisherman was unhappy about that. He disliked the unexpected, whether it was a storm, a surprise inspection by harbor police in Pontian Ketchil, or a delay. It was particularly dangerous in the smuggling business. Whether they were transporting drugs, weapons, or nuclear material, seamen did not like being out in the open sea. Here, they were equally vulnerable to patrol ships and pirate vessels.

Bin Omar hoped that Captain Kannaday had a reasonable explanation. Though processed nuclear waste was not the easiest material to obtain, Kannaday was not the only supplier in the region. Until today, he had simply been the most efficient. And the group with whom bin Omar was associated, the Kansai Unit, demanded reliability. The Asian group also demanded accountability. Bin Omar would have to explain the delay.

Despite that, bin Omar was at peace. His wife and other children were home and well cared for. And he was always at ease on these waters, which his family had sailed for hundreds of years. For whatever the fate of the angry men and the mad civilizations they built, he knew one thing for certain. The bin Omars would sail these seas for centuries to come.

TWENTY-FIVE

Tokyo, Japan
Friday, 9:34 P.M.

Shigeo Fujima was standing on the balcony of his apartment smoking a cigarette. The Japanese intelligence officer was tired and had come home early. He wanted to try to relax this weekend. Fujima had worked on several situations back to back. There was Chinese involvement in the attack on Vatican clergy in Botswana; increasing Chinese financial links with Taiwan; and the rapid growth of the Chinese space program, which was about to put a man into orbit. Chinese expansionism on earth, with a workforce of one billion people, was a direct threat to Japan and the entire Asian Rim. Especially with the Japanese economy so hard hit by the worldwide recession.

Fujima lived with his wife and two daughters in a spacious apartment near Yoyogi Park. They had been living here for nearly seven months. The elder Fujima daughter, Keiko, attended the International Trade and Industry Inspection Institute, which was just a five-minute walk from the apartment. Their younger daughter, ten-year-old Emiko, attended the Children's Play International School, which was a six-minute walk from the apartment. They were lucky to get the 2,000-square-foot, two-story place, though the Fujimas' good fortune came at a price. They lived here because the Japanese economy was in turmoil. A commercial photographer used to live here. When retail sales began to struggle, advertising was cut back. If agencies ran advertisements at all, they used text and computer-generated images rather than photographs. The photographer was evicted. The Fujimas moved in from an apartment that was half the size and nearly as expensive.

"These are sad times," he muttered to himself as he flicked his cigarette toward the street. They were difficult for the economy and they were barely manageable in areas of world security. He was lucky to be home this early. To be able to have dinner with his wife. To see the kids before they went to bed. Assuming Keiko got off the phone and Emiko unplugged herself from the computer, that is. He smiled as he turned back to the apartment. He could not really expect them to change their routine for him. Things were not as they were when he was a boy. If he had not gone to his father when he came home from his job as a train conductor, he would have been beaten with a strap.

"Maybe it's good to have things so predictable here," he thought aloud. His life at the office was anything but that.

Suddenly, Keiko came running from her room. Her long raven hair framed her vampire-pale face.

"Father, there's a man on my cell phone," the teenager said. "He wants to talk to you." She held out the purple phone.

"Someone called for me on your phone?" Fujima asked.

"Yes. He cut in while I was talking with Kenji. He said it's urgent. He sounds foreign," she added. "His Japanese is terrible."

Fujima took the phone and thanked her. He turned back to the balcony. "This is Fujima," he said.

"I'm sorry to call this number," said the voice on the other end. "It was the only one listed in the directory."

Keiko was right. The man's Japanese was awful. But the voice was familiar. "Who is this?" Fujima asked.

"It's Paul Hood at Op-Center," he said in English. "I'm sorry. I was using a god-awful translation program on the computer. My phonetic Japanese is not particularly good."

"Neither is your timing, Mr. Hood," Fujima said. "This call is extremely—"

"Unorthodox, I know," Hood said. "My apologies, Mr. Fujima. But we need to speak."

"I was just about to have dinner with my wife," Fujima told him. "And this is an unsecured line."

"I know that, Mr. Fujima," Hood replied. "So I hope you will understand when I tell you that materials are missing from your backyard. Materials that should have been left at the 130-5 site."

"I see," Fujima said. Hood was referring to radioactive waste. Suddenly, dinner did not seem so important. Fujima used his shoulder to hold the phone to his ear while he lit another cigarette. "Please go on, Mr. Hood," he said as he drew hard on it.

"We are looking for it with the help of Singapore and Australia," Hood went on. "But someone is watching us. They're using a Chinese satellite, and we don't believe it is the Chinese. We think it may be the traffickers. We need to know who might have access to that platform. I thought you might be able to get that information."

"I can tell you that right now," Fujima said. "South Korea conducts naval maneuvers in that region. North Korea has full access to three satellites in the region. The satellite you're interested in is called the *Fong Sai*."

"Who would run that operation for the North Koreans?" Hood asked.

Fujima heard his daughter yelling from behind. "Father, my phone! That man had the operator break in!"

Fujima covered the mouthpiece. "A moment, Keiko," he said. He returned to Hood. "The man you want is Colonel Kim Hwan of the North Korean Reconnaissance Bureau. He's a very low-profile fellow."

"Do you have any contact information for him?" Hood asked.

"We have his office telephone and E-mail," Fujima said. "I'm sure you have that on file."

"If not, I'll let you know," Hood said.

"Is there anything we can do?" Fujima asked.

"Not at the moment, thank you," Hood said. "We have people on the scene and more en route. If anything happens, we'll talk again."

"You had best use my home phone," Fujima said. He gave Hood the unpublished number. "It will help to keep peace here. You have a teenage daughter, as I recall."

"I do," Hood said. "Go and have your dinner. Again, I'm sorry to have interrupted."

"Not at all," Fujima said.

The intelligence officer clicked off the phone and returned it to his daughter. The young woman hit Redial and disappeared into her room. She closed the door with her foot. Fujima shook his head and ran a hand through his short black hair. It was damp with sweat. Anxiety never showed in his stoic expression, his dark eyes, his strong mouth. When he was worried, he perspired.

Fujima continued to smoke his second cigarette. He wondered whether he should go back to his office at Gaimusho, the Ministry of Foreign Affairs. He felt he should do some research into the 130-5 site. Perhaps get a schedule of the drop-offs, collect background data of the ships and their crews. But Op-Center was probably doing that already. It would be better if he rested tonight. That way he would be fresh for whatever happened the following week.

The slender thirty-five-year-old intelligence officer turned as his wife came from the kitchen. She told him that dinner would be ready in five minutes. He thanked her, winked, and said he would be in shortly. She smiled back. Then Fujima leaned on the railing and looked down at the street.

"What a world it is," he said.

Fujima's father would never have believed it. The nation that had dropped a pair of nuclear bombs on Japan was asking him for help to find missing nuclear material. And Fujima had given that aid. In the space of one generation, loyalties had shifted that dramatically. Yet that was not the most astonishing part. What was remarkable was that warlords and rogue groups could work in the shadows to create Hiroshima-level destruction. And not to end a war but to start one.

"What a world," Fujima said again.

For the moment, however, Fujima was going to leave the responsibility for it to someone else. Dinner and his wife were waiting. His daughters would join them.

He intended to enjoy them.

That, after all, was what he was fighting for.

TWENTY-SIX

Washington, D.C.
Friday, 8:57 A.M.

It was time for Bob Herbert's wake-up call.

After Paul Hood hung up with Shigeo Fujima, he brought up the dossier on Colonel Hwan. While he read the file, Hood had his assistant Bugs Benet put in a call to the cockpit of the TR-1. Hood was patched through to his groggy intelligence chief. As Bob Herbert answered, it occurred to Hood that in all the years they had been working together he had never had to wake Herbert. It seemed like the man was always on the job or socializing. The first-time experience was disturbing. Clearly, the Mississippi native was not at his most alert or Pride-of-the-Deep-South charming when yanked from a dead sleep.

"Sorry to get you up," Hood said after Herbert had grumbled something into the headset.

"The world better be ending," Herbert said. Those were his first coherent words.

"It isn't, though it might be roughed up pretty bad if we don't do something," Hood informed him.

"Now that I think of it, I don't give a damn about the world," Herbert said. "Just us. The U.S."

The intelligence chief sounded as if his mouth were full of sand. Hood waited a moment.

"Are you sure you're with me?" Hood asked.

"I'm here," Herbert said. "But damn, I wish I had coffee."

"Sorry about that," Hood said.

"It's okay. What's on the table?"

"A North Korean colonel named Kim Hwan," Hood said. "Have you ever heard of him?"

"Colonel Kim Hwan," Herbert muttered. "Yeah. I came across his name in the files I brought. He's a surveillance guy, I think."

"Right," Hood said.

"Is he with us or against us?" Herbert asked.

"He may have used a Chinese satellite to have a look at what we're doing in the Celebes Sea," Hood said.

"How do you know that?" Herbert asked.

"I asked Shigeo Fujima," Hood said.

"The prick finally took your call?" Herbert asked.

"He had no choice," Hood replied. "I had the operator cut in on his daughter's cell phone."

"Nice," Herbert said. "Well, Fujima would know who is running what in that part of the world." The intelligence chief was sounding much more alert now. "So Colonel Hwan is against us. Why?"

"That's what we need to find out," Hood said. "Coffey's team found an empty concrete block at the bottom of the Celebes Sea. The block was supposed to have nuclear waste inside."

"North Korea gets whatever nuclear material they need from China," Herbert said. "Why would they be interested in unprocessed waste material?"

"That's the go-for-broke question," Hood said.

"South Korea doesn't need to go buccaneering for it either," Herbert said. "We supply them. So Hwan wouldn't have been watching to see what the enemy does either."

"Makes sense."

"That suggests a third party," Herbert said.

"Which is where we run into problems," Hood said. "I've got Colonel Hwan's dossier on the computer. It's pretty thin stuff. He's a career man, no family, completely off the Western radar."

"Does he attend seminars, go to retreats, travel in a private capacity?" Herbert asked.

"We don't have that information," Hood said. "As I said, he's not even a blip to our intelligence allies."

"That worries me."

"Why?" Hood asked. "It could be he isn't a heavy-weight."

"It could," Herbert agreed. "More often than not, though, those are the real professionals, the ones who manage to stay hidden and anonymous. Let me think for a second."

While Hood waited for Herbert, he scanned the dossier. They did not even have a picture of the man. That seemed to support Herbert's interpretation. A low-watt intelligence officer would not mind being photographed. Hood came from the worlds of politics and finance. Voters were wooed according to complex demographics. Banking and investments were done with precision. Crisis management was different. It unnerved him to consider how often the only barricade between security and disaster was seat-of-the-pants thinking by men like Bob Herbert. In the same breath he thanked God that he had men like Bob Herbert around him.

"Okay," Herbert said. "Did Hwan go to school?"

"You mean college?"

"Yes," Herbert said.

Hood scanned the dossier. "He did. Hwan studied in Moscow and then in London. Why?"

"Nearly seventy-five percent of the people who are recruited for intelligence service jobs studied abroad," Herbert told him. "Other cultures and colloquial languages are familiar to them. If Colonel Hwan studied in London, he probably speaks English."

"How does that help us?" Hood asked.

"We can talk to him," Herbert informed Hood. "What time is it in North Korea?"

"Just after ten P.M.," Hood said.

"Spies collect information during the day and disseminate it at night," Herbert said. "Hwan probably gets up early to read intelligence reports that came in during the night."

"Why does that matter?" Hood asked.

"He'll probably be at home now, sleeping," Herbert said. "Can you get me that number?"

"I'm sure Matt can dig it from a computer system somewhere," Hood said. "Why?"

"Because sometimes a classic, low-tech approach is the best one," Herbert replied.

"I'm not following you," Hood admitted.

"How did I behave when you called me just now?" Herbert asked.

"You were cranky. Disoriented," Hood said.

"Exactly," Herbert said. "It's the old POW gambit. You drag a guy from his cell or cot during the middle of the night. His guard is down. His head is fuzzy. You don't even have to beat him. You hammer him with questions. A man who is scared and tired will respond to force. His mouth will engage before his brain can prevent it."

"So you call Colonel Hwan and wake him up," Hood said. "He's not a prisoner of war. He's probably not going to be very scared in his own home. What makes you think he'll tell you anything?"

"Because I'm a professional, too," Herbert replied.

TWENTY-SEVEN

The Celebes Sea
Friday, 11:09 P.M.

Lowell Coffey was belowdecks in the captain's cabin. The attorney was lying on the small bed with his arms at his side and his eyes shut. Though it was black outside, the shade was pulled over the porthole. Coffey did not want to open his eyes and see the swaying of the stars. It was bad enough that he had to feel the constant movement of the corvette, hear the waves brushing the hull. He had come down here a half hour before, after Jelbart and Loh had both decided to remain at the site. There was no point of going to Darwin or Singapore until they had some idea where their next stop would be. They could not do that until they located the vessel that had deposited the empty concrete block. It bothered him that the naval might of two nations had to wait for some slippery civilian ship to turn up on someone's radar. He felt as useful as Scylla and Charybdis after Odysseus had sailed through the Strait of Messina.

There was a rap at the narrow metal door.

"Come in," Coffey blurted. The attorney sat up slowly on the edge of the bed. Even so, he had to stop and prop himself on an elbow as his stomach remained horizontal.

A young sailor entered carrying a large radio handset. "Sir, there's a call for you."

"Thank you," Coffey said weakly as he extended his free hand.

The young seaman gave him the unit, then left and shut the door. Coffey lay back down.

"Yes?" he said.

"Lowell, it's Paul."

"Hey, Paul," Coffey said weakly.

"Wow," Hood said. "It sounds like I'm waking everyone today."

"No, you didn't wake me," Coffey said. "I'm just trying not to make any excessive moves. That includes my vocal chords."

"It's that bad?"

"Whatever the opposite of *water baby* is, that's me."

"I see," Hood said.

"What's been happening?" Coffey asked.

"Your ships are being watched," Hood said.

That opened Coffey's eyes. The attorney rolled onto his side. He ignored the complaints from his belly. "How? By whom?"

"By a Chinese satellite," Hood told the attorney. "It's apparently being time-shared by the North Koreans. We have an idea who may be running the actual surveillance, though we don't know who may have ordered it. Bob is looking into that now."

"You know, it could be nothing at all," Coffey said. "It may be a planned reconnaissance. I'm sure the North Koreans routinely watch the military activities of other nations in this region."

"They do, but military traffic is uncommon in that sector," Hood said. "This is not someplace they would have targeted without a reason."

"That reason being we may have been seen or heard or ratted out," Coffey suggested.

"In a manner of speaking," Hood replied. "We don't know yet how it happened. What's the latest over there?"

"Jelbart and Loh are still trying to find the ship that made the drop-off here," Coffey replied. "The only thing we're sure of is that it did not leave the way it was supposed to."

"How do you know that?"

"The ships that come here are required to file an itinerary with the International Nuclear Regulatory Commission," Coffey told him. "FNO Loh called Paya Lebar Airbase and asked for an air force F5 Tiger II flyover of the route. The jet didn't find any ship there. Jelbart informed the INRC and asked for their help. They were useless."

"What do you mean?"

"Roughly half the ships are spot-checked on their way to this site, when they are carrying nuclear materials," Coffey told him. "They are boarded and checked for radiation leaks, security, general seaworthiness. The ships are not checked after they leave the site."

"So no one knows if they have even made the drop," Hood said.

"Correct."

"That's insane," Hood said.

"I agree. So do Warrant Officer Jelbart and FNO Loh," Coffey said. "The problem is that maintaining a fleet is expensive. The INRC is financed by grants from the United Nations, environmental groups, and dues paid by nations that use the waste fields. That gives them about fifteen million dollars a year to oversee all international nuclear shipments, not just waste product."

"That's all?" Hood said.

"Yes, and that doesn't take into account whatever kickbacks are being handed out," Coffey added.

"That's a helluva low priority we give the security of nuclear material," Hood said with disgust.

"That's true, Paul. But to be honest, people who want to smuggle nuclear material are going to do so whether the INRC increases its activities or not," Coffey said.

"That does not mean we have to make it easy for them," Hood pointed out. "We wouldn't even have known about this incident except for the attack by the sampan."

"Not everything is as well-ordered as law and finance," Coffey said.

"Funny you should say that," Hood said. "I've been thinking about the nature of our business, and it should be more structured. We live in a high-tech world. We can watch someone key in a cell phone number from outer space. Losing ships and radioactive waste are inexcusable."

"Only in hindsight," Coffey said. "When I was in college, I interned with a criminal lawyer. I used to go to prisons with him to interview clients. Once we had perpetrators locked up, it was easy to kick ourselves in the ass and realize what we should have done to save lives. These people we're dealing with now, the smugglers and terrorists, are full-time sociopaths. How do you compete with that? How do you stop someone from putting botulism in an ATM deposit and poisoning the money supply? How do you prevent someone from filling a glass water bottle with acid and carrying it into a jetliner?"

"I don't know," Hood admitted. "But we have to figure it out. We're talking about hundreds of thousands of lives!"

"The numbers aren't the issue, Paul," Coffey said. "I've watched hostage negotiators work. To them, a single captive is their entire world. Anyway, the problem is not how we apportion resources. The problem is us. We still have the equivalent of a moral gag reflex."

"And that is?"

"We're civilized," Coffey said sadly. "Hell, I'm so civilized I can't even be at sea without feeling my guts in my throat. Our quarry does not have that disadvantage."

"You may be right about that, about everything," Hood said. "But I know this. If we want to stay civilized, we're going to have to find a way of identifying who's with us and who's against us."

"Ideally, yes," Coffey said. "The question is how."

"That's something Op-Center is going to have to look at a lot more carefully, Lowell," Hood said. "We need more comprehensive human intelligence and preventative interference."

"You mean profiling and spying on your neighbor," Coffey said. "We become the sociopaths we behold."

"I'll trust our civilized nature to keep that from happening," Hood said.

"If nothing else, that puts you on the high road," Coffey said. "Right now all that seems to get you is a better vantage point from which to watch all the fighting and destruction."

"I hate to say this, but you're sounding like Bob now," Hood noted.

"Frustration will do that," Coffey said.

"Only if you let it," Hood said. "Meanwhile, I'll let you know when I hear from Bob."

"Okay," Coffey said. "You know, maybe it's just the nausea talking. I'll try to hold tighter to my optimism."

"Thanks. We can use some of that," Hood said.

The attorney clicked off the phone. For a moment he felt like he did when he used to listen to a closing argument on behalf of a defendant he knew was guilty. He felt virtuous in theory but crafty in practice.

Coffey sat, this time more slowly. He felt a little better now, proving that seasickness was to some degree a state of mind. As long as he did not pay it attention, he was fine.

Too bad all our problems don't go away when we ignore them, Coffey thought.

He rose cautiously and opened the door. The seaman was waiting outside. Coffey gave him the phone and thanked him. Then the attorney followed him to the bridge. He walked closer to port side so that when the vessel rolled, he could simply lay a shoulder against the wall and slide forward.

The more he thought about it, the more Coffey realized what his problem was.

He had joined the National Crisis Management Center to help keep it honest, as it were. To keep it from becoming unaccountable, in case the leadership ever moved in the direction of J. Edgar Hoover's FBI. Despite his own protests and resistance, however, Coffey knew that Hood was right. More needed to be done to protect lawful people and nations. And that protection had to come from places like Op-Center. Bob Herbert had once described it as the cowcatcher that guarded the rushing locomotive. Op-Center was uniquely equipped to position itself between progress and disaster. It had men like Darrell

McCaskey, Mike Rodgers, and Bob Herbert to share experience in police work, the military, and intelligence. There were technical geniuses like Matt Stoll and the seasoned staff psychologist Liz Gordon. It had communications experts, political professionals, and an authority on satellite reconnaissance. Coffey knew international law. And Paul Hood was a skillful manager who knew how to synthesize all these talents.

If Hood were looking for order, Coffey was holding too tightly to it. Not all the answers were found in law books. Sometimes they were found in people. And he knew that this was a team of good people.

Hood was right when he said he would trust in their civilized qualities to keep abuses from happening. That thought made Coffey proud, and that pride was what had lifted his spirits.

The challenge was great. But there was one thing more important than that. Something they could not afford to forget.

The challenge was far from hopeless.

TWENTY-EIGHT

Over the Pacific Ocean
Saturday, 2:22 A.M.

Surprise was a wonderful but dangerous thing.

Whether giving or receiving, surprise was short-lived, explosive, and directed. Wielded deftly, it was an intelligence operative's greatest tool. It was also valuable as "incoming." Knowing there might be danger behind a door or around a corner or even at the other end of a telephone kept an agent sharp. Being unready for it could be lethal. Bob Herbert had learned that in Beirut. Since then, he had no trouble ramping up to high alert.

That zero-to-sixty acceleration was one of the qualities Bob Herbert cherished most about intelligence work. He did not have to know what time it was. He did not necessarily have to know where he was. All Herbert needed to know was who or what the target was. Once he had that goal, exhaustion, discomfort, and even lust slipped away. If he had not gotten into the intelligence game, Bob Herbert felt that he would have made a helluva chess grand master.

Matt Stoll got the colonel's home phone number for Herbert. Stoll did not even have to slip into the North Korean People's Army classified phone directory. The number was attached to an intelligence research file included with the *North Korea Advisory Group Report to the Speaker of the U.S. House of Representatives* from 1999.

"I've learned to search our own government databases before going to others," Stoll said.

If the number didn't work, Stoll said he would take the next, longer step to get it.

Herbert would have preferred verification up front. But he also wanted to get this done as quickly as possible. He had suffered through a traditional bomb attack. If the Beirut terrorists had possessed nuclear material, he and thousands of others would not be alive today.

While he waited, Herbert booted his wheelchair computer. He plugged the phone into a jack with two cables. He jacked one back into the aircraft comm system and the other into his computer. He activated the transcription interface, a program that would simultaneously create a typed recording of their conversation. Herbert also practiced speaking in as deep a monotone as possible. Herbert was not sure of the nationality of the individual who had spoken to Hwan. He wanted his voice to be as geographically neutral as possible. Accents were less about the spin given to vowels and consonants than about cadence and pitch. The deeper and flatter a voice, the less identifiable it would be.

Herbert's headset was still jacked into the aircraft's secure phone line. He input Colonel Hwan's number. The phone beeped several times before someone answered.

"Hwan," said a man with a high, nasal voice. There was a long moment before the man spoke. That meant he had lifted the receiver, then had to get into position to use it. Probably because he was in bed.

"We need more coverage," Herbert said. His voice was like a bow being drawn across a bass cello. And his goal was to keep the conversation in the third person singular. Herbert needed names.

"I'm in bed," Hwan said.

"We need it now," Herbert replied.

"You cannot have it now," Hwan replied. "And who is this? You are not Marcus."

"Marcus took ill. You know how it is here."

Hwan said nothing.

"He's been working too many hours, like everyone else on this damn project," Herbert added.

Again, Hwan did not bite. Perhaps the North Korean did not know what the project was.

"I'm Marcus's backup, Alexander Court," Herbert said. Court was the author of a novel Herbert had seen lying in the crew bay. He liked the sound of the name. Good pseudonym. "What about it, Colonel? Can we count on your help just one more time?"

"Alexander, remind Mr. Hawke that I agreed to give him one look," Hwan said. "I cannot afford to do more at this time. Don't make me go to his superior, Mr. Court."

"Maybe you should go to the boss," Herbert pressed. "Hawke has been making all our lives miserable."

"I suggest you complain to him yourself," Hwan said.

"He would never take my calls," Herbert said. He was pushing Hwan, trying to get a name.

"I doubt he would take mine either, even if I knew how to reach him," Hwan said. "Good night, Mr. Court."

"Colonel Hwan, will you reconsider if the boss himself calls?" Herbert asked.

"It would depend on what he has to offer," Hwan said. "If he is willing to part with one of his Sisters, I might consider it." He said that with a laugh.

"Which one?" Herbert asked.

"His choice," Hwan said.

The connection was cut.

Herbert sat still for a long moment. He felt drained. He had not gotten everything he had hoped for, but he had gotten something. An uncommon first name, Marcus. A surname, Hawke. The fact that Hwan had attached a "Mr." to it suggested strongly that it was not a code name, "hawk" without the *e*. And they were all working for a secretive, tough-to-reach figure who had more than one sister. Possibly young, apparently wealthy.

He unplugged the phone and logged on to the Internet. He forwarded the transcript to Hood and Coffey. Then he did a word search of *Marcus, Hawke, sisters*.

The words showed up in the same place, but in each case they were unrelated. There was an on-line bookstore with author Nigel Hawke, a biography of Marcus Aurelius, and a novel called *The Lost Sisters*. There were sports pages with a Hawke's Bay soccer team, the tennis-playing Williams sisters, and a basketball player named Marcus Fowler.

"It was too much to hope that I might catch a break," he muttered.

Herbert checked *Marcus* and *Hawke* separately. There were over four thousand references for each, too many to check. He decided to add geography to the search. He entered *Marcus, Hawke, sisters, Malaysia,* then replaced Malaysia with North Korea, North Korea with Indonesia, then Indonesia with Singapore. He still did not get a single link for even two of the entries.

Then Herbert increased his geographical search. He included Australia, followed by New Zealand. What he found in New Zealand was unexpected.

A surprise.

A good one.

TWENTY-NINE

The Celebes Sea
Saturday, 12:04 A.M.

Peter Kannaday remained on deck as the *Hosannah* sailed swiftly toward its rendezvous. He used to love this feeling of his yacht slashing through the water. It made him feel powerful and free. He had seldom done this at night due to the risk of collision. But with the radar and sonar equipment Darling had paid to install, darkness was no longer a problem.

Kannaday leaned against the port-side railing, his legs spread wide to help him keep his balance. He was pouring black coffee from a thermos. His hair was thick with sweat, and the strong wind chilled his scalp. The perspiration on his head and neck was partly from the hot coffee and partly from a sense that he was lost. He was no longer the captain of his fate or even his own ship. The professional seaman was not accustomed to feeling adrift.

Or frightened. But he was that, too.

Kannaday had spent his life on the ocean. Below its surface was nothing but mystery. He had always accepted that. And it was never a problem as long as he stayed above the water. Yet he was just becoming aware of how much of the rest of the world was hidden from view. Some of it was mundane, like hot coffee inside a thermos. Some of it was more threatening.

Like a knife concealed in a wommera, he thought. *Or radiation in a lead case. Even Jervis Darling at his estate.*

Also hidden were the true loyalties of men. Especially those who served with him, it seemed.

The captain had been awake for nearly forty hours. Tired as he was, however, he would not go to sleep. First,

there was a job to finish. Captain Kannaday did not want
to rest until the cargo had been delivered and he had reported that to Darling. He was also determined to stay on
deck. If the yacht were approached by any of the military
patrols investigating the 130-5 site, he wanted to be on
hand and ready to talk with them.

The second reason Kannaday had stayed on deck was
more important. And also more personal. It was because
of John Hawke and his security team. Perhaps exhaustion
was influencing his perception to some degree. But over
the past few hours it seemed as though the kingdoms of
the two men, like their crews, had become clearly defined.
The security personnel and belowdecks belonged to
Hawke. The upper deck and the seamen belonged to Kannaday. The communications center was neutral. No one
had actually said as much. It was all in the looks, in the
attitude of the crew, in the places men did and did not
go. They bonded like pockets of algae around a rock.

Kannaday wondered how much of the tension was due
to the strain between himself and Hawke. Most, he suspected. He doubted Hawke would have said anything
about their confrontation. Perhaps the men had heard it.
Or maybe they sensed it. A sailor who could not sniff a
change in the wind, feel a shift in the rolling deck, did
not survive for long.

But some of the tension also had to be due to their
cargo. The events of the past two days had reminded them
just how dangerous it was. Kannaday had visited the laboratory once to watch the entire purification process.
Those spent nuclear reactor fuel rods, black and glittering,
were among the deadliest materials on earth. They were
terrifying, beautiful, and curiously sensuous, like a rattle-
snake or a black widow spider. If someone were exposed
to one, death would be extremely unpleasant. Kannaday
had read up on radiation sickness before accepting this
assignment. A brief exposure to low-dosage radiation, between 50 and 200 rads, would cause mild headaches. The
same exposure to 500 or so rads would cause headaches,
nausea, exhaustion, and hair loss. With exposure to 1,000

rads, individuals would suffer vomiting, diarrhea, and complete exhaustion within an hour of exposure. The cells of the body would begin to break down, and a painful death would result within thirty days.

Fortunately, the scientists who had been processing a previous delivery in the laboratory had been wearing protective garments. And the few particles of radium torn away by the blast had been carried outward by smoke from the resulting blaze. The lab workers assured Kannaday that any exposure their own people had suffered was well under fifty rads. The crew took showers to clean off whatever particles they may have picked up. There were no reports of illness.

Still, it was clear now that the potential for catastrophe was ever present. And the nature of the danger magnified the fear of the crew. There was no defense against this foe. Once released, it was invisible and unstoppable.

Kannaday took another swallow of coffee. *So, if the cargo is so deadly, why are you so scared of Darling?* he asked himself. *And Hawke. Both men are physical, and one is not even here. They are far from invulnerable.*

To the contrary. They had one weak spot, he felt. Both were certain of their power over him. He had learned on the sea that nothing was certain. Seemingly small storms could explode in a moment. An apparently smooth surface could hide an undersea tremor that spat up hundred-foot waves. Overconfidence makes a man vulnerable.

There might be something Kannaday could use in all of this. The notion of the hidden weapon. Something that would work against Hawke, and even against Darling, if necessary.

He would have to think about that. First came the job.

Marcus signaled him on the point-to-point radio. He had just received a message from bin Omar. The Malaysian ship was twenty-two miles to the northwest. They would come alongside the *Hosannah* within the hour. Kannaday called the laboratory for an update. They were nearly finished processing the materials. They would be ready in time for the exchange. Kannaday thanked them, then went below. He wanted to inform Hawke in person.

Maybe it was the caffeine talking through a hazy mind, but Kannaday felt that was a bold step. The idea of going to the lair of the opposition made him feel energized. It made him feel stronger. It was the same reaction he had when he stood alone against Marcus and Hawke in the radio room.

Or maybe the events of the past few days had taught him something. After all these years of sailing, Kannaday had thought he understood what it took to be a man. He believed it meant a willingness to take on muscular challenges. To risk the elements and battle the sea, to master a sailing ship. Exertion made the male, danger made the man.

That was what he thought. He was beginning to see that he could not have been more wrong. Being a man meant doing things that did not come naturally, where the risk was in challenging one's own beliefs and traditions. In his case, fighting back with mind instead of sinew.

The exertion still made the male. But it was the knowledge gained that made the man.

And Kannaday was beginning to realize that knowledge, hidden inside, was what made men most dangerous.

THIRTY

Washington, D.C.
Friday, 10:07 A.M.

Paul Hood was just finishing a phone conversation with Mike Rodgers when Bob Herbert called.

The general was on his way back from a breakfast with Senator Dan Debenport of South Carolina. The senior senator was going to be taking over the chairmanship of the Congressional Intelligence Oversight Committee from the retiring senator, Barbara Fox. Hood would not be sorry to see her go. Fox had never understood that crisis management could not function according to a rule book. Op-Center could not always get approval from the CIOC for operations. Bob Herbert had a nickname for the constant clash between Op-Center and the CIOC. He called it the "bility breach." Hood demanded flexibility. Fox insisted on accountability. Those two things did not go together.

Debenport was a former Green Beret who had done two tours of duty in Vietnam. That was why Hood had sent Rodgers to chat with him. He hoped the two military men would hit it off. That would not only help Op-Center, it would also help Hood. Even when he kept Senator Fox out of the loop, dealing with the CIOC took more time than Hood cared to give it.

From the sound of things, Senator Debenport was willing to give Op-Center a great deal of leeway in terms of the kind of operations they could mount. But there was a caveat.

"We can have the freedom we want because Senator Debenport doesn't want the United States to stumble into crises that could have been avoided," Rodgers said. "To do that, however, he wants to work closely with us. He wants to make sure there is a flow of information between him, Op-Center, the FBI, the CIA, and the NSA."

"I'm not sure there's a net gain for us," Hood said unhappily.

"Added bureaucracy, you mean."

"That, plus the senator will be in a better position to interfere with operations," Hood said. "He can *tell* us that we have more elbow room. But if he disapproves of something, he can shut the action down. It may not even be intentional. He might have other things to do when a plan reaches his desk. He may red-light an operation until he has a chance to study it."

"We still have autonomy, Paul."

"Until he says otherwise," Hood replied.

"True," Rodgers said. "But I'll be able to talk to him. He and I have a lot of friends, colleagues, and experiences in common. That's more than we have with Senator Fox."

"I can't argue with that," Hood said.

That was when Herbert phoned. Hood immediately took the call. He could not conference Rodgers in because the general's phone was not secure. He did, however, plug the call through to Lowell Coffey. The attorney was on the bridge of the Australian corvette.

"Okay, Bob," Hood said. "What have you got for us?"

"I talked briefly with Colonel Hwan," Herbert said.

"I got your transcript and put some people on it. Nice work."

"Thanks. I've been doing some checking myself. If you read the transcript you know that he gave me a man's surname: Hawke, I believe with an *e*. And someone else's first name, Marcus. I didn't find any link between them. But then he mentioned the boss of the project. Hwan said that what he'd really like is one of the big man's sisters. Now, the colonel's not married, but I don't think that's what he was talking about. I found out there is an island group east of New Zealand. It's called the Chatham Islands. North of the Chathams is an island group called the Sisters."

"I've heard of those," Coffey said. "There was some issue about native rights and fern-tree preservation on the main island. Let me ask Jelbart what he knows about them."

Herbert chuckled when Coffey left. "And here I thought the law was boring," he said. "I didn't realize that the mind-swelling topic of fern trees was part of the mix."

"A battle is a battle is a battle, whatever the prize," Hood said.

"I guess."

"Is that all you were able to get from the colonel?" Hood asked.

"That's it," Herbert said. "I pushed, but I get the feeling he gives these guys as little of his time and effort as possible."

"Which suggests what?" Hood asked.

"That he's doing it for the money, not for the cause, whatever that is," Herbert said.

"Colonel Hwan is on the payroll, but his government is not part of the project," Hood said.

"You got it."

Coffey came back on the line. "Gentlemen, either we're way off target, or we've got one hell of a bombshell," the attorney said.

"I'm not sure which is better," Herbert said.

"Jelbart says that none other than Mr. Jervis Darling owns several of the smaller islands in the Sisters chain," Coffey said.

"The media big shot?" Herbert asked.

"That's the one," Coffey replied. "Jelbart is putting in a call to Darwin to check something else."

"Forget it," Herbert said. "I beat him to it."

"I'm lost," Hood said.

"I just went on-line and did a word search," Herbert said. "Darling has a nephew named Marcus."

"You've got to be kidding me," Hood said. "Why would a man with Darling's billions and all his media holdings be involved with something like this?"

"Boredom?" Herbert suggested.

"I don't believe that," Hood replied.

"What is the name of the guy who owns the ship that was

supposed to have made the drop at 130-5?" Herbert asked.

"Mahathir bin Dahman, a Malaysian billionaire," Hood said.

"*Another* billionaire," Herbert said.

"He's involved with everything from waste disposal to real estate," Hood said.

"This is smelling like what they call *executive action* over at the CIA," Herbert said.

"Which is what?" Hood asked.

"It started with the idea that businessmen from the military-industrial complex were involved in the JFK assassination," Herbert said. "They wanted to speed up U.S. involvement in Vietnam, along with the increased military buying that would entail. When Kennedy held the course, they got together and had him offed. Or so the theory goes."

"So there's an apparent executive action involving nuclear smuggling," Hood said.

"It could be," Herbert said. "The executive action profile says that men like Dahman and Darling can't be bothered with the inconvenience of the democratic process. Over time they begin to feel they're entitled to power. So they take it by any means necessary. That includes forming strategic alliances. If we have a union here, the question is who approached whom?"

"That's a big if," Coffey said. "You're making a lot of assumptions about some pretty powerful and reputable men."

"You bit," Herbert said.

"Pardon?"

"They count on that reaction to avoid suspicion, Lowell," Herbert said. "Paul, have Liz Gordon profile these guys. I'll bet she comes up with the same scenario I did."

"Even if she did, it would still be supposition," Coffey pointed out.

"Maybe, but we aren't in court," the intelligence officer reminded the attorney. "If we're going to find the missing nuclear waste, we have to make a few educated guesses."

"Bob, I agree that we have to pursue this," Hood said. "I also think we're getting ahead of ourselves. Lowell, let's assume Bob pegged this right. You're on the scene. What do you suggest?"

"To begin with, I can't imagine that the Australian government is going to move against Jervis Darling without overwhelming evidence," Coffey said. "And I mean airtight, overwhelming evidence."

"Certainly Darling would be counting on that, too," Herbert remarked.

"*If* he's involved," Coffey reminded them.

"You know, gentlemen, I'm thinking," Herbert said. "Why don't we step right up and ask him?"

"Just like that?" Coffey asked.

"It worked with Colonel Hwan," Herbert said.

"He's not Jervis Darling," Coffey said. "My dad deals with movers and shakers in Hollywood. They've got layers of people between themselves and the events they cause."

"Layers only work if you go through them," Herbert said. "I'll go around them."

"Before you do, maybe we should have some real ammunition," Coffey said.

"Such as?" Herbert asked.

"I'm wondering if there might be a paper trail from Darling to Dahman," Coffey said.

"Probably not," Hood said. "But there could be something else. Something I might be able to help with. This could be an executive action, as Bob suggests. Or it could be as simple as there being a hole in Darling's pocket. One that he's trying to fill. While we've been talking I've had a look at his stock reports. A lot of those media companies aren't doing as well as they once were. And he's a majority shareholder."

"I like that," Coffey said. "At least it's a starting point."

"Meantime, Lowell," Herbert said, "maybe you can get your local friends to do some recon to help me. See what kind of boats Darling owns, where they are, possibly check his phone records."

"I'd like to hold off on that," Coffey said.

"Why?" Herbert asked.

"Because there's the very real possibility that an all-out investigation will bump into people who are sympathetic to Jervis Darling or are on his payroll," Coffey said.

"So?"

"Bob, Lowell's got a point," Hood said. "We don't want him throwing those layers of intermediaries at us until we've had a good look around. Lowell, do you think you can talk to Jelbart or Ellsworth about this without sending up too many flares?"

"Jelbart, certainly," Coffey said.

"Bob, what about Dahman?" Hood asked. "Do we have any Malaysian sources?"

"Not really," Herbert admitted. "That's something you should ask Lowell's friend FNO Loh about."

"I can do that," Coffey said. "She seems trustworthy. Though I'm not sure we should open two fronts. There's twice the opportunity for leaks."

"I'm not sure we can avoid them," Herbert replied. "This rope apparently has two ends."

"That's true," Hood said. "Which means if you tug on one, you'll get to the other. I'm with Lowell on this. I think we should concentrate our resources on the Australian end for now."

"Paul, trashman Dahman may be the easier end of the rope to grab," Herbert said.

"But if we do get him, Bob, that will give Darling time to generate alibis and red herrings to keep the heat from him," Hood said. "Darling scares me more. He's got unlimited access to interests in the West, Bob. He probably gets a free pass through customs in most places."

"Billionaires with private jets often do," Coffey pointed out.

"If Darling's gone bad, for whatever reason, he's the one we have to worry about," Hood said. "If Dahman is involved, we can sweep him up later. Lowell, have that talk with Jelbart and get back to us."

"Will do," Coffey said.

"Bob, will you hang on a second?" Hood asked. "I need to talk to you about something."

"Sure," Herbert said.

As Coffey got off, Hood hit the Mute button. He wanted Herbert to think he was conducting other business. In fact, he wanted to take a moment to think about what he was going to say. Unless Bob Herbert himself did the closing, he did not respond well to having trapdoors shut on those dark, complex, underground tunnels that ran through his mind.

Hood tapped off the Mute button. "I'm back," he said.

"What happened?" Herbert asked. "Did I honk you off or something?"

"No," Hood replied. "Just the opposite. When you feel strongly about something, I don't like closing the door."

"Boss, I feel strongly about everything," Herbert said.

"I know," Hood said. "But Lowell was pissing you off. I wanted to get him on his way, then come back to what you're thinking."

"He pisses me off because he's a left-wing elitist," Herbert said. "But he may be right about this. I'm not sure I'm right about going after Dahman."

"And I'm not sure you're wrong," Hood admitted. "What if you went to Malaysia? Did some checking?"

"Frankly, I'd enjoy the hell out of it. If time were not at a premium, I'd push for it," Herbert said. "But since we don't have the resources to go in with me, I'm not sure it's the best use of my time, but I appreciate the counterproposal. Did you think I'd accept?"

"I wasn't sure," Hood said. "I thought you might."

"My independent Southern soul?" Herbert commented.

"Something like that."

"Well, I'm thinking you might be right about that one," Herbert told him. "I got into the spy game because I wanted to be Peter Gunn. Remember him? The TV private eye?"

"Vaguely," Hood said. "I was a *Gunsmoke* and *Bonanza* man myself."

"An ensemble guy," Herbert said.

"I never looked at it that way, but I suppose so," Hood admitted. "I wanted to run the Ponderosa."

"Gunn was a loner," Herbert said. "He always knew

what to say whether he was talking to a thug, a cop, or a woman. Just the smartest, most confident repartee. He was tough. He could take a beating or give one. And he never lost. That's what I wanted to be like."

"But?"

"But I don't have Gunn's writers," Herbert said. "I learned there is a big fat difference between fiction and reality. Just between us spies, I didn't get quite as much information as I wanted from Colonel Hwan."

"You got what we needed."

"Barely," Herbert said. "When that happens, I tend to push a little too hard on the next one. Thanks for reeling me in."

"You reeled yourself in," Hood said.

"You're wrong, but we'll leave it at that," Herbert told him.

The intelligence chief hung up. Hood sat back. It was funny. He never knew that Herbert had joined the CIA to be like a TV character. He wondered if things like that should be in a person's dossier. He found it touching. He was glad they had that conversation. Not just for Herbert's sake but for his own. There were times when Hood had his doubts about decisions. That came from not being a specialist like Herbert, Coffey, or Rodgers. There were other times, like now, when he was sure of himself. He thought back to something his mother's mother had said in her later years. Grandmother April was a dressmaker who learned her trade in Phoenix when Arizona was still a territory. After the family relocated to Los Angeles, she got work in the movies. Hood went with her to the studio one day and watched as she was making a ball gown for a movie. She asked for a bolt of gray. Her eleven-year-old grandson asked why she wanted such a boring color.

"Sometimes red and blue can't function together unless you have a neutral color between them," his grandmother had replied.

She was right. Which was why he felt pretty good right now.

Sometimes people needed that, too.

THIRTY-ONE

The Celebes Sea
Saturday, 12:36 A.M.

Coffey asked to see Warrant Officer Jelbart in private. With permission, the men walked over to the captain's small ready room. It was little more than a closet with a desk and chair, but it had a door. Coffey closed it. The men remained standing. Jelbart had known that the American was on a call to Op-Center. But Coffey had spoken quietly, and the bridge was filled with the usual conversation and radio communication, as well as the constant rumbling of the engines far below. Jelbart did not know what Coffey had discussed.

Jelbart was stunned when the American told him. He did not doubt the accuracy of the intelligence, but he refused to accept the conclusion.

"Mr. Coffey, why would a man in Salty's position become involved with *any* black-market activity?" Jelbart asked.

"Excuse me. Salty?" Coffey asked.

"Yeah. Nicknamed for a crocodile," Jelbart said. "And may I say, the shoe fits."

"Interesting," Coffey observed. "Crocodiles are not discriminating about their prey. They're survivors."

"What you're getting at won't fly," Jelbart said. "I'm sure they would be much more selective if they had billions of dollars to plan their menu."

"Perhaps."

"Mr. Coffey, forgive me," Jelbart said. "But do you have any idea what you're saying?"

"I do. Which brings us back to your question, Warrant Officer. Let's assume the information is correct. Why *would* a man in Mr. Darling's position do anything like this?"

Jelbart shook his head. "I cannot begin to imagine."

"Try," Coffey urged.

"Boredom, maybe? A challenge?" Jelbart said. "God knows he's got all the power, money, and influence he needs."

"Is his power base very solid?" Coffey asked.

"Lord, yes," Jelbart replied. "For many ordinary folks, Jervis Darling embodies the spirit of Australia. He has proven that anyone can build an empire. Politicians fight for his endorsement and photo opportunities."

"What about his personal life?"

"The business press doesn't like him, but the society pages love him," Jelbart said. "He and his young daughter go everywhere. Usually with some established actress or political matron on his arm. No supermodels or fluff."

"What happened to Mrs. Darling?"

"Dorothy Darling died in a hang-gliding accident four years ago," Jelbart said. "You may also be interested to learn, Mr. Coffey, that Jervis Darling has never been the subject of personal litigation. And it has nothing to do with the army of legal firms on his payroll."

"Tell me something, Warrant Officer. Are you under his spell, too?" Coffey asked.

"No," Jelbart replied. "But I admire the quality that my countrymen see in him."

"And that is?"

"Noblesse oblige," Jelbart said.

Coffey frowned slightly.

"I know that sounds strange to you Americans. But Mr. Darling presents class and benevolence in balance," Jelbart went on. "It makes him nonthreatening. And that makes him beloved. Sort of like Walt Disney or Thomas Edison. A man who started by creating small, special-interest magazines about archaeology, geology, prehistory. Merging them synergistically to create rich harbors for upscale advertisers. Using his profits to buy real estate, start a bank, develop the Internet. He's a local hero. People don't want to know about his flaws."

"Is all of this a way of saying we can't investigate him?" Coffey asked. "Or that you won't?"

"I don't know." Jelbart exhaled. "Your evidence is not overwhelming."

"I'm aware of that," Coffey told the officer. "But we do know that nuclear material is missing. We don't know where it is. Should we hold off until someone explodes a dirty bomb?"

"I'm not suggesting that," Jelbart said.

"You just don't want to involve Jervis Darling," Coffey said.

"Yeah. That's what I don't want."

"And we won't," Coffey said. "Certainly not at this stage. Hopefully not ever, if it turns out that our information is incorrect."

"What worries me is how do we verify that information? And then what happens if it is correct," Jelbart said.

"I'm confused. If Mr. Darling is proven to be a reasonable suspect, then I would think the law takes over," Coffey replied.

"In which case even solid evidence may not be enough to bring him down," Jelbart said. "Attorneys can battle the validity and admissibility of proof, you know that."

"Of course."

"Even if it does implicate Darling, his fall will do more than shake his empire," Jelbart said. "His investments, his reach, are everywhere."

Coffey said nothing. Jelbart shook his head.

"All of that aside, I would have to sell an investigation to Commodore Atlan, who is the commander, Maritime Patrol Group. He would probably want to take it to one or more of the ministers for defence. Darling will be a very tough target to sell and also to keep quiet."

"Do you need the authorization of Commodore Atlan to look into nuclear trafficking?" Coffey asked.

"Right now, all I am authorized to investigate is the destruction of a sampan that washed up on Australian soil," Jelbart said. "This is an issue of nuclear materials missing from international waters. When I file my report, the CDRMPG will make a determination about Australia's risk and, thus, her levels of involvement. Ironically, if Mr. Darling is involved, they will be less inclined to believe that Australia is at danger. He has always been a patriot."

"Maybe Australia isn't at risk," Coffey agreed. "What about Japan? Or Taiwan? Or the United States?"

"Do you want the truthful answer or the one you want to hear?"

"The truth," Coffey said.

"We are surrounded by nations who are distrustful of our Western culture, fearful of our freedoms, and covetous of our prosperity," Jelbart replied. "We move very, very carefully in this region because of that. Our neighbors look for any excuse to run us down to their people. So we tend to stay out of matters that do not directly concern us. I'm no coward, Mr. Coffey—"

"I never said that you were, nor did I mean to imply it."

"I wanted to be up front about that," Jelbart said. "I'd take on Satan himself if he swung his pointy tail at the Gold Coast. But all we know for certain is the following: that a Malaysian boat did not make its scheduled drop of nuclear materials; that a Singaporean sampan was apparently and inadvertently involved as a third party in the off-loaded materials; and that a North Korean officer is watching our investigation of the site. Your own intelligence, based primarily on a brief phone conversation with the officer, suggests that an Australian citizen might—*might*—be involved. Mr. Coffey, that is far from compelling."

"It doesn't have to be compelling. We are not writing a novel," Coffey said. "We are investigating possible criminal activity. We are obligated to follow reasonable leads."

"Well, there you've hit it," Jelbart said. "I don't find the lead reasonable. I'm not going to recommend a course of action based on some dilly theory. Marcus is not a common name, but Marcus Darling is not the only one who owns it. Jervis Darling is not the sole landowner in the Chatham Island Sisters group, nor even the largest investor there."

"It's the two of those together that make this a reasonable lead," Coffey said patiently.

"Tape recordings or fingerprints are reasonable. This is speculation," Jelbart said dismissively.

"Fine, call it 'speculative' or 'possible' or even 'remote.' Pick whatever word you like," Coffey said. "But it's not impossible. Op-Center is going to look into Darling's activities regardless. Will you be part of that? Or would you prefer that we come back to you if or when we find a more solid connection? At which point you will have to explain to your government why you did not pursue a possible lead about nuclear smuggling."

"Mr. Coffey, I don't give a ripe fig about saving face," Jelbart replied. "What I do care about is mindless activity. I'm too busy for that. If you want my help investigating Jervis Darling, give me one reason why someone like him would deal in nuclear waste."

"Maybe he wants to blow up one of his own holdings, get himself international sympathy," Coffey suggested. "Maybe he wants to blow up a rival's holdings and put him out of business."

"Talk about concocting novels," Jelbart said.

"You asked for ideas," Coffey said with an angry shrug. "I'm an attorney, not a theorist. But I can tell you this. If you're wrong, there could be a very heavy price to pay. Are you prepared to accept that?"

Jelbart stood in the small room. He listened to the purr of the ventilator fan above. The air smelled metallic. Part of that was due to the perspiration that had begun collecting on his upper lip.

"I assume you are going to brief FNO Loh and tell her about the other chap, the Malaysian," Jelbart said.

"We decided to wait on that," Coffey said. "Director

Hood felt that it would be an overreaction to involve Singapore at this early stage."

"Why?"

"Think Salty," Coffey said. "The animal, not the man. Tug the tail, and the head might bite you."

"What if I wanted her involved?" Jelbart asked.

"For what reason?"

"Triangulation," Jelbart said. "We don't do anything in the military without a three-point tag. Anyway, she will give us another set of eyes. Yours and mine obviously see things differently."

"Fair enough," Coffey said. "If you insist on her involvement, then we would have to go along with that."

"I insist," he said. "When you agree to that, I'll contact my superiors."

Coffey regarded the officer. "I need to know something, Warrant Officer. Which is it that's moving you? Respect or fear?"

"Neither," Jelbart said. "I said what I said so you'd know who Darling is. I want Loh involved to protect the RAAF and my career. As for me personally, I would feel this way if you were investigating a slushy in the ship's galley. I believe in fairness and the right to privacy, Mr. Coffey."

"As do I," Coffey said. "But we live in a dangerous world, Warrant Officer. And I also believe in the rights of people to live without fear. In this case, fear of being irradiated."

"I cannot argue with that, Mr. Coffey. Do you want to inform Op-Center before or after we chat with Loh?"

"After," Coffey said. "Asking permission isn't as important as having information."

Jelbart did not know if that were meant as a dig or if Coffey were simply being frank.

There was a firm rap on the door. Jelbart moved aside to open it. Communications Specialist Edie Albright was standing there with a radio.

"FNO Loh," she said.

"Thank you," Jelbart said. "There's timing for you," he

said to Coffey as he took the radio and raised it to his mouth. He hit Send. "Jelbart here."

"Warrant Officer, our shore patrols report no success in finding the Malaysian vessel from the 130-5 site," the woman said. "They regret to say the trail is very cold."

"I'm not surprised. They had a big head start in a bigger sea," Jelbart said. "FNO Loh, Mr. Coffey and I would like to have a private conversation with you. Is your line secure?"

"It is. What is this in reference to?" she asked.

"Mr. Coffey has information about someone who may be involved in this operation," Jelbart said.

"Mr. Jervis Darling?"

"Yes," Jelbart said. He felt as though he had been punched in the back. "What made you say that?"

"We have been watching him since he killed his wife," she replied.

THIRTY-TWO

The Celebes Sea
Saturday, 1:00 A.M.

The Malaysian fishing ship moved slowly toward the yacht. Kannaday watched from the deck. The fishing vessel had only one light on, a lantern attached to the prow. If they were spotted or pursued, the captain could douse the light and run dark on a different course. He would try to get behind the much larger yacht so that his movements would be blocked from radar. The yacht was at minimal lighting, which meant it was dark save for a light at the bow, one at the stern, and one amidships at the base of the mainmast.

But Kannaday did not expect any problems. Not from sea or air patrols, anyway. There was nothing on the radar. The only problem might come from Hawke. Kannaday had come up with a plan to deal with the security chief. He had worked out every convolution. There were two chances in three that it would go his way. He liked those odds.

Still, the captain was anxious. Kannaday had never had to deal with insubordination. Ego was never an issue with his crew. They were paid to do a job, and they did it. Moreover, unlike the incident in his cabin, this was going to be a public confrontation. Below deck, only Kannaday's pride had been at risk. On deck, his ability to command would be in jeopardy.

Kannaday stood at the port-side railing. He watched as the shipping vessel pulled within fifteen meters of the yacht. Neither boat went to anchor. The captains wanted to be mobile. Four *Hosannah* security men came from belowdecks. Each man was carrying a small barrel.

Hawke was behind them. He had been watching the loading of the mini-launch. The *Hosannah* had two, both suspended from the rear. The vessel would be loaded with the valuable cargo and then lowered. The *Hosannah* would take nothing in return. Payment on delivery was worked out through other means. Kannaday did not know what they were. Overseas bank transactions most likely.

Kannaday walked over to his crew. "Mr. Hawke, I'd like you to go with them."

"I always do," he replied.

"Not with our crew, with the Malaysians," Kannaday said.

Hawke turned to face Kannaday. The lantern was behind Hawke. Kannaday could not see his expression.

"Why would I want to do that?" Hawke asked.

"To ensure the security of the cargo. To reassure the chief," Kannaday told him.

"Did he order me to do that?"

"I'm asking you to go," Kannaday replied. The captain made a point of asking rather than ordering. He hoped that would make it go down easier. He also refused to say whether or not the order came from Darling. Hawke would not dare call to find out. That would appear openly mutinous. Hawke had to know that Darling would not be sympathetic to that.

How and why was not important. What mattered was to get Hawke into the launch. Kannaday would log the order and show Jervis Darling that he was still in command.

Hawke was silent as the men continued working behind him. He was obviously considering the same options Kannaday had contemplated.

"What if I decline to go?" Hawke asked. He moved closer to Kannaday. His eyes were steel resolve.

"Why would you do that?"

"My post is here, on the yacht," Hawke replied.

"Your post is where the captain sends you," Kannaday said. "Patrols are out there. You know that. They may be looking for us and anyone we meet. Or would you prefer that I radio the chief? Tell him that you do not consider the cargo to be worth protecting?"

"I'll send some of my security team," Hawke replied. "We do not need them here at the moment."

"They are not as capable as their leader."

"They are capable enough," Hawke insisted. He turned to go.

"Would you prefer that I call the chief and tell him that you are afraid to go?" Kannaday asked. The captain was speaking loud enough now that the other crew members could hear.

Hawke did not even look back. "Do that."

"Mr. Hawke, you will go aboard that fishing vessel or you will go below," Kannaday ordered.

"I have work to do," Hawke replied.

"Your work is finished," Kannaday told him.

"Not until we are back at the cove," Hawke shot back. He was still looking ahead.

Kannaday felt as if he'd been hit by a swinging spar. Hawke had defied him in front of the crew. The security officer had embarrassed him in front of the Malaysians, who were watching with night-vision glasses from the deck of their vessel. They would carry word to their boss, who would relay it to Darling. Kannaday's brain, spirit, and flesh were all affected by a disorienting sense of humiliation. Reason left him. His ego winked off, then came back like a nova. His flesh grew hot and prickly. Kannaday felt as though the dignity had been baked from him. He wanted it back. He had considered the possibility that Hawke would refuse the order. But he had not imagined exactly how it would feel.

Nonetheless, there was only one thing for Kannaday to do.

Without hesitation, Kannaday reached for the back of the security officer. He placed a strong hand on each of the man's shoulders. He did not grab just the fabric of Hawke's sweater. His fingers dug deep, wrapping tightly around the meat of the man's shoulders. Kannaday took a long step back, pulling Hawke with him. The captain immediately turned and dipped and slammed Hawke onto the deck. The security chief lay on his back. He whipped the wommera from his sash and pointed the blade up. Kannaday wanted to drop on the man's chest and pound him senseless. But he forced himself to step back. Kannaday did not want to give Hawke the opportunity to kill him in self-defense.

Hawke rose quickly. "You bloody bastard! No one puts his hands on me! *No one!*"

The men were less than ten feet apart. Hawke walked forward slowly, holding the blade waist high. The captain stood firmly on the gently rolling deck. His legs were wide and his fists were low at his sides. His eyes were on Hawke, who was now walking into the light.

There was no going back.

"Come at me again, damn you!" Hawke said.

"Back off, Hawke. You disobeyed an order!"

"You're not fit to give them!" Hawke said.

"Then relieve me of my command, Mr. Hawke."

The launch was loaded but did not lower into the water. The crew had stopped working. Everyone was watching the altercation between the captain and the security officer.

"I'll make it easy for you," Kannaday said. He stepped forward, took the wommera blade, and placed it against his heart. "Use it!"

Hawke glared at the captain. Kannaday did not know what the security officer would do. It was not as if the authorities of any nation or maritime group would care that a smuggler had mutinied.

Hawke pushed the tip through Kannaday's shirt. He continued to drive it forward. Kannaday knew he could not back down. Not with everyone watching. Not after he had given Hawke this opportunity.

Hawke stopped. He did not remove the wommera blade from Kannaday's chest. The knife hurt, dull and tight like a muscle cramp. But the captain refused to show pain.

"I do not participate in gestures," Hawke said. "Our customers can see to the security of their own vessel. I was hired to look after this one."

"In that case, your job is done," Kannaday said. "You may go below."

Hawke hesitated. The captain realized there was only one way to end this impasse.

Kannaday took a step back. The blade slipped from his chest. The captain ignored the laceration and the bleeding beneath his shirt. He turned and addressed the crew at the stern.

"Mr. Neville, take the cargo to the fishing vessel," Kannaday said to the launch pilot. Neville was one of Kannaday's men.

"Yes, sir," the seaman replied.

The men lowered the launch into the water. Kannaday walked to the railing and watched as the small boat settled into the smooth sea. The four men climbed down an aluminum ladder and boarded her. Neville turned on a small spotlight at the front of the boat. A moment later they pulled from the yacht and headed toward the fishing vessel.

Kannaday turned back to finish up with Hawke. His rage was gone but not his anger. It had been turned into strength of purpose. The captain did not know what he would say or do. Fortunately, he did not have to decide right now. John Hawke was gone.

So were his men.

Kannaday began walking toward the mainmast. As he did, he casually pulled a handkerchief from his pocket. He shook it out and slipped it under his shirt. He pressed it against the wound. The cut was bleeding moderately. A bandage should take care of it. He would tend to it when he went below. He wished his problem with John Hawke could be as easily resolved.

Kannaday was exhausted, but he dared not rest. When the launch returned, they would head back to Cairns. The trip would take nearly four hours. Hawke would surely attempt some form of retribution during that time. The security chief could not let the public rebuke stand. Not if he wanted to retain credibility with his men. And not if he wanted to maintain his own self-respect. Kannaday knew damn well what that was like. He was glad he had been able to turn this around.

Suddenly, Marcus Darling emerged from belowdecks. The radio operator hurried toward the captain. It was strange to see the younger Darling hurry anywhere. Nothing in life had ever seemed important to him.

"What is it?" Marcus asked breathlessly as he approached.

"What is what?" Kannaday asked.

"Mr. Hawke said you wanted to see me," Marcus said. "He told me it was urgent."

Kannaday felt as if he had been stabbed again, this time in the back of the neck. His sense of satisfaction evaporated like sea mist at morning. He looked at the younger man and swore.

Already aware that it was probably too late, Kannaday ran around Marcus Darling and headed toward the stairwell. Hawke wanted the radio room for a reason. And whatever that reason was, it would not be in Kannaday's best interests.

THIRTY-THREE

The Celebes Sea
Saturday, 1:01 A.M.

Monica Loh had never felt comfortable conversing with
outsiders. To her, that meant anyone who was not a member of her immediate family. She had always been able
to prove herself with actions. She felt confident in any
situation where physical or command skills were required.
She was proficient at judo, skilled with handguns, and
emphatically prepared to carry out orders. That was what
an officer of the Singaporean military did.

Conversation was a different matter. FNO Loh could
never anticipate every question, and she hated saying, "I
don't know." That was a sign of weakness. She was particularly uncomfortable talking with men. Rarely was the
conversation simply what it seemed to be. She usually felt
that they were talking down to her or tolerating her.
Sometimes they were looking at her body and not even
listening. She could always tell. Thoughts relaxed them.
When the mind was engaged, only their eyes were alert.
But when men were exposed to physical stimuli, their
entire body became tense, predatory.

Fortunately, Jelbart and Coffey had not been with her
when she told them about Dorothy Darling. The conversation was only about what she knew, which was not
much.

Loh told them how the thirty-five-year-old woman had
gone to Singapore with her young daughter Jessica-Ann.
They went to the famed Jurong Birdpark early one morning, two hours before it opened to the public, then went
off by SUV into the surrounding hills. Mrs. Darling was
a pilot and an avid fan of hang gliding. While her daugh-

ter picnicked with Mrs. Darling's personal secretary, Robin Hammerman, Mrs. Darling and her longtime flight instructor from Cairns drove their car higher into the range. They brought a powered hang glider—a tandem unit that looked like a large motor scooter suspended from a traditional hang glider. The unit was an early, home-made model. It did not have the ballistic parachute system that came with later designs.

Loh told the men how the engine of the hang glider caught fire shortly after liftoff. While Jessica-Ann watched, the blazing hang glider briefly circled the hills before plunging into a dense wood.

"That had to have left some serious psychological scars," Lowell Coffey suggested.

"The girl described the sight as a red-and-black bird," Loh said. "She said there were screeches coming from it."

"Jesus wept," Jelbart murmured.

"Was this information contained in an official investigation report?" Coffey asked.

"I only read the Australian newspaper reports, which were rather graphic," Loh told him.

"Many of the local rags tend to be that way," Jelbart admitted. "I don't like reading or repeating that rot."

"I did hear that Mr. Darling's bank accounts were flagged and watched," Loh said.

"By which nation?" Coffey asked.

"Australia," Loh said. "According to those newspaper accounts, which I've read, the man's wife was allegedly having an affair with the flight instructor. Prosecutors wanted to see who Darling might have paid to sabotage the engine. If they found anything that would have given them an actionable crime, they could have made a case for intent to cause death.

"The murder investigation was the start of the search, but the end was somewhat surprising," FNO Loh continued. "There was not enough of the engine left to examine, and investigators did not uncover any sort of payoff from Mr. Darling to whoever may have executed this crime. But they did find evidence of unusual financial activity."

"Unusual in what way?" Coffey asked.

"Mr. Darling was putting more money into Singapore banks at a lower interest rate than he could get in Australia," Loh said. "And he was keeping it in liquid assets only."

"Was that in the newspapers, too?" Coffey asked.

"No," she replied.

"Then how do you know?" he pressed.

"I briefly dated a banker. He liked to impress me with the names on accounts he was managing," she said.

"Hence the 'briefly dated,' " Coffey said.

Loh did not respond. But the American attorney was correct.

"This banker bloke told you that the government was watching Darling's accounts?" Jelbart asked.

"He did," Loh replied. "He did not tell me what they may have found out, if anything. I'm not sure he would have known."

"So you don't really know the extent to which the government is investigating Darling or what else they may have found," Jelbart said.

"No," Loh said.

"If they had evidence connecting Darling to the death of his wife, they would have gone after him," Coffey said. "Australia and Singapore have an extradition arrangement."

"I can't imagine him being careless enough to leave any kind of trail," Jelbart remarked.

"As American presidents and corporate CEOs have demonstrated with regularity, powerful people often feel bulletproof," Coffey pointed out. "Though I *am* intrigued, FNO Loh. You seem pretty certain that Jervis Darling had his wife murdered."

"By all accounts, he is a possessive man."

"And are all possessive men killers?" Coffey asked.

"I believe most people would be killers if they thought they could get away with it," she answered.

"I'm not sure I agree, but that's not important," Coffey

said. "FNO Loh, do you have access to the government files on Darling?"

"I don't know," Loh admitted. She found herself over-enunciating the words as she forced them from her mouth. "But I'll find out," she added.

"When you do, ask if they have anything on Mahathir bin Dahman, a Malaysian billionaire," Coffey said. He spelled the name for her. "Have you ever heard of him?"

"Again, only what I have read in the newspapers," she said. "He is heavily involved in the development of real estate."

"Any scandals?" Coffey asked.

"None of which I am aware," the officer reported. That was a somewhat milder form of "I don't know." It did not come out any easier. FNO Loh wished she did not feel as though she had to impress these two men. They certainly were not pushing her.

"All right," Coffey said. "Anything you can find will be more than we have now."

"Have you heard anything more about the sailor from the sampan?" Loh asked.

"The last report I had from the hospital was about ninety minutes ago," Jelbart said. "The patient was sedated and not speaking."

"Do they have anyone who can speak Malay in case he does say something?" she asked.

"The intercom is on, and there is a voice-activated tape recorder at his bedside," Jelbart said. "Anything he says will be recorded and played for someone who can translate. I'll make certain you hear it as well."

"Thank you," she said. Loh had to admit that for men, these two seemed all right.

"The question is, what do we do while we wait?" Coffey asked.

"If I may make a suggestion," Loh said.

"Please," Coffey replied.

"I will contact Singapore for those files. But we have a saying in the military: 'Do not wait. Advance.' "

"I'm sure that reads well in a textbook," Coffey said.

"It works in practice, Mr. Coffey," Loh replied. It felt good to say that with certainty. "I believe that we should try to collect our own intelligence about Mr. Darling."

"I'm a coastal police officer, not a spy," Jelbart said. The warrant officer was not complaining. It sounded to Loh as though he were frustrated. And a little concerned. "I'm also afraid that the more Australians who know about this, the greater the odds of Darling finding out. We're still talking about theories, and highly speculative ones at that."

"Our top spy will land in Australia a few hours from now," Coffey said. "He'll know what to do."

"I can tell you what we have to do," Loh replied.

"Can you?" Coffey asked.

"Yes." It felt good to be able to answer this one, too. Because the answer was not only right, it was obvious. "We should not waste time following the 130-5 trail. It is already cold."

"What should we do?" Coffey asked.

"Make sure that Jervis Darling is unable to kill," she replied. "Again."

THIRTY-FOUR

Washington, D.C.
Friday, 12:31 P.M.

"Boss, would you please authorize the uploading of a benevolent systemic virus?"

The man in the doorway was portly Matt Stoll. The young computer genius was standing there with his arms at his sides and his expression deadpan. Unless there was a crisis, Paul Hood had learned to take nothing the technical wizard said seriously. Stoll was not just a proudly archetypical nerd, he was a proudly archetypical nerd on steroids. It was not enough for him to be smart. He was aggressively intelligent, still driven by the curiosity and precociousness that must have made him an elementary school terror.

"A benevolent virus," Hood said, playing along. "What did you have in mind?"

"Something that would allow users of National OnLine Operations to enjoy a functioning Internet provider," Stoll said. "Every time I open an attachment, I get booted. Every time I download a photograph, I get booted. Every time I try to access data, I'm told that the system is busy."

"Matt, am I wrong in believing that we do most of our on-line work through U.S. Governet?"

"You are not incorrect," Stoll said in his characteristic monotone. "I am talking about a system I use at home. However, our computers here have the juice to really spruce up the service."

"Permanently?" Hood asked.

"No. For just an hour. To show those NOLO incompetents what they could have if they upgraded their systems and paid more attention to customers than to their stock prices," Stoll said.

"I'll tell you what," Hood replied. "No."

Stoll seemed unfazed. "They are an evil empire, sir. This is a crisis situation. It is within the parameters set by the NCMC charter to involve ourselves."

"The charter also specifies the process by which executives other than the director, deputy director, and acting directors may request operational status for a project," Hood said. "Write a report and submit it to the CIOC. If the committee backs this, you will have my full cooperation."

"I could have done it without telling you," Stoll pointed out. "You wouldn't have known about it unless you saw it on the news or read it in an intelligence briefing."

"Possibly. Why didn't you?" Hood asked.

"Because the individual we are investigating, Jervis Darling, is a major stockholder in NOLO-Australia," Stoll said. "I did not want any moves against a holding controlled by him to be traced back to me or to Op-Center. It might raise flags."

"Thank you," Hood said.

"You're welcome," Stoll replied.

The technical officer stepped from the doorway and left. The encounter was strange but not unprecedented. Telling someone the damage he *could* do was Matt Stoll's way of complaining. He was a tech guy and a perfectionist. He had vented about cable networks, long-distance phone carriers, and other high-tech systems in the past. It was like Mike Rodgers beefing about the bureaucracy at the Pentagon or Bob Herbert venting about what he could do with one-tenth the budget allotted the CIA or the FBI.

Stoll was right about one thing, though. "NOLO contondere," as it was referred to in the stock pages, was an ineffectual disaster. It made money because it was a monolith, nothing more. If he started thinking about that, Paul Hood would get pissed as well.

The phone beeped. It was Lowell Coffey.

"Paul, there has been a strange twist since our last conversation," he said. Coffey proceeded to tell him about the discussion with FNO Loh. "She spoke to the military intelligence people in Singapore who liaise with the prime minister's Office of Strategic Information," Coffey went on. "They confirm business ties between Darling and Mahathir bin Dahman. He's invested in the Malaysian's building projects, commercial aircraft plants, and water-processing facilities."

"Do you know what the paper trail looks like?" Hood asked.

"If you're asking whether this is public knowledge or not, it is," Coffey replied. "Darling puts money in Malaysian banks, and bin Dahman draws on that as needed."

"Is there a public record of Darling's holdings?" Hood asked.

"No," Coffey said. "The government has learned that Darling gets private stock for his money. Nothing actionable, though."

"It's a lot of stock, I'm sure," Hood said. "An improportionate amount compared to what other investors get. I'll bet that bin Dahman takes a big hit every time Darling invests."

"He does," Coffey said.

"This could suggest that bin Dahman is using real estate and privately held businesses to pay Darling for services rendered," Hood said. "Such as providing him with nuclear materials."

"It makes sense," Coffey said. "What's your view on Darling himself? He's got a helluva reputation down here. He's got a mega-fortune. Why would he risk all that to do something like this?"

"I've been wondering about that," Hood said. "Maybe it's tied into something you said a minute ago. He got away with murder and liked how it felt."

"You mean Leopold and Loeb, the sequel?" Coffey asked. "Bored rich man gets his kicks planning the death of millions of people?"

"You answered your own question."

"Yeah," Coffey replied. "Jelbart and I were talking

about this as a power grab, but you may have something there. You don't even have to run that one past Liz Gordon. It's simple but neat."

"It's a starting point, anyway," Hood replied. "Meanwhile, what's your next step?"

"We're sailing back to Darwin to wait for Bob, then I guess it's on to Cairns," Coffey said. "We're obviously going to have to take this investigation directly to Darling."

"I agree," Hood said. "And when you do grab him, I want you to do me a favor."

"Sure," Coffey said.

"Tell him he runs a lousy on-line service," Hood said. "Tell him for Matt Stoll."

Coffey was confused, but Hood told him not to worry about it.

Hood hung up. He felt more involved than he usually did in evolving situations. For one thing, unlike Mike Rodgers or former Striker leader Colonel Brett August, Coffey was keeping him plugged into every development in the field, however small. For another, the diverse resources of three nations were available to him. It was as true in crisis management as it was in mathematics: one point was simply one point; two points defined a line; three points created a plane, and a plane was something you could stand on. The United States, Australia, and Singapore created a plane.

There was something else that gave Hood comfort as well. For all his clout, Jervis Darling was still a businessman at heart. He was a potentially twisted one, yes, but a corporate tycoon nonetheless. Unlike the rogue generals and megalomaniacal politicians Hood and his team usually faced, he understood this breed. He could sit in their chairs and imagine the decisions they made.

But there was still a storm in the distance. One that Paul Hood could not anticipate. One that Op-Center and its allies might not be able to control. It had to do with the circus, of all things. Bob Herbert once told the CIOC that a crisis was like the big top.

"You can't afford to grab the ringleader and lose the other attractions," Herbert had said. "While we're all packed shoulder to shoulder in the grandstands, those rampaging elephants and runaway clown cars will crush us flat."

Hood hoped that if Darling were involved, he knew where the nuclear materials were headed and who was handling them. Otherwise, the toll in the grandstand could still be catastrophic.

THIRTY-FIVE

The Celebes Sea
Saturday, 2:02 A.M.

Peter Kannaday did not know what to expect when he reached the radio room.

He could not imagine to whom Hawke might be broadcasting. Jervis Darling? The Malaysian fishing ship? Someone else? Kannaday's mind leapt to conspiracies. Perhaps Hawke had pirates following them in order to seize the *Hosannah*. Or maybe an aircraft was en route to remove him. Or Kannaday.

As Kannaday swung down the stairs he learned how wrong he had been. Hawke was not even in the radio room. He and his thugs were waiting for the captain in the hall. Two men grabbed Kannaday, one hugging each arm. A third got behind him and grabbed Kannaday's windbreaker. He grasped it near the neck and put a knee against Kannaday's lower back. That prevented the captain from bending. A fourth man forced a rag in Kannaday's mouth. The captain tasted oil. It had come from the engine compartment. The men turned Kannaday so he was facing into the corridor.

Hawke was standing there.

The security man passed under the recessed light. His arms were at his sides. For the most part his expression was as inscrutable as always. Except for the eyes. They were volcanic.

Kannaday struggled for a moment before settling into tense compliance. He was not afraid. Though Kannaday had a pretty good idea what was about to take place. He was going to die. He was resigned, though still defiant.

Hawke stepped in very close. He put the heel of his left palm against Kannaday's chin and began to push up slowly. The captain's head went back. Kannaday's gaze shifted from Hawke's angry eyes to the low ceiling of the corridor. He felt the muscles tense along his shoulders and upper arms. The pressure was cutting off his air. He tried to draw breath around the rag in his mouth. Nothing was getting through. He began to feel claustrophobic, panicky. If Hawke pushed back any farther, his neck would snap.

Kannaday resisted. He began to struggle again.

"You want to breathe," Hawke said. "Let me help."

Hawke released Kannaday's chin. He stepped back and punched the captain hard in the gut. Kannaday could not help but breathe then. He sucked air through his nose and around the rank cloth. Hawke moved in on him again. He hit Kannaday with a roundhouse right to the jaw. It struck so hard that the cloth flew halfway from the captain's mouth. Kannaday snatched more air through his nose and mouth as he took another blow to the belly, a hard left. Hawke stepped in as he delivered it, twisting at the waist. At the same time he drew the other elbow back, tucked tight against his ribs. That gave the twist extra snap. Hawke knew how to drive the blows in. He knew how to make them hurt.

When he was younger, Kannaday had been in a number of dockside brawls. But those always ended up on the floor and consisted mostly of grappling and clawing. He had never been given a beating. Kannaday's jaw throbbed, and his ears were pounding. He was nauseated from the blows to the abdomen. His shoulders burned from the strong fingers of the man behind him.

A left uppercut rocked Kannaday's head back. He could actually feel his brain bump the top of his skull. His teeth bit through the cloth and snapped on his tongue. He tasted blood. The bone of his lower jaw literally rang, and the ringing spread to his limbs. If the men had not been holding him up, he would have fallen. Kannaday's jaw continued ringing as Hawke followed the uppercut with a right back fist to the mouth. Kannaday's head slumped to his right shoulder. His hurt tongue flopped over dislocated teeth. His eyelids sagged.

Hawke stepped in again. He grabbed Kannaday's aching chin and squeezed. The pain forced the captain's eyes to open.

"This is just the beginning of your tutorial," Hawke said.

He kneed Kannaday very low in the belly. Twice. The gag fell entirely from the captain's mouth now. So did thick drops of saliva mixed with blood. Hawke ignored the bloody spittle dripping onto his hand. He slapped him hard with his left hand. Against the right ear. Then Hawke cocked his left arm and jabbed a fist square into Kannaday's right eye. He drew his fist back and hit him in the mouth. Kannaday felt his lips split.

"Now, Captain," Hawke said. "Do I have your attention?"

Kannaday's head was drumming. His face felt hot wherever skin touched bone. He had only a greasy view from his right eye. All he could hear was his own rapid heartbeat and strained breathing.

Hawke was still holding the captain's chin. He moved his mouth close to Kannaday's left ear.

"I asked you a question," Hawke said.

Kannaday's chest was still bleeding from the wound inflicted earlier by the wommera. He was dizzy from the loss of blood and dazed from the beating. All he could manage was a weak nod.

"Good. Here is how the rest of this enterprise will play out," Hawke said. "You will stay in your cabin until we reach Cairns. Then you will go to the chief and tell him that the mission was successfully completed. When he asks why you look the way you do, you will tell him we had a disagreement."

Kannaday attempted to speak. He could not even move his mouth. It felt as though everything had been pulped together: tongue, teeth, lips. Instead, he just shook his head.

Hawke kneed him again, this time in the groin. Bloody spittle flew from Kannaday's broken lips. Hawke continued to lean close.

"We can keep this going for as long as you want," Hawke told him. "In the end, you will do what I ask."

Kannaday managed to exhale something that sounded like the word he intended. "Why?"

"Why?" Hawke asked. "Because if you tell him that you walked into another ambush, he will regard you as an ineffective commander. He will dispose of you, and I will get your job. Only I do not want it, Captain. I like having one man on the plank in front of me. I am only interested in money." Hawke moved back slightly. "Our friend Marcus will corroborate your story. He likes the way things are now, having to report to Uncle Jervis every now and then. I do not think he would enjoy serving a real captain."

Hawke had spoken slowly and clearly. Kannaday had heard all the words. But they were confusing. The captain had never known a man to fight for anonymity and a subordinate position.

"I would like to take you to your cabin," Hawke said. "My men will see that you are cleaned and patched up. But I want to make certain that we have an understanding this time, Captain."

Hawke's voice seemed to be echoing now. Kannaday had to fight to pick up the words.

"G-good," Kannaday said. It was the only word he could manage without using his lips or tongue. He was not sure anyone heard. He felt himself drifting. His good eye shut.

Hawke was still holding Kannaday's chin. He pinched hard. "Good?" Hawke repeated. "Then you agree?"

Kannaday nodded once. Hawke released his chin. The captain's head dropped so that his right ear was facing the ground. A moment later he felt his legs being lifted. He was being carried astern.

There was something oddly comforting about being semiconscious. Kannaday was living from second to second. He was preoccupied with pain. He had no responsibility other than to ride it out. The moments when the hurt subsided, even slightly, were almost euphoric. A part of him was actually grateful to the men who were carrying him.

A Marshall Plan for Peter Kannaday, the captain thought with lightheaded detachment. *First we break you down, and then we build you back up.*

Awareness came in short flashes. Kannaday was in the hall. Then he was in his cot. Then he was being bandaged and wiped down with a damp cloth. It felt refreshing but hurt at the same time. He realized that he was passing out and then waking as the men ministered to his wounds.

Finally, everything was silent and still. The pain was there, but it seemed distant.

As he lay there, Kannaday heard a soft buzz behind him. He recognized the sound. It was the engine of the launch. The crew must be heading to the fishing vessel. Or maybe they were returning. He had no idea how much time had passed. Perhaps he had been down here longer than he thought. In any case, Kannaday needed to get on deck to make sure the delivery went as planned. He was still the captain. Even the mutinous Hawke had said that much.

Hawke, Kannaday thought suddenly. Dreamlike memories of the beating came back to him. So did the rage he had felt when Hawke's men first grabbed him.

The captain should have killed the mutinous bastard when he had the opportunity. He would get the gun from his desk and kill him now. Marcus had betrayed the captain, too. Kannaday could not kill the boss's nephew. But he could lock the privileged little bastard in the radio room until they reached Cairns. Jervis Darling would understand that.

The captain sat up. As he did, his head imploded. The act of moving had reignited the beating. Hot prickles raced from Kannaday's forehead to his temples and down his neck into his spine. His flesh caught fire, and he was immediately sickened by the iron-rust taste of blood in his mouth. Kannaday shouted and shot back onto the cot. He breathed quickly, squeezing his eyes shut and whimpering as he tried to ride out the pain.

No one came to him. No one spoke. He listened past the blood that was surging through his ears.

He was alone.

THIRTY-SIX

The South Pacific
Saturday, 7:44 A.M.

Before Lowell Coffey turned in for the night, he phoned Bob Herbert. Coffey brought Herbert up to date on the latest development involving Jervis Darling. The veteran intelligence officer was not surprised by the idea that Darling might be involved in this undertaking. It was not the power-corrupts bromide that influenced Herbert. It was what Herbert called the big-shot syndrome. The idea that coin itself was no longer the coin of the realm. Resources were. He had tracked the phenomenon from his childhood, when the people who had color television sets were big shots. You went to their house to watch *Bonanza* or *Star Trek* or *King Leonardo* cartoons. Less than a decade later, oil became the prized commodity. Everyone wanted it. The Arabs had it. They became big shots. Kids in the early eighties who had Atari Pac-Man cartridges or Cabbage Patch Dolls were the talk of the class. Shortly after that, the Japanese had the technology everyone wanted. Enter the new generation of *bigeru shotsu*. Money was irrelevant. People would pay whatever it cost to get what the newest grand panjandrum was peddling.

With the collapse of the Soviet Union, high-grade nuclear materials became the hottest coin in the world. Just like the kid with a PlayStation 2, the person who had enriched uranium or plutonium or a nuclear weapon itself could be a star, if only for a moment. Herbert remembered thinking how a few years back atom bombs had briefly been the codpiece of India and Pakistan. One blew up a plain and hogged the headlines, the other blew up a mountain and did the same. Gross national product, religion, starvation, and disease just did not matter then. For those few days, big booming bombs was it. Megatonnage made you the Tom Cruise of the international stage.

Someone accustomed to wealth and control would find nuclear material irresistible. With it, he was a player. Knowing where it was, he was safe. Without it, he was simply an observer who could be erased along with every other pawn on the chessboard. That would definitely not appeal to a man like Jervis Darling. He liked to be a big shot.

Unfortunately, Darling *was* a big shot. Herbert downloaded gigabytes of data and read up on him. Darling had security, influence, money. He controlled international corporations that could be used to shift money and hide people and deeds. He also had the world's largest private collection of prehistoric fossils.

"The guy likes to remind himself what happens to giants who don't adapt," Herbert mused.

Worse than that, Darling was a beloved big shot. He was the Australian dream made flesh.

The hours raced by as Herbert sat in his little cubicle in the heart of the plane. As the engine roared and the sky brightened, Herbert consumed data as if he were a pigeon at an outdoor bake sale. He flitted from file to file, snagging a crumb of information here, another there. Everything Herbert read confirmed his initial suspicion: that this kind of trade was something in which a man like Darling would involve himself.

After the intelligence chief finished an initial read, he sat back in his wheelchair. "So how do we find out for certain whether you're behind this disgusting little transaction?" he wondered aloud.

They would continue to look for the people who had actually made the presumed trade. But Herbert knew they might not find the radioactive bread crumbs they were looking for. Already, one boat had been destroyed and another had vanished. For all they knew, they could be dealing with submarines or aircraft as well. Perhaps the materials had been dropped somewhere else for pickup at some later date. The canvas of possibilities was huge.

"No," he said. "Lowell had the right idea."

They had to go after Jervis Darling himself. Directly and quietly. If he had been in a movie, Herbert would have put on thick glasses and pretended to be a paleontologist with a rare fossil to sell. FNO Loh would be his assistant. Darling would be suspicious, of course, and quiz them about dinosaur genera. Herbert would have boned up on his prehistoric animals, and what he did not know, his erudite aide would. They would win Darling's confidence.

But this was real, and they needed a quick, comprehensive solution. One that would identify Darling as a participant. It would also, he hoped, stop the trafficking itself.

As the TR-1 banked into the light of the new day, Herbert saw a flash of orange on his computer monitor. A moment later he felt the delightful heat of the sun on the back of his neck.

And he got an idea. One that would not require him to pronounce *pachycephalosaurus*.

THIRTY-SEVEN

Washington, D.C.
Friday, 7:44 P.M.

Paul Hood stepped into the parking lot. It was a dreary and overcast evening, but the cool air tasted sweet. It always did after he spent a day in Op-Center's windowless, forced-air underground offices. He walked to his new Toyota Maxim for the forty-five-minute drive to his apartment. An apartment that was as empty as hell without the sounds of video games and ringing phones and the distinctive thumping of Alexander holding the handrail and wall and leaping down half a flight of stairs. But it was feeling a little more like home now. As much as leaving dirty shirts on the couch or renting the DVDs you wanted to see or eating chicken salad directly from Styrofoam take-out trays could make a place feel like home.

Hood was just getting into the car when his cell phone beeped. It was Mike Rodgers. The two men had not spoken since Rodgers met with Senator Debenport. The general had spent the day interviewing potential field operatives as well as intelligence personnel who might be able to help him put together his new HUMINT unit. Rodgers had wanted to see all four candidates in public instead of in his office. It was important to see how they blended in with crowds, how anonymous they could appear when they were not part of a group.

"How did the interviews go?" Hood asked.

"They were informative," Rodgers replied.

"Hold that thought," Hood said. Rodgers would know what that meant. As Hood sat behind the wheel he put his headset on. At the same time he tucked the cell phone into a scrambler built into the dashboard. It looked like a typical hands-free setup. However, the frame contained a chip that sent a loud screech along with the conversation. Only a phone with a complementary chip could filter out the sound. The chip in the car only worked with numbers that had been specifically keyed into the cell phone's memory. "Ready," Hood said. He started the car and drove toward the sentry post.

"I just want to say up front that this is not like putting together a military special ops team, where someone can demonstrate marksmanship on a firing range or hand-to-hand combat in the gym," Rodgers told him. "The entire process is a bit of a boondoggle."

"How so?"

"Because good intelligence people, by nature, don't talk. They observe and listen," Rodgers said. "As I sat there, I kept wondering if the silent interviewee was more suitable than the one who volunteered information."

"Interesting," Hood said. "Guess you go by your gut."

"Pretty much," Rodgers admitted. "Silence and disinterest have pretty much the same sound. On the other hand, David Battat talks a lot. Maria Corneja doesn't. Aideen Marley is somewhere in the middle. Falah Shibli speaks five languages but says less than Maria. It is all in what your gut tells you."

"How is Shibli?" Hood asked.

"Very well," Rodgers replied. "He's agreed to serve as needed, though he's decided he would prefer to remain in the Middle East. I got the sense that he's doing undercover work for the Mossad."

Falah Shibli was a twenty-nine-year-old Israeli of Arabic descent. He had spent seven years in Israel's tough Druze Reconnaissance unit, the Sayeret Ha'Druzim, before joining the police in the northern town of Kiryat Shmona. Shibli had worked with Op-Center in the Middle East. He would be a valuable resource for Israeli intelligence, since he could move freely among Arab populations.

Hood waved at Sergeant Ridpath in the booth. The noncom waved back and pushed the button that raised the heavy wooden bar. Hood drove from the lot. "So how did the new people impress you?"

"There's one guy I really liked," Rodgers said. "Sprague West. Fifty-five-year-old former Marine, Vietnam vet. He put in a quarter century with the NYPD, the first ten of those undercover. He infiltrated the Black Panthers, drug rings, broke up prostitution. My kind of guy. And cool, Paul."

"Silent?"

"Yeah," Rodgers admitted with a chuckle.

"Where is he based?"

"Here," Rodgers said. "He moved to D.C. when he left the force to be near his mother."

"Does he have other family?" Hood asked.

"Two grown daughters and three ex-wives," Rodgers said. "They weren't happy with what he did for a living."

"Great. We can start a support group," Hood said.

"The nontalker and the man who loves to listen," Rodgers said. "It could be interesting."

"Incredibly dull, more likely," Hood said. "What's your game plan with Mr. West?"

"I've invited West to come to the office on Monday," Rodgers said. "We'll talk more about specific assignments. His mom died last year, and he would like to get back in the field."

"Sounds perfect," Hood admitted.

"Meanwhile, what's happening with Lowell?" Rodgers asked.

Hood brought Rodgers up to date. When he was finished, the general was silent for a moment.

"Any thoughts?" Hood asked.

"Only about the Aussies and Singapore," Rodgers said. "They're tough nuts. Good partners to have in a big game."

"How big a game do you think this is?" Hood asked.

"I don't think there's a global conspiracy with Darling at the head, if that's what you mean," Rodgers assured him.

"Why not?"

"Men like Darling are autocrats, not oligarchs," Rodgers said. "Defenders band together for mutual protection. Aggression is a solitary activity. Even during World War II, Germany and Japan stayed a world away from each other. And they would have gone toe to toe eventually."

"So what's the scenario you envision?"

"Apart from the perverse challenge?" Rodgers said. "I see world capitals being attacked and crippled, economies paralyzed. You want to see where the targets may be? Look at where Darling has the fewest investments."

"I have," Hood said. "He's still invested heavily at home and in South America. But he's shifted a lot of his assets from Europe and the United States to the Pacific Rim."

"There you go," Rodgers said. "He's looking to rough up a London or Washington, Paris or Bonn. Change the financial and geopolitical dynamic. Does he have any children?"

"A young daughter."

"The heir to his efforts," Rodgers said. "What father doesn't want to give his daughter the world? You were ready to resign from Op-Center for your kids, for your family."

"True. But I would draw the line at killing millions of people," Hood said.

"Would you?" Rodgers asked.

"I don't follow."

"We've gone to war to protect our way of life, to preserve our view of the future for our children," Rodgers said.

"When we've been attacked," Hood said. "That's an important distinction."

"Maybe Darling believes that his world *has* been attacked, or at the very least threatened," Rodgers said. "He may feel that Australia has been minimized by the United States and the European Union. He may fear the growing political, financial, and military strength of China. Maybe the states around China are also afraid, and he has rallied the oligarchy to fight back. Maybe Beijing is their target. We just don't know."

"All good points, though instinct tells me this is more of a challenge to Darling than a political issue."

"That could be," Rodgers agreed. "It doesn't change the fact that he has to be stopped. Fortunately, as I said, the people on site are probably the best we could ask for. And we've got good ones in reserve, if needed. It won't come free, or even cheap, but we'll fix this."

Hood thanked Rodgers for the assessment. Then he hung up and cracked the window slightly. After being inside, he wanted to feel more of what his son Alexander called "real" air.

This was not a job for people who had families. Or liked to be able to sleep nights. It was one thing to worry about a corporate bottom line or a project deadline. It was far different to worry about lives, whether it was one life or ten thousand. Then again, Hood was inevitably encouraged, even inspired, by people like Mike Rodgers and Bob Herbert. Men and women who had vast experience, perspective, and something else. Something easily misplaced in the day's slush of ominous data and frightening theory.

Hope.

Optimism.

And the resolve never to let them go.

THIRTY-EIGHT

Cairns, Australia
Saturday, 9:45 A.M.

Jervis Darling had gone to bed after receiving a signal that the transfer had finally been made. It was three rings on his cell phone, twice in succession. Because Darling had installed an FDS, a file-disabling security chip, there was no record of who had called. If someone had been watching the yacht, there was no way they could triangulate the call. Ordinarily, communicating with the yacht did not concern him. But there had been disturbing news reports about the sampan attack in the Celebes Sea. There were unconfirmed reports that radiation was detected on the wreckage. If that were true, naval patrols might be monitoring communications in the region. They could be searching for radioactivity as well as looking for anyone who might have heard or seen the explosion. If the *Hosannah* were picked up for any reason, his nephew knew to play dumb. Marcus would say that he had been hired to run the radio shack by the yacht owner. Period. Jervis would then telephone the person in charge. He would protest the presumption that his nephew was in any way involved with nuclear trafficking. Peter Kannaday would take the fall for it. Yachts were easy enough to acquire. Blame was what Captain Kannaday was being hired to carry.

The *Hosannah* was not coming directly back to Cairns. It would sail the coast for several hours after dawn, like any pleasure boat. When Kannaday was sure they were not being followed, he would bring her in. That should happen around ten in the morning.

Darling spent the early part of Saturday morning as he

always did: having breakfast with his eight-year-old daughter. The meal of salmon, scrambled eggs, and raisin toast was Jessica-Ann's favorite. It was served in a large atelier adjoining Jervis Darling's bedroom. The room had been built for Darling's wife to pursue painting. It was too bad Dorothy did not stick to that as her principal hobby. As John Hawke put it after investigating her activities, "Your wife has been working with a new brush." Because a man is occupied, that does not give his wife license to amuse herself with someone less busy. Jervis and Dorothy Darling had exchanged vows, not contingencies.

Dorothy's wooden easel and tray of paints were still stored in a corner of the sunlit room. There was an untouched canvas stretching in its frame. Jessica-Ann said she wanted to paint on it one day. She liked coming here. The blond-haired girl had been one of her mother's favorite subjects. She said the smell of the paint made her feel as though her mother were still here. Darling could not deny his daughter that comfort.

Despite the loss of her mother four years earlier, Jessica-Ann was an outgoing, cheerful, and open young lady. Darling had seen to it that she did not want for companionship or activities. He also made sure that they spent as much time together as possible. Darling had no reservations about taking her to meetings at home and abroad. If he were leaving the country, he would simply pack up a tutor or two to travel with them.

Darling did not want to push his daughter into any of his businesses. For all he knew, she might want to be a painter, like her mother. She already liked to draw. She enjoyed sketching birds and insects. She imagined what the faces might be on the butterflies and fireflies she saw around the estate. That would be fine with Darling. He wanted to expose Jessica-Ann to all the possibilities. When the time came, she alone would decide what to do with her life. And she would make that decision in a world that did not revolve around Europe or America.

Jessica-Ann came to the table in a brilliant yellow

jumpsuit. Her long hair was piled under a cap sporting the name of the latest boy band she was into. Darling had a permanent skybox at all the arenas and stadiums in Australia. Jessica-Ann got to see every concert that toured Down Under. Her high cheekbones had a healthy flush, and she wore her big, perennial smile. The young girl had just gone for a morning squash lesson at their private court. She took a moment to mime for her father the proper way to serve.

"Let me ask you something," Darling said as she slid into one of the cushioned iron chairs. "Would you rather play with perfect form and lose or with bad form and win?"

"I'd rather win," she said without hesitation. "It would be even better to do it with bad form, because that would show I had *amazing* talent."

"I like the way you think," Darling said as Mrs. Cooper served their breakfast. Smelling the fresh salmon, Jessica-Ann's Siamese cat Spokane ambled over. The overweight cat was named for the first city outside of Australia that Jessica-Ann had visited. The cat moved aggressively along her leg, and Jessica-Ann slipped it a thin slice of salmon.

Darling and his daughter saw each other regularly during the week. But this was their special time. Business was not permitted to intrude. Thus, it was not until nearly ten A.M. that Darling took a call from the *Hosannah*. He was drinking coffee and having his first look at the online news services. Though it was not the call he had been expecting, it was not a surprise.

Peter Kannaday was not on the other end of the phone. It was Darling's nephew Marcus. He was calling from a landline. The yacht was able to plug into it upon entering the cove.

"You received the signal?" Marcus asked.

"I did. Why are you calling instead of the captain?"

"He's in his cabin," Marcus replied.

"I repeat the question," Darling said. He could tell when someone was being evasive. They tended to answer directly and quickly, as though the answer had been rehearsed.

"He had a run-in with Mr. Hawke," Marcus said.

"Is Mr. Hawke with you?"

"No," Marcus replied. "Shall I get him?"

"That isn't necessary," Darling told him. "What happened?"

"I'm not entirely sure," Marcus replied. "We made the rendezvous at the rescheduled time. As the launch was setting out, Mr. Hawke came below with several of his men. He asked me to tell Captain Kannaday that Hawke was in the radio room. I was to remain above deck until they came for me."

"How long were you up there?" Darling asked.

"About ten minutes," Marcus told him. "Mr. Hawke came up and told me it was all right to go below."

"And the captain?"

"Hawke said he had retired and was not to have any visitors or messages," Marcus told him.

"Are you sure Captain Kannaday is alive?" Darling asked.

"I went to the door and had a listen," Marcus said. "I heard movement but nothing more."

"He hasn't asked for anything," Darling said.

"Not that I'm aware of," Marcus replied. "He hasn't used the intercom."

"So Hawke has been running the ship."

"Apparently," Marcus replied. "He brought us in. I was asleep most of the time."

"Is anyone coming ashore?" Darling asked.

"Not yet," Marcus said. "Mr. Hawke asked me to call in. I have no further instructions or information."

Darling poured himself more coffee. It was already prepared to his taste, dark and sweet.

John Hawke was smart. Kannaday had obviously done what Darling had suggested. He had made noises like a real captain. Hawke must have threatened Kannaday in return. Perhaps they had tied him up or beaten him. But locked in his room, Kannaday was still the captain. If there were ever a fall to take, legally or with Darling, he would still have to take it. But that was Kannaday's problem. Darling's problem was that if he asked to see Kannaday, he would find out what happened. That Hawke had pushed him to the wall and won. Then he would either have to replace him or send him back to the *Hosannah*. If Darling left him in charge, then he himself would look weak. He could not knowingly leave a crippled captain in charge. Unfortunately, there was no one available to replace Kannaday except for Hawke. But if Darling asked Hawke to take charge, he ran the very real risk that Hawke would decline. John Hawke preferred the shadows to the light. His refusal would also make Darling appear weak. As Hawke had just demonstrated, he was not afraid to push back.

The next pickup was not for another four days. The yacht was scheduled to cruise with its "paying" customers until then.

"When you see the captain, tell him I'm pleased that everything went as it was supposed to," Darling said.

"What if I don't see the captain?" Marcus asked anxiously.

"Then deliver the message to the next in command," Darling replied. "That is typically how things are done, is it not?"

"Of course," Marcus replied. He hesitated.

"Was there anything else?" Darling asked.

"Actually, yes," Marcus said. "I'm not sure I want to go back on board."

"Why?"

"There's bad air on that ship," Marcus said. "First the attack, now this strangeness between the captain and Mr. Hawke."

"That shouldn't impact your work or your job performance," Darling said. "You're insulated from all of that."

"I don't feel insulated," Marcus complained. "Everyone on board feels it."

"Deal with it," Darling said firmly. "Set an example for the others. I need my radio operator."

"Yes, sir."

"Now go back on board," Darling told him. "Remember that fear is its own fuel. Have a positive attitude."

"I will, sir," Marcus said unconvincingly and hung up.

Darling placed the phone in its cradle. He glanced at his laptop without seeing it. He felt confident with Hawke watching things. He actually felt sorry for Peter Kannaday. Command was beyond the abilities of some people. Kannaday was one of those men. He was and would continue to be nothing more than the master of a pleasure boat. A rich one after another few years, but what did wealth matter without self-respect?

Darling wondered if Kannaday would settle into his role as a subordinate captain or whether he would try again to take on Hawke. Darling did not know the captain, but he knew human nature. He knew men. When it came to testosterone and reason, reason usually lost.

Kannaday would lash out again. Only this time it probably would not end with the captain being locked in his cabin.

Darling returned to the computer to read the latest rumors about a radioactive sampan found in the Celebes Sea. According to the reports, no one knew who the unconscious sailor was or what happened to him.

That was good. Even if he were conscious, it was unlikely the seaman had seen or heard anything useful. Hawke would have made certain of that. After all, Darling thought, he did do his best work in the dark.

THIRTY-NINE

Darwin, Australia
Saturday, 12:08 P.M.

At a few minutes after eleven A.M., the TR-1 touched down at the Australian Defence Force Basic Flying Training School in Tamworth, New South Wales. Within ten minutes, a rested and energized Bob Herbert was wheeling himself up a ramp into the belly of an RAAF Bell 204 helicopter. He had called ahead and specifically requested this vehicle. And not just because it was wheelchair friendly. It fit with the reconnaissance idea he was formulating. The Bells were heavy-lift choppers capable of transporting troops or, more importantly, being reconfigured for spray loads to help put out fires.

Ninety minutes and a smooth but loud ride later, Herbert was on the ground in Darwin. Before leaving Tamworth, Herbert had said he might need the helicopter for a few hours more. The pilot shut the rotor off and waited as Herbert disembarked. Lowell Coffey and a gentleman in uniform were there to meet him. The officer looked a healthy bronze. Lowell looked sallow.

The officer introduced himself as Warrant Officer George Jelbart. It was the first time a man had ever crouched to shake Herbert's hand. He probably did it as a courtesy, to make direct eye contact. But Herbert felt like he did when he was a kid being introduced to some friend of his father's. He half-expected the officer to tousle his hair when he rose. As they began walking toward the terminal, Coffey shot Herbert a furrowed, *That was strange* look. Herbert was glad Coffey had noticed. He was not sure how much was registering in the attorney's tired mind. It was clear from Coffey's bloodshot eyes and pallor that his little ocean odyssey had not agreed with him.

"I won't ask if you had a pleasant flight because those daylong trips are never enjoyable," Jelbart said. He had to speak loudly to be heard over the wind. "But we appreciate your coming. We have a van waiting out front. Our offices are just a few minutes' drive from here. There are beverages and sandwiches waiting. Is there anything else you'll want?"

"Not a thing, thanks," Herbert said.

"Mr. Herbert, the ADF commander told me that you rang ahead to request that specific aircraft," Jelbart said.

"Yes. The RAAF registry on the TR-1 listed it among your aircraft," Herbert told him.

"And you've asked it to wait for you," Jelbart went on.

"That's right."

"May I ask what you have in mind?" Jelbart pressed. "We have a number of helicopters here, you know."

"I do know that," Herbert replied. "But there was something special about this one."

"Would you mind sharing that information?" Jelbart said.

"We'll talk about it when we get to the office."

"All right," Jelbart said.

"Tell me something," Herbert went on. "Will FNO Loh be part of this operation?"

"She will," Jelbart said. "But I want to emphasize that whatever we do will not be a part of the official ASEAN or ANZUS logs. This is an entirely independent action."

ASEAN was the Association of Southeast Asian Nations. Established by the Bangkok Declaration of 1967, ASEAN was a socioeconomic as well as de facto security arrangement between Indonesia, Malaysia, Singapore, the Philippines, Thailand, and Brunei. Signed in 1951, AN-ZUS was a similar arrangement between Australia, New Zealand, and the United States.

"Why do you want to hide what we're doing?" Herbert asked. "Lowell, didn't you say that earlier, Ellsworth couldn't wait to have the U.S. officially committed to this investigation?"

"I did," Coffey said.

"That was pre-Darling," Jelbart said. "Any activities undertaken by those groups are part of the public record. If this proves to be a dead end, Mr. Darling must not know that he was being investigated."

"Makes sense," Herbert said. "Darling's got the clout to hammer careers flat and eviscerate budgets. He could probably bring down a sitting government if he set his mind and resources to it."

"Without question," Jelbart agreed. "FNO Loh agrees. Frankly, I'm uneasy even using his name in public."

"Then we won't use it," Herbert told him. "How does Captain Hook strike you?"

Jelbart smiled. "That appeals."

"Good." Herbert looked at Coffey as they reached the terminal. The automatic door swung in. "You've been pretty quiet, Lowell."

"Yes."

"You're also straw yellow," Herbert added.

"That, too," Coffey admitted. "Mr. Jelbart, you said I'd miss the swaying of the boat. I don't. I still feel as if I'm moving."

"That's because you were sitting and lying down on the boat instead of standing," Jelbart said. He seemed relieved to be talking about something other than Jervis Darling.

"Now you tell me."

"I once went to a seminar on homeostasis," Jelbart said. "It was mandatory for personnel who serve on the land, sea, and air. We learned that the body hastens to adapt to new stimuli, like ocean roll or weightlessness for astronauts. It's akin to the survival instinct or antibodies rallying against a disease. But acclimation works best if the individual is doing what he always does in both environments: walking, talking, eating, that sort of thing."

"What you're feeling, Lowell, is not the sway but the body's countersway," Herbert said.

"I don't understand," Coffey said quietly.

"What happens in a new environment is that the fight-or-flight mechanism is triggered, and adrenaline floods the bloodstream," Herbert told him. "When you went to sea, resources were pumped into all of your equilibrium centers. Your heart rate jumped, along with muscle strength and metabolism. It takes a while for that to return to normal. Over time, the on-off switch becomes much easier to control. Experienced seamen like Mr. Jelbart go from one to the other with no lapse at all."

Herbert had no idea whether Coffey had heard. He was looking straight ahead and showing no expression.

"I'm impressed you knew that, Mr. Herbert," Jelbart said.

"We got the same lecture when I joined the company years ago," Herbert told him. "Only they didn't call it a seminar on homeostasis. They used the acronym WYFLH."

"What does 'wiffle' mean?" Jelbart asked.

"Why You Feel Like Hurling," Herbert said.

Jelbart shook his head and smiled. Coffey did not react. He was too busy concentrating on putting one foot in front of the other.

The van had a civilian driver, and no one spoke about the mission during the brief ride. Jelbart informed Herbert that Darwin was the nation's gateway to Asia. The airport had recently been upgraded, and a four-billion-dollar railway had just been completed linking Darwin with Adelaide and other major cities in southern Australia. It certainly looked the part of an up-and-coming city. Downtown Darwin was more metropolitan than Herbert had imagined. Both automobile and pedestrian traffic were thick on the wide, sun-drenched avenues. Newly built towers twenty and twenty-five stories tall rose behind the thickly treed streets. Trendy, upscale stores filled the first-floor shops. It could be Cleveland or Charlotte or any other smallish metropolis in the United States.

Maybe that's one reason someone like Darling might want to shake things up, Herbert thought. Even though he had international corporations, he might not appreciate the globalization of his native land. That kind of resentment was not limited to Third World nations and radical regimes. Even the Canadians had their problems with American influence.

The van stopped in front of the Australian Central Credit Union Building. The group took the elevator to the tenth floor. They went directly to the MIC offices, where they were met by Brian Ellsworth. The solicitor was solicitous, though he lacked the rugged confidence of Warrant Officer Jelbart.

No, that isn't it, Herbert thought. *Ellsworth is afraid.*

They retired to a warm, sunny conference room and shut the door. Jelbart moved a chair aside, and Herbert rolled up to the circular conference table. He poured himself water and took a half sandwich from the tray in the center of the table. It was tuna salad. He took a bite and looked out the window. He could see the ocean from here. The tuna salad tasted very fresh. Maybe it was caught and made locally. This was really a small town with big-city aspirations and modern-world problems. No wonder Ellsworth was scared. On paper, there were solutions and options to twenty-first-century crises. In practice, Australians were still fighting the Japanese Eighteenth Army for New Guinea. They were strong, but not subtle. They were courageous but not patient.

Jelbart took coffee, a sandwich, and a seat. Coffey sat without eating. Ellsworth remained standing.

"Mr. Hebert has been fully briefed?" Ellsworth asked Jelbart.

"He has," Jelbart replied.

"Except for one thing," Herbert said. "The whereabouts of FNO Loh."

"She went back to the hospital for another look at the sampan wreckage," Jelbart said. "She will be joining us presently."

"I see," Herbert said. "Do you know if she was looking for something in particular?"

"She did not say," Jelbart replied.

"Forgive me, Mr. Herbert, but we need to move this along," Ellsworth said. "There are several ministers and one prime minister waiting for the outcome of our session. Warrant Officer Jelbart and I have been authorized to plan and execute a strategy for locating the missing radioactive material, as well as to gather evidence that will identify and help prosecute those who were involved in the removal and trade of said material. For obvious reasons, this strategy must be developed as quickly as possible. We are anxious for your input."

Herbert looked at Ellsworth. "I think I followed that," the intelligence chief said. He took a bite of sandwich. "There are two effective ways of doing this. One way is to set up a sting. We pose as men in the market for hot grease."

"Hot grease?" Ellsworth said.

"Fissionable material," Herbert said. "The stuff that makes things pop and burn."

"Jesus lord," Ellsworth said.

"We try to lighten up Armageddon to keep from being chronically depressed," Herbert admitted. "Anyway, the problem with that option is it would take weeks to set up a credible front. We don't have that kind of time. So I'm going to suggest a quicker, less orthodox plan."

"And that is?" Ellsworth asked impatiently.

"We smoke the bastards out," he replied.

FORTY

Darwin, Australia
Saturday, 12:31 P.M.

Monica Loh stood in the hospital room, behind the lead
shield, looking in. The door was shut behind her. The odor
was different than the last time Loh had been there. It was
musky, much less antiseptic. That was not surprising,
given that the patient had been lying here since his arrival
two days before. He was catheterized and taking only liquid nourishment, so there was little for nurses to do other
than change his position every six hours.

The sailor was still unconscious. According to the doctor, part of that was the result of the explosion and part
of it was due to the painkillers and sedatives being delivered intravenously.

Loh had asked the physician if the patient would be at
all communicative without the drugs.

"He would not be talking," the doctor replied. "He
would be moaning. Loudly. The burns he received are
quite severe."

So there was no information here and no clues from
the wreckage. She had just been downstairs. The pieces
of sampan had been examined for fragments of another
boat. Perhaps the target vessel had been damaged in the
explosion. There was nothing. The blast had occurred locally, on the sampan. Forensics had even pulled particles
of algae from the wood. They had hoped it might point
them to a specific area of the Celebes Sea where the sampan had been sailing in the hours before the blast. Unfortunately, the organisms the scientists had identified all
belonged to colonies that existed throughout the region.

A blank ship and, for now, a blank sailor. Word had

reached her while they were at sea. There were over 500 Lee Tongs listed at the Singaporean Office of Registry and Taxation. More than half of them were the right age to be this man. COSCOM was checking them out. But the research would take days, possibly weeks. If they could find this one, they might be able to learn who he spent time with ashore. Whether anyone else on the sampan survived. Dr. Lansing had told her he would jolt Tong awake again if she could prove that tens of thousands of lives depended on the answers the pirate would give. But the pirate had not said much before. Lansing and Ellsworth both agreed there was no reason to imagine a second try would produce different results. Loh felt it was certainly worth a try. If she thought that Tong would survive, she would have insisted that he be transferred to a hospital in Singapore. The doctors there might be no less reluctant to wake him than Dr. Lansing, but they would have no choice. Criminals have few rights in Singapore. The government would put public safety before the well-being of a pirate.

Instead of working with what might be scraps of information from the source, they were going to make plans based on ideas from an American spy. This Bob Herbert could be a brilliant intelligence operative. But whatever he came up with would still be exploratory. That was like sailing without charts. It was not something Loh preferred to do.

The FNO continued to look out at the bandaged, frail-looking Singaporean. He seemed so alone in the clean, white bed. She began to think just how alone he really was. She knew that people who were born without opportunity, such as a family business or store or political connections, had three options: they could dwell in poverty, turn to crime, or agree to indentures such as military service or a lengthy contractual apprenticeship. Ironically, if this man survived, he would return to Singapore in a worse position than before. Chances were good the owner of the boat would not come forward to press charges. The pirate would go free. But only the most menial, lowest-paying work would now be available to him because of his past. And because of that past, he would be watched by the police. His activities would have to be reported by landlords and employers. If Tong were involved in a fight, or stole food or clothing, or picked someone's pocket, he would be dealt with very harshly. Caning and imprisonment, most likely.

It would be better for everyone if Dr. Lansing revived him. FNO Loh could ask him a few final questions, and he could die having done something beneficial for society.

That is not for you to say, Loh warned herself. She had gone from making subjective judgments to making moral ones.

She turned from the pirate and walked into the deserted hallway. Darwin police were keeping nonessential personnel away from the pirate's room. They were checking the IDs of everyone who stepped from the elevator. There were already rumors circulating about what had happened on the Celebes. The Australian government did not want anyone to obtain confirmation that nuclear materials were involved.

An MIC officer was waiting to take FNO Loh to the meeting. They made their way to the elevator in silence. Loh was still thinking about the pirate. She was wondering what drove him to his trade. Confidence had to be one of those things. Everyone on a sampan crew works in an extended voyage. And only a crew that knew the sea well would attempt to sail it in a sampan. Especially if they were carrying explosives.

That boldness might spill over into the kind of vessel the pirates would attack, she thought. They were like longboat seamen who would not shy from chasing a whale. No ship would be too large for them tackle. No crew would be too formidable.

That was a small thought, but it could be a useful one. Maybe there were others she had overlooked. Loh actually felt a trace of satisfaction. Perhaps this poor man was not as blank as she had thought.

Lee Tong's misdeeds might help them catch a potential terrorist.

FORTY-ONE

Washington, D.C.
Saturday, 12:23 A.M.

Paul Hood could not sleep.

Dressed in Calvin Kleins and an old L.A. Rams T-shirt that had been given to him by former quarterback Roman Gabriel, Hood lay on his back in the queen-size bed of his two-bedroom apartment. He stared at the ceiling, watching for the occasional cone of light as a car drove past or an airplane flew by. The window was open a crack, and the blinds were raised. He had moved from a nearby hotel four months ago, but he had not gotten around to putting up shades. At least he was remembering to stock the essentials. The first night he'd had no toilet paper. He had to use the *Washington Post*.

The view was to the west, so Hood did not get the rising sun. Not that it mattered. He was usually awake before the sky was light. He had probably witnessed more sunrises than a generation of roosters. And he probably spent less time in the sun than anyone else in Washington.

The new, five-story-tall building was called The Newport. It was located on Tyburn Court in Camp Springs, Maryland, a short drive from Andrews Air Force Base. Hood had a corner apartment on the top floor. That gave him access to a sundeck on the roof, though he had never been to it. Whenever the kids stayed over, Alexander slept on a sofa bed in the living room, and Harleigh had the second bedroom. To ease the blow for Alexander of not having his own room, the living room was where Hood kept the PlayStation 2 video games.

The room was quiet. It was not noise that kept Hood up. Nor was it the situation in Australia. Hood had been through more than a dozen crises over the past ten years. He had learned how to ride them out by focusing on the upside. Civilization would survive. It was simply a matter of the cost. That did not make a crisis pleasant, only manageable. Besides, this problem was in the hands of very capable people. If they needed him, they knew how to reach him.

What troubled Hood, the more that he thought about it, was the extent to which he was needed. Not at Op-Center but in his personal life. Like the splashes of light above him, the patterns of Paul Hood's life changed less and less as the days wore on.

There was dust on the game console. He had noticed it tonight when he walked past the TV. The kids had not stayed with him in over three weeks. It had not seemed that long. Hood was not angry or disappointed. It was not even a question of his being at the house more. Teenagers grew up. They got involved in activities. They dated. Harleigh had two sessions with a psychiatrist each week. The girl was still suffering from post-traumatic stress disorder following her hostage ordeal at the United Nations. She had gotten over the initial phase, when all she wanted to do was stay in her room and see no one. Now she was back at school and beginning to play the violin again. She still went through frequent periods of lethargy and depression. She was also suffering from occasional headaches and psychosomatic stomach ailments. All of that was being taken care of slowly and carefully. Some of it was being addressed through psychiatry, some by Hood and Sharon. Most, however, seemed to be happening because she was hanging out with her friends. Perhaps that was to be expected.

Teenagers were like the cars and planes outside, Hood thought. They pulled away and threw less and less light on their parents. That was to be expected and accepted.

What bothered Hood was that he had come up with nothing to fill the empty places. Now that he thought of it, maybe losing those activities made him realize that there were other holes. Perhaps Op-Center was part of that problem. He had built an effective team, and he had not set new goals.

Maybe he should run for the Senate, he thought half-heartedly. He had enjoyed campaigning and giving speeches when he ran for mayor of Los Angeles. Maybe he should win an election, have himself appointed to the CIOC, and work on the other side of the intelligence fence. That would be a challenge. Especially if Mike Rodgers were named to replace him.

It was something to consider. Especially since Hood was one of the public heroes of the United Nations hostage crisis. He had saved children, including his own daughter. Voters would respond to that.

The more Hood thought about that, the more the idea appealed to him. Maybe he could even run for president. A few spy agency alumni had managed to reach the Oval Office.

The real question was how much he truly wanted that. Or the Senate. Or anything else.

And then late-night common sense poked him in the ribs and whispered in his ear. *The hollowness is not about whether you are needed,* it told him. It was not about what he did for a living. It was about how Hood was living. His former wife was dating. She was working and meeting new people. Not Paul Hood. Traffic patterns had changed, but he had not. He was waiting for the kids to come to him. He was waiting for crises and crisis managers at Op-Center to come to him. When they did not, he found himself lamenting how dull his life was. How sparse the lights on the ceiling were.

Running for office again was not a bad idea, Hood had to admit. But it was not a decision that should be made in the small hours of the night. Not with a head as clouded as his heart was empty. Not when there were smaller steps Hood could take first.

Such as? he asked himself.

Such as calling Daphne Connors back and asking her on a second date, he told himself as he shut his eyes and replayed the pleasures of the first date on the insides of his eyelids.

FORTY-TWO

Cairns, Australia
Saturday, 5:57 P.M.

Queensland North Rural Fire Brigade Deputy Captain Paul Leyland loved his life.

The brown-eyed Leyland stood on the wide balcony that surrounded the observation tower. He looked out at the world and lives that had been entrusted to him and his team. He felt the way the ancient mythic gods must have felt. They each had a particular responsibility, whether it was war, fertility, the underworld, or the hearth. For Deputy Captain Leyland, there was no greater responsibility than to safeguard this land, its people, and the future of both. And there was no greater reward than doing it well.

Leyland had a bald head that seemed to glow ember-orange in the fast-fading sunlight. Part of that was due to the tautness of his flesh. Part of it was the constant perspiration. Leyland hated hats. Feeling the sun on his bare scalp was one of life's great delights. That was why he preferred to be out here instead of sitting in the tower. There was an old joke about a bald head being a solar panel for the sexually active man. For Leyland, the part about the solar panel was true. The sun gave him life. As for the sweat, he had thick red eyebrows and a woolly mustache to protect his eyes and mouth. He rehydrated himself regularly from a canteen tucked in his utility belt. He used a vintage metal canteen instead of a plastic bottle like the kids who worked with him. Leyland liked the feel and taste of the hot, metallic water whenever he took a drink.

The five-foot-seven-inch former Royal Australian Air

Force Maritime Patrol Group pilot had been working for the QNRFB for six of his forty-two years. He had recently passed up a promotion to senior deputy captain because he did not want to go to an office or firehouse. He wanted to stay out here, with his devoted Little Maluka, in the Cairns Observation Tower. Nearly 170 feet in the air, he could see across the Atherton Tableland for limitless kilometers in every direction. The wind from the ocean was as constant as the blazing sun. Leyland could smell a fire before he saw it, even when the wind was blowing against it, which was a good thing. With its rustic farms, volcanic lakes, waterfalls, and rain-forest region, the upland area outside of Cairns was one of the nation's leading tourist attractions. The Kuranda Scenic Railway and the Skyrail Rainforest Cableway carried five times as many passengers each year as all the commuter railroads that served Queensland. Paul Leyland, his live-in crew of two, and Little Maluka were the Kadoovas, as they called themselves. The deranged ones who put the safety of their territory before their own well-being.

The observation tower stood on the top of a 500-foot-high hill. There was a paved, two-lane road and a landing pad for helicopters. The tower itself was made of unvarnished wood. Brick or cinderblock would have been safe from sparks in the event of a fire. But they would have been problematic on the hill. Because of the moisture, the ground was constantly shifting. The mortar would have cracked and left the structure unstable. A metal tower would have become unbearably hot. For Little Maluka and the others, anyway. Leyland could take anything. In fact, the Cairns native relished extremes.

Inside the tower was communication equipment and a two-meter-diameter alidade. The revolving, horizontal disc had a map on its face as well as upright markers for angular measurement. It could see in all directions from the tower. The topographic device was used to pinpoint the exact location of a fire. For Leyland, the alidade was the world in miniature. Looking at it made him feel even more like a god.

The other members of his team, John "Spider" Smolley and Eva Summers, were in the small log cabin at the base of the tower. Little Maluka, their koala mascot, was beside him. Usually he was in his large pen beside the cabin. At sunset, however, he liked to relax on the wind-cooled observation platform. The koala had been badly injured during a blaze and nursed to health. When the small marsupial was well enough to leave, he had decided not to. Why should he? Eva made sure Little Maluka had all the eucalyptus leaves he could eat. Leyland was the one who named him. *Maluka* was Aborigine for "the chief."

The cabin was air-conditioned, and there was a TV set with a DVD player. The twentysomethings spent most of their time watching television or talking on the radio. But they came to life when they had to. They risked their lives without hesitation. The three of them were usually the first ones on scene, working with volunteers to evacuate residents, construct firebreaks, and coordinate the activities of firefighters who flew in from other areas. Yet neither of Leyland's deputies felt quite as he did. That this land was Heaven and he was Saint Peter. If the red-tongued Devil showed up at their gates, it was a sacred duty to beat him back.

Little Maluka was lying on his soft back beside Leyland's boot. His eyes were shut. There was reddish white scar tissue around his big black nose and on his legs. The grayish fur would probably never grow back there. But that was all right, Leyland thought. It made the little guy look tough. Not that a koala needed to look tough. It had no real enemies here except for men. For centuries, they had hunted koalas for food and fur. Now there were laws to prevent that. The firefighter raised his foot. He touched the animal's exposed belly with his toe. The koala grunted, but he did not open his eyes.

"You're tough, all right," Leyland muttered. "You lazy slushy. Is that how you got hurt? Sleeping while the woods burned?"

"He's not a slushy," a female voice said over the radio. That was Eva. She was on the main radio in the cabin.

Leyland always kept his portable radio open. In an emergency, the second or two it took to turn it on could be decisive.

"You're right. Little Maluka could not work in a kitchen," Leyland replied. "At least kitchen help does the dishes. This boy doesn't do anything except purr like a fat cat."

"When the RFB starts a koala brigade, he'll be the first to enlist—hold on," she said, interrupting herself. "I have incoming."

Small, high-powered binoculars hung from Leyland's neck. He snatched them up and did a quick walk around the tower. If someone was calling in a fire, he might be able to spot it. He saw nothing.

"Captain, I'm putting the call through to you," Eva said.

"What is it?" Leyland pulled the radio from his belt. He put the cupped upper half against his ear. It was shielded so that he could hear if he were in a chopper or a loud roaring fire.

"I don't know what this is," she said. "They won't tell me."

"Who won't tell you?"

"They won't tell me that either," she replied.

"Better not be a smoodger," Leyland said.

"He doesn't sound like he's kidding," Eva assured her commander. "Here he is."

While Leyland waited, he stuck out his lower lip and blew perspiration from his mustache. It was something he did when he was annoyed. He was not accustomed to getting secret calls. He scanned the canopy of trees to the northwest. Fires occasionally started in the campground there.

"Captain Leyland?" the caller asked.

"Yes. Who is this?"

"Warrant Officer George Jelbart, Maritime Intelligence Centre," the caller replied.

"Is there a situation?" Leyland pressed. The man was

calling from a helicopter. He could hear the sound in the radio.

"There isn't a fire, if that's what you're asking," Jelbart replied.

Leyland relaxed. He lowered the binoculars.

"But we do have a situation," the officer went on. "We are coming in to discuss it with you."

"We?" Leyland asked.

"We'll discuss it when we arrive," Jelbart said. "We should reach the helicopter pad in about fifteen minutes. We'd like clearance."

"What kind of bird are you flying?"

"A Bell 204," Jelbart told him.

"There's room for you. You're cleared," Leyland informed him.

"We checked that before we left," Jelbart replied. "Thanks for the backup, though."

The caller clicked off. Leyland replaced the unit in his belt. It automatically switched back to base-audio. He was intrigued by the call but also frustrated. Leyland hated being in the dark about anything. He would have pressed for information, but he also disliked wasted effort. If the warrant officer had wanted Leyland to know more, he would have told him more.

"Eva, have Spider climb up to keep an eye on things," Leyland said. "I'm going to the helipad."

"Right away," she said after giving Spider the order. "What's going on?"

"We're having guests," Leyland replied. "Intelligence chaps from the Aussie navy."

"Sounds important," Eva said. "Is it?"

"When was the last time anyone visited who was not with the RFB?" Leyland asked.

"Never, in the three years I've been here," she replied.

"And not in the six years I've been here," Leyland said as he started down the ladder in the center of the tower.

"I don't follow," she said.

"*No one* comes out here if it isn't important," Leyland said.

FORTY-THREE

Cairns, Australia
Saturday, 6:22 P.M.

Lowell Coffey could not decide which was worse—riding in a boat or in a helicopter. The naval vessel rocked its passengers this way and that. The helicopter vibrated wildly and was deafening. Not that a qualitative comparison between the corvette and the Bell was going to help. His fight-or-flight mechanism, or whatever Jelbart and Herbert had decided it was, wanted him to flee. The only reason Coffey mused about the differences was to keep from dwelling on the discomfort itself. Toward the end of the forty-five-minute journey, it was a necessary distraction.

The relative motions being equally unpleasant, Coffey decided that the helicopter was marginally worse. On the corvette he could move around. Here, he was stuck between FNO Loh and Bob Herbert in a thinly cushioned bench designed for two. The pilot and Jelbart were in front of them. Herbert's wheelchair was in the small cargo space behind the backseat.

Herbert had contributed something else to the mission. His plan to gather intelligence about Jervis Darling.

For the first half of the journey, the plan had been in the forefront of Coffey's mind. For one thing, he was not sure it was a workable idea. But it was the only idea anyone had. That made it inevitable by default. For another, he was not sure it was a legal idea. But they were not going to court. Not yet. As Jelbart had said, the objective was to find the missing radioactive material. Pinning it on Darling could be done later.

Coffey also was not happy having to involve additional

outsiders in the operation. He did not doubt that the personnel of the Queensland North Rural Fire Brigade were
as brave as any soldier who ever shouldered a rifle. But
Jelbart admitted that the locals were fiercely loyal to Jervis
Darling. The magnate made generous donations to local
sports programs, environmental groups, municipal organizations, and charities. Since the reasons for the operation
were classified, the firefighters might not want to help spy
on their benefactor. And they could not afford to go
through channels. That would waste time and risk leaks.
This was going to have to be accomplished through tactful
persuasion. Bob Herbert could be persuasive, but tact was
not in his repertoire. Jelbart was a native, but he also
seemed to be a balls-ahead kind of guy. And Monica Loh
was both Asian and a woman. Exurban Australians were
cheerfully misogynistic as well as naturally suspicious of
all outsiders. But they were particularly wary of what
many called "the Asian Escalade." In less politically sensitive times it was known as "the Yellow Peril." The liberal soul of Lowell Coffey hated the term. Throughout the
Western world, it was applied primarily to the Japanese
before and during World War II. It was reborn when
China fell to Communism, and it grew in popularity with
the conflicts in Korea and Vietnam. To Australians, the
fear was not so much about the threat of military confrontation. It was the very real loss of jobs and economic
prosperity to all the nations of the Asian Pacific Rim.
Most Asian nations did not have the kind of compensation
packages that were available to Australian workers. A
company could hire twenty Taiwanese seamen or mill
workers for the price of three Australians. Many of these
workers toiled at home. But each year, hundreds of illegal
immigrants slipped into Australia along the nation's 7,813
miles of coastline. They went to work for industrial firms,
as fishermen, and in the food-processing industries. Most
of the money they made was sent home, doubling the hit
to the local economy. That made a considerable impact in
a nation of twenty million people.

The only diplomats on the team were Coffey and Ellsworth. Ellsworth had stayed behind to act as a liaison with other intelligence agencies. That left the burden on Coffey. Coffey, a man whose mind was being jostled as thoroughly as the rest of him.

The helicopter slipped over a ridge and dropped toward a white landing pad on top of a hill. As it settled down, Coffey decided that, in fact, he preferred the chopper to the corvette. The ride was a hell of a lot shorter. The chopper came to rest with the slightest bump. The pilot cut the rotor, and Jelbart jumped out. A man was approaching from along a dirt path. There was an observation tower some 400 yards behind him. While the pilot retrieved Herbert's wheelchair, FNO Loh and Coffey joined Jelbart. The Singaporean officer had been quiet and expressionless throughout the journey. Perhaps she felt uncomfortable being in Australia. Or she might have been focused on the mission. Or both. It could also be that after hanging around politicians and attorneys for his entire professional life, Coffey was unused to people who were silent when they had nothing to say.

Coffey waited by the helicopter until Herbert was in his wheelchair. Even without his chair, the intelligence chief was surprisingly mobile. His arms were thickly knotted with muscles. With remarkable ease, he could cross an aisle or hop onto a desk to assault someone on the other side. Those arms reminded Coffey of the climbing roots of a banyan tree. Herbert's strong fingers could probably dig holes in concrete. He swung unaided from the doorframe of the chopper into his chair. It was an inspiring thing to see.

The fire officer was nothing like Coffey had imagined. He had expected Paul Leyland to be a strapping and immaculate man. A *GQ* cowboy with outback trappings. He was not.

Paul Leyland was not especially presentable. His olive-green uniform was rumpled and spotted with perspiration on the collar, under the arms, and behind the knees. His skin was rash-red, not bronze. It looked like there were patches of fur stuck to his boot. He was well under six feet tall. He was not even wearing an outback shade hat. His bald head was bare and sweaty.

"I think we're going to be able to do business with this guy," Herbert said as they approached.

"What makes you say that?" Coffey asked.

"Two things. First, he smiled when he shook Officer Loh's hand," Herbert said.

"So? Maybe he just likes the ladies," Coffey suggested.

"Exactly," Herbert said. "He's not wearing a wedding band. He's up in his tree house most of the day. She'll be an asset."

"That's quite a leap of faith," Coffey said. "Jelbart said Leyland has a woman working for him."

"Yup," Herbert said. "That strengthens my case."

"How?"

"She's the only female firefighter in this department," Herbert told him. "He had to okay her being here. He likes having a woman around, *and* it doesn't matter if she's foreign. Which is my second point. It shows he's got an open and independent mind."

"I'm not signing off on any of that," Coffey said.

"Dinner at the 1789 in Georgetown says I'm right," Herbert replied.

"Does everything have to be a war with you?" Coffey protested.

"Not a war. Call it a dispute with hair on its chest. You in or out?" Herbert pressed.

"I'm in," Coffey said.

The men left the landing pad. They crossed damp grasses to where the others were standing. The group was brightly lighted in the glow of the footlights on the landing pad. Jelbart introduced them.

"I understand you're the offsider running the team," Leyland said as he shook Herbert's hand.

Coffey noticed that the captain did not smile. Herbert did, however. From the side of his mouth, at Coffey.

"Actually, Officer Loh and I will be conducting activities jointly," Herbert told him.

Both Jelbart and Loh looked at the intelligence chief. Loh was impassive. Jelbart seemed somewhat surprised. But he said nothing.

"I see," Leyland said. "So which of you is going to tell me exactly what these activities are? And would you like to go to the cabin to do it?" He pointed toward a small structure near the base of the tower. "It'll be getting pretty chilly out here in a few minutes. You might be more comfortable."

"We're a little squeezed for time," Herbert said. "And we won't be out here that long."

"All right," Leyland said. "What's on your mind?"

"Discretion, for one thing," Herbert said. "Nothing we are about to discuss can be repeated."

"I can keep a secret," Leyland said. "Just tell me one thing. Is what you want to do legal?"

"In theory, and if everything goes the way I hope," Herbert replied.

Leyland looked at him strangely. "That's like calling a match 'safe' until you strike it."

"Captain Leyland, I'm a solicitor," Coffey interjected. "The situation is equivalent to breaking down the door of a house that's on fire. Technically, you are trespassing. But by every other measure, it's the right thing to do."

"You burble like a solicitor," Leyland said. "So the answer is no?"

"The answer is that we are investigating a national security matter," Jelbart said.

"An international security issue," FNO Loh added.

"Correct," Jelbart agreed. "We can bat around the fine points of ethical versus legal law if you like. Or we can try to save a couple of million lives. Which will it be?"

Leyland looked at the group. "I'm out here to save lives. I'm listening, people."

"Thank you," Jelbart said.

"Captain, do you have any kind of personal or professional relationship with Jervis Darling?" Herbert asked.

"We trapshoot twice a week," Leyland said.

"That's fantastic," Coffey said.

"That was a joke," Leyland told him. "No. I have no personal or professional relationship with Mr. Darling. In fact, the only part of him I have ever seen is the arse end of his helicopter."

"What about firefighting?" Herbert asked.

"Our squad doesn't even *watch* his estate," Leyland said. "He has his own security and fire prevention service."

"So I've been told," Herbert said. "Still, I'm hoping there's a loophole somewhere. I need a reason to go into the estate."

"A reason to get on the property or in the house?" Leyland asked.

"In the house," Herbert said.

"You mean like asking to use the dunny?"

Coffey inferred from the context that *dunny* meant *lavatory*.

"No, it has to be somewhat more substantial than that," Herbert replied. "Assuming Mr. Darling is there, I need to be inside the mansion for about ten minutes while he is on the outside. Would you have a legal right to check the grounds for fire safety violations?"

"Only if there were a fire," Leyland said. "We have what's called the right of inquiry. We are allowed to investigate the cause of a blaze to make sure it doesn't happen again. But don't ask me to start a fire. It hasn't rained for two weeks. It could easily spread."

"We wouldn't ask you to do that," Jelbart said.

Coffey watched Herbert's expression go from hopeful to annoyed. Obviously, the intelligence chief thought he had his way in.

"Let me ask you this," Leyland said. "Is it necessary that you see Mr. Darling himself?"

"No. His presence is not required," Herbert said.

"He may not even be there," Jelbart pointed out.

"Then I have something that may work, though it's going to take a bush liar to sell it," Leyland said.

"We've got some of those," Herbert replied. "What's on your mind?"

"I'm thinking that Mr. Darling would rather deal with us than with a group that could really do him some damage," Leyland replied.

"Who?" Jelbart asked.

"Come with me," Leyland added. He started toward the tower. "I'm going to show you how to stamp your passport."

FORTY-FOUR

Washington, D.C.
Saturday, 7:31 A.M.

Matt Stoll was the only other person in the operations level when Paul Hood arrived. That was not unusual. It was a Saturday morning.

Hood came in on Saturday mornings now because he had nowhere else to go. He would get an update from Herbert or Coffey wherever he was. One thing on his to-do list was to call Daphne Connors and see if she was free that night. If he did not push himself, no one else would.

Stoll usually came in on weekends to write or try out software he did not get to use during the week. Unless there was a technology convention in town, the computer genius did not have an active social life. He had no interest in socializing with women who did not speak his language.

"She doesn't have to know gate propagation in high-res temporal resolution, though that would be heaven," he once said. "But she should know how many megabytes there are in her PC and what that means. If I have to explain it, then the sex is never very good."

Hood was not clear on who the sex was not good for or why. He was glad he was not on the need-to-know list.

As it turned out, the cherubic-looking Stoll was not here to tinker with a new program. He said he had gotten a call from Bob Herbert. The intelligence chief told him he needed something very specific.

"Bob wants me to rig him a Hoover," Stoll said in his joyless monotone. Excitement, whenever Stoll showed it, was in the speed his fingers moved on a keyboard. Right now he was typing very rapidly.

"Which is what?" Hood asked. He suddenly felt very sorry for any woman Stoll had ever met.

"A Hoover is a data vacuum," Stoll replied. "Bob wants to use his wheelchair computer as a drop zone for an external source."

"You mean we plug into Bob, and Bob plugs into something else," Hood said. "He serves as a conduit that allows us to read the 'something else.' "

"I couldn't have said it better," Stoll said.

"What is Bob planning to plug into?" Hood asked.

"Well, he called right before his chair was loaded into a helicopter, so he didn't go into a whole lot of detail," Stoll said. "Apparently, Bob's going to try to get into Jervis Darling's estate. He wants to jack into his phone system."

"Why? I thought we already hacked the Darling phone records."

"We did," Stoll said. "If he's using his own uplink for secure calls, they wouldn't show up on his public records. But if Bob plugs in directly, he's accessing the origin point of the calls. That will give him access to all the numbers in the telephone's memory."

"What if those numbers aren't programmed in?" Hood asked.

"Most phones retain the information somewhere," Stoll assured him. "The redial function usually stores ten to twenty numbers. It costs less to build a chip that eliminates numbers by attrition. They get scrolled from the system rather than erased. Most people don't know that."

"What about incoming calls?" Hood asked. "We need to ID them."

"If Darling's phone has caller ID or whatever the Australian equivalent is, those numbers will also be stored," Stoll said. "If he doesn't, we'll have to settle for the outgoing calls."

"Did Bob say how he intended to get access to Darling's private line?" Hood asked.

"For the record, it's not the line he needs to get access to," Stoll said. "It's the phone itself. Bob can't just splice into the fiber optics. That would put him outside the scrambler. Any data he got would be useless."

"I see. Okay. How does Bob plan to jack into the phone?"

"He didn't say," Stoll replied. "I'm sure Darling has an office phone with multiple lines. That would mean there's a data port. All Bob has to do is plug his computer into that. That will give us access."

"That's *all* Bob has to do," Hood said. "I'll give him a call."

"He said he was turning his phone off," Stoll told him. "He doesn't want it beeping while he's in with Darling. If it helps, Lowell told him the only legal risk would be invasion of privacy. Lowell is also pretty sure Darling would not press that issue. He said the reasons for the investigation would come out, and the publicity would be bad for Darling, even if he were innocent."

"The legal options are not what worries me," Hood said. "If Darling's into nuclear trafficking, he's probably also in bed with some ugly characters. They may not bother with lawyers."

"I don't blame them," Stoll said.

Hood scowled.

"I guess we could call Lowell to try to stop him," Stoll suggested.

"No," Hood said. "We need facts to support our theory, and this is probably the best way to get them. I take it Lowell is not going along."

"Right," Stoll said. "It was Bob, a fire warden, a lady officer from Singapore, and a koala."

"A koala? An animal?" Hood asked.

"Yeah. Search me what that's all about." Stoll smiled as he finished writing his program. "It's like the cast of the *Wizard of Oz*. And they're in Oz. Pretty ironic, don't you think?"

That it was. Right down to the big, blustering wizard spewing fire. Only this Oz was no dream.

Stoll activated the program. He ran a test on an Op-Center phone line just to make sure it was working. It functioned perfectly. They had all the numbers Lowell Coffey had phoned the day before he left. Hood looked away and ordered the list purged from Stoll's computer.

"I'll bet you didn't peek in the girls' locker room in high school, either," Stoll said.

"As a matter of fact, I didn't," Hood admitted. "I don't mind being a spy. I never liked being a voyeur."

"Interesting. We'll have to discuss the distinction," Stoll said.

"I can give it to you in two words," Hood said as he clapped a hand on Stoll's rounded shoulder. "National security."

"The voyeuristic instinct is a doorway to intelligence, and intelligence is the spy's basic unit of data," Stoll said. "Unless you look, how do you know Lowell's not working for the Chinese or some terrorist group?"

"He believes too strongly in the rule of law. Tell me, do you routinely check on all of us?" Hood asked.

"Nope. I'm not a voyeur. I was only asking you."

Hood felt like kicking himself. He should have known better than to take one of Matt Stoll's infamous buggy rides. They took you slowly around the park without getting you anywhere. Hood did not have the time or focus for this kind of discussion.

Stoll told Hood he would not know anything else until data started coming in. Hood asked his computer wizard to let him know the moment that happened, then left to go to his office. It was disconcerting to see the corridors so empty. It was like a manifestation of his own hollow life. Maybe that was something Bob Herbert had learned after losing his wife. You mourn, but you don't sit still. You fill that empty hall with anything you can. Even if it isn't necessarily good for you.

Of course, there's a difference between recreational and reckless, Hood thought. He was certain that Bob had considered the risks. He was also sure of something else. Herbert was probably enjoying the hell out of them. Hood only hoped that the intelligence chief was aware of the greatest danger.

Complacency.

A quiet, seaside estate was not war-ravaged Beirut or a skinhead stronghold in Germany. Those were the kinds of environments where Herbert was accustomed to waging war. They were unstable regions where instinct kept the mind and body on high alert.

Hood had to trust that his colleague knew what he was getting into. He also hoped that Herbert would come up with something else. Something that quickly sketched plans did not always allow.

An exit strategy.

FORTY-FIVE

The Great Barrier Reef
Saturday, 10:03 P.M.

He hurt.

Everywhere.

Peter Kannaday suffered pain with every breath. It was dull and warm and it was everywhere. He felt it spiritually as well as physically. The captain lay on his bed in a bruised heap, belly down, face to the wall. He had slept on and off since Hawke's thugs had brought him here. Kannaday's eyes and mouth were open, but it was dark. He did not see, nor speak, nor swallow. His stomach was rumbling from hunger. His tongue was swollen and dry. The only liquid he had tasted lately was his own blood.

Sometime during the night Kannaday had roused himself briefly to see if the door was locked. It was not. He checked to see if his gun was still there. It was not. He was free to walk the deck, broken and humiliated but unarmed. He would probably be able to radio Jervis Darling because he was free and he was still the captain. But what would he say? That he had been minimized, reduced to a figurehead? That he had not been able to enforce his authority or hold what was his? That he had no idea what to expect or what to do?

Kannaday closed his mouth. Even his neck muscles hurt. He must have strained them when he struggled with the men who were holding him. He had to get past the pain and think. It was clear that Hawke would not kill him. He wanted Kannaday as a buffer between himself and the law. But Kannaday had no idea what Darling might do. Darling did not like dealing with weak men. Kannaday would be kept around no longer than necessary.

Then he would be dismissed or, more likely, eliminated. Darling was a man of absolutes.

From the slow rocking of the swells, Kannaday could tell that they were close to shore. No doubt Hawke had reported back to the cove and was now following their cruising course along the Great Barrier Reef. Kannaday had time to act, but not a lot.

Kannaday forced himself to move. He got his arms under him and pushed up. Slowly. His upper arms trembled as he worked himself into a sitting position. He eased his back against the wall at the side of the bed. The solid support felt good. His head throbbed as blood fought to reach it. He closed his eyes and inhaled deeply. Miraculously, it did not feel as if any ribs were broken. He flexed his fingers. They were swollen. Maybe he had punched someone. He could not remember. The last thing he remembered clearly was running down the stairs. That moment was so immediate he felt as though he could go back there. Do things differently.

But it would still come out the same, Kannaday realized. Unlike Hawke, he had been predictable. On top of that, there was an unusual dynamic. Hawke was not after something that Kannaday had. He wanted to preserve the hierarchy exactly as it was. But with privileges. And he had succeeded. The fact that the rest of the crew had not come down to check on him was telling. If the cook had come by, Kannaday did not hear him. But he doubted it. Either the crew had been told to stay away or did so from fear.

Kannaday's body was beginning to accept the pain as a fact of life. It felt as though he had strained every muscle in his arms, torso, and neck. It was that kind of taut, deep-muscle ache. Kannaday knew that the more he moved, the more it would hurt. But he had no choice. He had to get out of here. Somehow, he had to take charge.

The captain waited another few minutes before trying to move again. He shifted to the edge of the bed and put his feet on the floor. He rose slowly. Most of the damage had been done north of Kannaday's waist. His legs felt all right. He felt a little light-headed as he took a few shuffling steps toward the door. The sensation passed after a few moments. It was not pleasant, but Kannaday had his footing. What he did not have was something just as important.

A plan.

Kannaday reached the door. He turned and leaned his back against it. Standing in the dark, he pondered his next steps, both literally and figuratively. As he did, something occurred to him. The events that had brought Kannaday here could be useful. After all, he made the same mistake twice. He had acted just as Hawke had expected him to.

Hawke would probably expect him to do it again. Especially after the beating he had taken.

Kannaday went back to the bed. He sat down. He tried not to think the way he usually did, as if he were going down a checklist of things to do before leaving port.

He let himself contemplate all the scenarios that would surprise Hawke. And Darling, for that matter. Everything from setting fire to the *Hosannah* to taking the dinghy and vanishing into the night sea.

How far are you willing to go? he asked himself.

More important than that, Kannaday needed to find out exactly what he wanted.

Kannaday was doing the job he had agreed to do. The crew had suffered a setback because of the sampan attack. Not a dramatic one, but Darling's reputation for absolute efficiency had been tarnished. Darling would be able to absorb the blow. The gentry knew how to talk to the gentry. He would explain it all to Mahathir bin Dahman. Darling would blame it on the serfs. But Darling would also want to make the head villain pay. Darling had known precisely how Hawke would respond to a threat or challenge. He had sent Kannaday back to be humiliated.

Kannaday realized that he was not interested in recapturing Darling's respect. He wanted to hurt Hawke, and he wanted to hurt Darling. The question was how to do that without hurting himself.

Or was it?

There is flaw in your thinking, he admonished himself. The question itself made him vulnerable. It cost him the advantage of surprise.

The question itself held the answer.

FORTY-SIX

Cairns, Australia
Saturday, 10:04 P.M.

They did things differently in Australia.

Bob Herbert had expected to be at the Darling estate by eight P.M. at the latest.

All they had to do was set the trap around back, go to the front, and knock on the door. But Leyland and Jelbart were not so impulsive. They insisted on taking several passes over the 500-acre estate in the helicopter. They used fire brigade night-vision goggles to study the terrain. They wanted to know where the security posts were and where there were places that could serve as emergency exits. The property was heavily fenced to keep out wild hare and deer. However, they found two spots where the bait could credibly be set inside. The security personnel would know those spots and probably go right to them. Jelbart wanted to time how long it would take for the teams to drive their golf carts to and from that area. Ordinarily, Herbert would have admired their thoroughness. But potential nuclear terrorists were on the run. He wanted to capture them. Herbert said so after they made their second slow pass over the estate. A pass they would explain to Jervis Darling or his security chief when they came to visit.

"We won't be able to capture anyone if our ruse is exposed," Jelbart pointed out. "*We'll* be the ones being investigated."

FNO Loh was sitting between Coffey and Herbert in the backseat. "I cannot believe that your government would discipline you. We are pursuing a reasonable lead in a case of some urgency," she said.

"The government would not bother us if we were pursuing the lead in a reasonable fashion," Jelbart replied. "We are not. We are invading a citizen's privacy. The law is very specific about things like that."

"Specific and constipated," Herbert said. "Remind me to quote the law to whatever guys are looking to slip nuclear material into populated cities and poison our water supplies."

"We're not certain that's the case," Coffey said.

"Certain enough to make me want to kick Darling's ass for quick answers," Herbert replied.

"And then what? If we become what we behold, then all of civilization goes to hell," Jelbart pointed out.

"If we don't, hell will come to civilization," Herbert shot back. "Don't take this personally, Jelbart, but I'm getting really sick of our leaders *re*acting instead of taking preventative action. Am I the only one who realizes that this isn't the twentieth century anymore?"

"What do you mean?" Coffey asked.

"Somehow, over the last forty or so years, the Western world evolved this screwed-up coddling mentality toward killers and terrorists. That *is* going to destroy us," Herbert said.

"This isn't about coddling killers; it's about individual voices and dignity," Coffey said. "And for the record, it came from us. From America. It came after the Vietnam War protests and civil rights movement proved effective. It came when police were required to read criminals their rights. Now everyone on earth wants a share of humanity. And I don't think that's a bad thing."

"That may have worked in the sixties and seventies, but it's a luxury we can no longer afford," Herbert said. "We don't stop eating tuna because a few dolphins get snared."

"What does that have to do with anything?" Coffey asked.

"Yes, what are you suggesting, Mr. Herbert?" Jelbart asked.

"That we hunt down bad guys aggressively," Herbert

said. He was yelling so that they could hear him over the rotor. But it felt good to yell because he was angry. "Once in a while you may grab an innocent. You apologize and make amends. But that's how you protect the majority of the people."

"So you think that we should just do away with human rights?" Jelbart pressed.

"No!" Herbert shouted. "The actions can be selective. I suggest we grant exceptional authority in emergency circumstances, like these. We have fanatical racists and radical sociopaths with access to nuclear fuel. We've got mass murderers in our high schools. When I was a kid, juvenile delinquents packed zip guns and switchblades. Once in a while they flashed their weapons, and once in a really rare while they used them. Usually on other hoodlums. Usually shitting their pants when they did. Now we have kids packing AK-47s and attitude. They're cool killers, Warrant Officer. You're trying to play soccer or football or whatever the hell you call it against a team that disregards referees, fouls, out-of-bounds lines, clocks, and rules. I'm telling you that if we don't identify and neutralize them, the game is over. With us the losers."

The cockpit was silent for a long moment. After making a final pass over the estate, Leyland spoke.

"I see a tree we can use," he said. He made another pass and showed it to the others.

"Maybe we should just hang ourselves from it," Herbert said. "Save Darling or whoever is behind this plot further inconvenience."

"You know, Mr. Herbert, I sympathize with you," Captain Leyland said as the helicopter turned back to the landing pad. "I look at every camper or tourist as a potential arsonist. But that does not make them one. Even if they're smoking or carrying matches, I can't go hosing them down. That's the price we pay for freedom. If we surrender that, we still won't have security. Not really. We will only have less freedom."

"Only if you're extreme about it," Herbert told him. "Look, we already have the fire. We have a guy who picnicked at the spot that's burning. He has matches. We should have the ability to sit him down and ask him questions before he can wash away the smell of the smoke."

"Obviously we agree with that to some extent, or we wouldn't be doing this," Jelbart said.

"We're doing it by sneaking in the back door," Herbert said. "I prefer a more direct approach."

"Like beating it out of him?" Coffey asked.

"No, like point-blank asking the guy what the hell's going on," Herbert said. "And if his answers don't match the facts we do know, we take him in. Ask him again. And again."

"The legal and political fallout would be disastrous," Coffey said.

"Only if we're wrong," Herbert said.

"That's just it," Coffey said. "You could still be right and lose. Those confessions wouldn't be allowed in court. It would cost the state tens of millions of dollars to defend against a wrongful arrest lawsuit, to name just one, and you still wouldn't have your man."

"Then he has an accident, as his wife did," FNO Loh suggested.

"Bingo!" Herbert said. "I like your style. That's the price of protecting the twenty-first-century world."

The debate ended as the Bell chopper set down. Leyland unfolded a detailed map of the area. He showed Jelbart the road to the area of trees they could use to set the trap. Herbert half-listened while Loh unloaded the wheelchair and helped him from the chopper. He was sick of talk in general. While they were crisscrossing the estate, radioactive material could be making its way to a terrorist factory. Or it could already be en route to Washington or London or Sydney. How stupid would they feel looking for perimeter access if a dirty bomb was built with this material and a few sticks of TNT? How would they live with themselves if 10,000 people died from radiation poisoning? Herbert had no interest in finding out. He would rather risk the wrath of Jervis Darling.

When Leyland and Jelbart had agreed on a place to

carry out the first part of the operation, the brigade commander summoned the gangly kid named Spider. The young firefighter was going to help Jelbart with the insertion. Then he would return to his post. That was already one more person than Herbert wanted to be involved.

When Herbert worked for the CIA, the objective was to streamline operations, not to pad them.

It was well after ten P.M. when Herbert, Leyland, and Loh slipped into the brigade's Humvee and headed toward the front entrance to Darling's estate. Loh had borrowed civilian clothes from Eva. They were a little roomy, but they would serve their purpose. As the trio left, Jelbart and Spider also departed. They drove out in a jeep to the tree they had selected in the flyover. A tree that was on public land but overhung the wall of the Darling estate.

The tree where they would take Little Maluka, the mascot of the Queensland North Rural Fire Brigade, to play his part in the deception.

FORTY-SEVEN

Washington, D.C.
Saturday, 8:47 A.M.

Hood was in his office, waiting for nine A.M. to arrive. That was when he planned to call Daphne Connors at home. While he waited, his phone beeped. He hoped it was the advertising executive. If Daphne called him, that would make his life a whole lot easier.

It was not Daphne Connors. It was Lowell Coffey.

"Well, we just sent two teams on a very unusual mission," Coffey said.

"Where are you?"

"At the observation post cabin of the Queensland North Rural Fire Brigade," Coffey said. "We have a new member of the team."

"Oh?"

"A koala that was burned in a fire," Coffey said. "They're sneaking him into the Darling compound through a back entrance. Then the fire captain, FNO Loh, and Bob are going in the front door to try to get him back."

"Who are Loh and Bob supposed to be?" Hood asked.

"Volunteers with the local International Wildlife Education and Conservation Group," Coffey told him. "They're going to position the koala as their local poster child. Tell Darling what bad press it would be if the little escapee was hurt on his property. While they're inside, Bob is going to try to split from the others to get to Darling's phone."

"Has he got a chance?"

"You know I would never bet against Bob," Coffey

replied. "But I have to admit he's got me worried. Bob's pretty pissed off."

"About what?"

"He was getting pretty hot about Darling, about the whole idea of a guy in our sights being innocent until proven otherwise," Coffey said.

"Hold on," Hood said. "I'm going to conference in Liz Gordon."

"Paul, I don't know if it's *that* serious—"

"Exactly," Hood said. "Let's talk to someone who will."

Hood put Coffey on hold and punched in Liz's home phone. She was there, obviously still asleep. The Op-Center psychiatrist did the Washington bar scene on Friday nights. Not to party, she swore, but to research a book she was writing on the dynamics of human flirtation. Maybe that was true. But Liz certainly sounded hungover when she answered the phone. She recovered quickly when she heard it was Paul Hood on the line. He brought her up to date and then plugged Coffey into the conversation.

"Lowell, Liz is on the line," Hood said.

"Good morning," Liz said groggily.

"Late evening here," Coffey said. "But good morning."

"Right. Lowell, did Bob seem unstable, impatient?" she asked.

"He seemed fed up," Coffey replied. "He was disgusted out of proportion with the situation we're facing."

"How bad did he lay into you personally?" Liz asked.

"Excuse me?"

"Did he insult you, criticize you, work you over?" Liz asked. "Putting it bluntly, Lowell, is this payback?"

"No!" Coffey said. "Even if he had, I can be objective. Give me credit."

"Not my job," she said. "Was there any physical manifestation? Was he pounding things, playing repetitively with anything on his wheelchair?"

"He was in the backseat of the helicopter," Coffey said. "I couldn't really see."

"Paul, was he airlifted from the Beirut rubble?" Liz asked.

"I believe he was," Hood said.

"This could be subconscious motor memory, the chopper sound and vibration triggering unresolved hostility," she said. "Bottom line, Lowell. Do you think Bob is dangerous?"

"That may be an overstatement," Coffey replied. "I mean, you want a guy in that position to be aggressive."

"So the answer is no," she said.

"The answer is no, he was sounding *almost* bloodthirsty," Coffey replied. "Not *quite,* but getting there."

"But he was not violent," she said.

Coffey said he was not.

"Paul," Liz said, "were there any reports of Bob overreacting on his last field operation? In Germany, I think it was?"

"It was Germany, and no, there was nothing," Hood said.

"What this sounds like is displacement," Liz said. "Shifting anger or desire from an original target to a more convenient one. Possibly triggered by the chopper, possibly by delayed post-traumatic stress. All of it tied together by Bob's natural frustration with the system and possibly some jet lag. It's difficult to ascribe exact causes without talking to Bob. But it doesn't sound as if he'll flip out on you. People who experience transference usually peak at the onset of symptoms. They're looking to dump. Something triggers it, and off they go."

"So we've seen the worst of it," Hood said.

"Probably," Liz replied. "Unless someone sprays lighter fluid on the fire. Is that likely to happen, Lowell?"

"From everything I've heard, Jervis Darling is a pretty cool fellow," Coffey said.

"What about the people Bob is traveling with?" Liz asked.

"Leyland is pretty lighthearted, and Loh is very quiet and serious, almost catatonic," he replied.

"That should help keep him in balance," Liz said.

"So we're okay to let this play out," Hood said.

"Given that nothing is ever guaranteed, I'd say yes," Liz told him. "I don't see him blowing."

"Not even if they're stonewalled?" Hood asked.

"Bob has a self-imposed objective, which is to get data from a telephone," Liz said. "If he fails to do this, he'll be angry. But his training will probably keep him in check. He will regroup and try again. The real danger is if he is personally exposed by Jervis Darling."

"As a spy and not an animal welfare worker," Hood said.

"That's correct," Liz said. "The assumed identity gives him a way of keeping his real feelings inside. If that's stripped away, he might become the person Lowell described. It's part of the fight-or-flight mechanism, and Bob Herbert is not prone to flight."

That was the truth. Hood had never been a big believer in psychiatry. But if he peeled away the jargon, the things Liz said made sense.

Hood thanked her and let her go back to sleep. Then he told Coffey that he was going to let this play out. Whether or not they liked Herbert's inquisitorial manner, there was no avoiding the bottom line. While there was still a trail to follow, they had to find out who made it and why.

Hood sighed. He no longer felt like calling Daphne. Until Herbert was safe, he did not want any distractions.

At least that was what Hood told himself.

FORTY-EIGHT

Cairns, Australia
Saturday, 10:49 P.M.

Monica Loh was accustomed to the dangers she faced at sea. There were storms, collisions, hazardous rescues, even mines dropped by insurgents from her country and its neighbors. Disasters were rare, but she and her crew were vigilant and confident.

The naval officer was alert but extremely uneasy as they pulled up to the massive front gate of the Darling estate. She was going into what the Republic of Singapore Navy classified as a search-and-discover mission. Yet she did not have all the information she needed to feel confident. Loh was posing as an animal welfare worker visiting from Singapore. Beyond that, they had not come up with much of a story for her. Nor did she have a clear idea what she was supposed to do, other than to go out back with Captain Leyland and look for the koala. Leyland expected they would find the animal pretty much where Jelbart and Spider left him. The koala was apparently rather sedentary. Loh also did not know what to expect from Jervis Darling or this man Bob Herbert. The naval officer admired Herbert's ideas and his courage. But he also seemed edgy and impatient. Would Darling notice that? If so, at the very least, their mission would fail. Loh had not even considered the ramifications if she were exposed. She had not sought authorization for this mission because it would be classified as a shore-based operation. That fell under the jurisdiction of the Defence Executive Command. It would have taken time to second her to the DEC, if the commanding officer would have permitted that at all. The group was highly protective of all land-based activities.

Leyland pulled up to the gate and lowered the window. He looked around for an intercom but saw none. The reason quickly became apparent. Darling did not need one. A jeep pulled up behind the Humvee. Spotlights were turned on the Humvee. Two men got out. Both were armed with Uzis. One guard approached the driver's side of the Humvee. He shined a flashlight on Captain Leyland. The other guard walked slowly around the Humvee. He checked on top and below, probably searching for explosives.

"What are you doing here?" the guard asked.

"I'm Captain Leyland with the Queensland North Rural Fire Brigade," Leyland told him. He took a leather holder from his shirt pocket and showed the security guard his badge. "These are volunteers with International Wildlife Education and Conservation Group. We're searching for an injured koala. We believe we spotted him from the air, out on the property."

"That was your chopper sailing over before?" the guard asked.

"Yes. Sorry for the disturbance. But it's rather important that we find the animal, and the night *is* growing a beard."

The guard shone his flashlight on the occupants. Then he stepped from the Humvee and pulled a radio from his belt. He turned his back on the occupants as he spoke quietly into the mouthpiece. After a short conversation, he came back to the window.

"The groundskeeper said he'll go and look for it," the guard told him. "You can wait here or—"

"I'm afraid that doesn't work for us," Leyland said. "The koala is ill, you see. It may spread sickness to other animals on the estate. Dogs, for example. Mr. Darling's daughter *plays* with those animals."

"Are you suggesting that we send a patrol out to shoot the thing?" the guard asked.

"I am not suggesting that," Leyland snapped. "We do

not want him shot. We want him reacquired for study. That is why these people are here. This is very important."

The guard considered this for a moment. He stepped away again and spoke into the radio. When he was finished, the guard informed Leyland that Mr. Darling's personal assistant Andrew Graham would meet them at the front door. Then the guard walked to the gate, swiped a card through a slot on the door, and the gate slid aside. Leyland drove through, following the winding, cobblestone drive toward the front of the mansion.

From the sky, Monica Loh had neither been surprised nor impressed by the size of the home. From the deck of her patrol ship she had seen many impressive oceanside and cliff-top estates. This was just one more. As they pulled up to the columned entrance, however, she felt as if she were in the presence of something oddly outdated and supine. Loh was used to oversized ships and aircraft, but they all moved. People worked on and around them. There was a sense of life to them. Not this place. Even the man who came to meet them was strangely inanimate. He was a thin man dressed in a charcoal sweater and black slacks. His actions were stiff, strangely guarded. One would naturally be wary of uninvited guests showing up this late at night. But that should manifest itself as impatience, annoyance. There was none of that in this man.

Loh and Leyland got out of the Humvee. The captain pulled Herbert's wheelchair from the back and opened it. He stood beside Loh while the intelligence chief swung into the leather seat.

"My sick koala's got more life than this pie-eater," Leyland said as the man approached them.

"I was just thinking that," Loh said.

"He's being watched," Herbert said quietly.

"By whom?" Leyland asked.

"I'm not sure," Herbert replied. He moved between the other two and nodded toward the top of one of the columns. "A small security camera is moving right along with him."

"I can't believe the big man himself would be doing that," Leyland whispered back.

"I can, if he's hiding something," Herbert replied.

The trio fell silent as the man neared. They could see him clearly in the clean white glow of spotlights clustered two at either end of the facade. He was a tallish, round-faced, dark-skinned man. In soft, overenunciated tones he introduced himself as Andrew Graham. He said he would show the others to the back, though he made an unhappy face as he looked down at Herbert.

"With respect, sir, it is all grass back there," he said to Herbert. "It might be difficult for you to navigate. Would you care to wait inside?"

Herbert looked at Loh. "What do you think? Can you handle Little Maluka without me?"

"I handled an orphaned Komodo dragon in Bandung," she said. "I think I can manage."

Herbert smiled. "If you need help, beep me."

Loh said the same, but with a look.

Andrew contacted the groundskeeper via cell phone. The burly young man arrived several moments later in a golf cart. While he drove Leyland and Loh around the side of the estate, Andrew helped Herbert up the short flight of steps into the mansion.

Loh was a veteran naval officer. Her bearings were surest when she was on the sea and, perhaps more important, when she was part of a unit.

Her feeling of uneasiness increased dramatically as their key player went into the house alone.

FORTY-NINE

Cairns, Australia
Saturday, 11:12 P.M.

The first thing Herbert did as he entered the long, marble-rich foyer was to look for security devices. There were motion detectors in the corners and a keypad beside the door. Obviously, they were not on now. There were no cameras here, only outside. That was good. If he were left alone, chances were good he could move about without being spied upon. Andrew released the chair as soon as they were inside. He extended a hand toward the living room. Both men began moving in that direction. Herbert felt as though he were entering a museum. It was absolutely quiet, save for the squeak of his wheels and the secretary's shoes. Large paintings and statues were barely visible in the vast room ahead. Herbert could barely make out other rooms in the dim light beyond.

"May I get you a beverage?" Andrew asked. "Sparkling water or something a bit more potent?"

"Thank you, no," Herbert replied.

"A snack, then?"

"Nothing, thanks," Herbert said. "I was wondering, though, if I might impose on you. Is there a phone line I can use? I'd like to send an E-mail to my office in Washington. I've been out on this search all night and need to get some information over to them."

"Of course," Andrew said. "That is not a problem."

"I'll charge the call to my personal account. It won't cost Mr. Darling anything."

"I'm certain it would be all right if you called your office directly," Andrew said.

"That's very kind," Herbert replied.

They entered the living room, and Andrew led the way to a study on the left. There were shelves filled with books and tools such as magnifying glasses, whisk brooms, and computer diskettes. The secretary gestured toward a large mahogany desk. There was a phone tucked among dozens of shoe boxes, cigar boxes, and plastic bags.

"Mr. Darling uses that unit for his laptop," Andrew said. "You can plug into the data port in back."

"Thank you very much," Herbert said.

"Not at all."

Herbert glanced around. "It looks to me like Mr. Darling does a little scientific work."

"He studies and collects fossils," Andrew said.

"Fascinating," Herbert replied. "I also thought I saw the dome of an observatory driving up."

"Perhaps you did," Andrew said.

"Is Mr. Darling also a stargazer?"

"Mr. Darling has many interests," Andrew replied as he turned toward the door.

The intelligence chief already knew that there was an observatory from the dossier on Darling. He was simply curious how forthcoming Andrew would be. The answer was: not very.

"Well, thank Mr. Darling for me," Herbert said.

"I shall," Andrew said as he left the room. He did not shut the door.

Herbert booted his computer as he moved himself to the near side of the desk. His back was to the door as he raised the armrest on the left side of his chair and unwound the cable tucked inside. He plugged that into the back of his computer and into the data port on Darling's telephone. If the magnate did hobby-related research in here, chances were good he took business calls here as well.

Herbert jacked in the six-foot cord and keyed the number Matt Stoll had given him. The link was established quickly through the small, slender antenna on the top right of the wheelchair. The antenna was attached to a booster on the back of the chair. Unlike standard cell phones, it could process high-speed transmissions. Herbert watched on his computer as it began searching Darling's telephone for the number log.

"That is quite a machine," said a voice from behind.

The voice was big and carried a mild Australian accent. Herbert did not have to see the speaker to know who it was. The intelligence agent smiled.

"It's a pretty standard Dell laptop," Herbert replied.

Darling smiled. "I was not referring to the computer."

"I know," Herbert replied. "Good evening, Mr. Darling."

"Good evening." Darling walked briskly toward Herbert. He was wearing a gray sweat suit that said Cairns Yacht Club across the chest. His eyes remained fixed on the chair. "Obviously custom made."

"Yes," Herbert said. "Designed by me and built by the same people who made FDR his chair."

The men shook hands. "And you would be whom?"

"R. Clayton Herbert," Herbert replied with a smile. Inside, though, he was anxious. He was also annoyed at himself. He did not want to give his full name if he did not have to. Darling could find out whom he worked for. But he also did not want Loh or Leyland calling him Bob after telling Darling that he was someone else. He should have given them a heads-up. It was one of those details you occasionally forgot when working with outsiders.

"Andrew said you wanted to send some E-mails," Darling said. "I don't want to keep you from that."

"It can wait," Herbert assured him.

The computer was still downloading as they spoke. Stoll had told him that once the file was found, it would take only a few seconds to snare the numbers. First, however, it had to make its way through whatever phone software might be piled in front of the log. Speed-dialing, voice-mail programs, call-forwarding, all of that. The search could take anywhere from a few seconds to several minutes. Stoll also said the computer would chime twice when it found what it was looking for. He would explain that to Darling as a reminder of some kind.

"In that case, I'd love to hear about your work with wildlife," Darling said. "You're a volunteer, I presume?"

"Yes," Herbert replied. "Actually, I'm here on a holiday. I was called into this search by my friend Monica. She's involved with IWEC in Singapore."

"I see. You're American, I gather," Darling said.

"Mississippi born," Herbert replied. "I live outside of Washington, D.C., now."

"Are you in government?"

"Personal security," Herbert said.

"Fascinating field," Darling said. "What do you think of the security we have at this estate?"

"From the little bit I've seen, it's pretty impressive," Herbert said. "You've got sentries and surveillance outside, motion detectors inside. It's a difficult combination to beat."

"Touch wood, no one has," Darling replied. He leaned forward slightly, squinting. "You appear to have everything you need for personal security *and* comfort. Your chair has a cell phone, a computer, what appears to be a satellite uplink, a joystick steering mechanism, and even cruise control, if I'm reading the joystick base correctly?"

"Yes," Herbert smiled. "I can do five miles per hour on the open sidewalk. They disconnect that function when I participate in marathons."

"Do they really?" Darling laughed.

"They do," Herbert said. The insincerity of this conversation was killing him. He wished Darling would get a phone call or something.

"Fascinating. You wouldn't think five miles an hour would be a threat to anyone."

"It isn't about the speed," Herbert said. "It's the idea of an assist. A marathon is supposed to be about physical endurance."

"Have you ever won one, Mr. Herbert?"

"I've never lost," Herbert replied.

Darling grinned. "I like that."

Where the hell is that chime? Herbert wondered.

Darling walked back behind the chair. "I'm curious, Mr. Herbert. That's a Ku-band uplink on the back of your chair."

"That's right," Herbert said. Alarms began ringing inside his head. This was not good.

"Why do you need an antenna to send E-mail?"

"I don't," Herbert replied.

Darling bent slightly to get a better look at the box. "But I notice the light on the power box is lit."

"Is it?"

"You didn't know?"

"That must have been from earlier, at the fire outpost," Herbert said. "I was downloading data."

"No, that couldn't be," Darling said. "It was not on when you arrived."

The outside security camera, Herbert realized with a jolt. He was watching their arrival.

"I must have turned it on by accident," Herbert said, smiling again. His soul ached as he reached behind the wheelchair and shut the antenna off. That cut the link to Op-Center. He unplugged the cable from Darling's telephone. He shut the computer, which would erase Matt Stoll's program. There would be no evidence it had ever existed.

Unfortunately, the computer still had not pinged. That meant none of the data had been downloaded from the telephone. This whole enterprise had been a freaking waste of time. Or worse, it could hurt them if Darling suspected that they were here for something other than a stray koala. Herbert had had a choice to make. He had made it.

Darling came back around the front of the wheelchair. He folded his arms again and paced back and forth. Jervis Darling suddenly looked as impatient as Bob Herbert felt.

"You know, R. Clayton Herbert," Darling said, "when people show up at odd hours for unusual reasons, it is typically a reporter hoping to get a story or a business rival trying to collect information. What is your reason, Mr. Herbert?"

"Actually, Mr. Darling, my reason is much more serious than nailing a story about you," Herbert said.

"Ah." Darling stopped pacing. He regarded Herbert. "You have the floor. And my attention."

Herbert hesitated. He was about to put himself, FNO

Loh, and Captain Leyland in jeopardy. Their careers, possibly their lives could be ruined. He had the right to do that to himself but not to the others. And what would he gain? Darling would not give him information. If Darling were guilty, talking might cause him to send his operatives deep underground. Or it might cause him to get angry and expose himself. Or it might cause him to have the lot of them shot for trespassing. There was no way of knowing.

Screw it, Herbert thought. He had come here to do a job. That job was to collect information and by so doing, save lives. The primary method had failed. Herbert was obligated to try another. Besides, when pressed, Darling might inadvertently answer one critical question: whether or not he was guilty.

"Mr. Darling, I honestly don't know jack-shit about animals," Herbert said. "I don't even like them much. Though there are some creatures I like even less. I do work in security, however. I won't tell you who employs me or how I know this. But here's the bottom line. Nuclear materials are missing from a radioactive waste site, and one leg of the trail leads here."

Darling did not react. Which, in a way, was a reaction. He did not ask what that statement had to do with him.

"No comment?" Herbert asked.

"Were you jacking into my telephone system in an effort to spy on me?" Darling asked.

"I was," Herbert admitted.

Darling looked down slowly. His expression was blank. He walked over to the phone and removed the unit from the desk. His slippered feet rubbed the hardwood floors of the study as he made his way to the door.

"Please show yourself out," Darling said over a very rigid shoulder. "Immediately."

"You're not calling the police?" Herbert asked.

Darling stopped in the doorway and turned. "Why bother? I don't know what data you hoped to glean from this telephone, but it is simply an estate intercom."

Herbert said nothing. That explained why his laptop did not *ping*. The phone had no numbers in memory.

"Do we have any other business?" Darling asked.

"Yeah," Herbert said. "I've got a suggestion for you. I know more than I just told you. So do the people I work with. We're going to get you and everyone you work with. My suggestion is that you cooperate with us."

"It's time for you to leave, Mr. Herbert," Darling said. "You are a man rich with suspicion, not knowledge."

"And you're a man with zero conscience," Herbert said angrily. "You and your associate Mahathir bin Dahman."

That was it. Bob Herbert had just played the only name he knew, the only other information he possessed. He hoped it was enough to rattle Darling into doing something careless or impulsive, such as attacking him so the fire chief could have him arrested. Or spitting out additional information in a rage. Or even better, cooperating.

It did not.

"Mr. bin Dahman is indeed an associate," Darling replied affably. "I'm lucky to have a partner of his local and international standing. And you are a sad, flailing fellow, R. Clayton Herbert." That was the last thing Darling said before he left the room.

Herbert wanted to punch something. Hard. Jervis Darling was guilty as Judas F. Iscariot. By not calling the police he had proved that to Herbert. But the impromptu interrogation had backfired. Herbert had gambled and lost, because now Darling was on guard. He could send his people into hiding, leaving Herbert without the two things Op-Center needed.

One was proof.

The other was the missing radioactive materials.

FIFTY

Cairns, Australia
Saturday, 11:27 P.M.

Jervis Darling returned to his bedroom on the second floor. He encountered Andrew on the way and told him to make certain Mr. Herbert left the house and that the others left the grounds as soon as they found their koala. Darling did not doubt the animal was there. They would have made certain of that before coming to the door.

Darling quietly shut the door and went to the back, to a large dressing room. He was numb and furious at the same time. The silence weighed thick and heavy in his ears. Darling sat at the restored Louis XVI desk and rang his nephew. He pulled over the only telephone in the mansion that had the number of the *Hosannah* in memory. He punched in his personal code, 525, to obtain a dial tone. Obtained by bin Dahman from the Russian air force, the secure phone was named the *konsulstvo*, or the "consulate." It was the secure phone in use at Russian embassies around the world. The *konsulstvo* was a large, square unit with a computer-style keypad on the top and a receiver on the side. The keypad was for writing codes. Hawke had done that before sailing.

"We rescued someone from the sampan."

Nothing the American had said after that really registered. Darling's answers had come from some independent, automatic-functioning part of his brain. Kannaday and Hawke had done more than suffer a setback in the Celebes Sea. They had permitted a security breach that led an investigator here. More than one, probably. Darling suspected that the woman who had come with them was with the Singaporean navy. Now that he thought about it, she had that stiff-necked, feet-wide-apart posture of a sea-man.

An American and a Singaporean. With Australian officials probably hanging to the rear because they did not want to tangle with Jervis Darling. Not until they had evidence. It made sense. Fortunately for Darling, whatever Mr. Herbert was doing at the study telephone would have netted him nothing. Not R. Clayton Herbert nor the people he worked for, whoever they were. That did not even matter. Any group ferreting around in Darling business was unwelcome. He would find out who they were, and they would be stopped. First, however, Darling had to make sure there was nothing to find. Starting with the *Hosannah.*

As Darling input the yacht's number, he burned inside. He wanted to strike out in all directions simultaneously. He was angry at Kannaday and Hawke. Their ineffectiveness caused this security breach. He would deal with Kannaday now, Hawke later. He also wanted to punish Herbert for invading his home. Darling would find a way to punch a hole in his life. And he would end the career of the fire captain who had assisted Herbert. They had not paid their dues on the world stage. Darling would not allow these wage slaves to question or delay him, let alone stop him. He would take this hit and move on.

Marcus was asleep when his uncle reached him. The elder Darling asked to speak with Hawke immediately. Marcus went to the security chief's cabin and got him.

"Yes, sir," Hawke said when he came on.

That was John Hawke. Called to the radio late at night for something that was obviously out of the ordinary. Yet his voice was the same flat instrument it always was.

"I want you to do the following as quickly as possible," Darling said. His voice was not as composed. "Destroy the lab completely and then the radio room. None of the equipment must survive. Then take the yacht to sea and sink it in deep water. There has to be a fire. Start it in the galley. Is there sufficient dinghy space for the crew?"

"Yes."

"Good," Darling said. "Get to it."

"Sir, Captain Kannaday will want to know why this is being done," Hawke said.

The devious bastard, Darling thought. Hawke had to be curious as well. Once again, the security chief wanted to keep Peter Kannaday between himself and Darling. Unfortunately, that was not going to be possible. Hawke was about to take two punches.

"Tell the captain that his security team failed to kill all of the men on the sampan," Darling said. "One of them was recovered."

The radio went stubbornly silent. That had been punch number one.

"It would be best if the captain were lost with his ship," Darling went on. "I do not want the accident to be perceived as an insurance scam. We do not need *additional* investigations."

That was punch number two. Hawke now knew just what the security lapse had caused.

"I will see to all of it," Hawke replied.

There was no hint of humility in the security chief's voice. Just determination.

Darling preferred that. He wanted results, not repentance.

Darling hung up the phone. He pushed it away and sat back.

Jervis Darling had spent a lifetime building corporations, amassing wealth and power, and, most importantly, evolving a worldview. He realized that only businessmen had the resources to move the world forward. Governments were too partisan and slow. Armies were too bestial and rigid. Only he and his kind had the vision to motivate the masses. First, however, they had to make themselves indispensable. They had to use mercenaries like John Hawke to surgically strike targets around the world. They would target factories, transportation centers, financial districts, and power plants. Existing governments and terror groups would take the blame. Especially since he would be hiring many of their members. And covering the events in his media outlets. Darling and his colleagues would eliminate competition to make their own resources more valuable. They would use that base to build de facto political power. From there, nothing was off limits.

Darling was still angry. But he was relatively unconcerned about the project or his goals. He had never undertaken a business or political operation that did not experience a few bumps. This was the first one the current action had suffered. He was confident that the undertaking would survive and move forward.

As confident as he was that R. Clayton Herbert would soon be wishing he had gone somewhere else this evening.

FIFTY-ONE

Cairns, Australia
Sunday, 12:00 A.M.

"I blew it," Bob Herbert said over the phone.

"What do you mean?" Hood asked.

"I gave a world-class, standing-room-only performance of how not to gather information."

"You're being way too rough on yourself, Bob," Hood said. "You did the best you could under extremely adverse circumstances." He was speaking softly but firmly.

"Paul, I *created* the friggin' adverse circumstances!" Herbert went on. "You want a list of do-nots that I would have reamed a newbie for? I did not case the site. I went to the wrong phone. And I gave the subject an overview of what we know without getting anything back except a vague confirmation that our suspicions were correct."

"This isn't lab science," Hood pointed out. "You took a huge risk against staggering odds."

"That's what the best is supposed to do, and my job title says I'm supposed to be one of the best," Herbert replied. "The best are also supposed to do one thing more. They're supposed to succeed."

"This is just one battle in the war," Hood replied. "And I'm not so sure we lost it."

"I've won battles before," Herbert shot back. "This is not what victory feels like."

Herbert was calling from his cell phone in the Humvee. FNO Loh and Paul Leyland had found the koala. They met Herbert in front of the mansion where they helped him down the stairs. The group left the grounds after conferring with Jelbart by phone. Herbert agreed with the warrant officer's assessment. Jelbart felt that Darling's armed guards would be unusually aggressive after what happened. They unanimously decided that the best thing to do was return to the observation base and regroup. Herbert and Loh were sitting in the back. Leyland was driving. Little Maluka was asleep in the passenger's seat.

"Bob, right now it doesn't matter how we got here," Hood said. "Let's look at where we are and what we're up against."

"All right," Herbert said and took a breath. That seemed to calm him somewhat. "We're facing a world-class thug who knows he's been found out. He also knows that at least one of his partners has been identified. And he knows that we have someone who may be able to ID the boat they used to carry the stolen nuclear material. He cannot be happy with any of that information."

"Agreed. So what does he do?"

"First, he has to make his own involvement deniable," Herbert said. "His phone records and financial transactions are probably clean. I'm betting it's the same with bin Dahman and whoever else is involved. Darling has to assume the pirate is heavily guarded and that we already took from him whatever information we want. So he probably won't bother going after him. The only place our boy's immediately vulnerable is the boat."

"We haven't been able to find the other vessel involved in this transaction," Hood said. "What chance do we have of finding this one? It may already have been hidden."

"That's very possible," Herbert agreed. "But I want to find it. I *really* want to find it."

"You want to get Jervis Darling," Hood pointed out. "That isn't the same thing."

"It will be if we find the boat," Herbert said. "Damn, I wish that pirate had seen something. At least we'd know what we were looking for."

"You could have him hypnotized," Hood suggested, half in desperate jest. "Maybe he'll remember more."

"That's good for quitting smoking, not interrogation," Herbert said.

"There is one thing," Loh said.

"What's that?" Herbert asked. "Paul, can you hear FNO Loh?"

"Barely," Hood said.

Herbert held the cell phone between them. He asked the Singaporean to speak up.

"The pirates would not have attacked a much larger vessel," Loh said loudly. "It's night now. Small vessels tend to go to anchor."

"How does that help us?" Herbert said. "There are probably a lot of small boats on the open sea."

"This one would not be stopped," she said. "If it's out there, and Darling is afraid of being caught, he would have it running somewhere."

"Good point," Leyland contributed. "But that still leaves a lot of area to cover."

"Not as much as you might think," Herbert said. "Chances are pretty good the boat won't be going toward Cairns. Darling won't want that ship anywhere near him."

"What if he wanted to hide it?" Hood asked. "What better place than his own facility?"

"That was probably the game plan before we showed up," Herbert said. "Now, Darling would never risk it. If there is a hint of radioactivity on board that vessel, it's as good as a fingerprint. We could identify the source from just a particle of material. Darling has to imagine that someone will come looking."

"We should get our ships back out to sea," Loh said.

"I agree," Herbert said. "But we should also get the chopper in the air and run a zigzag search heading seaward. If the vessel is back, Darling may have to send it out again. Just so he isn't caught. If it's not back, it's going to be racing to a safe haven somewhere else."

"Is there any kind of electronic surveillance we can do from here?" Hood asked.

"I'm sure the transport vessel is in a silent running mode by now," Herbert said.

"We can do a GPS sweep," Loh said.

"Right," Herbert agreed.

"I didn't get that," Hood said.

"Ask Stephen Viens to do a read on the global positioning satellite beacons in the region," Herbert said.

"The satellites, not the receiver?" Hood asked.

"The receiver itself, on the boat, is a passive site. All it does is tap into a continuous beacon from three satellites—four if you're adding altitude to the mix, which we are not. We can't pinpoint the boat by looking for a specific ID number. What we can do, though, is watch for the beacons themselves and triangulate them. Viens will know what I mean. Have him run a scan every minute or so. If we've got someone who's running at twenty-five knots or more, that will be worth looking into. Especially if they're heading away from Cairns."

"I like it," Hood said.

Hood said he would have Viens's office look into the GPS as soon as possible.

Herbert thanked him and hung up. Then he reached back and put the phone in his wheelchair. He felt a little bit better than before. At least they had a plan. And there was one thing an intelligence officer could always count on. Night was when vermin tended to move about.

"From what I've been hearing, that boat was armed," Leyland said. "What if it has some kind of surface-to-air missiles? Your chopper has no defense. They won't believe that Little Maluka got lost on his boardie."

"His what?" Herbert asked.

"His board. Surfing."

"You're right," Herbert said. "But if they shoot at us, we'll know one thing for sure."

"What's that?" Leyland asked.

"We found the right boat."

FIFTY-TWO

Washington, D.C.
Saturday, 11:00 A.M.

The phone beeped, and Hood snapped it up. He had just finished talking to Stephen Viens, who was rushing to the office. In his absence, weekend surveillance staffer Mary Timm was starting up the GPS sweep. It was not a complex operation, and the exchange officer was from the Communications Security Establishment of Canada's Department of National Defence. That was the branch of government that analyzed and catalogued intercepted radio and various electronic emissions from other nations. The CSE liaised closely with both the United States and Great Britain's SIGINT services.

"R. Clayton Herbert," said the deep and smoky voice on the other end of the phone. "That's Bob Herbert. He's on your staff, isn't he?" There was a hint of a Louisiana accent.

Hood did not like calls that opened with questions. Especially when the voice was not familiar. But the caller had access to Hood's direct line. That meant he had high-level security clearance.

"Who is this?" Hood asked.

"Bruce Perry," the caller replied.

Perry was the special assistant to the president for democratic elections. It was a post that monitored voting activities in foreign nations. Hood could not understand what Special Assistant Perry wanted with Herbert, or why he used that form of Herbert's name. He did a GovScan search of Perry's name. Those personnel files were little more than glorified résumés. They were available to officials who might need assistance in highly specialized areas.

"I don't believe we've ever met," Hood said, stalling while he scanned Perry's file.

"You may be correct," Perry replied. "But then, it isn't my job to keep track of peoples' activities."

Oh, Hood thought. *It's going to be one of* those *kinds of conversations.* And then he spotted the reason Perry was calling. The sixty-four-year-old was a former ambassador to Australia.

"All right, Mr. Perry," Hood said. "Yes, Bob Herbert is an officer here. You already knew that, or you wouldn't be asking. What's on your mind?"

"Mr. Herbert has just been to see Mr. Jervis Darling at his home," Perry said. "You've heard of Jervis Darling?"

"I read newspapers," Hood said. Darling had obviously wasted no time getting his puppets onstage.

"Newspapers do not tell the full story of this man," Perry said.

"I'm sure of that."

"Mr. Darling has put a substantial portion of his personal fortune into countless unheralded charitable activities, which include democratic advocacy programs," Perry went on. "He is a rock in that region, and Mr. Herbert had no right to call on him."

"In a democratic society we have all kinds of rights," Hood pointed out.

"The right to privacy is chief among those," Perry replied.

"Fair enough. I assume Mr. Darling called you. Did he say what Mr. Herbert was after?"

"He said there was some nonsense about misplaced nuclear waste," Perry said, chuckling. "The idea that Mr. Darling would know anything about that is completely ridiculous."

"Why?"

"Because, for one thing, Mr. Darling believes absolutely in the rule of law," Perry said. He was no longer chuckling. "He also happens to be an extremely moral man."

"Who may have had his wife murdered," Hood said.

"Oh, Jesus Lord!" Perry said angrily. "Don't tell me you believe that old smear!"

"Who would smear him?"

"He spent a great deal of money to find out," Perry replied. "He discovered that the Singaporeans had spread that rumor to try to keep him from investing in liberal political causes over there. God, Hood. I was with Mr. Darling when he received word of his wife's death. He was despondent. So was his daughter. The idea that he would have arranged it is frankly insulting."

"Mr. Perry, I'm not going to dispute what you've told me," Hood said. "Our information differs from yours."

"Then you are misinformed."

"You know something, Mr. Perry? I really hope so. I hope we're wrong about everything from the homicide to the nuclear trafficking. I hope you're doing this from deep conviction and a sense of honor."

"Mr. Hood, in the presence of God himself I would swear to everything I told you."

"You didn't tell me anything other than your beliefs, not fact," Hood pointed out. "But I thank you for sharing your perspective."

"You're welcome, Mr. Hood. I'd like to share this as well," Perry went on. "If Mr. Darling is bothered again without overwhelming evidence, charges will be brought against Mr. Herbert and yourself. Legal charges in Australia, ethics violations here."

"Bruce, you should have quit before you trotted out the threats," Hood said. "They always stink of guilt."

"I wouldn't know," Perry told him. "You collect intelligence, Mr. Hood. This is intelligence. Use it."

Perry hung up. Hood shook his head slowly as he replaced the phone. He jabbed the Delete key on his computer. That removed Perry's file from his monitor. That was the problem with government dossiers. They gave you plenty of data but not the man.

Of course, what intelligence services called 2DD—two-dimensional data, facts without body or analysis—was only one of the problems with government service. What bothered Hood more was how officials had to battle the enemies without while fighting the enemies within even harder. The longer he stayed in public service, the more Hood became convinced that leaders were a burden to society. If they all went away, the people would do just fine. A leader could not be ambitious and still serve others. People were fortunate when the ambitions of a leader, like Lincoln, like Franklin Roosevelt, happened to coincide with the general good.

Hood took a moment to check with Mary Timm. She was already on her second sweep of the region. If someone was on the run, she was willing to bet that they were not using the GPS.

"Which could mean what?" Hood asked.

"That the subject is either very near to land and can sail by eye or compass. Or else they have no intention of going near land, in which case a navigational aid would be extraneous," Mary replied.

That was not what Hood wanted to hear. He relayed the information to Herbert. The intelligence chief was unfazed.

"Any intelligence is useful," Herbert replied. "Even if it eliminates possibilities."

And there again was the paradox of government. Within just a few minutes, Hood's enemy and his ally had both said virtually the same thing.

And they were both right.

FIFTY-THREE

The Coral Sea
Sunday, 1:21 A.M.

Peter Kannaday's injuries did not prevent him from leaving his cabin. He stayed there hour after hour out of shame.

The captain alternately stood by the porthole or lay on the bed. He replayed the attack endlessly, considering things he should have done. He thought back to the days leading to that point. He wished that he had willingly formed an alliance with Hawke instead of being minimized. To do so now would be cowardly. To have done so before the attack would have been wise. Unfortunately, wisdom was not always there when you needed it. He began to wonder, after several hours, if maybe that was the way it needed to be. Lying on his back in the dark, he thought of the biblical prophets who went into the wilderness. They made the journey in order to be pounded down by the sun and starvation. The prophets bought wisdom by taking on pain, loneliness, and doubt. But the knowledge and self-awareness they acquired came with something else. Something indispensable. It nested atop the fortified backbone they needed to apply it.

Perhaps it was not too late to find courage. Realizing that, Kannaday even saw what form it should take. He had to leave the cabin and take a turn on deck. He had to show the crew and Hawke that he was beaten but not broken. He also needed to be more than just a captain. He needed to regain command.

Kannaday rose from the bed. The now-familiar aches made him wince, but they did not cause him to pause. He could not show hesitation once he left here. He had to be strong.

As Kannaday headed toward the door, he heard a key being turned in the lock. The door was already unlocked. He bolted for the knob and twisted. It did not turn. He patted his back pocket. His key case had been removed. He went to his desk for the spare. It, too, was gone. Kannaday went back to the door and banged once with the side of his fist.

"Who's out there?" he yelled.

There was no answer. The captain did not waste time or energy shouting. He looked around for something to pry the door open. Possibly the letter opener he had never used. Or one of the hooks from the closet. He would try the letter opener first. He went to the desk, but the opener was gone.

In quick succession Kannaday heard the 220 horsepower Caterpillar engine quiet, idle, then stop. The yacht slowed. This was not a scheduled stop. Then he heard the winches above him begin to turn. The dinghies were being lowered. The floor no longer hummed with the low vibration caused by the powerful motor. What the hell was going on?

Kannaday leaned on the desk. He punched on the intercom to the radio room.

"Marcus, are you there?"

Again, no answer. Which, in a way, was an answer in itself.

Just then he heard a commotion in the hallway. He went to the door and pressed his ear to it. Crew members were coming and going. He heard crashing but no shouts. The men were breaking things, but they were not fighting. It sounded as if they were in the lab.

"Sweet Christ almighty," he muttered.

They were in the lab. Destroying the equipment. Destroying evidence? But they were not throwing it over the side. They were smashing equipment on the floor. That could only mean one thing. It would be staying on board. And that could only mean one thing.

They intended that the *Hosannah* never be found.

FIFTY-FOUR

Cairns, Australia
Sunday, 1:42 A.M.

Warrant Officer George Jelbart was relieved and hopeful when the Humvee returned.

Hanging around in the observation tower with Spider was not Jelbart's idea of a fun time. Spider was one of those hard-talking Sydney street kids who were equally at home rock climbing on Cradle Mountain in Tasmania or picking fights with Southeast Asians who frequented the bars of Perth. Spider was not up here because he loved nature. Or because he wanted to protect and serve the people of Queensland. He was here because he loved the danger of fire. In Spider's eyes it was the ultimate enemy. A force that existed even in the vacuum of space. Jelbart wondered how the edgy, restless young man would react if he knew about the fire his own team was trying to prevent. Fire that could not be extinguished. Fire that was the ultimate deterrent until someone actually used the damn thing. Then it was the breath of hell itself. Jelbart had seen the disaster simulations put together by the American Pentagon. Those were programs that could not properly be called war simulations. After an initial flourish, both sides were effectively crippled. They included death tolls and destructive swaths for nuclear exchanges between India and Pakistan, China and Taiwan, Israel and any of its Middle Eastern neighbors. They included statistics for small, ten-megaton bombs exploded in major metropolises. They also included data for the exploding of small dirty bombs, nuclear material packed with traditional explosives such as plastique and dynamite. The best-case scenario involved the deaths of over 10,000 people.

Spider appeared oblivious to concepts of that magnitude. Nor was there any reason he should be aware of them. But his *mano a mano* nature seemed naive in the face of what Jelbart and the others were tracking.

Leyland parked the Humvee near the helicopter pad. He set Little Maluka down. The koala returned to the tower. Then Leyland called Eva and asked her to get the pilot from the cabin. The fire warden said nothing about their mission to his two associates.

"I expect you may get some fallout from all this," Jelbart told Leyland. He realized, after saying it, what word he had chosen.

"I can handle it," Leyland said. "He can't prove I knew what you blokes were up to. Besides, what are they going to do? Fire me?" Leyland winked. He had obviously meant to use that word.

"You're a good man," Jelbart said, shaking his hand.

Loh bowed slightly to Leyland. Herbert clasped the captain's hand with both of his. Behind him, the pilot readied the chopper.

"The koala idea was a damn good one, Captain," Herbert said. "I'm the guy that mucked things up. If they do kick you out, come to Washington. There's a job waiting for you."

"Thanks. You're definitely a bloke to go scrub-bashing with," Leyland told him.

Loh had opened the door, and Herbert wheeled over. The three climbed into the helicopter. They were airborne in under a minute. Jelbart glanced at the spotlit observation tower as it receded. It tightened the warrant officer's throat, just a little, to know that there were men like Captain Leyland. Men who did not limit their sense of duty to what was in their job description. That did not diminish Spider. But it certainly elevated Leyland.

Herbert leaned forward as they soared toward the starlit skies. "What the hell is scrub-bashing?" he asked Jelbart.

"That's when you make your own road through dense

brush," Jelbart replied. "It's a he-man's Sunday drive. If you get invited, it means you rate. You obviously made a good impression."

"Oh," Herbert replied.

The intelligence chief sat back. He looked confused.

Jelbart had not known Herbert long. But he knew how a man looked when he was frustrated. Herbert had that look. Leyland had to have noticed that, too. That could be why he said what he did, to give Herbert a little boost.

Jelbart smiled as they headed toward the coast. That elevated Leyland a little more.

FIFTY-FIVE

The Coral Sea
Sunday, 1:55 A.M.

Captain Kannaday was unable to pry open the cabin door. That was ironic. He did not want to get out when he could. Now that the door was locked, he desperately wanted to be on the other side.

Without access to the radio room, he could not call out. Here in the cabin he had very little at his disposal. A porthole just wide enough for his head. He could not crawl out. There was also the shower. If he plugged up the drain and tore the desk lamp from its cord, he could drop the loose ends into the water. Anyone stepping in the water would get a jolt. But the lamps in the yacht were run off a marine deep cycle battery. The 550 ampere charge would not kill them. He did not even think it would stun them.

And Kannaday would still be trapped in here.

He had a cigarette lighter, but the door was fireproof. He would not even be able to burn through it.

He swore. He could not understand what Darling and Hawke were up to. The captain's body had adjusted to the pain. He started to pace. He felt as though he were working sore muscles. He paused now and then to kick the door. The cabin had never seemed so small.

Suddenly, he heard a low growl from down the hall. The floor began to vibrate. It sounded as if someone were using an electric drill or router. They were kept in the event the yacht suffered damage in a collision or storm. But the sound seemed to be coming from below. There was a long, narrow crawl space between the deck and the red cedar outer hull. The area was accessible through a trapdoor in the corridor. Cables, extra gear, and emergency equipment such as the tools and flares were kept there.

The ship was in fine shape. There was only one reason to enter the crawl space with tools. They were putting a hole in the outer hull. The *Hosannah* was going to be scuttled.

"Hawke!" the captain screamed as he pounded on the door again. "Dammit, *Hawke!*"

Kannaday cursed himself for not having acted sooner. What was happening out there transcended discipline and retribution. Darling would only sink the ship if it could be used against him. Something must have gone wrong somewhere in the network. Darling needed to get rid of the evidence. Hence the smashing of the equipment. Darling also needed someone to take the fall. A corpse could not deny its guilt.

Kannaday was not especially close to the crew. Darling would not have had to offer them much to cooperate.

"You *bastards!*" he shouted.

Even if the men were listening, no one could have heard him. The winch and whatever tools they were using made too much noise.

The winch stopped. The two boats must be in the water. Kannaday could not be sure. His porthole looked out toward the starboard side of the yacht. A moment later, the rumbling sounds from the interior corridor also stopped. The captain heard voices and hurried footsteps. A few seconds later, all the noises on the vessel were coming from above deck. The men were rushing to the stern. They were obviously getting into the dinghies. Kannaday wondered if his own crew knew he was not coming.

Kannaday screamed in frustration. He ran at the door again. It was reinforced and watertight to prevent flooding. The impact hurt his shoulder, and he backed away.

Rubbing it, the captain paced anxiously in a tight circle. He looked around, trying desperately to think of a way out. There were aerosol cans in the bathroom. Perhaps he could puncture them, cause them to explode. But how, without hurting himself in the process?

Suddenly, the yacht became very still and stable. Kannaday heard the two masts creak. The waves were no longer moving it from side to side. That meant it was bottom heavy.

The yacht was going down.

FIFTY-SIX

The Great Barrier Reef
Sunday, 2:09 A.M.

Monica Loh knew that the search for Jervis Darling's vessel was probably hopeless.

The Singaporean patrol boat was moving at top speed toward the area. It was listening for the ship in a continuous sweep of all radio frequencies. The chopper was watching for the vessel. But a boat running silent and probably dark would be virtually impossible to find at night. Radar was unreliable due to the sheer number of hits they picked up: not just boats but reefs, sea creatures on the surface, even large waves. Modern equipment was occasionally too sensitive to be useful. She was guessing that by daybreak it would be gone completely. And with the ship hidden, they would lose their best chance to track this action to Darling and find the missing nuclear waste.

Jelbart was on the radio with his home base. When he was finished, the pilot contacted the RAAF Airfield Defence Squadron satellite base in Cooktown. That was the nearest refueling point in the region.

FNO Loh did not feel comfortable about the new world in which they were living. She did not yearn for a simpler era. Nor did she doubt her skills or those of her shipmates. They were smart and disciplined. What worried her were the agents who had joined groups like Interpol or the CIA because it seemed glamorous. Many of them did not expect nor ask for the grievous responsibility that had been placed on their backs. Loh hoped their efforts here would be an example to others rather than an exception. The civilized world did not have time to accommodate long apprenticeships.

"I just spoke with General Hopkins," the pilot informed the group. "He'll let us refuel there. That gives us ninety minutes of flying time. How do you want to spend it?"

"Warrant Officer, that's your call," Herbert said.

"I suggest we follow the reef northeast," Jelbart said. "HQ said that Darling's property holdings are mostly in the south and west. That would be out of reach for his boat. And his cove is completely open. My guess is he'll make a run for the open sea and a foreign port."

"Perhaps the same port that swallowed the Malaysian vessel," FNO Loh suggested.

"That's a reasonable guess," Jelbart admitted. "So we'll head north, which we'll have to do to reach Cooktown. Then we'll swing out toward the sea in a tight Z pattern and hope we spot our prey."

"Sirs, General Hopkins has also offered to launch a pair of A3 Mirage fighters if we need them for surveillance," the pilot added.

Loh waited to see Jelbart's response. The need for absolute security, to keep any leaks from Darling, versus the need for information.

"It's getting too late in the day for overcaution," Jelbart said. "Thank the general and say we would welcome the help. I'll have a look at the map and give him the air routes we'd like covered."

"Yes, sir," the pilot replied.

"I'll notify my patrol boat of our plan," Loh said.

Jelbart passed the headset back to her while he took a look at the flight book.

"I wonder if their base might be a tanker of some sort," Herbert thought aloud. "Something mobile."

"And protectable," Jelbart said. "Something that large could be a floating SCUD bank."

"It sure would be a helluva delivery platform for nuclear-tipped missiles," Herbert agreed. "Hell, there isn't a port on earth tankers don't visit."

Loh listened to the men as she placed her call. She hoped they were mistaken. It was bad enough contemplating the damage petty despots could do with intermediate-range missiles. Add money and international political clout, and there was no limit to the potential subterfuge.

Even if Herbert and Jelbart were wrong this time, they might not be wrong the next time. Or the time after that. Things were going to have to change radically in the way the military and intelligence services did business.

Fortunately, Loh had an idea where they might start. With a resource that was already in their lap.

FIFTY-SEVEN

The Coral Sea
Sunday, 2:09 A.M.

The yacht began to sink toward the stern. Kannaday stumbled back against the bed as the floor tilted. The incoming water was settling in the aft section. The captain heard the clatter of boxes and loose equipment below as the vessel shifted.

The crawl space, he thought suddenly.

Kannaday leaned on the wall. He braced himself with both hands as he stood. The far end of the storage area was directly below the cabin. If he could pry up the floorboards, he might be able to squeeze through.

The captain bolted toward the desk and pulled out the drawer. He did not have a letter opener or knife, but the drawer was held in by runners. He yanked it free, tossed it aside, and looked at the screws. A nail file would work. He went into the bathroom and got his nail clippers from the medicine chest. He flipped out the nail file and used it to work out the screws. There were two in each runner. The first one came free quickly. That was all he would need.

The runner was shaped like a squared-off *C.* Kannaday went back to the bathroom, unscrewed the metal spray head from the shower, and laid the end of the runner on the desk. Holding the showerhead in his fist, he used it to pound the end of the runner flat.

He had his lever.

Grabbing the runner, the nail file, and the showerhead, he dropped to his knees near the door. The floorboards were epoxy-coated mahogany. He wedged the nail file between two of the planks and dug a small hole between them. He inserted the flattened edge of the runner. Rising on the sloping floor, he used the showerhead to pound the runner down. He did it firmly enough to push the metal in, but softly enough to keep it from bending. It took just four whacks to put the runner through. Kannaday repeated the process along the entire side of the narrow plank. As he worked, the boat continued to shift. First it leveled, then it dipped to port, then the aft dropped again. Kannaday tried not to think about going under. Hawke would have taken them several miles out to sea. The water was an average of two hundred feet deep here. Once the *Hosannah* went down, Peter Kannaday would not be coming back up.

The captain had gone around most of the first plank when he stood and stomped on it. The plank split from the one beside it and dropped into the crawl space. Kannaday got back on his knees and worked on the ends of the plank beside it. When he had punched through those, he put the runner down, put his fingers into the opening left by the first plank, and pulled on the second. With three sides free, it came up easily.

Kannaday could hear the water rushing in. He did not stop. The batteries were in a watertight compartment, but he did not know how long they would last. If they died, he would be in the dark.

He managed to get the third plank up. Kannaday needed to remove at least six before he could think of trying to get in. As he watched the water rise, he realized that there would not be time to continue this way. Reaching behind him, he pulled his pillowcase from the bed. He wrapped it around his hands. Crouching, he reached into the hole he had made and pulled up on the next plank. He grasped the edge of the wood. The pillowcase prevented him from slipping on the moist mahogany. The wood refused to budge. He screamed in frustration and looked around. There was nothing.

Just then he realized that the contents of the crawl space were settling toward the stern. Swearing at his own stupidity, he got a flashlight from his desk, dropped to his belly, and shone the light in the opening he had made.

He saw the tool kit. It was banging around in the area just beyond the door of his cabin.

Reaching in, Kannaday stretched his arm in that direction. He could not quite reach it. He took the runner, bent the end into a hook, stuck it into the opening, and fished for the metal chest.

He snagged it.

Pulling it inside, Kannaday opened the large box and took out a hammer. Getting on his knees, he slammed it repeatedly into the planks. It took two blows each to crack them, one more to send them tumbling into the crawl space. As the water started to flood his cabin, Kannaday realized that he would have to go in headfirst. The yacht settled again slightly. This might be as level as the vessel got before going down. Taking the flashlight in his left hand, Kannaday lay down, took a long breath, then slid into the crawl space.

There was only about twenty-five feet to the opening cut by the crew. But it seemed much farther because of the debris that blocked Kannaday's way. There was no room for vertical or lateral movement. He could not shove the flotsam around, under, or behind him. He had to push the containers, equipment, shards of wood, and other objects ahead as he wriggled forward. It was like moving against a dam that grew thicker by the instant. He was finally forced to let go of the flashlight and use both hands. Fortunately, the crew had left the trapdoor open to facilitate the flow of water. The hall lights filtered through the opening in the deck. Kannaday used both hands to shove on the objects clustered in the crawl space. The captain was literally knee-walking forward as the algae-thick water rolled through the crawl space and lower deck.

The *Hosannah* continued to tilt and pitch. The geyser of seawater batted the debris back. He did not think he would be able to get much farther ahead. Kannaday's arms and chest hurt from the beating, and the exertion strained his lungs. Even though his brain knew it would kill him, his lungs insisted that he inhale. The captain had to fight that impulse. He was less than four feet from the trapdoor. It was like being under the ice-covered surface of a pond. Kannaday was close to freedom yet not quite there.

His temples were pulsing hard, and his vision was beginning to swirl. He did not have much time. The way the debris had piled up in front of him, there was only enough room to extend his right arm. Turning onto his back, he stuck his hand toward the trapdoor, turned his palm up, and grabbed the near side of the opening. He pulled hard. The edges of metal boxes, tools, and the other gear cut into him as he dragged himself up. It would not be enough to get to the opening. It was already underwater. He had to get through it and out of the crawl space.

He needed to breathe. In a few moments he was going to breathe, even if he took in only seawater. He worked his left arm past the pile of equipment, ripping his sleeve and rending his flesh as he stretched it toward the opening. He grabbed the edge and pulled with both hands now. He moved slowly up the side of the mountain of debris. His forehead was near the opening. It went through. His shoulders followed. Now he was pushing on the edge instead of pulling. He was in the water-filled corridor. He bent at the waist, drew his feet out, flipped over, and scrambled ahead.

He half-swam, half-jumped to his feet and gasped at the same time. He took in air. It was salvation, the common made uncommon. All other fears and considerations dwarfed in comparison. He splashed back down and felt for a wall. He found one on the starboard side. It was at a slight angle, tilting away from him. He leaned against it and got his feet under him. He rose, his shoulders rounded, water running from them.

Blood from his fresh wounds mixed with the seawater. The salt in the water stung, but it was not like the pain of the beating. He had earned these wounds by deed. He felt reborn.

Kannaday was just forward of the radio room. The water came up to his waist. At this rate, the boat would be underwater in about a half hour.

Suddenly, there was a snap like a dry twig breaking. The water must have reached the batteries. The lights went out.

The captain turned back toward the trapdoor. He looked down into the crawl space. His flashlight was still on, twisting in the rushing water. He waded back to get it. Now that Kannaday was no longer pushing the debris, it had begun to slide back into the aft depths of the crawl space. It knocked the flashlight around, but he managed to grab it before it drifted away. He turned and balanced himself against the sloping wall as he slogged through the water. There was something he needed. Something he was sure that murderers in the night would not take.

Kannaday entered the radio room. Most of the wrecked equipment was underwater. Smaller pieces, mostly wires and microchips, were floating on the shifting waters. But the box he wanted was still bracketed shoulder-high to the inner wall. The captain knew that Hawke and Marcus would not have bothered with it.

The box was bright red and the size of a lunch pail. Kannaday reached up, flipped the lid, and removed the contents. As the yacht moaned and lurched, he made his way quickly toward the stairs and freedom.

FIFTY-EIGHT

Washington, D.C.
Saturday, 12:38 P.M.

Like a federal Darwin exploring survival of the fittest in a bureaucracy, Paul Hood had identified countless functions for the director of Op-Center. Sometimes the job required a quarterback. Sometimes it called for a cheerleader. Sometimes there were other responsibilities. This happened to be one of those rah-rah times.

Paul Hood entered the small, bright room that was Stephen Viens's work area.

Officially, this area was Op-Center's internal security department. Viens and his one-person team watched for moles and people who might be tempted to pass secrets on to other nations. That was how it had been described when Op-Center's accountant Carolina Burdo drew up the annual budget. Unofficially, it was also where Viens used his years as satellite imaging supervisor with the NRO to get priority satellite time for Op-Center.

Viens's office was the only one in the underground sector that had a window. The window looked out into the corridor, but that did not matter. After years of working for the National Reconnaissance Office, Viens wanted a real-time view, even if it was of more work space. That included Mary Timm's small cubicle, which was located just outside his door. The young woman was reviewing data being fed to her by various surveillance satellites. She was collating that information and sending it to Viens.

Viens himself was seated with his back to the window. Before him, on a laboratory table, three laptop computers sat side by side. The surveillance expert looked over as Hood entered.

"Sorry to disappoint you, Paul, but we're not getting anything useful," Viens lamented.

"Are you getting anything at all?" Hood asked. He stopped beside Viens. There were very different kinds of maps on each monitor. Hood guessed that they were the sections of sea that Viens was studying. This sector of intelligence gathering was relatively new for Op-Center, which used to rely exclusively on the NRO for satellite surveillance.

"We haven't seen or heard anything that resembles a boat on the run," Viens informed him. "And we've covered a lot of territory along the Great Barrier Reef, the eastern reaches of the Celebes, the entire Banda Sea, and the western and southwestern Coral Sea."

"You did all that in ninety minutes?" Hood asked.

"Yes, but we had three processes going at once," Viens said. "Audio, visual, and thermal. One often eliminates the need for the other."

"How?"

"For instance, we've been monitoring the ARCON," Viens told him. "That's the Asian Rim Civilian Observation Network. It consists, basically and informally, of whoever is out there. The maritime police and navies in that region use specific frequencies for civilian communication. If the radar on a freighter or a cruise ship saw another vessel barreling through, the night watch would have reported it on an ARCON frequency. Since no one did, our program calculated how far the radar of reported vessels was sweeping. Odds were that our target ship was not moving through that area, so we didn't waste satellite time looking for it." Viens made a face. "I don't like the fact that we're using technology to figure out where people aren't, not where they are. But it's the best we can do."

"Michelangelo said that sculpting is taking away the parts of the marble that aren't the statue," Hood said.

"It also took the man about four years to paint a ceiling, if I'm remembering my Vatican history correctly," Viens said.

"You are," Hood told him. He had spent several nights reading about the Vatican during Op-Center's church-allied mission in Botswana. The Vatican's wealth included its vast art collection, and facts about it were in the files.

"Stop kicking yourself in the ass," Hood said. "You're searching with no idea of what to look for. At least we can tell Bob where not to look."

"I'll E-mail the clear zone parameters to your office," Viens said.

"Thanks," Hood said.

"But I'm still not satisfied," Viens said.

"That's okay," Hood said. "Just don't be down on yourself. There's a difference."

Viens grunted in what Hood took for agreement. He began collecting the data for Herbert.

Hood left the office. He had not managed to boost Viens's morale. Worse than that, there had been back-wash. The futility of the operation was starting to gnaw at Hood. Viens literally had access to a world of electronic data. He was usually in the forefront of any we-can-do-this movement. If he was worried, then there was real cause for concern.

Hood glanced down at Mary Timm as he passed her desk. He gave her a brave little smile and a wink. She smiled back. It was a big smile. Not just pretty but confident. It was a smile full of youth and uncorrupted hope. Even Mary's eyes were radiant.

Hood remembered when he used to feel that way. First as mayor of Los Angeles, and then when he first became the director of Op-Center. Even if he were being naive at the time, Hood always felt that things would work out. And invariably they did. Not always without cost, but they had a saying on Wall Street when he worked in finance. If the goods are worth it, the price was worth it.

These goods were worth it.

Things would work out again, somehow. He had to believe that.

Mary's smile lingered in Hood's memory. Sometimes just the simplest gesture was also cheerleading.

FIFTY-NINE

The Coral Sea
Sunday, 2:39 A.M.

The *Hosannah* was listing nearly twenty-five degrees to starboard when the captain came on deck. He was hunched forward as he emerged from the companionway. That helped him to keep his footing on the sloped deck. He was carrying the two items he had brought from below.

Kannaday glanced at the stars to get his bearings. He had sailed this region for years and knew it well. The prow of the yacht was facing northeast. The nearest land was probably Cape Melville. That was about a mile to the southwest. The captain turned and swung around the mainmast, then ducked beneath the spar. The dacron sail flapped in the night wind. The fabric made a hollow, mournful sound. Kannaday moved quickly past it. The launch motors were off. The men would be rowing. In the dark, in unknown waters, they were unlikely to be hurrying. Kannaday hoped they had not gone very far.

When the captain was below, drowning seemed imminent. Now that he was above deck on a sinking vessel, drowning also seemed imminent. Yet Peter Kannaday felt invigorated. He had bought himself another opportunity to confront John Hawke. He had a chance to buy back his dignity. Kannaday would rather have that than a life jacket.

The *Hosannah* took a sudden dip toward the stern just as Kannaday reached the aftermast. He grabbed the thick pole, hugging it tightly with his arms as loose halyards loudly smacked the mast and capstan. In his hands were the two objects he had taken from the radio room.

He waited. The boat would not go down yet. It could not.

It did not.

The vessel listed to port then settled again. Carefully making sure of his footing, Kannaday let go of the mast. He half-walked, half-slid toward the aft rail. The barrier was only knee high. But years on the yacht had taught the captain how to brace himself in unsteady seas. He braced his right knee against the post that supported the flag marking the ship's registry. Then the captain looked out across the relatively calm sea. A fine spray misted his skin. The salty water soothed his bruised jaw and stung the open wounds on his arms. The sea, the pain, and the joy. Anticipation and a driving hunger for something, whether it was wealth or survival or revenge. All of Kannaday's life seemed to be encapsulated in that moment.

The captain raised both arms straight ahead. His left arm was nearly perpendicular. His right arm was parallel to the sea. He fired the flare gun in his left hand. The pinkish fire rose on a puffy magnesium-white plume. The small, dark waves of the Coral Sea became a widening expanse of sharp shadow and light. The light areas dimmed as the flare rose in the sky. But the circle of illumination grew as Kannaday stared ahead. Finally, all but despairing that he had lost Hawke, Kannaday saw what he had been hoping for. About three hundred meters away, he saw the dinghies on the edge of the light. The sailors looked up at the light, then back along the high, smoking arc.

Kannaday swung his right arm in front of him. He stared along the barrel of the second flare pistol and fired. The recoil caused his body to twist slightly on the slick deck. Without waiting to see whether the projectile had struck, Kannaday pulled two spare 38mm cartridges from his pocket. He reloaded each plastic-barrel pistol, raised both, aimed, and fired in succession. The twin streaks flashed through the artificial light on a course toward the dinghies.

The first flare had struck its target, landing inside the farthest dinghy. The heat of the projectile quickly melted the inflated neoprene. The dinghy succumbed with a faint pop and a collapse to the right side. Kannaday's second shot missed both dinghies, but his third and fourth shots both landed in the companion vessel. The flares must have burned through the bottom. In the dying light of the overhead flare Kannaday saw the dinghy fold inward.

He loaded his last two flares and fired them into the sky. The heavens gleamed with white smoke and light. The glow illuminated a scene of a handful of men in the water, fighting to grab the few oars or the remains of the deflated dinghies. Even as the yacht groaned from somewhere under the water, Kannaday could hear their distant yells.

He had done it. Kannaday raised the pistols triumphantly, even as the yacht lurched to the starboard and dipped further toward the stern. He stumbled roughly against the flagpole, dropping the pistols as he fell. He clutched at the pole, nearly swinging over the side. He managed to stabilize his position and remain on deck. No sooner had he steadied himself than he felt a sharp stinging pain in his left shoulder.

He reached for it, simultaneously turning toward the bow. Kannaday gasped as he felt a dart in his flesh. He winced as he drew it out. He did not have to look at it to know what it was.

"A good security chief does not leave a job until it is done," said a voice from amidships.

A shape was barely visible in the dying glow of the flares. It was the form of a man. John Hawke stepped forward on the sloping deck. He was wearing a life jacket and carrying the wommera in his right hand.

"I heard the fuss you were making and decided I had better stick around," Hawke said. "All that pounding and hammering."

Hawke's right arm swooped back, then snapped forward. A second dart flew toward Kannaday. It hit him in the right thigh. It pinched and the leg buckled. He caught the flagpole to keep from hitting the deck. He hung there while he removed the second dart. The bastard could have hit him harder. He was simply playing with the captain.

"I waited for you at the bow," Hawke said. "I did not think you would make it out."

"You waited until I was out of flares," Kannaday said.

"A good security chief also knows when to make his move," Hawke replied as he began walking forward. "It's a shame you sent our men into the water, though. Not everyone has a life jacket, and it's a long way to shore." The wiry man leaned backward slightly as he approached. He remained surefooted on the sloping deck. "But it won't bother your conscience for long. Like many of them, you will drown. There can be no other mortal wound. Otherwise, you would already be dead."

Hawke was holding the wommera like a club. In a sinking ship, any number of objects could hit a sailor on the head and crack his skull. That was obviously the plan. To knock Kannaday out and then drown him.

Kannaday could not believe that he had underestimated Hawke again.

The captain had a problem and only a moment to solve it. His shoulder and leg had taken muscle damage from the darts. Hawke was uninjured. The security chief could probably overpower Kannaday. But if he turned to climb the rail, Hawke would reach Kannaday before he could get over.

Kannaday knew, of course, what he had to do. He had fought hard to regain some of his self-respect. He refused to surrender that. The captain of the *Hosannah* would not run.

The security officer was now a silhouette against the vivid splash of stars. Kannaday rested his lower back against the railing and raised his hands like a boxer. He kept his fists close to his chest. If Hawke intended to club him with the wommera, the captain wanted to try to block it. Hawke would probably go for the side he had wounded. That was why he had wounded it. Kannaday would be ready to twist and take the blow with his forearm.

Suddenly, from beneath the men, a third player entered the drama.

SIXTY

Osprey Reef
Sunday, 2:46 A.M.

The helicopter was moving in a northeasterly direction when Herbert's phone beeped. All eyes save the pilot's turned to him. Herbert could not see the eyes clearly in the dark. But he knew what was in them.

Hope. They wanted information, a shred of intelligence, a place to look. Anything. Jelbart lowered the binoculars he had been using. He and Loh looked to Bob Herbert's expression for a quick indication of whether Op-Center had learned something.

Herbert listened for a moment, then shook his head once. Without comment, Loh and Jelbart went back to looking out the windows. Ahead of them was Osprey Reef, which lay 210 miles from Cairns. It was a popular shark-watching spot for tourists. Herbert wished that were an omen.

The pilot turned to his passengers. "We're nearly at the point of no return," he shouted back. "If we don't start back in the next fifteen minutes or so, we won't reach the refueling depot."

Herbert acknowledged with a nod. He looked past the reef. It was odd. He had never felt trapped in his wheelchair. But he felt trapped now in a fast-moving helicopter unhindered by roads and mountains. That was because he lacked information and the means to get it. Ignorance was not bliss. It was a prison.

Herbert blinked his tired eyes. He raised them to the horizon. It had a slightly ruddy hue. He looked at his watch. It was not quite three A.M. It was too early for dawn.

"People, have a look at the eastern horizon," Herbert said. "What do you make of that?"

"It can't be sunrise," Loh said.

Jelbart turned his binoculars in that direction. "No. There are individual lights out there." He tapped the pilot on the shoulder and pointed. "Let's have a look before we go back."

The pilot nodded and swung the Bell toward the faint glow. Jelbart continued to study the lights with his binoculars.

"You know, those lights are the color of distress flares," Jelbart said.

Herbert thought the same thing. White flares were for a person overboard. Yellow flares were for working a line-throwing apparatus. Orange meant the user was stranded but safe. The colors were different so that the flares could provide light without needlessly summoning surrounding vessels.

Jelbart lowered his binoculars and pressed the headphones to his ears. He and the pilot were obviously receiving a message.

"One of the planes saw the light, too," Jelbart said excitedly. "Definitely flares, looks like a ketch is going down."

"Any fires?" Herbert asked.

Jelbart shook his head.

"Lifeboats?" Loh asked.

"Not that they could see," Jelbart replied.

"A ketch," Herbert said thoughtfully. "A boat like that wouldn't seem out of place here, would it?"

"No," Jelbart replied. He pulled the chart book from the sleeve on the door. He flipped to the page with the coordinates the pilot had given him. "That area of the sea is two hundred feet deep, with no reefs. Nothing a ship would be likely to strike. Not with enough force to sink it."

"Why would the smugglers sink their own ship, then send out flares?" Loh wondered.

"Especially so many flares," Jelbart pointed out. "There

had to be three or four to light the sky like that."

"They are not the kind of projectiles that would self-launch in heat or in a fire," Loh said. "They have to be triggered intentionally."

"Right," Jelbart said. "Though it appears some of these were ignited close to the water. Not in the air."

"Perhaps the boat shifted when they were firing," Loh suggested. "This may have been an act of desperation before it went down."

"You don't take a boat to deep water and sink it because you want to be found," Herbert said.

"Then why fire flares?" Jelbart asked.

"Maybe not everyone liked the idea of the boat being deep-sixed," Herbert speculated.

"A mutiny," Jelbart suggested.

"Dissent among smugglers," Herbert replied. "That's not a big leap of imagination."

"True. Well, we'll have our answers soon," Jelbart said. He turned to the pilot. "How much time until we get there?"

"About ten minutes," the pilot replied.

"If we don't go back for refueling, where's the nearest place on the mainland to set down?" Herbert asked.

Jelbart checked the map. "Moribura, which is about two hundred kilometers to the southwest."

"That would still only give us another ten minutes of hovering time," the pilot pointed out.

"My patrol boat is coming over at full speed," FNO Loh pointed out. "They should be on site in approximately one hour. They will maintain the integrity of the site."

"That may not be in time to help the people on board," Jelbart said.

"I can radio Darwin," the pilot said. "There's a Royal Volunteer Coastal Patrol base nearby. In Port Douglas, I think."

"Thanks, but that wouldn't help," Jelbart said. "The RVCP fields a Patrol 5 that does 18.5 knots, and they don't have air capability. Anyone in the water will be arm weary and damn near freezing before help arrives."

"I'm crying," Herbert said.

Jelbart ignored his remark. "Is there anything we can do before FNO Loh's patrol ship arrives?"

"Not really," the pilot said. "All I've got is an aluminum ladder and not a lot of flying time."

Herbert watched as the helicopter swept toward the boat. The light from the flares was all but gone now.

"It looks to me as if the prow is underwater," Jelbart said.

"Where were those flares burning?" Herbert asked.

"Off the stern," Jelbart told him.

"So that rules out one theory," Herbert said.

"Yes," Loh said. "The idea that someone fired across the water's surface because the vessel shifted. A forward dip would have thrown the projectiles skyward."

"Exactly," Herbert said. The intelligence officer was impressed. Monica Loh did not always seem to be listening. But she was. And she was thinking. Herbert had gotten accustomed to the way things were done in Washington. When people were silent, it was always for one of two reasons, both of them bad. Either they thought they had all the answers and were not interested in hearing any others, or they were afraid to speak because then they would have to take responsibility for suggestions that might become policy. Far too many federal employees put personal interest over national interest.

Herbert enjoyed being surprised by a person's quiet assets rather than by their hidden shortcomings. His wife Yvonne had been like that. When they started working together, the future Mrs. Herbert was always very quiet. Herbert instinctively, chauvinistically, wrongly thought of Yvonne in terms of her pay grade. She was a subordinate. She was backup. But the woman was anything but that. She was usually beside him or several steps ahead. It was odd. When the Beirut embassy was bombed, Yvonne had taken shards of wood and cinderblock in the back. Herbert had no proof of this, none at all. But he went down a moment before she did. He had always imagined that Yvonne became aware of the bomb going off an instant before he did, pushed him to the floor, and dropped on top of him. That was how the couple was found.

Whether or not they were approaching Darling's boat, Herbert no longer felt quite so trapped.

"It's too dark to see anything now," Jelbart said as he lowered his binoculars. "Wish I'd brought the bloody night-vision glasses."

"We'll be in range of the spotlights in two minutes or so," the pilot pointed out.

"We'll also be in range of any weapons they might have," Herbert said, leaning toward the pilot.

"I was just thinking that," Jelbart said.

"Sirs, we don't have any retaliatory capability," the pilot noted.

"I noticed that," Herbert said. "Mr. Jelbart, can you radio General Hopkins and ask to have the Mirages circle the area."

"Of course," Jelbart said. "Not that I think we need to worry. A sinking boat is not an ideal firing platform."

"I'll still feel better with a couple of fighters buzzing the boat, just to keep them honest," Herbert said.

"Sir, I'll try to position the under section of the hull between us and anyone who might still be on it," the pilot said. "That will make it difficult to target us."

"Sounds good," Herbert said.

"There are two things in our favor," FNO Loh observed. "All the scarring on the sampan was from small arms fire. Our adversaries may not be equipped with anything stronger. Even if they were, they are apparently out here trying to sink the evidence. That would include weapons."

Herbert nodded. That cinched it. He was in love with this woman.

The intelligence chief sat back and called Op-Center. He did not think Stephen Viens would be able to get useful satellite data in the next few minutes. However, he wanted Paul Hood to know what was going on. He also wanted to tell Hood exactly where they were.

Just in case they were wrong about the heavy artillery.

SIXTY-ONE

Washington, D.C.
Saturday, 1:00 P.M.

There was a point, about three years ago, when Paul Hood had identified a third component to his job. There was the quarterback role, there was the cheerleader function, and there was also the color commentator in the booth. The guy whose job was really to play devil's advocate.

Hood had assembled a team of professionals. Military experts. Intelligence strategists. Psychologists, diplomats, surveillance professionals. He was here to listen to what Mike Rodgers or Darrell McCaskey or Bob Herbert had to say. Whether he agreed or not, his answer had to be, "Yeah, but . . ."

He did that when Bob Herbert called from the Bell. After sitting at his desk and listening to the intelligence chief's description of the scene, Hood went into his, "Yeah, but . . ." routine. Only in this case his concern was genuine.

"How confident are you that the boat is not a decoy?" Hood asked.

"There wasn't time to pull that together," Herbert insisted.

"He had enough time to call the president's special assistant for democratic elections and get him to gnaw on me," Hood said.

"Bruce Perry?" Herbert asked.

"Yes."

"What did he do, give you the 'Why are you bothering this wonderful philanthropist' routine?" Herbert asked.

"Pretty much," Hood said. "There was nothing specific.

I wouldn't be surprised if Perry didn't know about the smuggling."

"I agree. Though it's interesting," Herbert replied.

"What is?"

"On a scale of executive influence, Perry is what? Two out of a possible ten?" Herbert asked.

"If you're breaking things down that way, I guess so," Hood agreed.

"Darling is used to dealing with the top levels of government," Herbert went on. "Perry is not as high as he could have gone *if* he had been prepared. He wasn't. This was the best he could do on short notice. Paul, I think we caught Darling with his trousers around his ankles."

Hood considered that for a moment. "That's not the conclusion I would draw," he replied.

"What then?" Herbert asked.

"I think that Perry may be as high as Darling *dared* to go," Hood said. "If he had called the Speaker of the House, and he could have—they've golfed together a number of times, according to the files—political survival instincts would have forced the Speaker to ask himself, 'What if Darling is guilty? Do I really want to go to bat for this guy?' "

"Okay," Herbert said. "That's another indication our boy Darling has something to hide."

"Right. But that doesn't mean Darling was caught off guard," Hood said. "This could still be a diversion to keep you away from the real transport. Or worse. Have you got night vision?"

"No. Nor weapons."

"Jesus," Hood said.

"Him I've got. On a chain, right near my heart," Herbert said.

It took a moment before Hood got the reference. He smiled.

"Look, Paul," Herbert went on. "We're almost at the site, and I haven't heard anything to make me want to turn back. If these guys do tag us with some kind of sucker punch, come back here in force. Dig up the boat, search it ass to chin, and find something to implicate Jervis Darling. Nothing is ever one hundred percent clean. Nothing."

"Bob, we've charged into places before and paid a heavy price," Hood reminded him. They lost Charlie Squires in Russia, and the bulk of the Striker team averting war between India and Pakistan.

"Yeah. And I paid a toll when I was just standing around an embassy minding my own business," Herbert said.

"Beirut was a war zone," Hood reminded him.

"Paul, these days, the world's a goddamn war zone," Herbert said. "Anyway, I have no right to turn back. Managing crises is part of the job description. If this is the boat the smugglers have been using, it certainly qualifies."

Hood was fresh out of "Yeah buts . . ." He had done that part of his job. Now it was time to do the next part. The secondary, more difficult part. To rein in his own natural conservatism. To refrain from overruling his field officer. To let him have his head.

To allow him to risk his life.

"All right. Just keep the phone line open, will you?" Hood asked.

"Sure," Herbert said. "You won't hear much, though. It's pretty damn noisy in here."

"That's exactly what I hope to hear, Bob," Hood replied.

"I don't follow," Herbert said.

"I want to hear a very loud helicopter returning from a successful recon mission," Hood said.

"Gotcha," Herbert said. "Thanks. We're getting ready to switch on the spotlight now. And Paul?"

"Yes?"

"If that bastard Perry calls again, put him on hold," Herbert said.

"Sure. Why?"

"With luck," Herbert said, "we'll have some news for you real soon."

SIXTY-TWO

The Coral Sea
Sunday, 3:01 A.M.

The yacht had assumed a life of its own. It seemed like a legendary sea beast as it moved and turned in the dark sea. It became a participant in the struggle between the two men.

As though resenting their entrapment, the waters in the lower deck of the *Hosannah* shifted. That caused the prow of the vessel to drop suddenly, hurling Hawke back and Kannaday forward. The men collided amidships, then tumbled hard against the mainmast. Hawke lost his wommera, and both men lost their bearings. They continued to slide forward as the yacht's aft section rose. The arms of both men pinwheeled at their sides. They tried to grab at anything that might break their fall. At the same time, the vessel began sliding deeper into the water. The forward portholes cracked, and large air bubbles popped from the openings. Each one caused the yacht to hop slightly, as though muscles were contracting. They forced the yacht up slightly, but only for a moment. The final, downward slide had begun.

Kannaday lost sight of Hawke. His hands found a flopping halyard, and he held tight. But his body was weak from loss of blood. He hung there while the yacht slid further into the sea. His ear was pressed to the slanting deck. He heard the roar of water as it pounded against the hull.

It was strange, Kannaday thought. He probably had only a minute or two more to live. Yet he felt oddly euphoric. He had returned from the dead to confront Hawke.

A life of wandering had ended in a flourish of purpose. It felt good.

Suddenly, through the spray of water, Kannaday saw a light. He wondered if this was the light of the afterlife people spoke of. He watched as the white beacon, sharply haloed with a rainbow, appeared to be growing larger. A moment later, Kannaday heard a drone. The sound rose above the rush of water that was coming from below. As the white light approached, Kannaday realized it was above him. This was not the glow of passing from one world to the next.

It was a helicopter. Perhaps its pilot had seen the flares and had come to investigate. Not that it mattered. There were too many people to rescue, and they were far from shore. He did not think many of these men could stay afloat for the two or more hours it would take for ships to reach this remote point.

Kannaday's fingers were cramped and trembling. He was holding tightly, but the rope was slippery and the angle of the yacht increasingly severe. The captain began to lose his hold. He moved his feet around. The steeper the angle, the more dead weight his own body became. He was looking for a place to brace himself. He found nothing.

The light floated behind the yacht. Kannaday slipped a little more. He let go with one hand and tried to wrap the rope around his wrist. There was not enough slack to do that. He was losing blood and felt his head swim. His fingers weakened, and he slipped farther down the line. But Kannaday forced himself to hold tight. He wanted to finish what he had started belowdecks. The long overdue reformation of Peter Kannaday. A captain was supposed to resist any effort to mutiny. In the end, he had done that. The unwritten law of the sea also dictated that a captain remain with his ship until passengers and crew had been safely evacuated. Kannaday intended to honor that, too, even though he hoped that John Hawke drowned with him. He knew that Hawke was still somewhere on the deck of the sinking ship. Kannaday had seen the security officer hanging to the bottom edge of the forward hatch. He refused to surrender the *Hosannah* to him. Even in the end.

Strong winds howled along the sides of the yacht as the vessel slid deeper into the sea. It was rotor wash from the helicopter. The light behind it rose slowly behind the ship. Kannaday saw the *Hosannah* silhouetted on the restless sea. It was a foreshortened, oblong shape.

Almost like a coffin.

That was the last thing Kannaday saw as the ship went under. It dragged him feetfirst into the cold water. His fingers remained wrapped on the rope as he submerged. He did not hold his breath, and he did not struggle. It did not matter to him what the maritime authorities made of the sinking. What mattered was that Peter Kannaday knew the truth.

He had died a captain.

SIXTY-THREE

The Coral Sea
Sunday, 3:08 A.M.

"I think it's safe to go around," Herbert said.

The American's voice was thick with sarcasm as the ship vanished. Jelbart turned his binoculars on the water where the boat had been.

"Did the name of the yacht sound familiar to anyone?" Herbert asked. "The *Hosannah*?"

"No," Jelbart said. "But it looked like a typical charter. You see them a lot in this region."

"There is someone down there," FNO Loh said suddenly.

"Where?" Jelbart asked.

"On my side," Loh said. "Floating facedown."

The pilot turned the helicopter around so Jelbart could see. "You're right," Jelbart said. "And there's someone swimming toward him. Officer Loh, can you get the ladder?"

The Singaporean reached behind her. She unhooked the rolled aluminum ladder from the small storage area.

"There are hooks on the floor," the pilot said.

"I see them," Loh replied. She unbuckled her seat belt and dropped to one knee. She fastened the top of the ladder to the steel hooks, gave a hard tug, then undid the nylon bands around the ladder. "Ready," she said.

"He's waving to us," Jelbart said. "It must be someone who did not want the ship to go down."

"That would be someone we definitely want to talk to," Herbert remarked.

"If we do get him, we'll have to leave immediately,"

the pilot said. "The extra weight is going to put a strain on our fuel consumption."

"I understand," Jelbart said. "Let's get him."

The pilot acknowledged. There may be other survivors out there. He did not like the idea of leaving them. Not at night in a cold, tortured sea. But he liked even less the prospect of having to ditch the Bell at sea if they could not reach shore.

"Officer Loh, would you deploy the ladder?" the pilot asked. He turned the chopper around.

Loh held on to the canvas strap beside the door, then opened it. She leaned out. The downdraft was stronger than she expected. She had to brace herself against the other side of the doorway.

The man was treading water beside the other sailor. He had turned the body onto its back. It did not appear to be moving. She used her left foot to kick the ladder out. The man was far enough away so that it would not hit him when deployed. The ladder clattered gently as it unrolled. Loh leaned out again.

"Can he make it without assistance?" Jelbart asked.

"He's trying," Loh replied. "He's swimming toward it but only using one arm. The other seems to be injured."

"I can't go any lower or we'll blow him under," the pilot said.

Loh watched as the man threw his right arm up. He grabbed the lowest rung and brought his left arm over. He was having trouble raising it. His left arm looked like it might be broken.

"He's struggling," Loh said. She turned around. "I'm going down."

"Officer, take these!" the pilot said. He handed her his gloves. "They'll help your grip."

"Thank you," she said as she pulled them on. Loh backed out the open door and started down.

The ladder vibrated as the naval officer made her way down. There were twenty rungs to the surface of the sea. She took them slowly. The rungs, FNO Loh's cheeks, and her clothing quickly became damp with seawater. The gloves proved to be a lifesaver.

Every few steps the officer looked down. She wanted to make sure the sailor was still hanging on. He was there, his right arm hooked over the rung. If he went under, Loh knew that she would have to drop in to retrieve him.

The descent went quickly. When Loh was one rung above him, she carefully stepped to the rung he was holding. His expression was tight. He appeared to be in extreme pain.

"Can you put your bad arm around my shoulder?" she yelled down.

"I think so," he said. He cocked his head to the side. "That man betrayed me! I want his body brought aboard."

"We can talk about this inside!" she said.

"You don't understand," the man said. "He's a traitor! You need to fingerprint him, find out what else he may be involved in."

"We're low on fuel," Loh told him. "There is a patrol ship on the way. They will collect his remains."

The officer ducked lower. The man seemed to hesitate. Then, reluctantly, he tried to raise his left arm. Loh reached back with her right hand to pull it around her neck. He clutched her collar with weak, bleeding fingers. She shifted slightly and hefted him a little higher. Then they started climbing. The man was not exactly dead weight, but neither was he as helpful as she had hoped. About halfway up she really began to feel the strain. Each rung was twice as difficult as the one before. The man was trying to climb with her. But each time he reached with his good arm, he rested his full weight on her back. She was surprised at how difficult this was. At the naval academy's annual fitness review, FNO Loh was still able to climb a rope thirty feet without using her legs. Of course, she did not try the escalade, as it was called, with a man on her back.

"Officer Loh, pass him up!"

Someone was shouting down at her. FNO Loh looked up. Bob Herbert was sitting in her seat. He was holding on to the strap and leaning out. His right arm was extended. She had to climb another three rungs to reach it.

The officer looked ahead and pulled herself up another rung.

"Officer, stop or we'll lose you both!" Herbert yelled. "Help him climb over your back onto the ladder. I'll grab him. I promise."

Loh did not acknowledge. She did not want to give up before the job was finished. That was not how she lived, and it was not how she had been trained. She looked straight ahead, at the landing strut. She tried to climb another rung. Her arms were so weak they were shaking. She stopped.

"Dammit, my legs may not work but I can curl fifty pounds with each arm," Herbert said.

The man leaned close to Loh's ear. "I'm going to try to reach your friend," he said.

"All right," Loh replied.

The Singaporean officer snaked her left arm through the rungs so her right arm was free. The man shifted to her right side and grasped the rung above her. She used her free arm to help him up. Bob Herbert was right. This was easier than trying to move them both. Meanwhile, Herbert reached behind the man and hooked a hand under his good arm. That gave the man all the extra lift he needed. With Loh pushing from below, he was able to make it into the doorway. Herbert pulled him in. Loh followed.

"You okay?" Herbert asked when Loh climbed in.

"Yes," she said. "Are you sure there isn't time to get the other man?"

"Very sure," the pilot said, glancing at the fuel gauge. "We need to pull out. Now."

The naval officer understood. She unhooked the ladder, pulled it in, and shut the door. She piled it against the door, then fell into the empty seat across from Herbert. She looked at him as the pilot swung the helicopter to the southwest. "Thank you, Bob."

"Yes, thank you," said the new arrival.

Loh and Herbert looked at him. The man was sitting in the seat that Herbert had vacated to help him aboard. He was soaked and shivering. He had his left elbow cupped in his right hand.

"Do you have a towel back here?" Herbert asked the pilot.

"I'm afraid not," the pilot replied.

"A bottle of water?" Herbert asked.

"I finished it a hundred miles back."

Herbert regarded the man and shrugged. "Sorry."

"That's all right," he said weakly. "I'm just glad to be here. I thought I was a dead man."

"How about that arm?" Herbert asked. "We can rig a sling for you."

"It's my shoulder, actually," the man said. "It was hurt when the boat was upended. It will keep."

"We'll get that taken care of ashore," Jelbart said. "In the meantime, talk to us. Who are you?"

"I am Peter Kannaday, captain of the *Hosannah*," the man said weakly. "And you people are?"

"I'm Warrant Officer Jelbart. The gentleman across from you is Bob Herbert, and the lady is Female Naval Officer Loh."

"Australia, America, and—Singapore?"

Loh nodded.

"I thank you all," the man said with a little nod to each.

"Tell me, Captain. What were you doing out here?" Jelbart asked.

"And who was that individual in the water with you?" Loh asked as she removed the damp pilot's gloves. She flexed her cold fingers. "You said he betrayed you."

"He betrayed me, and he betrayed Australia," the man replied coldly, his eyes fixed on something far away.

"How?" Loh asked.

The man blinked quickly as though waking from a trance.

"Captain Kannaday?" Loh pressed.

"Forgive me," the man said. Suddenly, he began to sob. "Officers, if you would indulge me. This has been a terrible night. I would like to shut my eyes for just a few minutes."

"Captain Kannaday, we understand what you've been through. But this is rather urgent," Jelbart said. "I need you to tell us who the man was and why you were out here."

"His name is Hawke," the man replied. "John Hawke. And he brought the *Hosannah* out here to sink it."

"Why?" Jelbart asked.

The man sat back and shut his eyes. He said nothing.

"Captain?" Jelbart said. "Captain!"

"Officers, I must rest," the man said. "Please. For just a few minutes. It won't change anything, I assure you."

Water dribbled down the man's temples and forehead, and his head slumped against the window. Loh leaned across the aisle and jabbed him with a finger. He grumbled but did not open his eyes.

"If this were Singapore, we'd wake him," Loh said.

"If this were Singapore, I'd help you," Herbert said. "We've got a nice, long ladder. What are the international laws about fly-fishing a guy from a helicopter to wake him?"

"It's called 'extreme coercion,' Mr. Herbert," Jelbart said. "What your legal system would define as 'cruel and unusual punishment.' "

"These are extreme and unusual circumstances," Loh remarked. Her tone was unsympathetic. She did not respect weakness. Especially from a man whose life she just saved.

"Nonetheless, this man is not the pirate we found," Jelbart said. "As far as we know, this man has not committed a crime. We have no recourse but to bring him in and question him at his convenience."

"There are times when we worry about etiquette and protocol too much," Loh said.

"I'm with Officer Loh on that," Herbert said. "We have two responsibilities here. One is to the captain. The other is to a few million people just like him. In one case, a guy may be inconvenienced. In the other case, tens of thousands may die. That's not even a contest to me."

"We can honor both," Jelbart insisted. "The captain asked for a few minutes. Let us at least give him that."

Herbert shook his head, and Monica Loh sat back. She wondered if Jelbart would have been so compassionate if Captain Kannaday had been American. Or Singaporean. Australians were notoriously protective of their own.

Because it was her nature, she also wondered whether Captain Kannaday were really asleep or whether he had been listening carefully to everything they said. Trying to decide what he should say.

She did not know. One thing she did know, however. Soon, someone on board was going to be apologizing to someone else on board for a serious miscalculation.

SIXTY-FOUR

Washington, D.C.
Saturday, 1:24 P.M.

Research was job number four for Paul Hood. That came after quarterbacking, cheerleading, and devil's advocacy.

Hood usually did research only on weekends, when Op-Center had just a skeleton staff. He actually enjoyed it. Searching for information exercised his linear thinking. It gave more logic to those "yeah but . . ." questions. It also shut out his emotions, his fears. He was totally in the moment.

Bob Herbert had left the cell phone open. Hood had put the call on the speakerphone, cranked up the volume, and listened to the conversation between the rescue team and Peter Kannaday. As soon as he heard that name, Hood conducted a computer search through Interpol and FBI files. Nothing showed up. That was good. It suggested the man was telling the truth, that he had been used and shanghied. Hood also did a wider off-line search and came across the registry filing for the *Hosannah*. There was information about Peter Kannaday. He was the owner of the yacht before it was "sold" to the apparently nonexistent Arvids March. It included copies of his license and dates when the yacht had visited various ports in the South Pacific and the Caribbean. Hood forwarded that information to Herbert's computer. If the *Hosannah* had been used to traffic nuclear material, the abbreviated log might help to track pickups or drop-offs.

Hood felt the way Warrant Officer Jelbart did. The man was a guest, not a prisoner. That was very easy to forget in times of high emotion, which occurred with some frequency whenever Bob Herbert was involved.

That's why you have to hold tight to what you once determined was right, Hood told himself. Otherwise, police officers became bullies, presidents became tyrants, and intelligence officers became both.

Hood sent the Kannaday file to Herbert with an audible prompt. He knew the intelligence chief would be sitting in the cabin, stewing. He wanted to make sure Herbert got the E-mail.

Hood heard the wheelchair beep over the phone. The data file had arrived. He still found it pretty amazing that information could be sent around the world so quickly, so completely, and so secretly. He remembered when he was still in school, and telexes were a big, innovative deal. That was about the time when Pong was the rage at airports and college lounges.

At least most forms of terrorism still had to be done the old-fashioned way. The killing tools of that despicable trade had to be moved slowly, by hand. And like a slug trailing slime across a slate walk, there was no way to erase all evidence of its passage. In days of depressing reality, that was a cheering thought.

It was at once sad and astonishing what passed for hope in the twenty-first century.

SIXTY-FIVE

The Coral Sea
Sunday, 3:33 A.M.

Herbert was stewing.

The intelligence chief did not think that Warrant Officer Jelbart was wrong about backing off Kannaday. He just did not think that Jelbart was right.

Captain Kannaday was hurt. Herbert had no doubt that the man was exhausted. But he did not believe the man was asleep. Kannaday's nap was the Australian equivalent of cover-your-ass. Whatever had happened on the yacht was illegal. Kannaday had said as much. He was not going to say anything else without a barrister or solicitor or whatever they called criminal attorneys Down Under.

It had also been imprudent of Jelbart to mention the pirate. That information had not been made public. If Kannaday were asleep, it would not matter. If he were awake, he might be less inclined to talk. The captain might say things that contradicted what officials already knew from the pirate. That would not be good for Kannaday.

Herbert's E-mail alert beeped. "Christ," he said.

"What's wrong?" Jelbart asked.

Herbert turned and snapped the cell phone from the armrest of the wheelchair.

"Paul, are you still there?"

"I am," Hood said.

"Sorry, boss," Herbert told him. "I forgot you were hanging on. What have you got?"

"A file on Peter Kannaday," Hood said. "I thought you might like to have a look at it."

"Absolutely," Herbert said. The laptop monitor was anchored in the left armrest of the wheelchair. Herbert craned around and swung the screen toward him. He punched the On button. It activated with a hiss. He opened and downloaded Hood's E-mail.

"Do you think the captain is really asleep?" Hood asked.

"Yeah," Herbert said. "And I'm going to be the next president of the United States."

"Do you believe anything he said?" Hood asked.

"I don't know," Herbert admitted. He was watching the monitor as the file downloaded. "I don't have enough information."

"And there's nothing you or Officer Loh can do to get that information," Hood said.

"Well, there is—" Herbert said.

"Lawfully, I mean," Hood interrupted. "Peter Kannaday is an Australian captain working in international waters. He was rescued by an Australian helicopter. They're going to have the first swing at him."

"Paul, we've got to fight that," Herbert said. "Maybe Lowell can pull some legal precedent out of his brain pan." The intelligence chief looked out the window as the computer continued opening the file. It was dark out there. But not as dark as Herbert felt inside.

"Come on, Bob. You know better."

"Unfortunately, I do," Herbert replied.

"Even if Lowell got us in to talk to Kannaday, he's not going to let an interview turn rough," Hood said.

"He'd rather see some psycho warlord get heavy artillery?"

"The Australians won't let that happen," Hood replied. "Give them some credit."

"In a perfect world, I would," Herbert said. "But if the authorities find out our other friend may be involved, I'll tell you exactly what they'll do. They'll circle the wagons around the big man. They have to. It would bring down his empire, do damage to the national economy. They'll scapegoat some secondary guy to keep their national treasure from being sullied. If that happens, we'll never get all the names we're after. And we'll never know if we've cut this caravan off completely."

Herbert did not want to mention Darling's name in case Kannaday was awake. If the man were going to talk, Herbert wanted him to mention Darling without being prompted. A lie or cover-up could usually be identified quickly. A half-truth was much more troublesome.

"I don't agree that they'll protect Darling," Hood said. "Something this big would leak eventually. They will have to cut a deal."

"I don't like the smell of that," Herbert said.

"It's done in business all the time," Hood said. "The alternative is closing your eyes or bringing down the whole system to get one man. In exchange for cooperation, regulators or investigators give executives a degree of immunity and time to turn the companies over to associates."

"Jesus, Paul," Herbert complained. "We're not talking about insider trading here."

"I recognize that—"

"I don't want to see this guy have his passport revoked and agree to the equivalent of house arrest," Herbert said. "That isn't right."

"I agree. And I don't want *you* to forget that this isn't about retribution," Hood said. "That's why a Richard Nixon resigns and gets a pardon, or a Kurt Waldheim has his visa shredded and any war crimes he may have been involved in are locked in a filing cabinet. It's about fixing a problem with a minimum of embarrassment, if possible."

"That's the solution of a bureaucrat," Herbert said. "I want this guy's tanned hide."

"*That* is the self-righteous indignation of the Lone Ranger," Hood replied. "Bob, if Darling is guilty, I'd love to see him get life in prison. But that probably won't happen. Right or wrong, you can't just remove a foundation of international industry like that. Maybe over time, but not immediately."

"Over time people will forget," Herbert said. "They'll forgive."

"That's possible," Hood agreed.

"It's inevitable," Herbert said.

"Not if he was trying to kill people," Hood said. "Al Capone was a folk hero until he ordered the Saint Valentine's Day Massacre. People will cheer someone who beats the establishment. They won't tolerate mass murder."

The computer beeped, signaling that the file had been downloaded. Herbert terminated the link and opened the file. He was angry. He was not angry at Hood. He was angry because Hood was right. Jervis Darling would probably survive a worst-case scenario.

"Bob?" Hood said.

"Yeah."

"You're unusually quiet."

"Sorry," Herbert replied. "I was thinking about what you said."

"And?"

"Like Mr. Jelbart, you've got a point. I just don't happen to like it," Herbert told him. "Is that what we do for a living? Risk our lives so we can settle for a compromise?"

"It seems that way," Hood said.

"It doesn't seem right."

"I agree," Hood said, "but that's the ante when your opponents are ready to risk *their* lives. Besides, in our business a trade-off that prevents a war is still better than a loss."

"I don't know," Herbert said. "I never respected football teams that went for a field goal and a tie. That's not what champions do."

Hood chuckled.

"What's so funny?" Herbert asked.

"Your choice of words," Hood said. "When I was mayor, there was a small bronze plaque in city hall. It was a quote from Daniel Webster that read, 'This is a hall for mutual consultation and discussion, not an arena for the exhibition of champions.' I believe that."

"You would, Paul. You have the patience for talk,"

Herbert said. His tone was not disparaging. He admired
Hood's diplomacy.

"Talk works," Hood said. "If you're doing that, you
probably aren't killing each other."

"I can do both."

"Only if you're screaming, not talking," Hood said.

Hood was right about that point. The problem was, Herbert had always liked his way of doing things. It worked.
Hood made it sound bad.

"Anyway, it isn't patience," Hood went on. "Talk is
my weapon of choice. It worked well with voters and with
my kids. Now it's a part of me. I couldn't change if I
wanted to." He added pointedly, "None of us can."

Finally, there was something Herbert could agree with.

Hood said that he would call Lowell Coffey and bring
him up to speed. Herbert thanked him and hung up the
phone. He sat back and thought about what Hood said.

None of them could change.

Hood was right about that. But with that comment came
Paul Hood's tacit acknowledgment that he accepted Bob
Herbert as is. That gave Herbert a little wiggle room. He
had not been told, expressly, to stay out of the investigation and interrogation.

What it did not give Herbert, immediately, was a place
to put his fist. He was furious with Jervis Darling, with
the polite but recalcitrant Peter Kannaday, and with the
coddling mentality in general. Herbert understood talk.
But to be honest, he still preferred war. It took less time
and it resolved disputes a lot quicker. Nor were the casualties any heavier, really. Just quicker. The combatants
lost to bullets what they would have lost to endless raids
and corrosive debate.

Herbert noticed Loh staring at him.

"What are you thinking?" he asked her.

"I agree with you," she said.

"About?"

"A stalemate," she said.

Herbert smiled. "I didn't think you would care for that."

"Not at all. I would rather fight and lose than feel as

though I did not give something my fullest effort," she replied.

Herbert smiled at her. That iced it. FNO Monica Loh had to become the next Mrs. Herbert. He was betting she had less patience for bullshit and insincerity than he did.

Almost absently, Herbert reached behind him and opened the computer file Paul Hood had sent. The intelligence chief angled the monitor toward him. He considered dreamily how he and Monica would be banned from every party and fund-raiser in Washington, D.C.

The file opened. Herbert glanced at it. His eyes shrank and his mouth widened. He stared at the screen more closely.

And he knew at once what to do with his rage.

SIXTY-SIX

Cairns, Australia
Sunday, 3:56 A.M.

The call was late.

Jervis Darling stood in the beige kitchen eating a half cantaloupe from the rind. He was no longer dressed in the gray Cairns Yacht Club sweat suit he had been wearing earlier. He had exercised on his rowing machine for forty-five minutes. Then he showered, pulled on a bathrobe, and sat in front of the television. He moved impatiently from satellite to satellite, watching nothing as the hours passed. At the same time, his mood shifted from disgust to anger to concern. He should have heard from his nephew or John Hawke by now. But the cell phone in his pocket had remained resolutely silent.

Darling finished the fruit. He cut the rind into slices and fed it into the garbage disposal. Things always seemed worse in the dark hours of night. Yet he could not help but think that something had gone wrong. Even if they had failed to sink the yacht, Marcus would have gotten in touch with him. The only thing he could think of was that miserable American.

Other than by dumb, idiotic luck, Darling could not imagine how Herbert might have found the yacht. Or what he might have done to stop Hawke. No one stopped John Hawke. As he finished pulping the rind, Darling began to consider what he should do. Earlier that evening he had called his old college friend Bruce Perry about Herbert. Perry had said he would handle it. The men had not spoken since. Darling did not want to call and ask him how the conversation went. Pressure was as good as an admission of guilt. The only thing that drove away an ally faster was failure.

Darling began to consider his next move. It might have to be a bolder preventative step than simply calling a friend at the White House. This was not a position Darling enjoyed. He was usually the one maneuvering CEOs or politicians into a corner.

Darling felt that he should wake Jessica-Ann and leave the estate. He and his daughter could go to the cove and take the yacht to his retreat in the Sister Islands. Or they could drive to the airstrip and depart by jet. If something had gone wrong, Darling did not want to be easily accessible. Since the Sister Islands were part of New Zealand, that would add another country—and another bureaucracy—between himself and any legal activities. He would let the barristers tackle any issues that might come up.

Though these concerns are premature, Darling reminded himself.

Darling still did not know for certain that anything was wrong. John Hawke could simply be hiding until dawn. He might have had a reason to maintain silence. Or he could be playing a psychological game of some kind. Darling would not put it past Hawke to make him wait. Hawke would do that from spite or to show some muscle. Just enough to be annoying but not enough to threaten. Hawke knew better than to cross that boundary.

After considering the situation for several minutes more, Darling decided that it would be a good idea to leave. He would take the jet to the nearest of his islands in the Sisters. Picking up the house phone, Darling woke Andrew and told him to pack a bag for himself and for his daughter. Next he called his pilot, Shawn Daniels, who lived in a cottage at the far end of the estate. Darling told him to be ready to fly out within the hour. The Learjet was always ready and accessible for unexpected business trips.

Finally, Darling went to wake his daughter. He moved quickly but unhurriedly to the living room and up the winding marble staircase. Jessica-Ann would be groggy, and she would sleep through the flight. She would wake up to invigorating sunshine and clean sea air. Wake from the restful sleep of the innocent. Darling wished that were something he could enjoy.

Not that it matters. Things will look better in the morning, he assured himself.

If they did not, he would have them fixed by the afternoon. Either through talk or through deed.

A man with radioactive materials at his disposal always had options.

SIXTY-SEVEN

The Coral Sea
Sunday, 4:01 A.M.

Monica Loh sat in the deep vinyl seat of the helicopter's dark cabin. She was watching Bob Herbert. His face was in shadow, but his posture was tense, aggressive. He was leaning forward, anxiously pressing a thumb into his palm. Loh did not wonder what he was thinking. She knew. He wanted to get information from Captain Kannaday using any means possible. Herbert had said as much when he was on the telephone.

But then something changed. Herbert glanced at his computer monitor and sat up. His hands relaxed. He turned toward Captain Kannaday and regarded him for a long moment. Then he looked at her.

"Wake him," Herbert said.

Loh turned and gave Kannaday's shoulder a firm shake. He opened his eyes slowly.

Warrant Officer Jelbart turned. "What is it?"

"I wanted to ask our guest a question," Herbert said.

"I thought we had decided to let the captain be for now," Jelbart said with a hint of annoyance.

"I let him have his power nap," Herbert said. "Now I want to know something. Something simple."

"You are free to ask anything you like," the man replied.

"Thanks. But you're saying you may not answer," Herbert said.

"As I said, I am extremely tired. I don't want to say anything that is inaccurate or may be misinterpreted."

"I understand," Herbert said. "How about this, which is pretty tough to screw up. Where were you born?"

The man looked at him.

"What's wrong?" Herbert asked. "Is that too tough?"

"Are you serious?" the man asked.

"I've been accused of that, yeah," Herbert said. "Have you got an answer for me?"

"I was born here. In Australia," the man replied.

"In which town?" Herbert asked. "On what date?"

"Why?" The man grinned. "Are you going to buy me a gift?"

"One that keeps on giving," Herbert told him. "A lifetime sentence in a maximum security prison."

"Really?" the man said. "For what?"

"I think you know," Herbert said.

"Bob, we decided we weren't going to do anything like this," Jelbart said angrily.

"*You* decided that," Herbert said. His eyes remained on Kannaday. "Where were you born and when?"

Loh did not think Herbert would bully someone unless he had a solid reason. Apparently, he did. She watched Kannaday's reaction. He was unfazed. After a few moments the captain closed his eyes. His head sank back on the seat and was lost again in darkness.

"Bob, why do you want to know that?" Jelbart asked.

"Why?" Herbert replied. "Because this man is not Peter Kannaday."

"What?" Jelbart said.

"I just saw a photograph of Captain Kannaday," Herbert said. He angled the monitor toward Jelbart and cranked up the brightness. "There is a picture attached to his license."

Jelbart looked from the computer monitor to their guest. "I'll be a nong—an idiot, to you. Bob is right. This isn't you."

"Rot," the man replied without opening his eyes. "There's obviously a mistake in the file."

"I don't think so," Herbert said. "There were two men on the deck of the yacht. One man dies. The other man assumes his identity."

"Why?" the man asked. His eyes were still shut. He seemed utterly unconcerned.

"What better way to earn our trust than to pose as a virtuous sea captain fighting smugglers? We give that trust, along with safe passage to shore. Then, as soon as you get there, you slip away."

"The photograph is as mixed up as you are, Mr. Herbert."

"Then answer the question," Herbert pressed. "Where and when were you born?"

Loh was watching the man carefully. He did not flinch. Nor did he tell Herbert what he wanted to hear.

"I'll tell you what," Herbert said. "You're a cheap fake and a lowlife smuggler, but I won't hold that against you. You're not the guy I want."

The man said nothing.

"The man I want is Jervis Darling," Herbert continued. "You give him to me, and you walk."

The man opened his eyes slightly. "You can't offer that kind of deal."

"You don't deny that Mr. Darling is behind this smuggling operation?" Jelbart asked.

"*Mr.* Darling," the man said with contempt. "You'd call the fallen prince Your Highness," he suggested.

"Obviously, you do know Darling, then," Herbert said.

"Only by reputation," the man replied. He closed his eyes again and settled deeper into the seat.

Loh was surprised. Herbert seemed unusually calm. Like a grand master with a checkmate move that no one else saw.

"You look like the kind of tough monkey who isn't afraid to face death," Herbert said. "Much as I'd like to, I won't threaten to throw you out the helicopter door or anything like that. What I am going to do, however, is change the plan. And since we found you in international waters, I don't think Warrant Officer Jelbart has the will or authority to object."

Jelbart nodded. The floor was Herbert's.

"We are not going to take you to Cairns," the intelligence officer went on. "We are going to land at Cape Melville where the local police will meet us and hold you.

We will turn you over to FNO Loh. When her patrol ship arrives, you will be taken to Singapore, to the military police, and the ultimate justice of the magistrate's court."

The man looked at him. "Balls to you," he replied.

Herbert shrugged. "Suit yourself, tough little monkey. Either way, I get Darling. Pilot? Make the change."

The pilot looked at Jelbart. The warrant officer nodded.

"We will get the information we want," Loh added, "because the chief interrogator will have it flogged or drugged from you. The military police have that authority under the Singaporean Nuclear Emergency Response Act of 2002. It defined nuclear trafficking as an act of terrorism. In Singapore, individual rights are suspended when evidence points to imminent deeds of mass destruction."

Herbert gave her an appreciative look for the added push.

The man opened his eyes. They did not seem quite as relaxed as they were a moment before.

"We're nearing the coast," Herbert pressed. "What's it going to be? Jail here and cooperation, or jail there and electrodes on the earlobes and God knows where else?"

The man looked out the window. The coast was coming into view.

"I'm guessing you've been pretty slick till this point," Herbert said. "But your luck has hit a wall. Trust me."

The man regarded Herbert. "I won't go to jail," he said. "I did not run the ship, and I did not run the operation. I was just a mate."

"Are you John Hawke?" Herbert asked.

"Yes," he replied.

"What was your job?"

"Security chief," he answered unapologetically. "I had no contact with sellers or purchasers, and I did not interact with the contraband. Peter Kannaday ran the ship. Jervis Darling ran the operation. His nephew Marcus operated communications and is back there in the water."

"Those flares?" Loh asked.

"They were fired by Kannaday to sink the dinghies,"

Hawke replied. "He wanted to prevent anyone from getting away."

"Why?" Herbert demanded.

"Because we were told by Jervis Darling to sink the ship," Hawke said.

"To hide evidence of what?" Herbert asked.

"A nuclear processing laboratory on board," Hawke replied.

Herbert smiled.

"But I will not repeat any of this for the record if you send me to prison," Hawke said. "I go free, or you have no testimony."

"The deal is this," Herbert told him. "You talk or you go to Singapore. We'll encourage leniency, but that's the best you'll get."

"That's not good enough," Hawke snarled.

"The only other option is to walk out the door right now," Herbert told him. "Frankly, I think five to ten years with cable TV is a better deal than a long drop into a cold sea."

Even in the dark, Loh could see Hawke's expression tighten. He looked as if he wanted to put a fist through Herbert's chest. But that would get him nothing. He would still have to deal with Loh and Jelbart.

John Hawke's mouth sagged into a frown. His eyes lost their cruel luster. The slight man lowered himself back into the seat and looked out the window. He appeared to be lost. Herbert was right. This was probably the first time the man had ever been cornered. And it happened without a blow thrown or shot fired. The security chief had been undone by words.

Just words.

Herbert looked as pleased and surprised as Hawke looked sullen.

SIXTY-EIGHT

Cairns, Australia
Sunday, 4:45 A.M.

The sun was beginning to brighten the skies behind the hills as Lowell Coffey waited for the helicopter. The attorney had managed to get a little sleep in the fire station before Hood called to tell him about Captain Kannaday's rescue. Spider was asleep in the next cot. Coffey stepped into the brisk morning to take the call. When it was done, he breathed in the crisp air.

Washington, D.C., had never tasted like this. Nor Beverly Hills. Both cities were hot and fuel-scented. The only other place the attorney had spent any time was the Middle East. That was dusty and arid.

Queensland was not just soul reviving. It was a treat for the eyes and ears. It was a deep, rich green and silent, save for the occasional bird or cricket and the wind that carried the sound.

"Jesus!"

Coffey jumped when his phone beeped again. He fished it from his belt. It was Bob Herbert, telling him that the helicopter had landed at an air base to refuel. They would be arriving in Cairns by five-thirty. He also wanted to inform Coffey that the man they had on board was not Peter Kannaday.

"It's a thug named John Hawke, who has confessed to sinking the yacht and helping Jervis Darling smuggle nuclear waste from ship to ship. The yacht even had a processing lab on board."

"He told you all this on the helicopter?" Coffey asked.

"Right."

"No attorney?"

"We fished a barracuda from the Coral Sea and used him," Herbert said. "No, we didn't have an attorney."

"And you have no evidence," Coffey asked.

"No."

"Then you have no right to hold him," Coffey replied.

"What the hell are you talking about?" Herbert asked. "We have a shitload of circumstantial evidence."

"No," Coffey said. "What you have is a 'confession' that he can deny ever having made. Word against word is a hollow legal exercise."

"Oh, come *on!*" Herbert said. "Four people heard him!"

"Four people can plot," Coffey said. "They're no more valid than one, legally. The Rule of Evidence applies here just as it does in the United States. The Evidence Act was amended in 1995 to link it to the Drugs, Poisons, and Controlled Substances Act of 1981."

"To do what?" Herbert asked. "Protect drug dealers?"

"To preserve justice," Coffey replied. "Where is Hawke now?"

"He's still in the helicopter."

"Smart."

"What?"

"He wouldn't want to get out on a military base," Coffey said. "If he did, you could theoretically hold him for trespassing."

"Lowell, this is a joke, isn't it?" Herbert demanded. "You're pulling my bum leg."

"Bob, I am completely serious," Coffey said.

"That's *not* what I want to hear," Herbert snapped.

"Sorry. But unless you can get someone who will identify Hawke as an accomplice, you have no reason or right to hold him," Coffey said. "Until you get to the yacht and locate evidence, until you can connect Hawke to smuggling activities or to the sinking, he's an innocent man. When you land here, he can demand to be released. And you'll have to let him go."

"I don't believe this," Herbert said. "The prick played me. He fed me what I wanted to keep from going to Singapore."

"Is that where you told him you'd take him?" Coffey asked.

Herbert said it was.

"*That,* at least, would have been legal," Coffey said.

"Wait. What do you mean 'would have been'?" Herbert asked. "Can't we still do it?"

"Sure, but it probably won't do you any good," Coffey told him.

"Why?"

"You landed in Australia," Coffey said. "Hawke is Australian. Under international law, that gives the authorities here first crack at him. If you took him to Singapore now, the courts there could not move against him unless Australia first declined to do so."

"Which they won't," Herbert said. "Not if Darling is involved."

"That's what your guest is obviously planning on," Coffey said.

"Shit," Herbert replied. "We land at the fire station, Hawke walks, Darling helps him get lost, and we don't have a witness."

"Except for those people at sea, who probably got no closer to Darling than that koala."

"I can't let him go," Herbert said. "What the hell do I do?"

"You need a witness in order to hold him," Coffey said. "When is Loh's patrol boat due there?"

"Any minute," Herbert said. "But we don't know what condition the crew will be in or even how many key people survived. So much for words."

"Excuse me?"

"I took Paul's advice and talked to Hawke," Herbert said. "What I should have done was follow my gut."

"Which told you what?"

"To empty a bullet casing of gunpowder on his tongue and interrogate him with a match," Herbert said.

"I'm with Paul on that one," Coffey said.

"I figured."

"No, Bob. You did the right thing," Coffey said. "If

you had tortured Hawke, he could have landed and had *you* arrested."

Herbert was silent.

"The more important thing now is, do you think Hawke was telling the truth about Darling?" Coffey asked.

"I do," Herbert told him. "He had nothing to lose. Hawke needed to keep me hooked until we reached a nonmilitary landing site. The best way to do that was with the truth."

The phone went silent. Herbert's frustration was almost palpable. The tranquillity of the morning was gone.

"You say I need a witness," Herbert said. "Can we stay at the base until the patrol boat arrives?"

"Yes, but if Hawke suspects anything, he can legally request an escort off the base," Coffey said.

"How would he get one?" Herbert asked.

"You can't deny him a phone call," Coffey said. "Muscling a citizen who is not even a prisoner plays poorly in court."

"Lowell, you're not helping me," Herbert said.

"I'm trying," Coffey said. "I want to stay focused on the case, not on the fact that Hawke knows how to manipulate the Australian legal system. He's probably had countless run-ins with the courts. He knows his way around."

"Now that you mention it, every damn thing Hawke told me implicated someone else," Herbert said. "Jervis Darling, Darling's nephew Marcus, Captain Kannaday. According to Hawke, all he did was run security. Yet he never even confessed to firing a bullet."

"What about other potential leads or witnesses?" Coffey asked. "Do you have anyone on the mainland?"

"No one that I can—" Herbert began. He stopped suddenly.

"What is it?" Coffey asked.

"I just thought of something," Herbert said. "There *is* someone who can nail this guy."

"Who?" Coffey asked.

"Later," Herbert said.

"Wait, *Bob?*"

There was no answer.

"Bob, are you coming back to the station?" Coffey asked.

The dial tone returned. So did the external tranquillity of the morning. Inside, however, Lowell Coffey was not happy. He was bothered by the subtleties of his profession. The details were legitimate and necessary, but they could also allow a nuclear terrorist to go free.

Coffey loved the law and admired those who upheld it, in the field and in the courts. He did not think of himself as the barracuda Herbert had alluded to. What he did feel like, however, was a dolphin. Smart and swift.

And powerless.

SIXTY-NINE

Cairns, Australia
Sunday, 4:59 A.M.

The Bell rose swiftly from the RAAF Airfield Defence Squadron satellite base in Cooktown. It angled toward the southwest. John Hawke had been silent since his confession. His expression was still dour. He did not make eye contact with anyone on board.

Bob Herbert was less genial than he had been before they landed. Jelbart asked him if anything was wrong. Herbert said there was not.

Bob Herbert was lying.

The intelligence chief was sitting in the cabin, waiting. Figuring out exactly how he was going to play this. After Herbert had spoken with Coffey, he called Stephen Viens at Op-Center to ask for specific satellite intelligence. While he waited for Viens to arrange that, FNO Loh received a call from Lieutenant Kumar on her patrol boat. They had reached the scene of the sinking. The yacht was gone, but seven individuals had been pulled from the sea. The yacht crew had provided their names, but there was no way of knowing whether they were telling the truth. Kumar did not know whether Marcus Darling was among them.

Loh told the patrol boat to return to Darwin. The fate of Marcus Darling worried Herbert. It certainly complicated what he was about to do.

The helicopter finished fueling and took off. Flying time to Cairns was fifteen minutes. That was not a lot of time.

This was going to be tight.

After they had been airborne for three minutes, Herbert's phone beeped. He answered quickly. Viens was on the other end.

"I've got what you want," Viens said. "Do you have access to your computer monitor?"

"I do," he said.

"I've got the image, and I'm forwarding it to you, real time," Viens said. "I figured you would know what you were looking at better than I would."

"Good thinking," Herbert replied. "Stay on the line. I may need you to relocate."

"No problem."

The intelligence chief turned the monitor so he could look at it. If Hawke happened to glance over, he would see nothing. The screen was at an extremely sharp angle.

The satellite image was a fairly tight view of the Darling mansion. The house was at a forty-five-degree angle. In the green night-vision image, Herbert could see that there were lights on upstairs and downstairs. That suggested a good deal of activity in the house.

At five o'clock in the morning.

It only took a kitchen light to make breakfast, and probably not this early. Something was not right.

"Stephen, I want you to go to the Idlewild," Herbert said. "Got that?"

"The local airfield?" Viens asked.

"Yes. To the northeast."

Herbert wanted to use a term with which Hawke was likely to be unfamiliar. He did not want to give the man time to think up a new strategy. The original name for New York's Kennedy Airport seemed a good bet.

"You got it," Viens said. "I'll have to walk the satellite over, though. That's not one of the coordinates we have programmed in."

"Understood," Herbert told him. "Just walk as fast as you can, please."

It had occurred to the intelligence chief that Jervis Darling would expect to hear from either John Hawke or his nephew Marcus after the yacht went down. Absent an all-clear call, Darling might not want to stick around. Embittered former employees might want to talk. Darling would probably want to get out of Australia. Being in another country would add another layer to any legal or political fallout. Herbert could not permit that.

Of course, there was still the question of Marcus Darling. Marcus may have contacted his uncle to say that someone had been snatched from the yacht by helicopter. Perhaps after they were safely aboard the patrol boat. A rescue of Kannaday or even Hawke could be bad news for Jervis Darling.

It took a few seconds for the satellite to begin shifting. The image jerked toward the top right. It changed once every second after that. It was a slow, exasperating process.

How quickly the miraculous has become inadequate, Herbert thought.

Each live picture was a fresh frustration for Herbert. He wanted to see the airport *now.* He wished the fire tower had a clear view of the field. That would make things easier.

Herbert knew from Darling's dossier that he had a 1994 Learjet model 31A. The Australian used that for local hops. Darling kept his larger Gulfstream G-V at the airport in Darwin. Herbert would be able to identify the smaller plane with no problem.

A moment later, the small jet appeared on the airport landing strip. At this hour, it was the only active vehicle on the field. It stopped at the end of the runway. The pilot would go through his final preflight check. Then he would request clearance from the tower. A few moments later, Jervis Darling would be gone. The helicopter would never be able to catch him. And Lowell Coffey would definitely oppose scrambling the jets from Cooktown to force the Learjet down. Especially if Jessica-Ann Darling were on board. The media would take huge bites from a story headlined, "RAAF attacks schoolgirl."

Herbert looked at his watch. It was approximately seven minutes until the helicopter landed in Cairns. They would never reach the airstrip in time. He no longer had time to be subtle. He leaned toward the flight deck.

"What's the range of the radar at the airstrip in Cairns?" Herbert asked.

Jelbart looked at the pilot. "What have they got there, an EL/M-2125?" he asked.

"I believe so, sir," the pilot replied.

"They've got high-resolution views to the horizon on all sides, from one degree above the surface," Jelbart said.

"Meaning they'll see us as we fly toward Cairns," Herbert said.

"Like they were looking out the window," Jelbart said.

"What will they do if we come screaming in at them?"

"Buzz the tower?" Jelbart asked.

"I want to make a run toward the field!" Herbert said. "What will the tower do when they see us coming?"

"They'll shut the field down until they've contacted us," the pilot informed him.

"Then do it!" Herbert ordered.

"You want me to streak the airstrip?" the pilot clarified.

"At maximum drive! *Now!*" Herbert yelled. "Absolute radio silence."

As Herbert spoke, he disconnected the telephone receiver from the cord on his wheelchair. He held the plastic receiver in his right hand. With his left hand, Herbert gripped the plastic strap above the door. He did not want to use the seat belt. He needed a little mobility.

Jelbart protested. But his complaint was lost in the roar of the powerful 500 TTSN engine. Everyone was thrown forward or back as the Bell dipped, revved up, and raced ahead.

As Herbert expected, John Hawke was thrown toward him. Herbert swung the telephone receiver at the back of Hawke's neck. The security officer went down. Just to make sure Hawke was not feigning sleep again, Herbert leaned down and slugged him again. Hawke would have a difficult time proving he did not hurt himself when the helicopter abruptly changed directions.

Monica Loh had had the foresight to buckle her seat belt. That wonderful lady did not miss a thing.

Scooting back up in his seat, Herbert looked at his phone. The receiver was cracked. He would apologize to Viens later for disconnecting him. He would also have to frame the phone and give it to Paul Hood.

In this instance, at least, he and his boss were in complete agreement.

The telephone could be one hell of a weapon of choice.

SEVENTY

Washington, D.C.
Saturday, 3:06 P.M.

Hood was looking at the computer monitor on his desk. Stephen Viens had just sent him the same image that Bob Herbert was seeing. Hood saw the gleaming white Learjet poised for takeoff on the end of the runway. The aircraft was just sitting there.

"So that's Darling's jet, and Bob's going to try to keep him from taking off by mucking up the field's airspace," Hood said.

"That's pretty much it," Viens said.

"And then what? Did he give any clue?"

"No," Viens admitted.

"He wouldn't have wanted to say much," Hood thought aloud. "Not with a suspect in the cabin."

"I wonder if the Cooktown airbase will scramble jets to try to chase him away."

"They might, but Jelbart could handle that," Hood said. He shook his head. "Stephen, this is one of those times when you just have to trust the people you have in the field. But I do have one problem."

"What's that?"

"The poor Mississippi kid wants the rich Australian's hide," Hood said.

"I see," Viens said.

"I want the nuclear material," Hood went on.

Hood continued to watch the monitor. He did not think that Herbert would forget why he had gone to Australia.

And then he saw something on the monitor. Something new. "Stephen, can you bring me in closer?"

"I was just about to suggest that," Viens replied.

"You see it, too?"

"Yes," Viens said.

"Can you make it out?" Hood asked.

"Not yet," Viens told him. "Give me another few seconds to kick up the zoom and resolution."

The green-tinted image began to change. The Learjet became larger in the lower right-hand corner of the monitor. The white of the fuselage looked irradiated in the night-vision lens. The tarmac expanded. And the black, bloblike object in the upper left became slightly clearer.

Hood stared at it intently. He saw what the object was. And he was very sorry that Bob Herbert's phone was not working.

SEVENTY-ONE

Cairns, Australia
Sunday, 5:07 A.M.

The sun was beginning to brighten the charcoal gray tarmac at the tiny airfield. Inside the sleek Learjet, Jervis Darling sat in a deep, cushioned seat over the wing. The gentle hum of the engines comforted him, as always. He loved the feeling of bridled power. Especially when he controlled the reins. Bundled in his overcoat, his daughter was asleep in the seat beside him. Once they had reached cruising altitude, Darling would carry the young girl to the small bedroom in the back of the aircraft.

As the jet continued to idle, Darling became impatient. He punched a button on top of the armrest. That activated the intercom to the cockpit.

"Shawn, what's the delay?"

"Mr. Darling, the tower has put us on temporary hold," pilot Shawn Daniels replied.

"Find out what it's about," Darling snapped. "I want to be airborne as quickly as possible."

"Sir, that may not be possible," Daniels told him.

"What are you talking about?"

"There's activity on the tarmac," he replied.

"What kind of activity?" Darling demanded.

"The tower has not given me that information, sir," Daniels replied.

"Damn the tower," Darling said as he unbuckled his seat belt. He moved through the narrow cabin, ducking his head slightly under the low ceiling. He opened the cockpit door. Pilot Daniels and copilot Kristin Bedard moved slightly to either side so he could see out the windshield.

A helicopter was parked at the end of the runway. The rotor was still churning, and a side door was open.

"Do you know who that is?" Darling asked.

"No, sir," Daniels told him. "It's a Bell helicopter, but I can't see the identification number."

Darling squinted into the darkness. Something was being off-loaded. He could not tell what it was.

"Mr. Darling," the pilot said. "I could be mistaken, but that looks like a wheelchair."

"He wouldn't dare," Darling muttered.

"Sir?"

Darling ignored the pilot. He continued to look out the window. After a moment, the helicopter rose slowly from behind the object. Darling could see clearly now. It *was* a wheelchair. The wheelchair of R. Clayton Herbert. And it was coming toward him.

"Can you take off around him?" Darling asked.

"Sir?"

"Can you go around him, over him, *through* him?" Darling yelled.

"No, sir," the pilot said. He seemed surprised.

"Ask the tower why no one is coming to take him off the field," Darling demanded.

"Sir, they've plugged me into the cross talk between themselves and the helicopter," the pilot said. "Apparently, Warrant Officer George Jelbart of the Maritime Intelligence Centre has just commandeered the landing strip for a military action."

This cannot be happening, Darling thought.

"The tower is asking the helicopter for a reason," the pilot went on. "The warrant officer is saying there is a question about the cargo of the jet." The pilot seemed surprised. He glanced back at Darling. "I can cut in if you like, sir. Do we have a response for them?"

"Yes," Darling said. "Tell the tower I am going out to remove the impediment. If they have a problem with that, they can take it up with the prime minister, whom I intend to wake once we are airborne."

"I will tell them, sir," the pilot said.

Darling backed into the cabin. He motioned to copilot Bedard, who jumped from her seat and opened the door. She lowered the retractable stairs.

"Sit with my daughter in case she wakes," Darling told her as he swept onto the tarmac.

The night seemed endless, but Darling's patience was not. The new world power structure was inevitable.

It might as well begin here and now.

SEVENTY-TWO

Cairns, Australia
Sunday, 5:16 A.M.

A Learjet looks a helluva lot bigger when you're rolling right up to it, Herbert thought.

That was not the only thought he had, but it was a powerful one. Waves of heat from the turbines were rising in the dawning sun. The machine was hot, volatile, dangerous. The pointed nose was like a lance aimed directly at him. The low hum of the engines was what Herbert imagined tigers would be like growling from behind brush. All it would take was a gentle nudge from someone inside to send the beast charging toward him. The helicopter had moved to an emergency access road beside the tarmac, leaving Herbert alone. Now that the Bell was out of the way, Herbert had no doubt that Jervis Darling would like to run him over. The intelligence chief hoped the pilot and copilot would be disinclined.

As Herbert rolled himself forward, the cabin door of the jet swung open. Someone charged down the steps. Herbert could not see the figure clearly, but it could only be Jervis Darling. He approached aggressively, with a shoulder-driven swagger. It gave Herbert a moment's hesitation. Darling was not that many generations removed from the people who first cut civilization into the rough terrain here. They were convicts and their keepers, for whom hardship was constant. As he had discovered before, it was going to take a lot to cow him. Hopefully, the extra ammunition Herbert had would give him the kill shot he needed.

"Get out of my way!" Darling said as he approached.

"Leave, or I will call the chief constable and have you removed."

"Call him. Then I'll have to explain why I was here." Herbert stopped moving forward. He pressed down on the brake to lock his wheels. There was no wind. He could hear Darling breathing as he approached.

"Your delusions don't interest me," Darling said as he stopped in front of Herbert.

"My 'delusions' will interest the police," Herbert said.

"Let's see," Darling said. He took out his cell phone.

"Why don't you start talking, Mr. Darling? It'll save us a lot of time."

Darling speed-dialed a number.

"Even if I am removed, you're not going anywhere," Herbert said. "The helicopter will see to that. You're not leaving here, and if you're planning on going to your cove, the helicopter will get there before you do. And you can't afford to wait. That's why you were leaving now."

Darling turned his back on Herbert. He began walking away, the phone to his ear.

"The reason you didn't hear from John Hawke is because we rescued him from the yacht," Herbert went on. "He told us everything he knew about the operation. I'm sure I'll get more from your nephew. The Singaporean navy scooped him and several others from the Coral Sea. Probably an underachiever, right? I'm willing to bet he'll finger you to buy leniency for himself. That's what sycophants do."

Darling stopped. He closed the phone. He turned.

"What do you want, Mr. Herbert?" Darling asked. "I don't mean to leave the airfield but to go away. To leave me alone."

"You can start with the location of the nuclear materials you've been shuffling around."

"They're in your *mind!*" Darling said angrily. "We're not going to talk about your fantasies. Only about the reality of this moment. I'll ask one more time. What do you want?"

"I just told you."

Darling shook his head. "Mr. Herbert, I've tried to be reasonable with you. I've failed. Now I hope you'll get off the tarmac. Because I can fly that jet, and I intend to take off."

"You'd run over me?"

"Mr. Herbert, if everything you've intimated is true, one more criminal act would not make things worse," Darling pointed out.

The Australian turned and left. Herbert had one more round in the chamber. It was his silver bullet.

"I did not accuse you of murder," Herbert shouted. "But only a man who had already committed one would say that he has nothing to lose."

"I suggest you move!" Darling yelled over his shoulder.

"How will your daughter feel when she learns you had her mother murdered?" Herbert said.

Darling kept walking, but only for a moment. He turned and threw the cell phone at Herbert. It fell short, exploding on the tarmac. The Australian stalked back toward Herbert.

The kill shot had hit its target. Now Herbert needed one more very specific result.

"You *shit!*" Darling yelled. "You deformed *shit!*"

There was the verbal abuse. That was the start of the final phase, like Hitler shouting orders in the bunker as his world burned. If Herbert did this right, the rest was inevitable.

"Your ambition is as limited as your mobility!" Darling went on. "You have no eyes, no soul to dream, *nothing!*"

"You want to talk about a soul? I lost my legs in a terrorist attack," Herbert said. "I lost my wife then, too. I would give anything to have her back. But you had your wife killed out of vanity. Because it was convenient. Who's the deformed *shit?*"

"You don't know *anything* about my life!" Darling yelled.

"This may come as a shock, but the world is not Darling-centric," Herbert said. He was pushing. He needed one more thing.

He got it.

The Australian reached Herbert's side and threw a hard right backhand across his face. Herbert took the hit.

"You don't know anything about life itself!" Darling went on angrily. "Go back to your grim little cubbyhole and review reports and study the activities of individuals who make history! But don't be a spoiler. You have no idea what you're doing!"

"I do," Herbert said. "I just got a lunatic to slug me. The tower saw it. My people are calling your friend the constable right now from the helicopter. You're going to be arrested for assault. Then your government and mine are going to stop you from slipping radioactive material into subways and office buildings around the world."

Darling shook his head violently. "I was trying to *help* the world! Why should history be written by America or China? What happens to the rest of us? Where is our place in history?"

"Some of us would have been happy building an international empire and having a couple of jets to tool around in," Herbert said.

"Which is why you *don't* have those things!" Darling replied. "You settle. You dream small!"

"Really?" Herbert said. "I just sank you with a few words. That, Mr. Darling, is not small."

The sun cleared the horizon, and Jervis Darling seemed to shrink in it. In a moment, his shadow was taller than he was. The billionaire's arms went slack, and his chin fell.

"Where I come from, everything isn't about changing the world on an epic, historic scale," Herbert said. "Some of it is about improving ourselves, becoming better people. Better spouses. Better parents. That is not small either, Mr. Darling. It's a very big dream and an even bigger project. You ought to try it sometime."

The Australian looked at the yellow-orange sun. His face was lined, older in the stark light. Head cocked oddly to one side, he turned and began walking slowly toward the aircraft.

"Mr. Darling, where are you going? I need you to stick around," Herbert said.

"You need to leave."

"That isn't going to make the problem go away," Herbert said. "Too many people know."

He continued to walk toward the airplane.

"Mr. Darling!"

"One thing you still have to learn," Darling said, "is that people know what you tell them. I am not finished."

Herbert frowned. Something was up. Something unsettling.

And Herbert had an idea what it was.

SEVENTY-THREE

Cairns, Australia
Sunday, 5:24 A.M.

"The tower saw the attack on Mr. Herbert," the pilot said to Jelbart. "They've called the police, as you requested."

"Good," Jelbart said. His own headset was off.

"Now they want to know why Mr. Herbert and Mr. Darling are on the tarmac at all," the pilot went on.

"I think that should be obvious," Warrant Officer Jelbart replied. He was watching the two dark figures on the slowly brightening airfield. "They're having a conversation."

"The tower recognizes that," the pilot said. "They want to know why."

"I took my headset off so I didn't have to listen to their spew," he said.

"I understand," the pilot said. "But the controller has already remarked on the number of Commonwealth Department of Transport safety violations this action embraces. This includes the fact that the Cairns airfield is an emergency landing strip for the region. And that is the only runway."

"Tell them this *is* a bloody emergency," Jelbart replied impatiently.

"Look!" Loh said suddenly. "Darling's going back!"

The urgency in the female naval officer's tone was not matched by the billionaire's slow gait. A moment later, Herbert pointed toward the jet. He began wheeling after Darling.

"Tower, please hold," the pilot said. He turned to Jelbart. "What are we supposed to do?"

"Block him from taking off," Jelbart said.

"No, wait," Loh said. "I don't think that's what Bob wants us to do."

"What are you talking about?" Jelbart said. "That was the plan."

"I know," she said. "But it looks as though Bob is pointing to Darling. Give me a minute. I'm getting out."

"To do what?" Jelbart asked.

"Please, just wait," she said.

FNO Loh opened the door. She ducked from the helicopter and jogged toward Herbert. The roar of the rotors was like the bellowing of the sea. The tang of burning jet fuel permeated the air. It dominated the smell of the ocean blowing in from the east. In all, it was like the familiar sound and smell of the main deck of her patrol boat, a call to arms.

Herbert saw Loh approach. He motioned toward the billionaire, then grabbed his own wrist.

She was right. He wanted Loh to try to stop Darling.

The naval officer turned toward the jet. She was running hard now. Darling had reached the steps and looked back. He saw her and, without expression, climbed into the cabin. She was not going to get there before he shut the door. Still racing, she turned toward the helicopter. She gestured upward and then toward the nose of the Learjet. The pilot obviously understood. The helicopter took off and rapidly overtook her. The pilot circled wide of FNO Loh to keep the prop wash from knocking her down. He stopped about two hundred meters in front of the jet, some twenty meters above the tarmac. The Bell hovered there. The Learjet was not going anywhere. If it started to taxi, the helicopter pilot could stop it by placing a landing strut on the windshield.

Loh passed the cockpit and reached the wide door. It was just forward the wing on the port side. She could hear the door being locked as she arrived. She pounded on it.

"Mr. Darling, come out!" the Singaporean shouted. "You will not be able to take off!"

The combination of the helicopter rotor and jet engines generated a great deal of noise. Loh was not sure he heard her. She stepped away from the aircraft and peered into the cockpit. The sunlight was glinting off the windshield, making it difficult to see. She shielded her eyes. The Singaporean had intended to signal the pilot to let her in.

But that would not be possible.

The cockpit was empty.

SEVENTY-FOUR

Cairns, Australia
Sunday, 5:30 A.M.

When Darling reentered the aircraft, he asked pilot Shawn Daniels to join him in the cabin. The captain exited the flight deck.

"Is everything all right, sir?" Daniels asked as he slipped on his cap and made sure his tie was straight. "Are *you* all right?"

"I am . . ." he said, but then his voice trailed off. How could he explain to this man what he had just lost? His empire. His dreams. His self-respect.

Copilot Kristin Bedard was already in the cabin. She was sitting with Jessica-Ann. The young girl was awake now and talking to the copilot. They were making up voices for the two prehistoric animals that made up the Darling Enterprises logo. The flying pterosaur and sea-going ichthyosaurus were painted on the bulkhead wall of the Learjet. It had always been Darling's notion that if you mastered the air and sea, you controlled the land.

Copilot Bedard rose when Jervis Darling arrived. He sat in the seat beside his daughter. Daniels and Bedard moved several feet away. They stood with their backs to the two. Darling touched the tip of his daughter's nose. He used to do that when she was a baby. He smiled as she twitched.

"Daddy?"

"I'm here," Darling said. "Did you have a nice sleep?"

The girl nodded. She gently scratched her nose with her forearm.

"I want to ask you something," Darling said. "I want to know if you are happy, sweetie."

The girl nodded again.

"What are you happiest about?" her father asked. His voice was soft, hardly more than a whisper.

She was silent. He could not tell if she was thinking or falling back to sleep. Then she suddenly said, "Frenchie."

"Your pony?" That was not what Darling had meant, but he went with her lead. "Frenchie is nice, isn't she?"

Jessica-Ann nodded once.

"And the thing that I'm least happy about are the dinosaurs," she added before her father could rephrase the question.

"Why?" Darling asked.

"They scare me," Jessica-Ann replied.

"They shouldn't," Darling said.

"They do."

"I told you that a lot of them were very peaceable. Do you remember which ones?"

"The plant eaters," she said.

"Right," he smiled.

"But they could step on you by accident," Jessica-Ann said. She was more animated now.

"They would never have done that," Darling said. "They had young ones all around. They were very smart, and they were very careful."

And they are all gone, he thought. They were so successful for so long. Many were large and powerful. Yet they were annihilated. It was an inevitability of nature.

Darling touched his daughter's cheek with the back of a finger. "I'm glad you like your pony, Jess. But I guess what I really want to know is if you have a happy life."

"You mean everything?"

"Yes," he smiled.

The young girl nodded vigorously.

"I'm glad," he said.

"Now can you tell me something?" she asked, looking up at him.

"Of course," he replied.

"Where are we going?"

Darling felt tears pressure the backs of his eyes. Tears

crept around to the front. He nonchalantly touched them away with his fingertips.

"Actually, sweetie, I'm going somewhere," Darling told her. "I've got a big job for you."

"Okay." She made a face. Her brows dipped. "Daddy, I think someone's knocking on the door."

"Don't you worry about that," Darling said. "What I need you to do right now is go home with Shawn and Kristin."

"Go home? That's not a job," she said.

"It is," Darling said. "A very important one. You're to go home with them and tell Andrew something. Tell him that Daddy has to go somewhere, and you could not go."

"Where are you going?"

"Where do you think?" he asked.

Jessica-Ann thought for a moment. "To visit Mommy?"

Darling started slightly. That caught him off guard. The young girl looked up at him.

"What made you say that?" he asked.

"Your voice sounds the same as it did when you told me Mommy had her accident," the girl replied. "Are you going to her grave?"

"No," Darling said. "There's something else I have to do." He helped her sit up as he eased from the seat. Still holding her hand, he had her stand on the cushion. "Give Daddy a hug," he said as he put his arms around her.

She wrapped her lean arms around his shoulders and put her head on his chest.

Darling could smell the shampoo she had used the night before. *Apricot,* he thought. He remembered when Jessica-Ann was much younger. Her mother would frequently go out for the night, often longer, and he would give their daughter a bath. He would wash her hair. Then he would put her to bed. Now she was doing those things herself.

When had that happened?

What matters is that it did happen, he told himself. That was the wonder of growth and evolution. It took place even without a global cataclysm.

Jervis Darling hugged Jessica-Ann tightly. The changes

he had wanted for her world would not transpire. Or she would have to make them happen herself. Perhaps she would. She was his daughter. Darling had been stopped by a man whom he should never have underestimated. Herbert was a functionary. A gear in a machine. But he won, the same way the dinosaurs had been undermined by the tiny mammals that moved underfoot. Darling's network would be uprooted and stopped. It was ironic. Here he was in his private jet, with the world before him. Yet there was really only one place for him to go.

Darling turned from his daughter without releasing her. He called quietly to Shawn Daniels. The pilot and copilot came over. Darling handed his daughter to the woman.

"I want you two to take her home," Darling said.

"Yes, sir," the pilot said. "Will there be anything else?"

Darling grinned humorously. "That remains to be seen."

He walked them to the door and leaned close.

SEVENTY-FIVE

Cairns, Australia
Sunday, 5:38 A.M.

"Please back away," someone said from inside the Learjet. "We're coming out with Ms. Darling!"

Bob Herbert had reached the side of the jet. He and FNO Loh moved back several yards. The voice from inside had not belonged to Jervis Darling. Herbert looked along the fuselage at the five windows. He did not see Darling inside. He also did not imagine that Darling would be coming out with the others. Herbert realized what had struck him about Darling's behavior a few minutes before. It was like the sudden arrival of the hurricane's eye. This was not over. To the contrary. What was happening now had the feel of women and children being allowed to leave the Alamo before the final assault. But there was nothing Herbert could do. The girl and anyone else who wanted to leave had to be allowed to do so.

"I want my Daddy to come!"

Herbert's eyes snapped back toward the door as it opened. His feeling had been accurate. Darling was letting the flight crew and his daughter go. Herbert glanced at the cockpit. Someone was moving inside. The intelligence chief bet it was Darling.

The stairs unfolded, and the pilot and copilot stepped out. The pilot was carrying Jessica-Ann. The girl was trying to see around him, into the plane. She was calling for her father.

Herbert heard a police siren over the howl of the jet engines and the beat of the helicopter rotor. They were coming to arrest Jervis Darling. That required Darling to be here.

Herbert was about to tell FNO Loh to rush the stairs. The woman was ahead of him, of course. As soon as the copilot stepped out, the naval officer maneuvered around her. The crew stepped aside as they made their way to the tarmac. Loh entered the cabin.

"He's in the cockpit!" Herbert said.

Loh nodded. Herbert wheeled to the side so he could see her. She pounded on the door.

"Mr. Darling, we will not let you depart," she said.

Herbert had watched the crew run off. They had hurried to the small, fenced-in parking lot. Darling's driver was still there. He was probably instructed to wait until his employer was airborne before departing. Herbert was glad. He did not want Jessica-Ann to see this.

"Mr. Darling! Open the door!" Loh insisted.

Herbert turned back to the cockpit. He could see the top of Darling's head. He was seated in the pilot's seat.

The jet began to move.

"Officer Loh, get off!" Herbert cried.

The Singaporean officer continued to hit the cockpit door.

Herbert did not know whether Darling was playing chicken. Even if he managed to get past the helicopter and take off, he would have difficulty maintaining equilibrium with the door open. A jet that size would be impacted by sudden shifts in air pressure, by fluctuations in temperature.

That assumes Jervis Darling is thinking rationally, Herbert thought. For the past few minutes, the Australian had been in the throes of a fight-or-flight response. Reason is not a strong component of that.

Herbert looked up at the helicopter. He gestured for the pilot to move in. The flier expertly maneuvered the chopper closer. He turned the aircraft perpendicular to the jet and lowered the port-side strut toward the windshield. Herbert could see the Learjet wings fluttering from the chopper's downdraft. The jet continued to move forward, gaining speed. The two vehicles were about ten yards apart. They would collide in moments.

Herbert had never felt so helpless. He wanted to run onto the Learjet and help Officer Loh kick in the door. Instead, he rolled back as the two vehicles hit. The jet slowed with the impact but continued to move ahead. The helicopter was knocked slightly to its starboard. The rotor tilted precariously.

It was surreal, like watching a pair of prehistoric behemoths do battle. The pilot swung away and righted the helicopter. He rose in a tight arc and prepared to drop down again.

Herbert motioned aggressively for him to stop. As much as the intelligence chief wanted Darling, he did not want to damage the jet. Darling might still try to take off. Herbert wanted the man in prison, not in the morgue.

Someone came running from the tower. Two police cars were just entering the airstrip behind the jet. So was another vehicle, with a familiar driver. Paul Leyland was at the wheel with Spider riding the running board.

The fire brigade had been called by the tower, and a squat red rural Nissan Patrol Light Attack fire truck was racing forward. There was a 600-liter water tank mounted to the back. The Queensland firefighters used it to battle blazes away from hydrants.

And that was when Herbert got an idea.

The intelligence chief motioned to the chopper to try again to stop the jet. Herbert lowered his hands slowly, indicating a measured attack. It was risky, but he needed to delay Darling. As the chopper came down, Herbert wheeled quickly toward the fire truck.

"The hose!" Herbert yelled as he rushed past the wing of the Learjet. "Get the hose!"

Spider could not quite hear him. Herbert was dying. He reckoned that he had less than a minute to pull this off.

"We need the hose!" he shouted. He gestured broadly at the canvas hose, which was coiled on the side. Then he pointed to the wing of the Learjet.

Leyland sped up. He overtook the police car and came to a smoking stop beside Herbert.

"Hit the engine intake with water!" Herbert said.

Leyland obviously sized up the situation. He shot toward the Learjet. Herbert did likewise. He wanted to try to get Officer Loh out.

While the fire truck was in motion, Spider shimmied along the running board to the hose in back. Obviously, his ability to cling to the side of a moving vehicle had helped him earn his name. He unhooked the hose, pressed the button to open the tank, and climbed the ladder to the top of the tank. He stood on a small platform there. As the truck neared, Spider leaned forward at a forty-five-degree angle. When the truck was within two hundred meters of the jet, Spider flipped a switch at the base of the nozzle. He pointed the hose toward the rear-mounted engine. Water shot from the hose so forcefully that Spider ended up standing erect. The powerful spray smashed into the back of the jet engine.

The jet was well ahead of Herbert; he was not going to get to it in time. The water was sucked through the superheated turbine. It turned to steam, simultaneously cooling the internal metal components. The engine cracked audibly and crisply, like nearby thunder. Smoke mingled with the wispier steam, first from the front and back and then from cracks in the side. A moment later, shards of silver and white metal shot from the front and back of the engine. Then the engine casing itself burst like a hot dog on a grill. The jet lurched, hopped slightly on the port side, but continued to move forward. The helicopter had approached more cautiously this time. It kept the jet back with repeated nudges rather than a single hit. It was a more successful means of keeping the aircraft from gaining speed.

Spider left the smoking husk and turned his spray on the starboard engine.

That turbine spat and sizzled as had the first one. Herbert continued to wheel himself toward the jet. From this angle, Herbert could see flames lighting up the interior of the starboard engine. They must be coming from a split casing of some kind. They flared for only a moment before the water smothered them. A moment later, the second engine ruptured with a single loud bang. Spider killed the hose as the casing peeled from the center outward, the top and bottom pointing toward the fuselage. The jet coasted for a moment, then angled toward the tower and stopped. Both engines were still smoking, the white smoke turning black.

Spider redirected the hose to the first engine. While he did, Leyland stopped the truck and jumped out. A small oxygen tank and mask were slung over his shoulder. He reached the stairs a moment before Herbert did. They had dragged along the tarmac and were cracked along the bottom. Leyland bolted inside. The cabin was filling with dirty white smoke. Herbert could not see anything.

The next few seconds seemed to pass in slow motion. The helicopter moved away from the jet and set down on the landing strip. Warrant Officer Jelbart emerged and ran forward. The police car arrived. Two officers in sharp blue uniforms emerged. One of them was using his portable radio to summon an ambulance. The air traffic controller arrived, breathless and waving his undone shirtsleeves and shouting profanities. But all Herbert could hear was the dying hiss of the engines. All he could see was the wide, open door of the jet.

Finally, Leyland emerged from the smoke. He was alone. He backed down the steps, peering at the interior.

Urgently, Herbert wheeled himself forward. "Paul, what's wrong?" he demanded.

Before Leyland could answer, Monica Loh emerged from the roiling cloud. Jervis Darling was beside her. His arm was thrown around her shoulder, and his head was nodding forward. Leyland remained in front of the barely conscious man as Loh walked him down the stairs.

When they reached the tarmac, Leyland and one of the police officers took Jervis Darling from FNO Loh. They carried him to the police car and lay him on the backseat.

Herbert went over to Loh. He scooted sideways on his seat and offered her a corner to sit on. She declined. Her face was covered with sweat. It seemed to make her dark eyes shine even more brightly. As Jelbart arrived, Loh looked at the shattered engines, then down at Herbert.

"That was a very clever backup plan," she said breathlessly.

"Backup plan?" Herbert said. "What do you mean?"

"I finally got the door open," she said with the faintest trace of a smile. "Jervis Darling was not going anywhere."

Herbert loved this woman. God, how he loved her.

SEVENTY-SIX

Washington, D.C.
Saturday, 4:00 P.M.

"I'm not sure which took the larger hit," Lowell Coffey said to Paul Hood over the telephone. "Jervis Darling's Learjet or Australian statutes for crime and misconduct."

"How bad is it?" Hood asked.

"For us? Pretty favorable, actually," Coffey said. "I took Leyland's car and only just got to the airport, so I'm still catching up. Basically, the Queensland Crime and Misconduct Commission has taken over this case from the local police. They're flying in an assistant commissioner to investigate."

"Because of Darling's involvement?"

"Partly that, but mostly due to the nature of the charges," Coffey said. "Jelbart briefed them by phone. They're classifying the destruction of the jet and the attack on the airfield as a single action, and attributing it jointly to the Queensland fire team, Op-Center, the Republic of Singapore Navy, and the Maritime Intelligence Centre."

"Good God."

"Yes, but having everyone named is good for us," Coffey said. "It gives weight to the idea we'll be putting forth, that there was probable cause to detain the jet. It's also good that the QCMC is classifying this as a 'reactive' investigation, which is a fancy term for 'after the fact.' That suggests there may be a valid reason for what we did. It's not quite as extreme, but it's like stopping a guy who enters a bank wearing a ski mask and carrying a gun. The act is not considered a crime. It's called a contravention."

"I follow," Hood said.

"The best news is, the QCMC is also responsible for

overseeing the transport of hazardous materials through the area. Based on Warrant Officer Jelbart's report, they're instituting what they call a 'proactive' investigation into the smuggling activities."

"Which means what, exactly?" Hood asked.

"Basically, it means they can hold Hawke on Jelbart's say-so," Coffey said. "They've got him in the hospital. He hit his head at some point on the flight to Cairns. It seems he was the only one not wearing a seat belt when the chopper went into some kind of dive."

This was an open line, so Hood did not say what was on his mind. Not that he had to say it. He was sure the same thought was on Coffey's mind.

"What about Darling?" Hood asked.

"They booked him for assault, though they're taking him to the hospital as well to make sure he's all right. He took in a lot of smoke. He's extremely disoriented."

"Have they got solid security for Hawke and Darling?"

"The local police are handling that now, but Jelbart has some of his people flying in," Coffey said. "They should be here momentarily."

"At six in the morning?" Hood said. "They don't drag their feet over there, do they?"

"No, they don't," Coffey said. "The efficiency of every division, from the fire brigade to the local police, has been incredible."

Hood knew why. The Australians were surrounded by nations where the black market was a dominant financial force. Australia itself was mostly open coastline. If they did not maintain a warlike preparedness along every meter of that, it would not take long for corruption to set in.

"That said," Coffey went on, "we're all betting that Hawke will get off with minimal jail time."

"It wouldn't surprise me," Hood said.

"He'll take the brunt of the fall for Darling in exchange for guaranteed early parole," Coffey went on. "To put Darling on trial would be counterproductive. It would become a circus that would hurt the economy and detract from the main issue, which has to be breaking up the smuggling network and finding the nuclear material. Jervis Darling himself is effectively finished. He'll be quietly forced to resign the boards of his companies, his not-for-profit companies will be dissected for laundering the nuke payouts, and he may serve some token jail time. After that, he'll probably go live on one of his islands."

"With or without his daughter, I wonder," Hood said.

"The courts won't have much say over that," Coffey said. "But Darling will want her to get a great education. That means boarding school in Australia or Europe. They won't be together much."

"No mother and an MIA father," Hood said. "Did she see much of what happened at the airfield?"

"I don't think so," Coffey said. "But she had to have heard the engine explosions, the sirens. She knows the plane didn't take off."

"I wonder how she's taking this."

"I saw her in the small terminal building when I arrived," Coffey said. "She was sitting with Darling's co-pilot and driver. They were talking to her. She looked shell-shocked."

"I wish there was something we could do for her," Hood said. There was sadness in his voice, in his soul. He thought of his own daughter, Harleigh, living without him. He could not imagine what kind of man would create a situation that would expose his daughter to this kind of emotional peril.

Then again, this was the same man who reportedly took the girl's mother from her, Hood thought. Normal values did not apply. The good news was that Jervis Darling would not be taking anyone else's parents from them. Ever.

"I'm sure Ms. Darling will be looked after in the short term," Coffey said. "The people who were with her seemed very attentive. Though I have to wonder. Was it fear or affection that made these people loyal to Darling?"

"A little of both, I'm sure," Hood said. "But it was probably the free pass that had the most impact."

"What kind of free pass?" Coffey asked.

"I used to get that when I was mayor," Hood said. "That's when people are around someone of influence, so they have no problem getting into restaurants or clubs or the most popular attractions at amusement parks. They don't have to worry about speeding tickets or bureaucracies or bad service. If they get into trouble, strong, decisive help is just a name-drop or phone call away. I'm sure you saw some of that at your dad's law practice."

"Yes, only in Beverly Hills it was called kissing cheek, and nobody liked to do it," Coffey told him.

"You were lucky, though. You had money. You had a choice," Hood said. "A lot of people don't. For them, playing the sycophant to a Jervis Darling or a Mayor Hood is like consolidating their debt. The humiliation comes from one place, not dozens."

"Well, I should probably get back to the others," Coffey said. "It looks like Herbert and Loh are ready to break huddle. Tell me, though. Did you enjoy having people kiss your ass?"

"I hated it," Hood said. "I discouraged it. But people kept doing it. That's one reason I'm here instead of there."

"We'll see who sticks by Darling now," Coffey said. "As the philosopher says, 'A failure is a stranger in his own house.' "

Hood hung up. He stared at the phone.

That was cruel and true, he thought. It was bad enough to fail. But one also had to endure it alone. It was impossible to feel any sympathy for Jervis Darling. But while Hood should be savoring the successful mission, he found himself responding emotionally to the idea of failure. He was uncomfortable by the nearness of it. By the sadness of what Jessica-Ann Darling would have to face. It forced Hood to think about the mistakes he had made with his own family. He wondered if that sense of inefficacy would ever completely disappear.

Maybe it's not supposed to, Hood decided. Maybe that's what prevents a man from repeating his errors.

Hood picked up the phone. There was one thing of which he was certain. The antithesis of having his ass kissed was having it kicked. By himself. Neither one of them did him any good.

He had to put the past behind him.

He had to call Daphne Connors.

Now.

SEVENTY-SEVEN

Cairns, Australia
Sunday, 7:10 A.M.

John Hawke and Jervis Darling were taken into custody separately. Even after their departure, the helicopter still had a brief delay in Cairns. The pilot wanted to ascertain that there had been no damage to the landing strut.

The report was favorable.

"Metal is still stronger than glass," the pilot reported proudly to Herbert after examining both the landing surface and pylons.

The team said farewell to Leyland and Spider, both of whom had earned the respect of Bob Herbert.

Leyland waved off the suggestion that he and Spider had acted heroically. "You told us where to go and what to do."

"Bugger, all we did was pull the trigger," Spider said.

"Of a bloody *hose,*" Leyland added. "It's not like that's going to put someone's eye out or anything."

"You ran down a jet," Herbert told them. "That took guts. You prevented Darling from taking off and finishing the operation he started. That's a hero by my yardstick."

Leyland shrugged. "We really didn't have much choice, did we?"

"Sure you did," Jelbart said.

"No, I mean I don't think Mr. Darling would have believed it if we said we needed to get a koala out of the engine."

Herbert smiled. He had not known this man very long, but he was going to miss him. Maybe the intelligence chief would stop by and see him when he came back to visit Monica Loh, which he absolutely intended to do.

"Paul, I've got just one more question for you," Herbert said.

"Ask it," Leyland said.

"Why'd you hire the only female firefighter in the district?"

Coffey rolled his eyes.

Leyland smiled. "The truth is, she was the best firefighter in the district."

Herbert scowled. Coffey smiled.

"That hair on your chest cost you a prime rib," Coffey said to the intelligence chief.

Leyland leaned toward Coffey. "And frankly, I like watching her climb the ladder."

Herbert smiled. "Dutch," he said to Coffey.

Coffey nodded.

When the pilot said they were good to go, Lowell Coffey took the seat formerly occupied by John Hawke. The flight back was quiet and introspective. Everyone was tired. More than that, they were oddly dissatisfied. Herbert could see it in their faces. No one could call this a Pyrrhic victory. "The good guys," as he had described the team to Loh, had not suffered any physical losses. But there was a spiritual loss. Business and government had always been closely related. Business and crime regularly crossed paths in money laundering, intelligence gathering, and other activities. Business had even encouraged wars to increase productivity and profits. But this was the first time to Herbert's knowledge that a small band of businessmen had planned to use nuclear material to change the balance of power. The thought was as sickening as it was disquieting. They would never know if they had nabbed everyone who was part of the operation. Or every pellet of enriched uranium, or whatever substance they were shipping.

"Bob, I want to ask you something," Monica Loh said after nearly a half hour.

"Sure."

"Were you really going to let Hawke go before?"

"You mean on the way to Cairns, when I was asking him to rat out his boss?" Herbert asked.

"Yes," Loh said.

Herbert's answer was precise, if not articulate. He snickered.

"Now you tell me something," Jelbart said from the front seat. "I try to stay on top of local laws and such, but I've never heard of the Singaporean Nuclear Emergency Response Act of 2002. Is there such a thing?"

For the first time since Herbert had known FNO Loh, she smiled. It was not quite a snicker, but then she was probably not as jaded as Herbert was.

"I thought not," Jelbart said. "Well played," he added.

"Now I'd like to ask all of you a question," Herbert said. "What do you think Darling was trying to do back there?"

"You mean take off or take his life?" Jelbart asked.

Herbert nodded.

"I've been wondering that myself," Jelbart said. "He sent his daughter away. That suggests he did not expect to survive."

"He was moving her out of danger," Coffey said. "That doesn't mean anything. He could have sent for her later. His priority was to get out of the country and wage a legal war. He'll probably do that anyway. This thing smells of a plea bargain."

"Do you think that's inevitable?" Jelbart asked.

Coffey nodded. "We won't be able to prove everything that we suspect, and Darling won't be able to duck every blow that's thrown. That will demand a compromise. Besides, everybody will want this over as soon as possible. Darling because he will suffer less damage, the government because there's always the risk that Darling or Jessica-Ann could be perceived as victims."

"Not to mention the fact that it will cost a bomb to try," Jelbart said.

Coffey looked at Herbert. "What do you think?"

"About Darling trying to off himself?" Herbert asked. He shook his head. "When you strip him of the financial armor, he's a coward. Cowards don't kill themselves."

"I disagree," Loh said. "I would think most individuals who take their lives do so because they are afraid to face adversity."

"I wonder if the statistics support that," Herbert said dubiously.

"I don't know," Loh admitted.

"When it comes down to it, sucking on a gun barrel is not for the faint-hearted."

"Life is not for the faint of heart," Loh replied. "Surrendering that life is, I believe, an act of the gravest cowardice."

"I think you're both wrong," Coffey said. "In law school they teach us that most crimes of passion are conceived and executed in a space of five minutes. Suicide included. I don't think the brain or backbone play a part in it. Suicide is usually an act of despair."

"And a rather comfortless topic as well," Jelbart added.

The cabin fell silent again. Herbert and Loh looked at each other with challenging eyes. Like Herbert, she was obviously a woman who did not like to let things sit. Monica Loh could fight, interrogate, debate, and she looked damn fine. Herbert wondered where the flaws were.

Oh yeah, he thought. *She lives in Singapore.*

Also, he had no idea what she thought of him. He wondered if he were better off not knowing.

Shortly before landing, Jelbart received a call from Brian Ellsworth. News of what had happened at the Cairns airstrip traveled a lot faster than the Bell 204. International media were waiting for them. So was Ellsworth. He greeted the team at the helicopter. Police kept the reporters away. Ellsworth congratulated them for the job they did, then cautioned the team to ignore the questions being shouted by the press.

"Whatever you say will be reported and distorted, both pro and contra Mr. Darling," Ellsworth said. "That can only help his case."

"Prejudice the judicial process," Coffey said. "Make it

look like the government has prejudged Darling."

"Precisely. One thing I must ask you," Ellsworth said as he slipped his cell phone from inside his jacket. "The prime minister is waiting to hear from me about the missing cargo. He wants to know what the chances are of getting those materials back."

"That depends," Herbert said. "First we have to find the people who distributed the stuff. Then we have to get them to talk."

"We also have to hope the materials haven't already been passed around," Jelbart added.

"I wouldn't worry about that," Herbert said. "These guys work like diamond and art thieves. The neighborhood is too hot to try transferring it now. We've got a week or two to find out who they are. Everything depends on how you handle Darling, Hawke, and the other members of the crew."

"You may have to cut them deals you aren't going to like," Coffey said.

"I'm not going to like anything that doesn't have them hanging by their feet over a pit of rattlesnakes," Herbert said.

"Well, Mr. Coffey, we are sure to be engaged in various dances with Mr. Darling's legal lancers," Ellsworth said. "I actually worry about them nearly as much as I worry about the smugglers."

Herbert understood that. He resisted shooting a nasty look at Lowell Coffey. Ever since an attorney in Lebanon had helped free one of the men responsible for the Beirut embassy bombing, attorneys had been one step above terrorists on Herbert's favorite-people list.

"With a little forethought, we should be able to find the nuclear material," Loh promised.

"How can you be sure?" Ellsworth asked.

"Did you ever play volleyball, Mr. Ellsworth?" she asked.

"In school. Why?"

"There are times when you rally for position, and there are times when you spike," she said. "This is a time to spike. We need to follow the trail while it still exists."

"How?"

"Give me one of the sailors," Loh said. "Any one of them, though I suggest a less hardened member of the crew. We will find that trail and the missing materials. We may not even have to take him to Singapore. Just the idea of it seems to make people talkative."

Ellsworth thought for a moment. "Officer Loh, your vessel has the crew now. You might want to decide which of those men actually fired at your sampan. That would make a strong case for Singapore having the right to arrest and try those individuals."

"Thank you, Mr. Ellsworth," she said. "I will communicate that to the lieutenant in charge."

Ellsworth turned his back on the reporters as he made the call to the prime minister. Loh went to use the telephone in one of the waiting sedans. While they did that, Herbert excused himself. He wanted to have a minute with the pilot. He wheeled himself over to the helicopter cockpit. The pilot jumped out. The man seemed glad to see Herbert.

"I just wanted to thank you for all your help," Herbert said, extending his hand.

"Thank you for the adventure, sir," the pilot said.

"You know, I'm ashamed to admit this, but I don't even know your name," Herbert admitted.

The pilot grinned. The grin stayed there for several seconds. Herbert was puzzled.

"Did I miss something?" Herbert asked.

"No, sir," the pilot said. "Actually, my name is Bob Herbert."

The intelligence chief grinned. "You're joking."

"Swear on the Bishop Barker. Only my family pronounces it *Erbert*," the pilot told him. "I may have to change that, though," he added as he saluted Herbert. "It's been a rare honor, sir."

Herbert returned the salute, then shook his head with disbelief. He turned to rejoin the others.

Civilization might be in jeopardy, and rats like Darling

helped make the world a hell. But that exchange made Herbert feel as though he could fix those problems single-handedly. Men like Pilot Bob Herbert gave him a reason to keep slugging. They also gave him hope.

By God, this war is far from lost, Herbert thought, as he made his way to the waiting sedan.

SEVENTY-EIGHT

Darwin, Australia
Sunday, 7:13 A.M.

Herbert and his team were shuttled to Jelbart's office, where more reporters were waiting. The three sedans entered the building through an underground garage. They rode a freight elevator to Jelbart's floor. Loh had the feeling, for a moment, that she was on an aircraft carrier. She felt at home and in charge. It was nice. Herbert was such a dynamic character. He had taken command of this mission and not let go. At first Loh thought it was the same kind of male arrogance she had always encountered among soldiers and intelligence personnel. Then she discovered that ego and testosterone had nothing to do with it. Herbert took charge for one reason only.

He knew what he was doing.

There was something exciting and refreshing about that. For that reason alone she was sorry to see this brief operation end.

Upon reaching Jelbart's office, Loh contacted her patrol boat. It had remained at the site of the sinking. Lieutenant Kumar said he had wanted to secure the yacht before it was swept away by currents or evidence was degraded by the salt water. At the same time, he took the initiative and interrogated the individuals they pulled from the Coral Sea. Faced with the prospect of being taken to Singapore for questioning, Marcus Darling would probably choose to reveal a great deal about the operation. He also spoke expansively about his uncle's involvement in it. Hearing from Kumar, Loh wondered if Mr. Coffey might be wrong. It did not sound as though Jervis Darling would be in a position to bargain for leniency.

Loh told Kumar that she would be arriving early the next morning. Jelbart wanted to revisit the site with his own ship. He said he would ferry her out there. They would be leaving in about two hours. Loh would clean up and rest on the ship. She had something else she wanted to do before she left. She went to Jelbart's office to arrange it. Then she headed toward the elevator.

Herbert and Coffey had been on the phone with their superior in Washington. She walked past the conference room they were using. Herbert saw her go. He excused himself and went after her. The intelligence chief wheeled alongside the officer as she walked down the hall.

"Are you leaving now?" he asked.

"At ten o'clock," she told him. She pressed the elevator button.

"Jelbart sent out for coffee and doughnuts. Do you want to wait with us?"

"There is something else I must do," she replied.

"By yourself?"

She looked at him. "I would prefer to."

"Oh."

"But I was wondering about something," Loh went on. "I have three weeks' leave in two months. I have never been to America. I was thinking I might like to fly to Washington."

"That sounds like a very good idea," Herbert smiled. "I would love to show you around."

"I would like that," Loh smiled back.

"Just make sure to stay away from our deputy director, Mike Rodgers," Herbert said. "He'll send you on a mission."

Loh frowned. "I don't understand."

"You will," Herbert assured her. "I'll have to introduce you to Maria Corneja. She'll explain."

All of this was very confusing. But FNO Loh liked the idea of a world ripe for exploration. She also liked the fact that Bob Herbert seemed genuinely pleased by her suggestion. That surprised her. He had not seemed like a man who would enjoy leisure.

But then, you are not a woman who likes to socialize, she thought. Perhaps all it took was the right person.

The two parted with a long handshake. Herbert held her hand between both of his. They were strong hands, but gentle. She was glad Herbert had taken charge of this, though the good-bye could easily take far longer than expected. And she had something to do. Loh smiled warmly and left quickly.

"Monica!" Herbert called after her.

She turned. "Yes?"

"Thanks for everything," he said. "And I don't mean just the crisis management."

"You are welcome."

"Good luck with whatever you're off to do."

"Thank you," she said.

And then she went off to do it.

SEVENTY-NINE

The Coral Sea
Sunday, 7:45 A.M.

Although the Singaporean patrol ship was not a fully equipped salvage vessel, it did carry air buoyancy bags. These were to be deployed in the event the ship itself suffered a critical breach. Descending well before sunrise, divers placed the bags in the higher stern section of the *Hosannah*. It was a difficult salvage, due to the darkness. However, Lieutenant Kumar did not want to risk the boat sinking further. The air compressor filled the bags one at a time. Finally, with six bags inflated, the aft section of the *Hosannah* broke the surface.

However, with the ship's return came something else. Something the crew did not expect.

A body.

The divers recovered the remains. Kumar went to the cabin, where several of the rescued seamen were being kept. He asked the young man Marcus Darling to come to sick bay and identify the body.

Marcus seemed numb and pale as he looked at the still-damp, slightly bloated corpse on the gurney.

"Who is he?" Kumar asked.

"That is Captain Kannaday," Marcus said softly.

"Was he part of the ring?" Kumar asked.

"At first," Marcus Darling said. "Then . . . something happened."

"What happened?"

"He changed," Marcus said. "He turned on Mr. Hawke."

"I see." Kumar motioned to the medical officer. The

man handed him a white towel. The lieutenant opened it gingerly and showed it to Marcus.

"We found this tangled in the ropes beside him," Kumar said. "Did it belong to him?"

"No," Marcus said. "That belonged to Hawke."

"What is it?"

"A weapon," Marcus told him. "A wommera. You use it to throw darts."

"That might explain the wounds on his body," the medic interjected. "Was there a struggle, Mr. Darling?"

"I don't know," Marcus told him. "We were in the water."

Kumar covered the weapon and set it on the gurney. "It appears as though Mr. Hawke may earn himself a murder charge as well."

Marcus snickered. "That's funny. Hawke was always so careful. They all were."

"All it takes is one active conscience to undermine the cleverest criminal plot," Kumar said.

"Well, I'm sure that is a real comfort to Kannaday here," Marcus said. "Instead of being wealthy, he's dead."

Kumar looked disdainfully at the man beside him. "I believe it must have been a significant comfort to him. Buddhism teaches that the quality of a moment can be valued more than corrupt longevity. The ripples are felt throughout the world and time."

"Thanks for the lesson," Marcus said.

"In fact, Mr. Darling, it was advice."

"Was it?"

"Yes," Kumar said. "We have reason to believe that you were one of the men who shot at the sampan."

"I did what? I don't even know how to fire a gun!"

"You can tell that to the chief interviewer in the Maximum Security Changi Prison in Singapore," Kumar replied.

"Changi? You're not taking me to the logs," Marcus said.

"I have consulted with my superior, who is with representatives of your government. They agree that it is within our rights to ascertain your innocence," Kumar replied.

"This is wrong!" he shouted. "I want a lawyer!"

"You will have one, though it may be a few days before he can see you," Kumar said. "Singapore's courts are always very busy."

"I want one of my uncle's lawyers!"

"I'm told they are going to be fully engaged as well," Kumar said. "May I suggest a compromise, however?"

Marcus asked what that would be.

"Tell us who your captain dealt with," Kumar said. "Do that, and we will return you to Cairns."

"I thought this was about shooting the sampan," Marcus said.

"It can be," Kumar said.

"You bloody bullock," Marcus said.

"I am not bloody," Kumar replied. "Not yet."

Marcus huffed for a moment, then said he would have to think about it. On the way back to the cabin, he agreed to cooperate with Kumar. The lieutenant radioed to inform FNO Loh that he had a successful chat with Marcus Darling. The young man seemed willing to cooperate. Kumar also told Loh that they had located the real Peter Kannaday.

Back in sick bay, the medical officer finished cleaning the body of the seaweed that had collected on it. He picked it away carefully, using long tweezers and cotton swabs. Then he covered the body with a sheet and left it on the gurney. There was nothing else he could do. The body could not be touched until an autopsy had been performed onshore. He turned off the light and locked the door. It had been a long night of caring for the half-drowned sailors. He needed to rest.

Captain Peter Kannaday was alone. He was at sea, where he belonged.

And one thing more.

He was at peace.

EIGHTY

Darwin, Australia
Sunday, 7:46 A.M.

Lee Tong had never felt ill or disoriented when he was at sea. Not even the first time on the wonderful old timber carrier. Now he was on land, and it made him sick to move. Anything more than a slow, short breath caused deep waves of nausea. Which was strange, because Tong was also hungry. The young man could not remember the last time he had eaten.

In fact, Tong could not remember much of anything. He remembered closing in on a boat and being shot at. He remembered an explosion. After that, he remembered nothing.

Tong appeared to be in a hospital room. It was white with yellow walls and a large screen of some sort. People came in now and then, but he did not know who they were or what they were saying. Most of the time he did not bother to look or listen. Lying in the cool bed, floating in and out of sleep, was physically less disturbing. Yet even that was not a haven. He dreamed of better times, of a happier youth. The future had never held much promise for him. But when Lee Tong sailed the ocean with his father, at least there was the prospect of success. There was hope. He preferred that to the reality of failure. In the moments after he woke, Tong would wish desperately to go back and try again. But then the truth washed over him. He was here. Hope was gone. People did not get a second chance.

"Lee Tong."

The young man thought he heard someone say his name. The voice was muffled, but it did not sound like a voice from one of his dreams. He forced his eyes open, just barely. Someone was looking down at him from the foot of the bed. A woman. She had a darker face than the others, but was also wearing a mask and gown. Through his nearly shut eyes she looked gauzy, like a ghost.

"Can you hear me?" she asked.

She was speaking Malay. It was beautiful. He nodded once. The nausea reminded him to stay as still as possible. He obeyed.

"Good," the woman said. "I am Female Naval Officer Monica Loh of the Singaporean Navy. You are suffering from mild radiation poisoning. It came from the vessel you attacked. But I've just spoken with your physician. You will recover. Do you understand?"

Tong nodded once, very, very slowly. The nausea was a little kinder this time. He opened his eyes a little wider. Some of the haze lifted from the woman. She was real.

"Mr. Tong, you were the only member of the sampan crew to survive the explosion," the woman went on. "We will need you to testify about the nature of the firefight. Whatever you remember, we want to know." The woman took several steps around the edge of the bed. "But that is not why I came to see you. I know what you were doing out there. We cannot prove you did anything wrong. However, I would like to keep you from doing anything illegal in the future. When you are released from the hospital, I would like to see you about a civilian job with the navy. There are a number of defense technical positions and administrative support positions for which you can be trained. I hope you will consider them."

Lee Tong was awake. He knew that because he felt queasy. But he thought he heard the woman say she wanted him to work for the navy. He had neither the education nor the kind of background recruiters sought. No one in his family had served in the military. It did not make sense.

"Why . . . ?" he asked weakly.

"Why do I want you?" Loh asked. "It took a great deal of skill to navigate a sampan that far out to sea. We can always use talented men and women, and I don't just mean the navy." The woman smiled under her mask. "I heard someone use the phrase 'the good guys' to describe us today. I like that. I want you to be one of them, Mr. Tong."

He looked at her and smiled back weakly. He nodded once. The nausea was worth it.

The woman nodded back and left.

The navy, Tong thought. Even in a civilian capacity, naval service would give him the kind of respect his father had always wanted for him. His only regret was that his shipmates were not here to collect their share of respectability. They were good men and loyal friends. He would miss them.

The young man's eyes blurred again, this time from tears.

As he slipped back into sleep, Lee Tong's last thought was that he no longer had to dream of happier times. He could imagine them.

For they were no longer behind him, but ahead.

EIGHTY-ONE

Washington, D.C.
Saturday, 6:29 P.M.

Paul Hood was about to leave his office when the phone beeped. The caller ID identified it as Bob Herbert. He picked up.

"Lowell went on to participate in what's left of his conference in Sydney, then decided to hang with the hostess and her husband," Herbert said. "But I'm coming home. I'm flying commercial later in the afternoon. First class."

"I hope you've got the frequent flier miles for it," Hood laughed.

"Nope. Op-Center's treat. I don't think chasing Darling's plane earned me enough to upgrade," Herbert said.

"I'll see if we have any money left in our 'off to save the world' account," Hood joked.

"If not, you can dig it out of the goodwill fund. We made some good friends here, Paul. Strong allies. And I have a rotten feeling we're going to need them all sooner rather than later."

"I have that feeling, too," Hood said. "There's a new world out there with a lot of enemies we haven't begun to identify."

"Well, we've made a good start identifying a few of them," Herbert said. "I understand Marcus Darling has caved. He's reportedly opened his Palm Pilot rogues gallery for the Singapore navy."

"In exchange for what?"

"Being handed to Australian authorities instead of Singaporean grill masters," Herbert said.

"Lowell will probably not approve, but nicely done," Hood said.

"Lowell did not openly *dis*approve, which is pretty good for him. This thing scared him, too. Speaking of enemies," Herbert went on, "did you hear anything else from Mr. Perry?"

"Not so much as a snarl," Hood said.

"Hardly a surprise," Herbert said.

That was true. Lowell had nailed it before when he said that a failure was a stranger in his own house. The corollary to that is, 'No one leaves the house faster than a politician.' Hood toyed with the idea of calling Perry at home and busting his chops. He decided that would not be necessary. Perry was probably anticipating just such a call. That was revenge enough.

"Well, I'm going to be sitting around Jelbart's office for a couple of hours, helping him write reports. A lot happened, and we weren't taking notes. What are you up to on what is still early Saturday night?"

"I have a date with a lady," Hood told him.

"Oh? Is this the advertising lady you saw the other night?"

"I started to call her, but there was someone else I wanted to see tonight," Hood said.

"And she is?"

Hood smiled. "My daughter."

Herbert did not say anything. He did not have to. The intelligence officer had just gone through this event with Darling and Jessica-Ann. He would know where Hood was coming from.

"Are you going to see Sharon, too?" Herbert asked.

"Only in passing," Hood said. "She agreed to switch weekends with me so I could see Harleigh tonight."

"Nice. Make sure you give her a hug from Uncle Bob," Herbert said.

"I will," Hood assured him. "I'll tell her you're bringing what? A stuffed koala?"

"It's a deal," Herbert said. "And a boomerang for Alexander. I won't even bill Op-Center for it."

Hood smiled. "Thanks, Bob." He looked at the computer clock. He did not want to be late. He wished Herbert a safe flight and left his office. He rode the elevator up one flight.

It is indeed a deadlier and less predictable world than ever, Hood thought, as he stepped into the twilight. But in it was one constant.

Loyalty.

With it, you possessed what was best in men. Loyalty to loved ones, to friends. Loyalty to ideals, to country. With it, you had long, powerful arms that could reach for the heavens.

Or a daughter.

Which worked out fine, Hood reflected, as he climbed into his car. For in the end, who were the heavens for?